TRUTH BE TOLD

Rachel Skerritt

Library of Congress Number: 00-192434
ISBN #: Softcover 0-7388-4207-9

This book was printed in the United States of America.

To order additional copies of this book, contact:
Xlibris Corporation
1-888-7-XLIBRIS
www.Xlibris.com
Orders@Xlibris.com

CONTENTS

PART TWO

PART THREE

CHAPTER ONE

Kahlila

There is one thing I should have learned last semester: if the class is Black Studies, it sure as hell ain't starting on time.

Kahlila had just finished running down the hall against the current of students, squeezing through tiny patches of open space and knocking her backpack into other rushing bodies. She arrived in the doorway of Room 314 nervous that the professor might have already begun to lecture.

Bewildered and breathless, she stood staring at the two people occupying desks in the classroom. Neither was the professor, and one of them was fast asleep. That's when she remembered the rule about Black Studies classes, relaxed, and took a seat near the right tip of the U-shaped desk formation.

Her watch read 10:40, but she always set it five minutes fast. People were starting to float in, and she engaged in some people-watching after getting out her notebook and pen. A few white students came in looking even more frantic than she had, thinking they were late. They clearly didn't know the rule. Most of the black students looked like upperclassmen, and they sauntered in like class started at 11:00, and not 10:30.

Kahlila eyed the non-sleeping guy who'd arrived before she had. His desk was cluttered with several paperback books, along with a huge bulkpack of xeroxed articles. He kept opening and shutting them, underlining text, and jotting down notes.

Is he kidding? Those books better not be for this class. How's he gonna go buy all the books before we even get the syllabus?

It didn't take long for Kahlila to realize that buying all of the books for a class right away was not a smart move. Not only might someone be able to loan them out, but she got burned last semester when she bought books that the professor never even used. Her new policy was buying books one at a time, as they were assigned. Clearly this highlighting idiot wasn't down with the program. But he didn't look like a freshman, so he should know better by now.

The U of desks was completely occupied after five more minutes and a few students were even sitting on the outskirts. Friends were talking in hushed tones. Kahlila's watch now read 10:46. Her impatience was increasing.

Rule Number Two: No matter how late the students are, the person who arrives last is always the professor.

As if on cue, Dr. Howard Harkonn strode into the classroom and shut the door tightly behind him. He pulled up a chair-and-desk-in-one at the opening of the U, took off his black leather jacket, threw his Polo shoulder bag on the floor, and began talking before he was even seated.

"Welcome to Black Collective Responsibility. I hope all of y'all aren't here because you think this class is going to be easy. What time is it? Almost quarter of? Damn, we're already behind!" He had a big grin on his face, causing a lot of the females in the class to return the smile.

Kahlila was one of them. He was definitely a cutie, if you could call a member of the Franklin University faculty cute. The fact that he had crazy knowledge only made him look even better. Some of the students looked confused when he started talking, as if they couldn't believe he was a professor. They clearly weren't in the loop, because Dr. Harkonn was at every event having anything to do remotely with Blackness on Franklin's campus. Black Activist League? Hark was their advisor. Step show? Hark was the M.C. (He was a Q-Dog back in his own college days). Kwanzaa Ceremony? The man was pouring libations. Yup, Dr. H. was the man at Franklin, and he sure as hell looked better than any Skip Gates

To Mom, Grandma, Dad, Nadine, the Skerritt and Peters tribes, Keira, Joanne, Sonia, Dawud, Ben, Jamaal, and my students at BLS and U-City. Thanks also to my Penn peeps for the inspiration: Patrice, Rhonda, Brandi, Luam, Jen, Nikki, Dayle (my talking journal), Sean, Kendall, Kenyatta, Malik, B, Lee.

happy new year, 1996

there is a feeling
whenever the ball drops in times square
that one must resolve to do something—
to change something—
to make something happen
in the next 365 days.

i'm not giving in—
because if i make
a resolution—
it won't be sincere—
because i don't know who
or what
i want to become.

and if i don't have a clear idea of
what i'm doing
or where i'm headed,
what's the point of setting a goal?

if there is no passion in my promise,
then i won't care if i break it.
so when i go back on my word
on january third
apathy will tear through my body
like folks tear through corbel
on december 31st.

so until i find my passion—
my reason for being—
i'll hold off
on resolving to be anything more
than someone who's trying to find
a reason to resolve at all.

maybe that's my resolution—
this year, i'll find
whatever it is that
will make me want to be more than i am.

i hope it doesn't take all twelve months
to find this magical thing.
i'd like some time to enjoy it
once it's found.

PART ONE

or Cornel West ever could. Kahlila snapped out of her revelry in time to hear his course description.

"... particularly pertaining to the Black college student. What do we owe the community where Franklin is located? What is our responsibility to our hometowns? Our families? To each other at this institution? I'm glad to see some Caucasian, Latino, and Asian brothers and sisters up in here, because responsibility crosses racial lines and many cultures have unique views on this topic." The Asian girl on the outskirts of the U was nodding vigorously.

"Now, I don't think it makes sense to waste time going through the syllabus. Franklin's a top school according to U.S. News and World Report, so I presume you had to pass some sort of literacy test to get in here." He flashed his playful smile. "Read it on your own. E-mail me with questions by next class.

"Now we're gonna get down and dirty next time, but today I just want us to get to know each other. There is going to be quite a bit of discussion in this class, and I think it's important for us to know names and what brought us all here. I guess I'll start—Howard Harkonn. Morehouse '78–B.A., political science. Yale '83–Ph.D., American Studies. I've been a prof here in the Black Studies Department for twelve years now—I got tenure, so I can do and say on this campus whatever I damn well please."

The class chuckled, aware of Franklin's ridiculous policy regarding tenure. Publish eighty million books and tenure is yours, and once you have that you're untouchable. Got any actual teaching skills? Who cares? As long as you're raking in the grant money, you're a keeper.

"I designed this course last semester," he continued, "because I'm sick and tired of brilliant students, particularly African American students, getting the degree, running off into corporate America, and never giving back. Never even *looking* back, I dare say. Now I see some business students in the back looking really pissed off, but that's the point. I want differing opinions in here; I want to be challenged. This is going to be a good semester. I can feel it."

That grin again, and that twinkle in his eye. "Before we go

around, I want to introduce my teaching assistant for the semester, Dave Robinson. Because of the volume of work in this class—yes, be very afraid—I'm going to need some help with grading. He will also be leading discussions from time to time and he has his own office hours. You can come to either of us, depending on your schedule. Dave, you want to say a few words?

Kahlila had been staring at Dr. Harkonn's wedding band during his Dave introduction, but she finally looked up once the T.A. began speaking. *Oh, thank goodness. It's the guy with all the books. At least he has an excuse for being such a herb.*

"What's up everybody. Like Hark said my name is David Robinson—yeah, like the basketball player. Y'all can call me Dave though. I'm a second year Ph.D. student in Sociology with a focus on urban environments. I basically feel like rich institutions such as Franklin owe the schools, community centers, businesses, and residents of the neighborhoods where they decide to set up shop. When I grow up, I'm gonna find a way to hold them accountable. I look forward to meeting you individually, and we can discuss these issues further if you're interested."

Students then began to give their own personal bios. Kahlila caught snippets as she planned her own self-description.

"Senior English major from Long Island . . ."

Now what facts about herself were important enough to mention? She couldn't stand when people gave pointless information during activities such as this one. *Who cares if you have two older sisters, or if pink's your favorite color?*

"I'm a junior, and I'm trying to get enough classes for a Black Studies minor, so . . ."

Damn it, why is everyone in this course an upperclassman? Because all of the freshmen are busy taking Calculus, Bio, and the Freshman Writing Requirement. Bullshit. All bullshit.

"I'm actually a grad student in the School of Education. I'm auditing this class because it really fits in with my dissertation topic . . ."

Kahlila felt the butterflies in her stomach coming. She'd heard the legend of Howard Harkonn, but they'd never officially met before. What if he told her that freshmen weren't allowed in his seminar? He was nodding appreciatively in response to everyone else's impressive academic credits. What did she have that was comparable?

Damn. I'm next. Here goes.

"Hi guys. I'm Kahlila Bradford and this is my first year at Franklin. It's been . . . real so far." *Polite laughter. That's always a good thing.* "Um, I took a year off after high school to work at a high school myself. In my whole academic career, the thing that really grabbed me was the concept of schooling and how messed up the whole system is. I don't know what my major is going to be yet, but as my career I'm basically trying to address why our kids aren't learning as much as they should be. This class really intrigued me from the title alone. So I thought, why not?" *I'm rambling. Stop here.*

She was scared to make eye contact with Dr. H. but she finally forced herself to do so. He was doing more than nodding. He was actually opening his mouth to speak.

"Ms. Bradford, correct? Well Ms. Bradford, I'm glad that someone has had some experiences out in the trenches. You'll have to bring us back down to earth if we start pontificating too much in here. Theory must always be accompanied by practice. You're officially in charge of keeping it real."

Dave Robinson chuckled. A few girls in the class shot dirty looks her way. Kahlila wasn't sure what her own expression looked like, but her face was on fire. She moved her head up and down and concentrated on the motion. *I hope this head movement resembles nodding.*

Kahlila didn't hear any other student introductions. She forced herself to tune back in when she heard "assignment." That was college language for "homework." It had taken her a while to learn Collegese—by the end of first semester she'd finally stopped saying "teacher" instead of "professor," but she still sometimes forgot to ask students what year there were instead of what grade they were in.

"Now like I said before, I don't believe in theory without practice. So this class is not going to be just sitting up in a classroom twice a week having intellectual battles. You will be required to find some type of outside experience that explores the concept of giving back, of responsibility. You can mentor, tutor, clean the neighborhood, organize a scholarship fund, whatever. Your fieldwork will comprise a significant portion of your grade. Many of your writing assignments will stem from your experiences. Brainstorm and research for next class. Come with a list of five possible placements that interest you. And buy the bulkpack. Read the first article. I hear the author is truly brilliant. A Howard somebody." He winked at no one in particular.

"Now get out of here, will ya?"

At this point, I'll do whatever you say. She looked at her watch: 11:48. Might she have to add a rule that Black Studies classes never last the full 90 minutes? She could only hope.

CHAPTER TWO

Dave

There is one thing I know for sure: if I don't lighten my load this semester, something is gonna give.

Dave Robinson pushed hard on the door of Cummings Hall and stepped into the glaring January midday sun. He barely noticed the change in weather from the day before. It had been raining and sleeting all week, but today the sun came out like it had been busy getting a makeover. Hailstones could have been pelting him on his baseball cap for all he knew; he was too busy thinking about his hectic schedule, and why things were so out of hand.

How the hell did Hark convince me to T.A. this class? Shit is gonna be real, and this ain't the semester for all that.

Dave had always prided himself on time management. Even back in undergrad, when no one had their stuff together yet, there was Dave with his planner and a smile. He always knew what his next step was, and he had the stride so that he never had to break a sweat to achieve his goal. His personal life was organized in a similar fashion: each relationship and friendship had been analyzed and slotted in such a way that they rarely required unscheduled maintenance or repair. But sometime recently, things had begun to unravel. So this clearly wasn't the semester for him to be taking on so many projects, because Dave had decided that sometime in the next sixth months, he was going to figure out exactly where his life was going.

He looked around him and it seemed as if the entire campus just stepped out of their ten-thirty class. *Better put on my head-*

phones so I don't gotta speak to anybody. He debated whether to play his D'Angelo CD or the radio, but he decided not to listen to music at all. He needed to hear himself think.

Class that morning had gone well. The students seemed to have their heads on straight for the most part. But why were there so many? That meant more papers to grade, and more people to talk with during office hours. He was going to have to seriously consider resigning his position as graduate advisor for the Social Change Committee. But how could he realistically do that? Those undergrads counted on him to get things done. They had big ideas and lofty goals, but absolutely no clue how to execute them. If he wanted the group to make things happen, he couldn't just desert them. *If I could stop taking classes, I would. But considering that's the reason I'm here, I guess that wouldn't quite work.*

If he wanted to leave Franklin with both his Ph.D. *and* a sense of accomplishment, then his academic and political endeavors had to remain as they were. The social arena was the only place where there was room for change. And the only person who really fell under the "social" category was Joy.

Dave saw his nondescript brown brick apartment building in the distance and picked up his pace. If he focused on everything he had to do once he got in the house, he could stop thinking about what Joy meant, or didn't mean, in his life. *Look over the reading for class this afternoon. Make some phone calls to find a guest speaker for that rally next month. E-mail Hark about class this morning.*

He was turning his key in the lock before he knew it. Lloyd was slouched on the couch, watching T.V. and working on a laptop simultaneously.

Dave slammed the door behind him and walked toward his roommate. "Sup, nigga. Pretending like you're getting some work done, I see."

"Whatever, D. You know I'm not the person living in this crib who's all stressed and overworked. I handle mines."

How does this dude know I'm stressed? I swear Lloyd be reading minds sometimes. "And you know I take care of shit as well. But this semester is gonna be real though. I was just thinking about it on the way home." Dave threw his things down next to the couch and sat in the oversized chair alongside it.

"Oh, right. You're coming from Hark's class. How did that go? I know that's not helping your stress level, working for that crazy negro."

"True dat. He's definitely buggin'. But the class looks like it might be kinda tight. The folks seem ahight. Hark was out of control though. Yo, why did he tell some chick in the class that she was officially in charge of keeping it real?"

Lloyd chuckled. "He said that? Who was he talking to?"

"Some freshman."

"Damn, a first year is up in Hark's class? I feel sorry for her—she doesn't even know what she's in for."

"True, but he's harder on the heads who he thinks should know better. He might give her a little slack 'cuz she's young. And it's second semester, so maybe she's gotten her shit together already. We'll see I guess." Dave picked up the remote control and started flipping through the channels.

"Stop there," commanded Lloyd once Dave hit ESPN. "Seriously though, you'll be straight. Things will work themselves out. But on the real, is it the Ph.D. you're sweatin', or is it the M.R.S?"

"What the hell is the M.R.S?"

"The missus, D. Are you finding joy in Joy these days?"

Dave smiled as he searched for an answer. *Damn, the philosophy major in Lloyd sure does creep out when you least expect it. He just starts poking around, spouting out some lyrics and then bam—he's hit exactly what you're trying not to talk about.* "Joy's cool."

Lloyd knew when to let things go, and he picked up on the brevity of Dave's response. "Well good, 'cuz she called about a half hour ago."

"Aw, man. I promised her I'd come over for dinner tonight."

"That's too bad. Your team's playing tonight. I figured you might want to hang out here and watch the game."

"And who exactly is 'my team,' Lloyd?" Dave asked sarcastically even though he knew the answer.

Lloyd played along. "Why, the Spurs of course."

"How many times do I gotta tell you," he began his overused speech. "Just 'cuz I got the nigga's name doesn't mean I gotta sweat him."

"True. But it's like you make it a mission NOT to like the guy. He's pretty much the most likable guy in the NBA. No scandal, impressive education, that big ass grin, loves his momma . . ."

"Lloyd, I ain't watchin' the game so chill. I'll start backin' the Spurs when Robinson gets a new haircut, and you know he ain't parting with the fade in this lifetime." Dave started flipping channels again absentmindedly.

With his usual impeccable timing, Lloyd asked, "So, you gonna return her call or can I get on the phone?"

"Why are you all up in the business? And who do you need the phone to call? I know you ain't calling a girl considering your ass *still* can't get over the one back in New York, even after the chick done went and fell for some Indian yoga master."

"'Done went and fell for?' Okay, we're not in Alabama, Dave. Quit that country garbage. And your effort to take the attention off of yourself in this conversation is so transparent that I'll do you a favor and humor you. Tell me exactly how you manage to make my whole Sonia saga sound like some twisted sitcom. I mean, she's half Indian. So the fact that she's with an Indian guy isn't all that deep. And he's not a yoga master. She met him in the building where she takes her yoga classes." He shook his head as if disappointed that his friend couldn't remember the exact details of Sonia's sordid story.

Before Lloyd came to Franklin, he was at Columbia undergrad seriously committed to Sonia, an English major at Barnard. He wanted to do the distance thing, but it fizzled after the first semester of his Ph.D. program. As a symbol of protest, he shaved off his dreads, stopped playing the piano, and swore off women. A full year later, he was still musically uninspired and single.

And his hair remained confined to a two to three inch radius from his head.

"My bad, Lloyd. I'm just sayin' that you need to get back out there. It's been a year. I mean, damn."

Lloyd heaved a sigh before responding. "Yeah, but it's not even about Sonia anymore. You know how this program kicks my ass, just like yours does. It's so easy not to find the time to have a life. If you hadn't brought Joy with you from Boston, you'd probably be single now too."

Shit, I can't argue with that. Wouldn't life be much easier right now if all I had to think about was taking my classes, T.A.'ing Hark's joint, and making this campus more Negro-friendly. He chose to respond to Lloyd's comment with a "yeah," and turned his focus to Sports Center. They watched in silence as Lloyd occasionally typed a few words on his laptop and as Dave reviewed the readings for his 3:00 class. After forty-five minutes and a grilled cheese sandwich, Dave finally managed to motivate and went into his bedroom to call his girlfriend.

Lloyd eyed Dave as he rose from the couch and slowly walked away with the cordless phone in hand. Snippets of conversation sneaked out to the living room. "Yeah, tonight's still cool." Mumbling. "I miss you too, baby." As Dave sat on his bed, he watched his roommate through the crack in the door. Lloyd was twirling a piece of his short Afro, looking slightly frustrated. Dave avoided eye contact, knowing that it might prompt a smart comment from his boy. *Whatever, nigga. Yeah, my relationship ain't all fun and games. But at least I'm in one.*

CHAPTER THREE

Desiree

I wonder if people realize that they are being watched constantly. Or are they so self-involved that they are oblivious to everyone else?

Desiree Thomas sat gazing out of her third floor bedroom window with a pair of binoculars pinned to her face. She didn't remove them when she heard the apartment door slam shut.

"You're kidding me. Did you even go to class?" Kahlila stood in her suitemate's doorway looking mildly shocked and slightly annoyed.

Ignore her. She knows not how damn aggravating she sounds. "It *is* January, is it not?" Desiree asked, half talking to herself. "Why do white people feel the need to put on shorts and/or sandals in the middle of winter as long as the sun is shining? It's really a God damned shame."

"I'm used to that, remember? In Boston, white folks put on their Birks when the temperature hits 50 degrees. But I asked you a question, sweetheart."

"Oh, class? I popped my head up in there. I'm gonna drop it though. Two papers and a final? You must be crazy. Tests *or* papers. Dez don't do both, baby." She got up from her bed and followed Kahlila into her bedroom. "How was *your* class? Maybe I'll take it with you."

Kahlila threw her backpack down on her bed and sat down at her computer. "That would be cool since there are absolutely no freshmen up in there at all. It looks like it's gonna be good though."

"Hell yeah, it's gonna be good! Fine-ass Harkonn teaching the class, you know I'd be up in the front row *every* Tuesday and Thursday."

"Whatever, Dez. I don't think you'd like it for real. There's gonna be mad work. We have to do volunteer work somewhere as a class requirement."

"So?" Desiree responded indignantly. "It's not like I'm incapable of working hard, Kahlila."

"I never said that. But you just told me that you're gonna drop your class because there's too much work required. So why would you wanna take Hark's?"

Well damn, Kahli. If you didn't want me up in there you should have just come out and said so. "No, you're right, girlie. I'll find something a little lighter—maybe a once-a-week type joint. So let's discuss more important matters. What's up with Da Krew's party tonight?" Desiree forced her tone to a higher pitched, cheerier decibel.

Kahlila was too busy reading her new e-mail messages to notice the abrupt subject change. "Is that tonight?" she asked absentmindedly.

"Shouldn't you know? Last time I checked, you were the one sleeping with one of Da Krew members, not me." Her voice dripped with sarcasm.

"Dez, first of all, that juvenile nickname of theirs is played so I wouldn't even gas them up by using it. Second, I think that if you could slip the fact that I'm having sex into conversation eighteen times a day, you would," replied Kahlila as she began typing an e-mail response to her mom.

"Damn straight I would. Life is so much more interesting now that you're not so frickin' virginal."

"I'm glad you think so, because I'm really not having all that much fun. So I'm happy *you're* enjoying all this."

"That's a shame, hon. It'll get better though. It's only been a few months. Or maybe Tarik just isn't representing . . ." She placed a lilt at the end of the sentence to hint that it was more of a question than a statement.

"It's possible," Kahli said over the fluttering noises of her keyboard.

"Kahlila, as happy as I am that you've finally joined us in the land of the fucking, I can't understand why your first is someone you're not even really liking all that much."

"I just don't see sex as that big of a deal. I was never on that whole 'wait till marriage' kick, but I just wasn't really ready in high school. So I came here, and Tarik seemed cool so I figured why not."

Seemed cool? That nigga got tested for every damn STD known to man just to get in your pants. Cool is an understatement. "Well Kahli, you better watch out because that boy is catching crazy feelings and y'all are truly on different pages."

Kahlila heaved a sigh. "I know. I never thought I would be so superficial to be holding on to something because nothing better has come along yet."

Desiree shot her a skeptical glance. "Let's not give ourselves too much moral credit, now. We're horny ass adolescents, and as much as you hate to admit it, you're as superficial as the rest of us. Tarik was a playa-player before you. He was legendary on this campus before you worked your spell. You love being the one who broke him."

Kahlila refused to look her way, her gaze intent on the computer screen. "Not true! It's causing me more stress than satisfaction, actually. Although . . . I guess it is kinda new for me, being pursued so hard. I like it—I can't front."

She began typing furiously as if to cover the sound of her confession. Desiree stared at her perplexed. *I can't figure out for the life of me if this girl really doesn't understand why guys would sweat her, or if this whole innocent role is all an act.* Her eyes focused on Kahlila's flying fingers, watching her chunky silver rings reflecting the light of her desk lamp. She scanned up to the sweater Kahli was wearing—an afghan-type oversized knit with Native American inspired designs. She actually looked almost Native American in the sweater, her deep reddish-bronze skin tone accentuated by the copper colored shirt. Though the sweater was baggy, her closer fitting bellbottom corduroys revealed her true size, which was quite slim.

Desiree's gaze moved back up to Kahlila's face, where her eyes were still glued to her e-mail. They were narrow, almost suspicious-looking, but possessed a wide-eyed innocence at the same time. Her high cheekbones were accentuated by her hair, which was parted in the middle and tightly pulled into a ponytail. She always tied her hair back, and that annoyed the hell out of Desiree. *That girl could do so much with her hair, but never even bothers. I don't even think she needs to perm it.* Her one flaw was her smile, which turned her mouth a little crooked whenever she grinned really wide. In pictures, she always half-smiled so that her mouth wouldn't shift to the right. But the irritating part was that even her damn slanted smile was cute.

It wasn't like Desiree was jealous or anything. She had guys sweating her left and right. The seniors voted her "flyest freshman" in "Extra, Extra," the unofficial black senior newsletter. It was a senior tradition to publish a newsletter every fall, with private jokes from the four years past, and the "Extra Awards," something everyone looked forward to reading. Categories ranged from "Biggest Gossip" to "Most in Need of a Clue" to "Player of the Year." No one was surprised by Dez getting "Flyest Freshman." Her creamy beige skin, curvy figure, and long highlighted hair pretty much guaranteed her the win. If there was any doubt, the fact that she had already dated a few senior guys by the time the newsletter came out in November made her a shoe-in.

Little did Desiree know, but the senior males often talked about Dez and Kahli as a pair. The two of them definitely turned heads as they walked into the dining hall, two distinct definitions of attractiveness. Desiree, with her long chestnut hair, the lighter brown streaks framing her face, her part angled so that her bangs swept down near her right eye and then tucked behind her ear. Kahlila, with her almost jet black hair smoothly pulled back into a shiny bun, exposing her three silver earrings in each ear. Desiree's tailored shirts and tight pants contrasted Kahlila's funky, baggier style. Dez loved black and red, while Kahli preferred brown and green. And guys liked them both. But it was Desiree whose phone had been ringing off the hook since they stepped on campus in September. So why was Desiree so annoyed by Kahlila's newfound, and still limited, popularity? *Tarik is definitely a hottie, but it ain't like I'm trying to get with him.*

". . . and why are people having parties on Thursday nights, like it ain't still the work-week? Thank goodness I didn't register for any Friday classes. Did you, Dez? Desiree! Hello?! Dez—I just admitted to you five minutes ago that I was enjoying the attention from Tarik. Shouldn't you be gloating instead of sitting there all dazed and confused?" Kahlila finally stopped typing and turned in her chair to face her friend.

Desiree regained her composure in time to answer. "Why should I be tripping off something I already knew? So let's get back to the original point of this conversation. Are we going tonight?"

"Yeah. Tarik will be pretty pissed if I don't come, and I'm in the mood to dance anyhow."

"Good, because I'm in the mood to drink and you know the two go hand in hand," Desiree smiled at Kahlila knowingly. Despite all of their differences, their party behavior was very similar. Dez looked like that girl who would be chilling on the wall, sipping on a drink and waiting for dudes to step to her. Kahli could have been labeled the girl who bopped her head to the hip hop vibes in her own little corner. But Dez and Kahli were always in the center of the floor, waving their hands drunkenly in the air during the hip hop sets and grinding to the reggae vibes. It was probably their spontaneous dance routines that first caught the eyes of many male admirers and female haters.

"Yeah, we'll be straight chillin' tonight. Maybe if we get enough alcohol in your system you can kick it to your boy Trevor." Kahlila returned Desiree's omniscient smile.

How does this girl know I'm feeling Trevor already? He hasn't even been on campus a full week yet! Trevor was Tarik's ace from back in high school who transferred to Franklin this January to play basketball. Tarik had played for the team as well until this year, when he decided to quit because his grades were not at all cool. The word around campus was that Tarik had already earned the "baller" status, so basketball really wasn't doing anything else for him. It wasn't like he was going to play pro-ball after college, and it wasn't like Franklin had a chance in hell at an NCAA tournament win, so he might as well concentrate on his finance major. *Well, no sense in holding back on this whole Trevor thing. She can probably hook me up anyhow.*

"I guess Tarik told you I was asking about him, huh? Yeah, Trevor's a cutie. What has J.T. said? What's his first impression of Trev?" J.T. was Kahlila's friend from high school who also played basketball for Franklin.

"Trev? Calm down, girl. You don't know him all like that yet to be shortening his name. And I don't think J.T. knows him that well yet either 'cuz Trevor has to sit out this year so it's not like they're practicing together or anything. But you know how girls are on this campus when it comes to some fresh meat. Our numbers are small and we get real desperate. So you better strike while the iron's hot, before someone else does." Kahlila turned her body back to her computer, where a few new messages had popped up on her e-mail screen.

"I know you ain't doubting my skills!!" Desiree jumped off of Kahlila's bed and ran to the stereo. She pressed the power button and began to dance before she even recognized the song on the radio. The bass filled the room. Thump, pause. Thump-thump-thump! When she recognized the song as the new Total release, she got even more hyped. She ran over to Kahlila and pulled her out of her chair. After some reluctance, Kahlila became Kema, one of Total's group members, personified. Desiree had already taken Keisha's part, and no one was trying to be "manly-ass" Pam. They started booty bumpin' around her cramped room. By the time they reached the second chorus, they'd worked out a choreographed number, complete with finger pointing, hip swirling, and seductive poses.

"There's so many things, that I wanna do/ Take you all around, it's all up to you/ If you take my hand, and just follow me/ There's no telling what we can be, just you and me."

The sound of the front door closing barely registered as they crooned about needing "No One Else" but their fictional mates. Suddenly their roommate Robyn tore through the room in time to attempt Da Brat's rap. She threw her things down on her side of the room that she shared with Kahlila and strolled into their routine like she was on Soul Train. The fact that she had no clue as to exactly what Da Brat was saying didn't stop her from rapping in gibberish and getting the imaginary crowd amped. She got her gangsta act together by the end of the rap segment.

"Long as you pleasin' me, I'm all you need nigga/ Decoy—watch Brat kill and destroy/ You the last one to fuck wit So So Def and Bad Boy!"

Kahlila and Desiree tried to continue singing the chorus, but they soon collapsed in hysterics on Robyn's bed. Robyn was still on her feet, sporting a pair of sunglasses she'd picked up off her dresser, and reaching out to her fans in the front row. Dez's spirits had picked up. She looked over at her friend, who was laughing so hard at Robyn's antics that the corners of her eyes were watery. *Kahli is my girl, for real. I need to stop trippin' and quit giving her a hard time.*

Desiree swung her legs over the side of the bed, ran over to the stereo and turned it off abruptly. "Ahem! Are we gonna be the three dopest women at the party tonight?"

Robyn and Kahlila looked at each other and grinned. “Hell yeah!!” They answered in unison.

“Ladies, we have costume decisions to make. To the closets!!”

And the three friends scattered.

CHAPTER FOUR

Joy

After five years, I still try to look perfect whenever he comes over. Is that a good or bad thing?

Joy Rainer struggled to get her bangs to lie flat. For some reason, a few strands decided to flip and stand up, instead of obeying the direction of the comb. She made a face in the mirror. Maybe it was a positive that Dave still gave her that excited feeling, that he still had the ability to bring out the butterflies in her stomach. But at the same time, she should be able to answer the door with a scarf on her head and feel completely at ease. But she couldn't. Dave deserved nothing but her best.

She decided to try a brush instead of a comb, which proved effective. Her bangs now lay evenly across her forehead, with longer pieces on either side, resting on her cheeks. The back of her hair was twisted up and secured with a green barrette that matched her long-sleeved green ribbed turtleneck. She gave herself a once-over in the mirror, felt satisfied, and floated into her living room to turn on some music.

With Faith Evans' "I Remember" playing on her stereo, she bustled around the apartment, straightening up. She was always so neat that straightening up involved rearranging things as opposed to actually cleaning them. Finally, tired of trying to improve upon perfection, she flopped down on the couch and let the music take her to another place.

Sometimes Joy couldn't even believe where she was, and how she'd gotten there. Three thousand miles from home, in a serious relationship with a Harvard grad . . . little old Joy? She knew that's what the folks in Seattle must still be saying: She's still on the East Coast with that wonderful man? Well good for her!

Yeah. Good for me. She still had to pat herself on the back occasionally for getting up the guts to leave home for college in the first place. She'd applied to Boston College just for the hell of it. She heard they had a good nursing program, and since she got fee waivers for her applications, she figured that it couldn't hurt. When they accepted her and gave her a generous financial aid package, it actually became a realistic option. They even paid for her to visit.

When she got there, she fell in love with the cosmopolitan cobblestone aura of Boston. Boston's simultaneous big-city and small-town feel won her over after one trolley ride on the Green Line. The admissions office set her up with a black host, a junior named Carla who really did a great job of selling the idea of coming to B.C. Carla admitted that the school was short on people of color. But between Northeastern, B.U., M.I.T, and the million and one other schools in the city, there would always be new people to meet. And since B.C. was usually so dead, she could concentrate on her studies during the week.

It was all she needed to hear. September arrived with the blink of an eye and suddenly there was Joy, on the other side of the country, alone. The lack of brown faces didn't do as much for her academic performance as Carla had predicted. Instead, she was overlooked when students formed study groups and picked lab partners. Still, she managed to persevere scholastically because she absolutely loved nursing, and her passion motivated her to work hard despite the lack of support from her peers.

Socially, she retreated to a remote place inside herself, where she would occasionally engage a friend or two in light conversation. But freshman year, it never really stretched beyond that. The few parties off-campus that she allowed herself to be dragged off to were disappointments. She realized that the drunken, freaky party scene was not her thing. In high school, she'd been with the same person since she was old enough to date, so the idea of meeting random guys and getting their phone numbers was intimidating, if not downright scary.

But in the end it was Gary, her high school sweetheart, who convinced her to stick it out. She returned to Seattle that summer after freshman year with a 3.8 GPA and a bad case of homesickness. Gary was having a great time playing football for UCLA, and was already in a new relationship with a cheerleader from San Francisco. But Joy and Gary spent a lot of time together that summer, talking about their new experiences, their fears, and their ambitions. Gary spent those summer months telling Joy how impressed he was with her willingness to go so far away from home. His votes of confidence meant a lot to her. She always remembered what he told her the night before she was to return to B.C. for the fall.

"Joy, you have this sexy, subtle appeal that draws people to you. You hold so much inside of you that folks get curious about what it is that you're guarding so tightly. Get out there—not into the bump and grind party scene necessarily, but explore. Use your independence in a way that forces you out instead of keeping you so boxed in. The friends you make will be the luckiest people in Massachusetts."

She went home and wrote down his advice before she forgot it. Early the next afternoon, her plane landed in Boston. When she was all moved in and unpacked, she took the piece of paper out of her pocket and read the words. She got up, folded the piece of paper and tucked it into her journal. Then she walked out of her dorm room, found a T schedule in the lobby, and headed out of the front door.

She didn't even know where she was going. She just thought about the beauty in Gary's words, and knew that she wanted to hear more of the same. She vaguely remembered people hyping up this jazz/poetry club in Harvard Square called Lyrics that was supposed to be off the hook. But she wasn't aware that Lyrics was her destination until it stood right in front of her.

Once the neon sign stared her in the face and the chromatic bassline drifted out onto the street, Joy wasn't so sure. How would she look sitting by herself in there? What if some shady guy harassed her?

"What is there to think about? I heard this place was the shit," said a nearby voice.

Joy was about to turn around and deliver an evil stare, but the face that met hers stopped her glare in its tracks. A tall, brown-skinned brother with a twinkle in his eye was smirking at her, his hands deep in the pockets of his brown leather jacket. She hoped he wasn't expecting an answer, because she had no witty reply and wasn't trying to say anything stupid.

He must have finally realized that if the conversation was going anywhere, he had to be the one to carry it further. "Tell you what. We can go in, give it fifteen minutes, and bounce if it's wack."

"And then what?" Joy managed to squeeze out a couple of words.

"I'll be on my merry way. So let's hope it's good." He winked at her and Joy knew there was no chance that she was letting him go any way other than hers.

Lyrics did actually turn out to be wack. It was Open Mike night, and the wanna-be poets had Joy and her companion falling out of their chairs.

In between sets, they chatted and got to know each other. To Joy, Dave Robinson was better than a dream. He was a sophomore at Harvard studying history, who had decided to head down to Lyrics that night because he was procrastinating on a paper that was due in two days. But it wasn't his resume that reeled her in. It was his dark eyes, smooth skin, and L.L. Cool J lips. It was the fact that he ordered coffee, confessing that he hadn't touched a drop of alcohol since the tenth grade. It was his laid-back confidence, his ability to listen so that you felt like you were the only person in the world who mattered. By the fifth bad poem of the evening, Joy had decided that Dave was the one.

Their relationship developed quickly and Joy felt like she had finally emerged from within herself. They shared everything—when she started doing clinical rounds, she told him about the terminally ill 14-year-old patient who was the bravest person she'd ever met. She told him about the first birth that she watched, and how that was the moment she knew that having a child could be the only thing that would complete her happiness one day. He told her about his passion for history, his belief that all the answers to future problems lie somewhere in the past. He shared his disgust with the culture of Harvard, the need for everyone to prove that he is more intelligent than the next person. He just didn't understand why people couldn't just rap about issues and build together.

Though Joy was happier than she had ever been, feelings of inadequacy began to nag at her. Dave was this highly intellectual being whom everyone looked to at Harvard to speak on all types of subjects. He read for pleasure, spent hours researching various topics in the library, and co-wrote papers with renowned professors. Joy took care of sick people.

He always seemed so proud of her career decision, but she sometimes felt a barrier between their two worlds. Does he really understand the importance of what I do? And do I really comprehend the significance of what he's doing? Or does it even matter?

Their relationship was supposed to be over after senior year. It was never said, but Joy felt it for months before graduation. He'd been accepted into the Ph.D. program at Franklin, and he was so excited to explore a new city and meet new people. He asked Joy about her job prospects and she sensed a feeling of relief when she expressed interest in returning to the West Coast. In actuality, Joy didn't care where she ended up. But she didn't want to lose the man whom she believed would one day complete her happiness.

In the end, she didn't have to. Something had saved her from losing him. But when she thought about the something that kept them together, a sick feeling began to turn her stomach. She shifted positions on the couch, trying to shake the doubts out of her head. *He loves me more than he's ever loved any woman. He's the most faithful, attentive man I've ever known. Stop replaying the past. Call it fate and thank God for preserving our relationship.*

A knock saved Joy from her mental pep talk. She hurried to the door and threw it open. She searched Dave's eyes for the twinkle that she'd loved so much five years ago. But his eyes seemed almost glazed over, and his smile was more polite than it was dazzling. Still, the man she loved more than life stood before her. And for her, that was enough.

"Hello, my love. Ready for dinner?"

"Hey baby. I am *too* hungry so hell yeah, let's eat." He walked through the door, kissed her on the forehead, and walked ahead of her into the kitchen.

Joy watched him go, his long strides carrying him quickly towards the food. *Yeah, folks at home wouldn't believe how lucky I am. I hardly believe it myself.*

CHAPTER FIVE

Tarik

"First things first, I poppa, freaks all the honeys. Dummies, playboy bunnies, those wantin' money . . ."

Tarik Reynolds was having a ball. Jamming to Notorious B.I.G. while playing the bartender role, he was sampling each concoction that he served. The music was tight, and every last one of his boys was somewhere in the house chillin'. Now that Trevor was at Franklin, his circle was complete. Da Krew was in full effect, and there was no stopping them, or their live ass parties.

But where's my girl at? Now of course, he would never say "my girl" out loud, but Kahlila was his girl in his heart, and everybody at Franklin knew it. Kahlila Bradford had been a freshman who niggas whispered about the first month of school. She seemed a little too sweet to even want to try and kick it to, although she also seemed a bit too smart to fall for the usual game in the first place. But for Tarik, she was a little too *fly* to swear off before he got further details.

If any guy was gonna kick it in her direction, it was gonna be T. He had been named "Player of the Year" in *Extra, Extra* as a sophomore, which was a huge accomplishment since that title usually went to seniors. It wasn't that he'd gotten with the most girls on campus. It was that he'd gotten with all of the quality, high-post girls whom everyone else had deemed untouchable. Charisse, the girl with the man back home who looked just like Lisa from

Saved by the Bell—Tarik was the shoulder she cried on when she and her man broke up, and he proved to be the reason she was crying again two months later. Meka, the girl Victoria's Secret asked to model for them *before* they asked Tyra Banks, who happened to think that college men were way too immature for her taste—Tarik was dodging her phone calls after two dates. And then there was Dana, the pre-med student who was always in the library. He noticed that when she took the book away from her face that she was actually a cutie, and he made it his mission to get her to take a major study break. Turned out she was the biggest freak he'd ever been with. Guess reading about all that anatomy paid off.

What made Tarik even smoother was that he never opened his mouth about his conquests. Being an athlete, that was especially impressive because dudes were constantly comparing stats in the locker room. But whenever questions started getting thrown his way, he would just smile and say things like, "Big money, we all know *you're* the true player in the room," or "Whatever nigga, I'm just tryin' to play ball, do my work, and be up outta here." Despite his protests, he'd always get called out: someone would have seen a girl leaving his room in the early morning hours, or he might have been spotted at a flower shop buying a long-stemmed rose. "Aw, man, you caught me," was Tarik's unfailing response when posed with an eyewitness account of T in player mode.

In reality, he liked for his buddies to find out his various projects. But he made an extra effort to keep his pursuit of Kahlila a secret. If heads knew that he'd targeted her as a potential, he might have to start dealing with competition, and he wanted to be the only contestant on her show. It wasn't hard to get to know her because she showed up to every party on campus with those two roommates of hers. When he found out that her third roommate was Shannon, a junior who he'd been cool with since their freshman year, he began to ask her questions about Kahlila. Did she have a man back home? Had she messed with anybody here on campus on the low? Though he was happy to hear that the answer to both questions was a no, he heard some news that was even more disturbing.

It turned out that a frequent visitor to Kahli's dorm room was J.T. Steinway, this white kid who played on the basketball team. J.T. was a sophomore, and he and Tarik played together for a year before Tarik quit the squad. He'd seen J.T. having lunch with Kahli a few times, but he didn't know how serious their "friendship" was. Rumor had it that they went to high school together or something. Some folks said she even came to Franklin because of him. Tarik figured that once Kahli heard about his reputation from J.T., she wouldn't want anything to do with him.

Still, Tarik persisted and made conversation when he'd see her at parties and meals. Though she would bring up J.T.'s name on occasion, she never asked Tarik anything about his past that would imply she knew something. He began to call her and take her out. She rarely turned down an invitation from him and she always seemed receptive when he called. He began to think that the challenge he set for himself was no challenge at all. But when she casually mentioned one day at dinner that she was a virgin, his heart began to beat a little faster. He was turned off and turned on at the same time. He'd been having sex for quite a few years, but he never got with a virgin before. The notion was exciting, but also a bit daunting. Was he ready for all that commitment shit that he'd have to deal with, being her first? She'd no doubt be stressing him for a relationship.

And what made him think that she was giving it up anytime soon in the first place? It's not like she said, "I'm a virgin. Would you like to do something about it?" But at the same time, she didn't sound like she was sitting on her principles either. She mentioned it like it was just a characteristic that she possessed, like long eyelashes or dark hair. And it's not like you can't dye your hair another color. It's not like things can't change.

They started really talking in the beginning of October, and by the end of November, Tarik was getting anxious. They'd messed around quite a few times, the level of intensity growing each time.

She'd even spent the night at his place once. It wasn't even like she was putting the brakes on during their physical encounters, either. Tarik was just nervous to push too far, afraid that she might cut him off. But one night in early December when she came over, he just knew that was the night it was going to happen. And it did. Simple as that. He was a perfect gentleman: took his time, asked if she was okay, made sure he had condoms on hand, held her afterwards.

But the experience definitely wasn't what he expected. He'd heard horror stories from his boys about chicks crying in pain and lying awake in bed afterwards, feeling all guilty and wanting to be reassured that they were still the good little girls their parents raised. But there wasn't any of that with Kahli. Sure, from the struggle at the outset he could tell that she wasn't lying about being a virgin. But she sure as hell didn't cry and she didn't seem to need any comforting when it was all over. She fell asleep before Tarik did. The next day she woke up all cheery, talking about random breezy topics and certainly not addressing anything related to the night before.

Tarik waited all day for her to call, but then he thought that maybe he should be the one to check up on how she was feeling after such a deep experience. When she answered the phone, he wanted to talk about it. "Was it what you expected? Do you regret it? Are we gonna do it again?" But he never asked, and she never volunteered her perspective. He only knew it was going to happen again when she was naked in his bed a few days later. But her phone calls didn't increase. Her demands on the relationship didn't either. The only thing she asked was that he get tested for S.T.D.'s because she was planning on getting on the pill. He was at Student Health the next day, feeling like a punk in the waiting room. Tarik felt all the rules about doing a virgin going in reverse. *He* was the one wanting more.

He never told her, but he stopped seeing other people. He thought about her constantly. He even mentioned her to his mom and dad. Still, when anyone asked, he would answer, "We're just chillin'." And she would do the same.

Sometimes he worried that since she never expressed how she felt about him, it meant that she didn't feel anything. But he consoled himself with the reminder that *he* was definitely sprung even though he never told her how he felt either. Plus, he knew that she wasn't messing with anyone else; it just wasn't her style. She was faithful, fly, and fiercely intelligent. And she was his.

And when he looked up from his passion punch as he shouted Biggie's lyrics, there she was pushing through the crowd with Desiree and Robyn in tow. *Damn, even Shannon came out with them. It really must be a live party.*

Kahli smiled at him over the heads of several sweaty bodies as she carved a path to Tarik. He examined her from head to toe as he managed to catch glimpses every once in a while when the crowd parted. She was wearing a little green tank top with really thin straps and a pair of very baggy faded jeans. Only Kahli would have the green and baby blue sneakers to match. By the time she reached him, he'd taken it all in and was happy with what he saw. He held out one arm to give her a hug. Her tiny waist felt nice in his embrace, and he was already hoping that she was planning to stay over.

"Hey bartender," she whispered in his ear. "Got any specials for me?"

Before he could answer, she was moving out of the way so that he could greet Robyn and Desiree. As he was giving Dez a hug, he peeped Shannon over Dez's shoulder looking at him with disdain. *Whatever Shannon. They may be freshmen, but they're the finest freshmen at Franklin.* Tarik couldn't figure out why Shannon had such little tolerance for her young roommates. His only hypothesis was that they reminded her of herself two years ago, when she was the flyest freshman on campus with her cute little girl crew always at her heels. Now, even though she still looked good, Shannon's popularity had dwindled and she wasn't even friends with any the girls that she hung around freshman year. But whatever the reason was that she always looked so salty around her roommates, she really needed to check herself 'cuz that shit was annoying.

Robyn and Dez were yelling over the music, trying to get Tarik to make them something strong but tasty. "Strong *and* tasty? Sounds like you're describing me in a glass," he answered slyly as he winked in Kahli's direction and lifted his shirt to reveal his six pack. She rolled her eyes and folded her arms, amused but determined not to show it.

Tarik lined up three plastic cups and filled each one with a concoction of peach schnapps, vodka, orange juice, and cranberry juice. Kahli's friends grabbed for them eagerly and headed into the mass of people to dance. Kahli and Tarik watched for a moment as they blended in with the crowd. Only their arms were visible, held high so as not to spill their drinks.

"Walk like a champion/ Act like a champion/ What a piece of body girl/ Tell me where you get it from . . ."

Robyn and Desiree were walking all over the floor to Buju Banton's song, winding up and turning heads. By the middle of the song, the cups were empty and they had both hands free to grab onto the dance partners who had approached them from behind.

Tarik turned to Kahli and handed her the third cup. She took a sip and nodded appreciatively. "Not bad. So do you have to make drinks all night long?"

"Nah. Just until Trev comes and relieves me. I got like a half hour left."

"Trevor, huh? Well I'll have to send Dez over when he gets here."

"Word? That's straight."

"When the east is in the house/ Oh my God—danger/ When the east is in the house/ Oh my God . . ."

The crowd roared as the DJ flipped the script from reggae to hip hop. Kahli's ears perked up as well, and she looked like she was itching to get out on the floor herself. Before Tarik could suggest that she go catch up with her friends, she took matters into her own hands. "All right, sweetie," she said. "Find me when you get relieved."

As she turned her back to him and got swallowed by the mob, he was slightly thrown for a second. But he was soon comforted knowing that she wouldn't be doing anything scandalous while he was stuck behind the bar. Heads might dance with her or whatever, but they knew their boundaries and if *they* didn't, Kahli did. She always had a polite sort of way of checking brothers who were trying to push up on the dance floor. She rarely even had to say anything; she'd just step away a little bit or turn out of a hold, never once losing the beat. And it wasn't like Tarik didn't have fun at parties without her; chickenheads were always flocking around, dropping flirtatious lines and touching him suggestively. Another thing that T liked about Kahli was that she never tripped about that type of thing. Someone could roll up to him while they were in the middle of a conversation and kiss him on the cheek, and she wouldn't even bat an eyelash. She was that confident. *Either that, or she just doesn't give a fuck.*

He quickly erased that thought from his mind and set off to mixing up some drinks for the folks forming a line around him. When he looked up again, he noticed that Shannon was still standing there. Her long braids were pulled up into a high ponytail, and she was looking a little like Janet in *Poetic Justice*. Except Janet always had that sweet little innocent expression going, and Shannon looked hard as nails.

"So, you done babysitting?" she said with a sneer.

"Whatever Shannon. Not even your smart comments could ruin my buzz. I'm feelin' no pain tonight."

"No one's tryin' to kill your high, T. I'm just teasing you. Your party is hype, as usual."

Tarik had to smile at the compliment. Everyone knew that Da Krew gave the phattest flows on campus. Not even the Greeks could compete with them. First of all, their house was perfect for a party. Their basement was huge, with ample room for a bar and a DJ. Nice and dark, everyone who wanted to bump and grind chilled down there. The first floor had a living room for lounging, a kitchen for talking to people in bright light, and a bathroom for those party emergencies that drinking induced. There was even a spare room for coats, which meant that no one had to go up to the second floor unless they were invited by one of Da Krew for a private session.

"So what's going on upstairs? Anyone smokin' up there?" Shannon was always trying to get down with some free weed, and tonight was no exception.

"Well if they are, they better not be in my room stinkin' it up."

"Since when don't you smoke? Don't tell me Kahli is trying to turn you into a good little boy."

"Actually, I never smoked. It has nothing to do with Kahli. It's just that liks do me just fine." He turned and handed out cups to a few folks who'd been waiting a while for service.

"Well I'm glad that you're not making any sacrifices for that girl," Shannon said, trying to regain Tarik's attention.

It worked. "Huh?" he asked as he whipped back around from taking orders.

"I'm just saying, you may not want to take this whole Kahli thing so seriously."

Tarik waved off the comment. "Who's talking about taking anything seriously? We're just chillin'. But . . . if you know something you think I need to be made aware of, just say it."

Shannon raised her eyebrows. "I have nothing to say, really. We just need to get together sometime and chat about some things."

Before Tarik could inquire further as to what she was hinting at, she'd disappeared into the crowd. *What the hell is that girl talking about? Did she hear Kahli talking about some other dude? No, that's crazy. How am I gonna believe anything Shady Shannon has to say to me anyhow?*

All of a sudden it seemed like everyone in the whole place was trying to get tossed, because Tarik was getting bombarded with drink orders. He was opening bottles of rum, vodka, and whisky as fast as he could. He saw a hand grab an almost full bottle of gin and pour it in a cup with some orange juice. T was ready to ill on the person when he realized it was his boy Trevor, swinging by to give him a hand with the high demand.

"Damn, you came at the right time, dawg," Tarik yelled over the music.

"Yeah, I figured I let you suffer here long enough. You need a break. I was caught up though, checking out the sights y'all got at this school."

"And what do you think so far?"

"Oh, y'all got some bunnies down here, no doubt. The sisters up at Brown were garbage. The white girls were all right, but it looks like I'm gonna be straight chillin' at this school, for real."

Damn, Trevor's still going for the white girls. I thought he'd grow out of that shit after high school. Tarik had never been with a white girl before. It wasn't that he had something against interracial relationships. It was just that all the white girls who ever showed him interest were those stereotypical ones who sweated athletes and wanted to rebel against daddy by bringing a darkie home. He'd decided back in junior high that he wasn't going to be anybody's token. His boy Trev, on the other hand, felt like if someone was in his face trying to give up some ass, why not take it? Tarik and Trev had been boys since the sixth grade, but they definitely didn't always think alike.

"Oh yeah, we got a selection here, no doubt. Matter of fact, I already got one that's sweatin' you."

"Word? Who is it?" Trevor was scanning the room, looking for his secret admirer to pop out from the shadows.

"That girl Kahli who I've been kicking it with has a friend named Desiree. She's kinda fly. A freshman."

"Word? Freshmen are always fun. They fall for anything and they haven't gotten all cynical yet. Is she down though? I mean, could I hit that?"

"Yo, chill Trev. You haven't even met her yet." He felt a little uneasy hearing Trevor talk about Desiree in such a crude manner. Tarik and Dez had gotten to be fairly cool since he'd started chillin' with Kahli, and although most dudes on campus saw her as a sex object, he saw her more as a little girl.

"I trust your taste though, T. We go back to middle school, man. You ain't never tossed me an ugly chick yet."

Tarik had to smile thinking about all the girls they'd set each other up with over the years. Trevor was the dark skinned bald Michael Jordan type, while Tarik was more Grant Hill. If they met a girl who was more attracted to the other's stylo, they simply swapped. They had numerous jokes about their exchange program over the years, and Trevor was right. It hadn't failed them yet.

"Nah, this girl looks good. She's here tonight. I'm gonna go find Kahli and I'll send Dez over to say hi. You straight over here with these alcoholics?"

"Hell yeah, son. I'll get up with you later."

They gave each other a pound and Tarik began his way through the crowd. He realized that spotting Kahli wasn't going to be as easy as he thought. The basement was dark with the exception of a couple of blue lights which only served to make anything white glow. And the room was absolutely packed. *How much did we charge tonight? Looks like our rent is paid for next month.* Even though Tarik wasn't doing too well in his finance major at Franklin, he proved excellent with budgeting Da Krew's loot. They made a profit off of every party, even though they notoriously never ran out of alcohol and let in mad people free.

He was standing in the middle of the basement, which was beginning to feel like a furnace. Bodies were everywhere. In the corners, on the walls, on the floors, in circles, in lines. Skin was everywhere.

Arms, shoulders, legs, backs. *You really wouldn't think it was the middle of winter, the way people are dressed in here.* Tarik himself was only wearing a Nike T-shirt and jeans, and even that was making him hot.

Finally, he spotted her. To his relief, he didn't have to see her dancing with some random head. She was in triangle formation, groovin' with Dez and Robyn. They were apparently feeling Junior Mafia, especially Lil' Kim. When she started rapping in "Get Money," they were screaming the words right along with her.

"Is you wit me?/ How could you ever deceive me?/ Payback's a bitch muthafucka, believe me!/ Nah, I ain't gay/ This ain't no lezbo flow/ Just a little something to let y'all muthafuckas know . . ."

Tarik stepped into the middle of their triangle, staking out his space on the dance floor by doing an elaborate two step that forced people to either side. "Ladies, why so bitter? Y'all are feeling some Lil' Kim tonight."

"Damn straight, we are," Dez chimed in as she danced. "Niggas are shady, and they need to recognize . . ."

"Well since niggas are so shady, I guess you wouldn't want to meet my shady friend Trevor this evening."

Desiree stopped dancing and moved in closer to Tarik to hear more. Kahli shook her head and smiled. Robyn laughed and headed upstairs for a breather.

"Tarik, you know I'm trying to meet him so stop fuckin' with me. Where is he?"

"He's at the bar and he's expecting you."

"Cool. Thanks." And just like that, she was headed in Trevor's direction to strike up a conversation. Tarik had to hand it to her—that girl was no joke. Most freshmen would have been all silly about that shit, giggling and saying they were too scared to go talk to the big bad basketball player. Not Dez. She knew her package was tight and wasn't afraid to talk to anybody.

That's what Tarik liked about their little clique. None of them really acted like freshmen. Well, that wasn't entirely true. They did act like freshmen in that they could never eat at the dining hall by themselves, and they always made a spectacle at parties. But each of them had qualities that set them apart from the other corny girls starting out. Dez was ten times more confident than most other girls in her class. She'd talked to mad dudes already, but had yet to get played, or come out looking stupid. Robyn was always on top of shit, managing to get her work done and still have fun. Most freshmen were either partying all the time and ruining their GPA, or locked in their rooms with no social life whatsoever. Robyn had achieved the perfect balance. Kahli? Well, Kahli was just Kahli. She was the bomb student, yes. And she definitely knew how to party. But her maturity was more of an indescribable comfort with who she was and what she expected of those around her. Basically, she tolerated no bullshit from her friends, and set the highest standards for herself as well. She made Tarik want to be better than he was, which was a first for him. He'd pretty much thought that there wasn't much to be improved upon before he met her.

Tarik snapped out of his daze when he heard females squealing at the DJ's next pick. The speakers amplified breathing sounds on top of a hot beat, and he recognized it as L.L.'s joint "Doin' it Well." Suddenly Kahli was on him, her arms around his waist, her hips on his, swaying him to the music. "Finally. I get you all to myself," she said in his ear. She cupped her hands around her mouth so no one could see what she was saying, and then she nibbled his ear. *She is clearly drunk off her ass.* Kahli was only ever that aggressive in public when she had alcohol in her system. But it didn't bother Tarik. He was feeling it, and they were moving together as one by the time LL hit the first verse.

Kahli was instantly inspired when she heard the girl begin to rap and their dance immediately became a theatrical performance. She was mouthing the words along with the chick singing, getting Tarik all kinds of excited. He'd heard that the girl who really sang the song was fat and ugly, so listening to her sexy voice and watching his sexy girl was the perfect combination. Kahli had stepped away from him so that he could take in her full performance as she looked into his eyes and spoke to him.

"I'ma call you big daddy and scream your name/ Matter fact I can't wait for your candy rain . . ."

It was here that Tarik had a decision to make. Was he going to laugh it off and keep dancing normally like everyone else in the hot-ass basement, or was he going to play along with her and take the dude's part? *What the hell. I'm tossed anyhow.*

"No doubt/ I'm the player that you're talkin' about. . ."

By the time Kahli was asking if he "could really work it out," he wanted a chance to prove that he could. Tonight. She was turning around and sticking her ass in his face, feeling on his chest, and getting him all hyped. *She better be staying over tonight. Got me acting all foolish at my own party, putting on a damn show in the middle of the dance floor.*

He couldn't take the suspense anymore. "So, you stayin' over tonight?"

"Sweetie, you know Thursday is the one night I can't stay. I gotta do the breakfast shift at the Caf tomorrow morning and I can't wake up that early in your bed. I just end up being super-bitch and treating you like shit."

"Baby, I can deal with your grumpiness tomorrow. But I want you tonight."

She put her arms around his neck and kissed him full on the lips. "Tomorrow night I will stay over. I promise. But I actually need to jet because if I stay any longer you're gonna convince me. Plus I'm gonna be a zombie tomorrow if I don't get some sleep." She was slurring her words a little bit, and Tarik knew that once she started slurring she only had a good hour left before she passed out.

"Well you might as well go collect your friends. You keep grinding up on me and I'm gonna have to hold you here hostage." He managed to force a smile as she took his hand and dragged him through the crowd searching for her friends. The basement had thinned out a little. It was getting late—some people had gone home, and others had moved upstairs to talk, or up-upstairs to do more than talk.

Tarik and Kahli ended up back at the bar where they began their evening. In front of them were Desiree and Trevor, talking it up like old friends. People had finally gotten tired of drinking, so Trev had shut down the bar and was sitting behind it with Dez. You could only see their heads since they were sitting down and the bar was so high. Her face was almond colored, her hair hanging forward so as to reveal just a nose, mouth and half an eye. His was chocolate, his head cleanly shaved and his teeth as white and straight as could be. Their faces were close together as they laughed and flirted.

Kahli nudged Tarik with her elbow. "Two best friends with two other best friends? Our lives are about to get super corny, T."

He looked at her in surprise. *That sounds like something I would say.* "Well let's not jump off the boat. Trev is never 'with' anyone. Looks like they might hook up, though."

"Hook up?" Kahli interrupted indignantly. "Dez is not the type to just mess any random dude, contrary to popular belief. I thought you knew that!"

"Damn Kahli, I *do* know that. I'm just saying that it might not turn out all that serious."

"Yeah, whatever. Let me go get this girl before the shuttle service stops running." She walked closer to the bar and squeezed behind it with Dez and Trev. She'd met Trevor before briefly, so he took her hand politely as she smiled and began a conversation with Desiree.

As Tarik watched from his distance, he could tell that Trev had already started his spell. Dez looked reluctant to leave and a bit annoyed that the end of their night was going to be supervised by

394-SKER

her girl. Kahli didn't seem to notice, which was very unusual for her. She was usually really good at reading people.

T watched his boy take a napkin from the now defunct bar and locate a pen on the floor. Dez wrote down her number, and slid the napkin his way. They both stood up, hugged, and Dez went upstairs to get her coat. Kahli was headed back in his direction.

"All right, sweetie. Sorry I couldn't stay tonight. I'll make it up to you tomorrow." She winked and headed upstairs. The fact that she didn't hug or kiss him goodbye must have meant that the alcohol was wearing off.

As soon as Kahli was out of sight, someone was waving a white square in front of his eyes. It was Trevor and his napkin of conquest.

"Yeah, nigga," he said a bit too loudly. "That bitch looks good as hell! She's mad cool too."

"Yeah? So if she's so cool, why she gotta be a bitch?" Tarik put a smile on the end of his sentence to lighten the sting.

"No you didn't just say that. You must be sprung on her friend more than I thought. You gonna check me over some dumb shit? O.K., player. But on the real, if your girl hadn't come along, Dez might have been in my bed tonight."

"NIGGA, PLEASE!!!" Tarik laughed so hard that he was doubled over, his hand on Trev's shoulder for support. "Keep dreamin'."

"Like you're any better. Kahli's supposed to be your girl and you *still* sleeping alone tonight." Trevor returned his friend's laughter.

He got me there. "But I ain't gonna be sleeping alone tomorrow night. And Dez ain't gonna be in your bed then either."

"Doesn't mean I'm gonna be sleeping alone." He fake punched Tarik in the shoulder, gave him a wink, and headed upstairs.

Tarik passed him talking trash with some of their boys on the way to the third floor. He was exhausted. He passed out before he could even think to call Kahli to see if she made it home okay.

denying impulse

standing at the door
saying our goodbyes
knowing
that if either of us moved toward each other
even an inch
that no one could tear us apart . . .
for that night, at least.

"good night" we utter
as the door closes.
i conjure up your spirit
to lie with me that night.

my body couldn't move an inch,
so my imagination was forced to move mountains.

CHAPTER SIX

Hark

College is a breeze. Kahlila was feeling better than terrific as she walked into Dr. Harkonn's class on Tuesday morning. Her weekend had begun with Da Krew's party on Thursday, continued as she put in some hours at the job on Friday, stayed over at Tarik's that night, slept in on Saturday, went to the movies with Robyn Saturday night, and got up early on Sunday to get some work done. She slept like a baby on Sunday night, ready to take on the first full week of spring semester classes.

By Monday afternoon, Kahlila had attended all of the classes she'd registered for. She'd managed to hook up quite a schedule for herself, complete with engaging classes and a heap of free time to be used for making money and loafing around. Her poetry class wasn't going to be too much work, and neither was her geology class. *How much work can a class called "Rocks for Jocks" be?* American History was definitely the class with the most reading. She still hadn't figured out how the professor was going to cover three centuries in fifteen weeks. She considered dropping it and finding another history course to fulfill the requirement, but she really felt like she needed to have a better sense of U.S. History. Her recollection of presidents and wars was pretty hazy. Slavery and Civil Rights she pretty much had covered, but she was sure there wouldn't be much time spent on either subject in Franklin's American (revisionist) history course anyhow.

The only class she still didn't have a real grasp on was this one. Black Collective Responsibility? She had an idea in her mind of what that meant, but what if her idea wasn't the same as the professor's? And how was she supposed to concentrate in this class anyhow with that beautiful man standing in front of the room? Also, Kahlila was generally outspoken in class. She never talked just to hear her own voice, but she was rarely intimidated and didn't have a problem speaking her mind. Except around a bunch of black folk.

Kahlila had been one of the few black people in her academic classes for so long, it no longer even felt strange. Being the spokesperson for the race was a burden she'd placed on her shoulders way back in junior high, when she was taken out of her neighborhood middle school and given a full scholarship to a private school in the suburbs of Boston that she attended through grade twelve. There were other black students there, but once she started taking honors and advanced placement courses, she saw them less and less.

She was self-conscious for the first time in a long time when she sat in Hark's class last Thursday. There were so many eyes on her—brown-skinned upperclassmen whom she'd yet to meet, at least beyond a "hi" as they passed each other on campus, or an "excuse me" at a crowded party. They would be forming an opinion about her based on what she said in this class. She didn't want to sound like a nerd, but she didn't want to be an airhead either. *It's funny how I could care less what these folks think about me when I'm running around campus with Dez or Robyn. But I can't bear to be humiliated here.*

As she walked into the classroom for the second time, she vowed that she was going to be quiet at least for today, just to get a feel for the environment. Was it hostile or was it freshman-friendly? She'd read Dr. Harkonn's article that he assigned for homework, so she wasn't assed out if he called on people at random to participate. But she wasn't going to go out of her way to play the "Guess My I.Q. Game." That game was reserved for when she had to throw down in a debate defending affirmative action, or the need for Booker T.

House to exist on Franklin's campus. *There shouldn't be any need to start preachin' today.*

To encourage herself to stay silent, she sat on the outskirts of the U-formation, making herself practically invisible from most angles in the room. She'd barely reached in her backpack before Dr. Harkonn swept into the room and began to lecture.

"Good morning. Lots to talk about today. Hope y'all read my article, or else somebody up in here is about to get played!" He received some sheepish looks after that comment, and even more poker faces.

"So . . . who wants to volunteer to give a brief synopsis of my article?"

Dead silence. The kind that could only follow a question in a class full of people who didn't want to look stupid in front of other people who shouldn't even really matter. And as he'd warned, Dr. Harkonn selected a sacrificial lamb. The guy he chose was looking intensely at his notebook, a sure sign that he was avoiding eye contact.

"You sir," said Hark as he rapped on the student's desk. "Just provide us with a quick summary of the reading you were assigned."

"Huh? Oh. Um, I didn't have a chance to buy the bulkpack yet."

Everyone in the room was on the edge of his seat, except the guy on the spot, who was slouched down in his. This was the moment of truth. Students seized moments like this to test the mettle of professors. How was he going to deal with this recalcitrant student? If he was lax about it, you knew not to take the course too seriously. But if he wasn't . . .

"What's your name, son?"

"Uh, Doug. Doug Jordan."

Dr. Harkonn walked back over to his own chair, picked up his Polo bag, went in it, and pulled out a small notebook. He took a pen off of his desk, opened to a blank page, and began to write. And write.

Kahlila watched in horror, as did all of her classmates. *He's definitely writing down more than Doug's name. Hark is no fuckin' joke.*

"Now," he said, putting away his notebook and pacing the front of the room. "Who would like to summarize the article for us?"

Do not raise your hand. Do not raise your hand. It took everything in her power not to save another person from humiliation by volunteering to answer the question. Just as she was about to crack, another sister took control and spoke up.

"It recounted the history of the relationship between Franklin and the neighboring community since the 60's," she said loudly without even raising her hand for permission to speak.

"Thank you," said Dr. Harkonn, only partially satisfied. "And can you describe the nature of this 'relationship,' as you call it?"

"Well," she began thoughtfully, "If the word relationship implies something positive, then I guess that wouldn't be the right term. Basically, the neighborhood around Franklin before the 60's was a thriving, working class African American community. They had their own businesses, owned their homes, raised their families. Then Franklin wanted to expand its campus and got the city to force folks in the neighborhood out of their homes so that they could build on the property. That started relationship of distrust between Franklin and the community that still exists today."

She took a deep breath and continued. "In your article, you traced the tension from then until now. Right now, we're attending a university worth millions of dollars surrounded by a bunch of our people who are living in poverty and whose kids have no chance of going to the college that is two blocks away from their housing project. It's really a shame."

"Indeed," agreed Hark. He made sure he took the time to ask for her name before moving on.

"So someone else please tell me how this article relates to the title of this course—Black Collective Responsibility." Everyone once again assumed their nervous faces as he looked sternly around the room.

"It doesn't." The noise of thirty bodies shifting filled the room as students turned to see who made the comment.

The culprit was a brown skinned brother with glasses, wearing khakis and a button-up shirt. Kahlila had never seen him before, so she figured that he was an upperclassman and had already grown out of parties. He was wearing a smug expression, apparently pleased that he had everyone's attention.

"What's your name, son?" Dr. Harkonn inquired.

"Winston Gabriel, Professor."

"Well Mr. Gabriel, can you expand on why you feel that the history of Franklin and the community has nothing to do with the notion of Black Collective Responsibility?" Hark looked eager to hear his response.

"I certainly can. I think the slant of this class is that we as privileged college students of color need to give back to those who aren't so privileged. Your article is using the argument that Franklin owes the community, so therefore we as Franklin students owe the community as well."

"So where do you see the flaw in this argument, Mr. Gabriel?" Hark suddenly didn't look as anxious to hear the rest of what Winston had to say.

"Because, Dr. Harkonn, I don't feel as if it's our responsibility to bring up the community just because we're black. It's hard enough trying to do well for ourselves here, never mind worrying about other people. I believe in picking yourself up by your bootstraps. If students in the public schools around here wanted to go to Franklin, they could go. I mean, if they get straight A's, how is Franklin not going to let them in? So clearly, the community isn't working as hard as it could to overcome obstacles. We all had to fight battles to get where we are. Why can't they? If we keep doing everything for them, they're never going to learn to do for themselves. The best thing we can do is to let them work out their issues on their own."

Dr. Harkonn was wearing a smile that Kahlila couldn't quite decipher. But that could have been because she could barely think straight. Her blood had begun to boil about two sentences into Winston's little tirade.

How the hell is homeboy gonna say that shit? Winston. It figures. He looks like a fuckin' Winston.

"Yes, Ms. Bradford?" Dr. Harkonn was staring directly at her.

Why is he calling on me? Then she realized that her hand was raised. She stared at her arm in the air as if it betrayed her. *Nice going, Kahli. Can't even keep your damn mouth shut for one day.*

"Um, yeah. I just want to ask Winston exactly how he expects kids who go to the public schools around here to prepare themselves for a place like Franklin." *Try to sound as cool and collected as possible.*

Winston pushed up his glasses, slightly agitated. "The same way that *we* prepared. Work hard, earn good grades, participate in extra curricular activities . . ."

"Oh I see," Kahlila interrupted. "So you work your butt off to get straight A's in high school while working forty hours a week to help out at home since you're living below the poverty line. Miraculously, Franklin accepts you. When you get here, you realize that the only thing your high school has prepared you for is failure. You're taking Calculus when your high school only taught up to Algebra 2, and you're getting assigned a novel per week when it took five months to get through a book with half as many pages in your 12th grade English class. See Winston, hard work isn't the only ingredient to succeeding at a place like this. You need resources too."

"Fine, but I don't see why Franklin needs to be the one shelling out the resources."

Okay, he's really pissing me off now. It's getting harder and harder to sound educated. I just want to bop him upside the head. "Franklin needs to give money because they have it. And because they tore down the houses in an African American community that was self sufficient and thriving. They have no more small business. They have no more restaurants. Franklin caused that, and that's why the institution needs to make reparations. As for why we as individuals need to give back . . . well, we're black college students. There is not one of us who hasn't gotten help somewhere along the way. How can you sit there up in your ivory tower and say that you don't see why you should have to go down the street and mentor a kid at Franklin City High? Do you really feel like you're that much better than the tenth grader at Franklin City? Guess what, Winston. If that kid had a few more dollars and a Princeton Review course, he might be sitting in your seat right now."

Kahlila's heart was beating so loud that she wondered if the girl sitting next to her could hear it. Her voice was getting louder and she thought it might be shaking. She hated when folks made her this angry in class. She'd gotten used to a lot of the racist white kids in her high school coming out of their faces, but this dude was black! Or at least he looked like he was. *Maybe this is some old Soul Man shit and he's popping tanning pills or something.*

Dr. Harkonn sensed the heightened tension in the room and cut in before Winston could respond, although it appeared as if Winston was at a loss for words. "I think what you're saying, Ms. Bradford, is that the obligation of the university is both an economic *and* a moral one."

All Kahlila could do was nod. She was looking around and she realized that everyone was staring at her. She suddenly remembered her promise to herself to keep quiet. She felt embarrassed in spite of the fact that she was receiving nods of approval from other students, and Winston was getting sucked teeth and rolled eyes.

"Now our T.A. Dave Robinson's area of specialization is community and university relationships," Hark continued. "Dave, do you have anything to add to Mr. Gabriel and Ms. Bradford's discussion?"

Kahlila strained to get a glance at the geeky T.A. sitting near Hark at the front of the room. His sweater was resting nicely on a pair of broad shoulders, and his side profile was looking kind of chiseled. *Did he look that cute last week? Goodness, between him and Hark, I'm not gonna get any work done in this class.*

Dave looked as if he was debating whether or not to comment.

"N'ah. I pretty much feel like Kahlila about covered it. I personally think that even universities that didn't tear town anybody's property in order to expand still owe their surrounding communities. And a large part of that obligation is moral."

He knows my name? Kahlila didn't really hear what he said after he dropped her name like she was his homie. She gave an appreciative smile and quickly looked back down at her notebook.

Kahlila was no more good for the rest of class. Her mind was all over the place. She'd just remembered that she was supposed to meet J.T. for lunch after this class, and was trying to mentally readjust her schedule to fit in some errands she had to run. She was also wondering why Hark hadn't mentioned the other homework assignment from last week. She'd found five schools in the area where she would love to spend a few hours a week, and was eager for him to place her at one so she could get started.

But class ended without the professor asking them for their mini-research project. Kahlila watched everyone around her zipping up backpacks and straightening their seats. She got up as well, suddenly eager to catch up with J.T. Dr. Harkonn's voice boomed through the room. "E-mail me your list of five possible volunteer experiences and I'll e-mail you back the one I think is best. Make contact with the organization by next week." There was a collective groan from the class.

Kahlila had almost reached the door when Dr. Harkonn stopped her. "Ms. Bradford, do you have a moment?"

Shit. Maybe he noticed I was spacing out in class. "Sure," she nervously responded, taking a seat at the desk next to his.

Dave approached them as Kahlila was sitting down. "Yo Hark, you want to just meet with me later on or something?"

"Actually, I want you at this meeting as well," and he motioned for Dave to join them.

Now Kahlila was really confused. She decided to stop guessing what he wanted and just waited for him to start talking.

Dr. Harkonn wasted no time as soon as Dave was seated. "Ms. Bradford, you don't know me too well yet, but Dave could tell you that I always cut to the chase. So here's the deal: Coca-Cola just gave me a $10,000 grant to run some type of summer program for neighborhood kids. That's all the stipulation they gave me. So what I'm thinking is that you two could organize and run this program for me." He sat back, waiting for a reaction from his listeners.

Dave raised his eyebrows, obviously intrigued. Kahlila's confusion was written boldly on her face.

Hark sat forward and resumed speaking. "Dave, I'm sure you can see why I thought you might be interested in this project. It's right up your alley, what with university and community partnerships being your future dissertation topic. Ms. Bradford, I think you're probably thinking 'why me.' Am I correct in my assessment?"

"Yes. You're absolutely correct." Kahlila leaned forward in her chair as well.

"Well first, I know you're a first year student. It looks like Coca-Cola is going to give me this money for the next two years, as long as the program goes well. So I want an undergraduate who is going to be here for the duration of the program, so they can train others, et cetera, et cetera. Also, you said on the first day of this class that you had experience in schools. What exactly have you done?"

Hark and Dave were both looking at her, awaiting an answer. *How did I get stuck in the middle of a spontaneous interview?* "I did after school tutoring at my neighborhood middle school when I was in high school. And I took last year off and served as a college counselor at my neighborhood high school."

"Was it the same high school that you went to?" Dave asked, appearing genuinely interested.

"Actually, no. I went to a private school right outside the city," she responded almost apologetically. She sometimes felt like people formed opinions of her based on the school that she went to. And she certainly didn't want to look sheltered in front of these two very down-to-earth scholars.

"I see," said Dr. Harkonn. "Sounds like you've been feeling a sense of black collective responsibility for a long time. I've seen you at a lot of functions and discussions since you've arrived in September, and you seem like an excellent candidate to assist Dave in this project. That is, if Dave will do it." He looked pointedly in his T.A.'s direction, extending a look as if to say that there was only one correct response.

"I'm down, Hark. Sounds like it's gonna be tight." Now they both turned to Kahlila, delivering that same facial expression.

"Well, Ms. Bradford?" Dr. Harkonn prodded.

This is crazy. I know Mom is gonna want me home this summer. Where am I gonna live? Are any of my friends staying here over the summer? Am I qualified to run a summer program?

"I'd be honored to do it, Dr. Harkonn," Kahlila heard herself responding.

Hark got up to leave as soon as she answered. "Excellent. Now y'all know I'm busy. I have time to write you two a check and that's it. The rest is all you. So get together, begin to plan. Keep me posted." He threw his jacket over his arm, swung his bag on his shoulder, and walked out of the room.

"Wow. He's intense," Kahlila said almost to herself once he was gone.

"You'll get used to him," said Dave wisely as they gathered their things and walked towards the hallway.

When they reached the door of the classroom, Winston Gabriel popped out of nowhere and began to walk with them. Neither Dave nor Kahli acknowledged his presence.

"Kahli, right?" Winston tried to initiate conversation as he struggled to keep up with their fast pace through the crowded corridor.

"Kahlila. My *friends* call me Kahli." She stared straight ahead. Dave looked away to hide a smile.

"Ouch. Didn't you verbally attack me enough back in class?" He flashed a grin.

I guess he would be attractive if he weren't such a hard core Republican. "Well if you felt that way, why were you waiting for me?"

He hesitated before his words came spilling out a bit too fast. "I don't usually talk to freshmen, but you impressed me today. I was hoping we could exchange numbers or something." Winston glanced over at Dave, a little annoyed that Dave was witnessing his whole display.

"That's funny," Kahli slowly responded with a sly smile. "I don't usually talk to elitist upperclassmen who've forgotten where they came from. So if you'll excuse me . . ." and she sped up, throwing open the front door of the building, fighting the urge to look back at the expression on his face.

The guilt was starting to gnaw at her gut when she heard someone call her name. *If it's Winston, I'm gonna apologize.* She turned around to see Dave jogging to catch up with her.

"Do me a favor," he said as he fell into step with her. "Remind me never to get on your bad side."

Kahli covered her face with her hands. "Dave, I am so ashamed. That was a very non-Kahli-like thing to do. I'm usually a really nice person."

"It's all good. It gave me a good laugh. I wouldn't count on him giving you a second chance though."

"Oh, I don't want one. My boyfriend wouldn't like it much at all." Kahlila surprised herself with her response. She'd never called Tarik her boyfriend before. Maybe it was the great weekend they just had. Or maybe it was the fact that she couldn't just say "Tarik" because Dave probably had no clue who Tarik was.

"See? Women trip me out. Why couldn't you just tell poor Winston that you were involved with someone?"

"Because if I said that, he might have thought he would have had a chance if I were single."

"And he wouldn't have?"

"Hell no!" Kahlila turned to look at Dave in his face. *And what a nice face it is.* "Why would I want to date Clarence Thomas?"

They both burst out laughing. "Tragically harsh, Kahlila. Anyhow, so where are you from?"

"Boston."

"Word? What part?"

Kahli was surprised by the question. Only people from Boston knew the individual sections of the city. "Roxbury. Do you know Boston well?"

"Pretty well. I went to undergrad up there, and I volunteered at a Boys' Club in Roxbury."

"Wow—small world. So where did you go to school?"

"Harvard." He looked reluctant to answer the question, like he hated to say the name.

"I see. So you're just slummin' it down here at Franklin, huh?" Kahli teased.

"N'ah. I was slummin' it up there in Cambridge. The company is much better at Franklin, trust me. Well, I gotta turn off here. Expect e-mail from me in the next few days."

"Cool. Do you need the address?" She swung her backpack forward and began rummaging in the small front pocket for a pen.

"N'ah, I'll just look you up. Bradford, right?"

"Right." She continued on the path to the cafeteria, very content with the way her day was going so far. She'd dissed an upperclassman, made friends with a grad student, and snagged herself a summer job. Kahlila suddenly felt very grown-up, and started to take longer strides on the cobblestone campus path. The toe of her right foot didn't quite clear the bumpy bricks beneath her, and she took a huge stumble forward. Her head was catapulting towards the ground when she managed to catch herself with an awkward left-foot save. She looked around to see if anyone saw. Everyone did. She tried to fall back into her long strides, but her confidence was blown. *Now THAT was a very Kahli-like thing to do.* She forced herself to smile as she made her way to lunch.

CHAPTER SEVEN

J.T.

I'm just gonna have to tell Kal when she gets here—as a white guy, I can't tolerate this C.P. time bullshit.

J.T. had been waiting at the dining hall for ten minutes for Kahlila to arrive. But his frown flipped up when he thought of a stinging joke to deliver when she did show up.

The midday lunch rush consumed J.T. on all sides as he sat in the midst of the commotion with his coat draped on the chair opposite him and the newspaper strewn all over the table. People looking for seats were shooting him evil looks as he tried to reserve a seat for Kahli. Usually evil glares changed to friendly smiles when students recognized him as Joshua Travis Steinway, the sophomore basketball sensation. Sometimes random guy groupies would throw him a "Hey man, awesome game last night," and shake his hand enthusiastically. Girls would toss him a casual, "Nice picture in the paper today, Josh." He'd always return the compliments with a winning Crest grin a modest thank you His mind was usually saying something completely different, though. *Look at this uncoordinated corny ass. Probably never picked up a basketball in his life. And this damn sorority bitch would look a lot cuter if she wasn't swinging from my nuts.*

J.T. was in the middle of a pseudo-friendly exchange with a guy from his Chem class about his jump shot when Kahli rushed up to the table. When she saw that he was engaged in conversation, she dropped off her belongings at the table and went up to the serving line to get her meal. He watched Kahlila's back as she retreated into the crowd before he turned back to his classmate. *This asshole sees that Kal is here and we're trying to eat together and he's still down my throat about some bullshit.*

He managed to get rid of him by the time Kahli returned with a tray and a newspaper of her own to read. She made herself comfortable before she gave him a big smile. "Hey babes. Are you in here today?" She was flipping her paper over to the Sports Section, as was their routine whenever they had lunch during basketball season.

He just smirked as her eyes fell on the huge photo of him posting up for the tie-break in the last three seconds of Saturday night's away game.

"Where There's a Will There's a (Stein)Way?" Kahli burst out laughing. "These headlines get cornier with each passing week. Remember '(Tarik) Reynolds Wraps up His Career?' Who writes this crap?" She closed the paper and put it in her backpack to read later.

"I can always count on you to kill my moments of glory, Kal." J.T. was only pretending to be offended. He knew that Kahli was his biggest fan. She had clippings of articles about J.T. all over her walls, dating back to high school. She only missed a couple of games during his high school seasons, even after she quit cheerleading. And since she came to college, she was at every Franklin home game cheering him on. She and Tarik were probably the two loudest people in the whole arena. Tarik's heart was still with the team, and Kahli loved to see her best friend on the court. Kids had started calling J.T. "Bird" in high school, after Larry, but Kahli firmly objected. She thought that Bird's game was too awkward looking to be compared to J.T.'s. "You really don't play like a white boy, J.T. It's as simple as that." That was probably the biggest compliment Kahlila had ever given him.

"Whatever. Sorry I'm late though. I have so much to tell you," Kahlila said as she took a big swig of iced tea.

"Fuck. I forgot to use my C.P. time joke. Well let me get some food and then you can catch me up," he said as he rose from his chair.

"Joshua, you were here for so long. Why didn't you get food before?"

"One, I didn't want to lose this table. Two, I wanted to read the sports page first. Is that okay with you, mother?"

"Just hurry up, will you?" Kahli was getting annoyed and chomped loudly on her salad.

J.T. walked away from the table smiling. As he picked up a tray and silverware, he thought about how worried he had been when Kahli told him she was coming to Franklin. He'd been having a great first year, and was communicating a lot with Kahli by e-mail and seeing her when he went home. Since she took the year off, she was applying to schools after he had already started at Franklin. There had never been any question about where J.T. was going. His dad went to Franklin, their basketball team was decent, and he had the grades to get in. When Kahli told him that she was applying, he just knew she would end up at Harvard or Stanford. And it looked like she was off to California until she came to visit Franklin for a weekend last spring.

By the end of a hectic schedule of campus tours, lunches with professors, parties, and information sessions on every topic imaginable, Kahli was sold. And J.T. was scared. Was she going to be too attached to him once she got there? Would she make her own friends or would she expect to fall right into his social scene? Also, Kahli was a good looking chick, which meant that dudes would be trying to take advantage. J.T. would have to play the big brother role and warn her about all the dogs on campus, always making sure she wasn't getting herself into trouble.

But Kahli had grown up a lot in the year that she spent away from J.T. He realized that from the moment she arrived on campus in the fall. She'd chosen to live in the Booker T. Washington House, which was 95% black. The non-black 5% consisted of white girls who liked black guys and miscellaneous students who applied for housing late. She got her apartment key at 1:00 in the afternoon, and when J.T. stopped by to take her to dinner, she'd already made plans with her roommates to get something to eat. When he called her later to tell her about a party the football players were having, she was on her way out to a Kappa party off-campus.

Kahli turned out to be the perfect supplement to an already terrific college experience. They lived separate lives in two fairly disjointed worlds, but they visited each others' existence frequently. When J.T. described Kahli to his friends, he called her his guardian angel. She kept him in line academically, memorizing his course roster and making sure he went to class. She also gave great girl advice, and females who dated J.T. soon learned that if you made an enemy of Kahli, you were history with Josh.

As J.T. waited for a cafeteria worker to refill the bin of mayo, he remembered how worried he had been that Tarik was going to destroy whole program. They'd struck the perfect relationship, and he didn't want to have to be the bearer of bad news by telling her what a player Tarik was. He decided to hold off and see how serious it was between them before he blew up T's spot. When Kahli had sex with him, he was all prepared to break down the Tarik cycle: find 'em, fuck 'em, and fling 'em. But Tarik didn't fling Kahli. And J.T. noticed Tarik making an effort to be cool with him. *If he didn't give a fuck about Kal, he wouldn't bother trying to say shit to me aside from some random basketball comments.* But there Tarik was, all up in his face, asking if Kal finished her paper and if J.T. had any ideas for a good Christmas gift. *All right, player. I'll give you a chance with Kal. But if you fuck it up, your ass is mine.* It went unsaid, but J.T. spoke those words with his eyes every time he saw Tarik, and he was pretty sure T got the message.

By the time J.T. finished circulating the cafeteria, he'd collected three glasses of orange soda, two sandwiches, a bowl of cereal, a slice of cake, and a jelly donut. He put it in front of Kahli's tray of salad, iced tea, and jello.

"Kal, please tell me that's not all you're eating."

She looked up from the newspaper she'd taken out of her bag

while J.T. was getting his food. "Nah, this is just my first round. I'll get a pizza or something."

"Good. Now what's all this shit you have to tell me?" He gnawed into his salami and cheese and washed it down with a gulp of Minute Maid.

"I just got offered a job!" She waited expectantly for follow-up questions.

"You have a job. You work at this shithole ten hours a week stacking trays."

"I know that, shithead. I'm talking about a summer job," she replied, sucking her teeth.

"Doing what?"

"Helping run a summer program for neighborhood kids."

This girl is always on top of things. "How did you manage to find a job in Boston when you're hundreds of miles away?"

"The job isn't in Boston, idiot." She was thoroughly enjoying the confused expression J.T. was wearing.

"It's here? At school?" He dropped his spoon into his cereal so hard that the milk splattered on the half a sandwich left on his tray.

"Yup. My Black Studies professor is gonna be my boss. And the T.A. for that class is going to work with me to organize the program."

"So you just got offered the job, right? You didn't accept yet . . ."

"Oh, but I did." Kahlila dropped a piece of jello into her mouth, thoroughly satisfied with herself.

"And you didn't check with Mom?"

"She's not gonna trip." She said this with confidence, though J.T. recognized the look of worry that she was trying to mask.

"Well, you're right. She *is* gonna be fine with it." Now J.T. was the one looking smug.

"And how are you so sure?"

"Because I'm gonna be here looking out for you, as usual."

"WHAT? You're staying at school this summer and didn't tell

me?" She looked around to see if anyone had noticed her outburst. A few folks were staring, but it was hard to tell if it was because she was loud or if it was because she was sitting with a white guy.

"I was actually scared you were gonna be pissed that I wouldn't be able to hang with you at home."

"This is so hilarious! So why are *you* staying, anyway?"

"Coach was pushing us to stay here and work out. Plus, I'm behind in my pre-med requirements. And sciences courses are notoriously easier in the summer." *I hope this answer will satisfy her curiosity.*

"Well, I'll be wicked happy to have you here," she said with a put-on Boston accent. She forgot herself for a moment and gave him a huge crooked smile.

J.T. didn't respond. He just smiled back and started on his cake.

Once they were both as full as they could be off of cafeteria food, they got up to leave. As they walked towards the door, Kahli gently ruffled his spiky hair. "So, staying this summer has nothing to do with that little chicky you've been chilling with lately?"

Shit. "Who, Kristy? N'ah. I don't even know what she's doing this summer."

"You're a horrible liar! She's gonna be here—it's written all over your face!"

J.T. turned beet red. "So what if she is? Don't you like her?"

"Actually, yes. Kristy's O.K. with me. She doesn't have anything to say about our frequent lunches. And she seems pretty cool with the fact that mad heads swear we're getting it on."

A sly smile crept over J.T.'s face. "You mean that's not true?" He asked innocently as he grabbed her and wrapped his arms around her waist.

They walked in that position towards the exit, J.T. holding on to her and trying not to step on her heels. They both laughed as they tried to fit through the front door of the dining hall without detangling themselves.

Suddenly, the mood changed. J.T. heard the voice before he saw where it was coming from.

"So you think you can diss me when I try to talk to you and then you can pull some bullshit like this?"

J.T. looked over at Kahli, who was absolutely mortified. He followed her gaze to the guy standing a few feet in front of them. He was a brown skinned, preppy looking kid with glasses, just looking heated for no reason.

Does this have something to do with me? J.T. removed his arms from Kahli's waist before he spoke. "What's going on, man?" he asked.

"Um, nothing dude," the guy replied with a fake California surfer accent.

No this little prick isn't trying to start shit. "What the fuck is your problem?"

Kahlila was starting to look really anxious now. "Joshua, stop. Winston, just chill out. Look, I'm sorry about earlier. I was out of line."

"Hell yeah you were." He began to walk away, and relief slowly spread across Kahli's face.

"*I* forgot where I came from? Fuckin' sellout."

Winston sai it just loud enough for the comment to drift back to both J.T. and Kahli. His back was to them, but J.T. could swear he saw that asshole smiling through the back of his head.

Kick his ass. Beat the shit out of him. J.T. turned to look at Kahli, who looked like someone had just knocked the wind out of her. He'd never seen her look so helpless, not even the time when someone stole her leather jacket from her locker in tenth grade.

He's dead. He rushed at Winston before he even knew that he was doing it. He connected with him and kept rushing. Winston was thrown into the brick exterior of the dining hall, and managed to put his hands up in time to save his face. It was still a hard shove, and a crowd had formed before Winston even had a chance to turn around and face his assailant.

When Winston did turn around, J.T. was in fighting stance, ready to swing. He couldn't see Kahli anymore, but he imagined that she hadn't moved from her original position. He couldn't think about her right now, though. He was busy sizing up his opponent. The last thing he wanted to do was lose a fight in a public space; he hadn't done that since elementary school. Even though it was a while ago, he could remember that it wasn't a good feeling.

Apparently, Winston's last loss must have been more recent than fifth grade, because he really wasn't trying to embarrass himself. He sidestepped J.T. and slowly walked through the group of people blocking his way. Once he was at a safe distance, he turned back to J.T. "There was really no need for that shit, man. I wasn't even talking to you."

J.T. chuckled. *He's not even fuckin' worth it.* He just watched Winston as he ambled away on the path down campus. The guys in the crowd were already cackling with laughter at how Winston had punked out. Girls were trying to get the lowdown on how the whole thing started. "What happened, Josh?" a million high pitched voices were asking at the same time.

J.T. ignored the pats on the back, the questions, and the laughter. *Where's Kal?*

She answered his unspoken question by squeezing through two wanna-be comedians who were physically re-enacting the entire scene. She didn't look as shellshocked as she did a few minutes before, but she still looked really sad. Sadder than when her dad didn't show up for her high school graduation. She was marching in the procession, only half paying attention to the band's horrible rendition of Pomp and Circumstance. She was squinting and trying to scan the crowd to find her father. She finally located the huge crowd of people who'd come to support her. Kahli's and J.T.'s families were sitting together, and they took up about five rows of seats. She made eye contact with her mom, and her mom shook her head no. Kahli had just nodded, like it didn't phase her. But the sadness and disappointment shone in her eyes.

J.T. looked at Kahli and the shine in her eyes was the same. He did exactly what he did that bittersweet day in June. He took her hand, and they marched off together while the crowd around them watched.

CHAPTER EIGHT

To: angelabradford@aol.com
From: kahlila@classof99.franklin.edu
Date: Jan 16, 1996 7:35 p.m.
Subject: big news . . .

Message:
hi mom-

you'll never guess what happened. you know my class with the amazing professor i told you about? he offered me a summer job running a program for public school students. i'd be working with a grad student who seems pretty cool. before you go asking me a million questions, i don't know where i'm living yet, how much i'm making, or much of anything really. but i really want to do this. what do you think?

love,
kahli

To: kahlila@classof99.franklin.edu
From: angelabradford@aol.com
Date: Jan 16, 1996 9:14 p.m.
Subject: big news . . . —Reply

Message:
kahlibear,

sounds wonderful. i'll restrain my motherly urges to delve for details. honey, i thought about begging you to come home for the summer. but then i remembered the words of your namesake:

"your children are not your children. they are the sons and daughters of life's longing for itself. they come through you but not from you, and though they are with you yet they belong not to you. you may give them your love but not your thoughts, for they have their own thoughts."

it's so hard to let go, baby. but you're a grown-up now. have i told you lately that you make me so proud?

love you,
mom

To: drobinson@sociology.franklin.edu
From: joy_rainer@yahoo.com
Date: Jan 17, 1996 3:35 a.m.
Subject: just thinking about you

Message:
david,

i just got home from the late shift at the hospital. i want to call you but it's way too late and i don't want to wake you up. wish you were here with me. i sleep so much better when you're in my bed. although i like it the most when you're in my bed and i'm not sleeping ;-). lunch tomorrow?

i love you,
joy

To: kahlila@classof99.franklin.edu

From: drobinson@sociology.franklin.edu
Date: Jan 17, 1996 10:05 a.m.
Subject: getting started . . .

Message:
hi kahlila,

how are things going? i'm on overload—i committed myself to way too many projects this semester, and now with our summer program to plan, i'm kinda buggin. i'm actually not gonna be in hark's class tomorrow because of a schedule conflict, so i won't see you till tuesday.

so i'm thinking we should get together outside of class and begin discussing the logistics—like what age kids do we want for the program, what kind of theme should the program center around, who we're hiring, etc. etc.

by the way, i was at this undergrad meeting yesterday (i'm the group's advisor) and folks were talking about how winston and some white dude were fighting over you? i'm usually not interested in campus drama but this sounded intriguing . . .

peace
dave

To: joy_rainer@yahoo.com
From: drobinson@sociology.franklin.edu
Date: Jan 18, 1996 10:23 a.m.
Subject: just thinking about you—Reply

Message:
joy,

sorry i couldn't help you sleep (or not sleep—wink) last night. i could have used a massage myself. i'm stressed as hell. lunch today—not looking too good. i'm gonna eat on the run—too many errands.

sorry—i'll call you tonight.
love,
david

To: joshuatravis@classof98.franklin.edu
From: kahlila@classof99.franklin.edu
Date: Jan 18, 1996 1:40 p.m.
Subject: defending my honor . . .

Message:
babes-

haven't heard from you since "the incident." i hope you're not still trippin about it. although you know i'm not a proponent of violence, thanks for having my back. seems like the story is all around campus, and of course folks have put their own spin on it.

winston didn't show up to class today. i'm not looking forward to seeing him again. write back and let me know you're okay. don't make me come by.

-kal

To: drobinson@sociology.franklin.edu
From: kahlila@classof99.franklin.edu
Date: Jan 18, 1996 2:01 p.m.
Subject: getting started . . .—Reply

Message:
hi dave,

class was good today. sorry you missed it. hark assigned everyone their community service placements. the good news for me is that our little summer project counts as my community work, which means i can fully devote myself to planning.

my schedule is much less hectic than yours, so give me a few possible dates and times that are good for you.

regarding winston—he just said something really fucked up to me, and my friend j.t. pushed him. that was it. so if you hear it again circulating through the rumor mill, make sure you dead it.

peace
kahlila

To: kahlila@classof99.franklin.edu
From: desiree@classof99.franklin.edu
Date: Jan 18, 1996 2:56 p.m.
Subject: read this!!! (fwd)

Message:
kahli,

i'm gonna be out all day so i probably won't run into you at home. but this couldn't wait. i'm forwarding you this message i got from trevor. can you believe it??? :-)-dez

> desiree,

i really enjoyed our phone conversation the other day. i had been thinking a lot about your beautiful face since the party. then when i talked to you and saw that you had a personality to match—well, i'm blown away. please allow me to take you somewhere nice as all hell this weekend. get back to me soon before i have to start begging.

>

> bye gorgeous,
> trevor

To: kahlila@classof99.franklin.edu
From: joshuatravis@classof98.franklin.edu
Date: Jan 18, 1996 3:38 p.m.
Subject: defending my honor—Reply

Message:
k-dawg,
i'm fine. i've just been busy. stop worrying. i don't know what got into me the other day though. truth be told, i don't think it was even about sticking up for you. i know that sounds fucked up, but it's true. i felt like i was sticking up for myself—like how was i gonna let that asshole say that because you were chilling with me you were a sellout. no. fuck that. i haven't seen him since then either, but if i do, he better not say shit to me.

yo, i ran into tarik and he told me that you filled him in on the story. i thought he'd be all pissed off, but he seemed cool about it. did he give you static?
-j.t.

To: desiree@classof99.franklin.edu
From: kahlila@classof99.franklin.edu
Date: Jan 18, 1996 4:13 p.m.
Subject: read this!!!—Reply

Message:
girl, we'll talk later. that shit is real. i don't suppose i can say

anything to tarik about it . . . nevermind, i'll just talk to you tonight.-
kahli
To: kahlila@classof99.franklin.edu
From: drobinson@sociology.franklin.edu
Date: Jan 19, 1996 10:12 a.m.
Subject: getting started . . . —Reply—Reply

Message:
how does next week wednesday sound? late afternoon, early evening . . .

so what's the deal with you and el blanco? is that the boyfriend you were referring to?

peace
dave

To: drobinson@sociology.franklin.edu
From: kahlila@classof99.franklin.edu
Date: Jan 19, 1996 1:27 p.m.
Subject: aren't you nosy . . .

Message:
funny, i could have sworn that my personal life had nothing to do with a summer program for kids.

el blanco, huh? you gotta work on your comedic skills. and if you're gonna use a foreign language, i'm better at french. j.t. is not my boyfriend. do you want the long or short version of who he is exactly?

-kahlila

To: kahlila@classof99.franklin.edu
From:drobinson@sociology.franklin.edu
Date: Jan 19, 1996 2:41 p.m.
Subject: aren't you nosy—Reply

Message:
kahlila,

sorry if i overstepped my boundaries. it's just that my e-mail account is so clogged with business-related shit that i wanted to have a message i could actually enjoy.

so do i want the long or short version? i want every bit of juice, and don't strain the pulp.

peace
dave

To: joshuatravis@classof98.franklin.edu
From: kahlila@classof99.franklin.edu
Date: Jan 19, 1996 2:45 p.m.
Subject: defending my honor—Reply—Reply

Message:
thanks for getting back to me so soon. you know how i overreact. re: tarik, he was mad cool about the winston thing. maybe it had something to do with the fact i told him seconds before orgasm. kidding. get some work done this weekend. i know that paper is due next week. robyn said she saw you with some chick coming from the movies, and she couldn't tell if it was kristy. what's the deal? i'll call you for details tomorrow.

-kal

To: drobinson@sociology.franklin.edu
From: kahlila@classof99.franklin.edu
Date: Jan 19, 1996 3:00 p.m.
Subject: aren't you nosy . . . —Reply—Reply

Message:
the juice AND the pulp, huh? well i'm not exactly sure about what you were trying to do with that slightly off-kilter metaphor, but i take it that means you want the long version. o.k.—here's the deal. j.t. and i went to high school together. we sat next to each other in 9th grade english class and just hit it off right away. in tenth grade we were boyfriend and girlfriend for a hot second, but it just sorta fizzled. we never even broke up, really. just gradually we reverted back to being purely friends. by eleventh grade he was one of my best friends, and by twelfth grade he was part of my family and i was part of his. he came to franklin and i took a year off, and now we're both here. that's pretty much it.

-kahlila

To: kahlila@classof99.franklin.edu
From: drobinson@sociology.franklin.edu
Date: Jan 19, 1996 4:10 p.m.
Subject: aren't you nosy . . . —Reply—Reply—Reply

Message:
interesting story. sure doesn't sound like the last chapter has been written.

p.s . . . .off-kilter?

To: drobinson@sociology.franklin.edu
From: kahlila@classof99.franklin.edu
Date: Jan 19, 1996 4:58 p.m.
Subject: yes, off-kilter!

Message:
sorry, my mom uses that expression. she's very strange. so wednesday sounds good. just pick an exact time and place. you can tell me in class tuesday.

-kahlila

To: kahlila@classof99.franklin.edu
From: drobinson@sociology.franklin.edu
Date: Jan 19, 1996 5:17 p.m.
Subject: yes, off kilter!—Reply

Message:
yeah, i'll let you know on tuesday the deal for our meeting. but i was thinking that we might want to jot down some ideas and exchange them before that time. if you think i'm being anal just let me know but i'm just amped to get started. and the better i plan, the less stressed i'll be.

so if this is cool with you, how about we exchange some preliminary notes sometime around sunday?

To: drobinson@sociology.franklin.edu
From: kahlila@classof99.franklin.edu
Date: Jan 19, 1996 6:50 p.m.
Subject: yes, off kilter!—Reply—Reply

Message:

i'm actually really anal at times too so don't worry about it. and i'm really excited to start planning as well, and my mind is already racing with ideas.

i'll be in my room studying all evening on sunday, so if you'll be in the area you can stop by with your notes and i'll have mine ready for you. i live in booker t. washington house, room 308.

To: kahlila@classof99.franklin.edu
From: drobinson@sociology.franklin.edu
Date: Jan 20, 1996 10:04 a.m.
Subject: Sunday night at 8:00?

Message:
i think the title speaks for itself.
damn, typing your e-mail address makes me feel old. class of 99? wow.

To: drobinson@sociology.franklin.edu
From: kahlila@classof99.franklin.edu
Date: Jan 20, 1996 11:24 a.m.
Subject: Sunday night at 8:00?—Reply

Message:
i'll be in my room at 8:00 tomorrow. and don't worry—you're not that old. if it's any consolation, you look good for your age :-)

kahlila

CHAPTER NINE

Lloyd

"Shit!" Dave muttered the expletive so loudly that Lloyd sauntered into their living room to find the source of the problem.

"What's goin' on?" Lloyd had just woken up from a nap, which caused him to look even more confused and disoriented.

Dave was staring at his planner as if it betrayed him. "I don't look at this damn book for one day and I start forgetting shit. It's 7:30, I'm supposed to be at Joy's right now, and I just realized that I was supposed to do something at 8:00."

Lloyd was disappointed in Dave's dilemma. He was hoping for something a bit more interesting—a reason to get out of bed, or at least a problem to chew on while he made a snack.

Might as well try to help anyway since I'm up. "How long is what you have to do at 8:00 gonna take?"

"Like twenty minutes or so."

"So just call Joy and tell her you're gonna be late." *There. Problem solved.*

"Naw. That's not gonna work. Joy's been kinda irritated lately 'cuz I've been putting her off. If I call with this, she's gonna be heated all night. She's probably already pissed 'cuz I'm late."

Lloyd wanted to tell Dave like it was: *D, even if she fronts like she's mad for a hot second, it's not like she's gonna allow a real argument to go down. She's too scared of losing you.* But Dave was sensitive about Joy stuff, so Lloyd decided to take a different approach.

"Yeah, I remember those days. You definitely don't want to cause any unnecessary drama. What do you have to do at

8:00, anyhow?" He found his way to the living room chair and sank into it.

"Remember that summer program I told you about? Well, I gotta drop off some preliminary notes to the person I'm working with."

"D, that does not sound urgent. I'm sure he'll be cool with getting the notes tomorrow."

"She. And I'm really not trying to fold when I was the one pressed about writing these notes in the first place."

Dave is my boy, but the nigga is truly anal. "You didn't tell me Hark hired a *female* to work with you. Who is she?"

"This freshman Kahlila who's taking his class. The one he put in charge of keeping it real."

"Stop playin'. I don't know what's more interesting—that Hark hired a freshman to co-direct a summer program, or that you're actually pressed about how you come off looking to her." Lloyd could have pushed it further, but he could tell that Dave was getting frustrated.

"Lloyd, if you're not gonna offer any suggestions . . ."

"Fine. Look, you supposed to go to this girl's crib? Or dorm, I should say, 'cuz we know that freshmen gotta live on-campus."

"Yeah . . ." Dave was starting to look hopeful.

"I'll go over there for you. But you owe me for real. Like a half month's rent or some shit."

"Yo, good looking out. I got you. Not with no money shit, but I got you. She lives in Booker T., room 308," Dave said enthusiastically as he read the information from his planner.

"Figures. Just what I need on a Sunday night. Gotta ruin my calm, going to a house full of black undergrads most likely actin' like fools."

Dave chose to ignore the bitterness. "My notes are right on top of my desk. And she should have some for you too." He was halfway out the door before he finished his sentence.

Lloyd was left by himself in the living room, playing with his hair and trying to shake off the residue exhaustion from his nap.

Damn it if I didn't just get had by my own boy. Got me to save his ass so that he could participate fully in his unhealthy relationship. I gotta find something of my own to get into so I can stop noticing how jacked up D's situation is. He tried to shake Sonia's smile out of his head as he walked into Dave's room to get the notes.

Weeks in college fly by so fast, but the weekends go even quicker. Kahlila was sitting at the head of her bed with a book in her lap, but she wasn't reading. She was trying to figure out how Sunday came around already. It seemed like just yesterday that she was putting in her Friday morning shift at the cafeteria, thinking about all of the possibilities that stretched before her for the next three days. Suddenly it was twelve hours and counting before her Monday morning class.

She'd procrastinated as long as she possibly could. Her phone call with Tarik lasted a good two hours, and they eventually ran out of bullshit to talk about. J.T. was at Kristy's house, Robyn was at the library as usual, and she didn't know where the hell Desiree was all day. Shady Shannon was actually home for a change, but Kahli wasn't so desperate to put off her work that she would knock on her door and have a chat. Shannon was almost a visitor in their apartment. Desiree had nicknamed her Shady Shannon by the second week of school when it became clear that she was in their room because of a housing error and that she wasn't interested in making friends at all. They saw her for a few minutes every few days when she stopped in to pick up some clothes or use the phone. She rarely slept in the bedroom she shared with Desiree, and none of them had the guts to ask her where she usually laid her head at night.

Fuck it. A conversation with Shannon has got to be better than all these damn readings on Christopher Columbus. As Kahli put her book aside and rose from her bed, she heard the front door close. Desiree appeared in Kahli's doorway breathless, as she'd done a million times before when she had a story to tell.

Kahli heaved a sigh of relief and plopped back down on her bed. "Girl, you wouldn't believe what I was about do to put off doing my reading . . ."

"Whatever, whatever. Shut up. I have to talk to you." Dez's words were harsh, but she was grinning from ear to ear. Her hair was in an unusually messy ponytail, and she was wearing a Franklin sweatsuit.

"Does your Kool-Aid smile have anything to do with your date with Trevor last night? And before you answer that, where were you all day today looking like such a scrub?"

"For your information, I was feeling so energized that I went to the library to get some work done," she replied as she pointed to the backpack that she'd dropped in the hallway outside of Kahli and Robyn's bedroom door.

"You're kidding. Did you see Robyn there?"

"Oh, was she there today? I didn't see her. Maybe she went to the medical library instead."

"Maybe . . . but forget that. I want to hear all about this date!"

"Well, I want to tell you! Kahlila, he is soooo wonderful. I had the best time," she said dreamily as she stared past her friend and out of the window, as if she could see Trevor's face in the moon.

"So what did you do? Where did you go?" Kahli asked impatiently.

"He'd made reservations at this fly little Italian restaurant. Are you hearing me, Kahli? Reservations!! What guy at Franklin have you ever met who has made reservations anywhere?"

She has a point there. While Kahlila couldn't really complain about Tarik, he wasn't the best date planner. They'd occasionally hit a movie or get something to eat, but plans were always spontaneous and never romantic.

"I hear ya, Dez," Kahli said. "Most Franklin guys call a date showing up to your crib with a Blockbuster video in their hand."

"Blockbuster?!" Dez said incredulously. "Please, Kahli. Niggas be borrowing videos from their boys. They ain't spendin' money on Blockbuster."

"True!" Kahli laughed, forming a mental picture of some sorry negro at her front door with a tattered copy of Jason's Lyric. "Or even worse, they time the date to coincide with a new release on cable."

"Oh, now that's a shame," Dez shook her head in mock displeasure.

"But back to Trevor. Then what did y'all do?" Kahli made herself comfortable on her bed, lying on her stomach and propping up her head with both elbows.

"We ate and we talked. And we talked. And you'll never guess what we did after dinner." Dez leaned forward in her chair for dramatic effect.

"Well if I'll never guess . . ." Kahli was tired of waiting. She wanted the meat.

"We went ice skating!!!"

"Damn," said Kahli, wide eyed. "A brother on ice skates. That's not something you see every day. Why ice skating?"

"I'd mentioned to him on the phone a few days before that I used to love to ice skate when I was little. So he found this really nice rink about a twenty minute drive from here. Did I mention that he has a phat ride? But anyhow, he was a horrible skater. It was pretty funny watching him grip onto the side of the rink. And we got to hold hands and be really cute."

Is this the same Trevor that Tarik introduced me to? Trevor sure hadn't seemed so sweet and sensitive the two times that Kahli had been around him. But maybe she made a hasty judgment. "Dez, I don't think I'm ready for whatever came next on the date."

She giggled. "No, that was pretty much it. He drove me home, we kissed, he said he'd call today. Which means I gotta go check my messages."

"Warning. Shady is home so don't expect any privacy in your room." Kahli laughed as Desiree threw one of Kahli's stuffed animals against the wall upon hearing the news.

Kahli tried to take Dez's mind off of her unwanted roommate. "So what time did you get in last night, anyhow?"

"Late," Dez answered quickly. "You and Tarik were probably already sleep."

"How did you know Tarik was here? Has he really been here that much lately?"

"Yeah, girl. Just a lucky guess." Dez hurriedly stood up from her chair and walked out of Kahli's room, grabbing her backpack and taking a deep breath before opening the door to her room and facing Shady Shannon.

Excellent. Now I have more reason to procrastinate. I can call Tarik and hear what Trevor said about the date. She picked up her cordless, pressed Memory 3, and waited as the phone rang.

Lloyd was flashing his Franklin I.D. in the lobby of Booker T. fifteen minutes after Dave's initial request. As he walked up the steps, images of himself as a high school senior projected onto the walls. Of course the images weren't really there; the walls were covered with flyers and posters in reality. But he saw himself clear as day, his curly Afro growing out of control, his rimless glasses, and that T-shirt with the big music note on it. That's what he looked like the last time he'd been inside Franklin's Booker T. Washington House.

1990. April. Deciding on schools. Columbia or Franklin. Why don't I visit and decide that way. Franklin's minority recruitment weekend. Booker T. Washington House? What's that? The black dorm on campus, another prospective student told me. Wow. I'd never been around that many black folks at once. Mom tried to expose me. Felt bad that she couldn't help me find myself. Guess her white skin and blond hair were impediments. Her signing me up for jazz piano at age six was the best she could do. That and making sure that pictures of Dad were all over the house. Dad before the cancer, not after. Wanted me to remember him as strong and healthy. Died when I was three—glad I can remember him at all.

Walked into the House with anticipation. My host by my side. Hadn't been very friendly on the walk to the dorm. Was he expecting someone more like him? More black? "No, I don't play basketball." "I like all kinds of music." "I'm not really the party type." My answers didn't seem acceptable. More of the same when I met his friends. Always the palest face in the room. Never wearing the right clothes. Never saying the right thing. Didn't know the songs they were talking about. Didn't know the T.V. shows they watched. What the hell kind of game is spades, anyhow?

Can't the weekend end? I can't see myself here. There's no one like me here. A lot of nice looking females. And I never see this many black girls in upstate New York. But they aren't lookin' at me. They're looking at the tall brown skinned brother with the high top fade and the Cross Color jeans. They sure as hell aren't paying any attention to the short yellow boy with the messy hair and crazy clothes. In my white school, my white neighborhood, and my white family, I always felt so conscious of my blackness. At Franklin, I can't even find it.

Guess it's Columbia.

The sound of Lloyd's fist pounding on the door of Room 308 abruptly turned off the slide show of his past flickering on the walls. When the door opened, Lloyd had his eyes closed, as if to completely wash away the residue of his flashback. He opened his lids only to find a pair of curious eyes looking back at him. These eyes belonged to a girl wearing a tank top and a pair of pajama pants. Her hair was pulled back, leaving his eyes to fully take in a face that made it hard to look anywhere else. Her skin radiated a warm, red glow that made Lloyd wonder if she'd been in the sun lately. An island during Christmas break, perhaps? She had a slight frame, her delicate arms folded across her chest, and her tiny hips thrown to one side. Though her stance seemed to convey some sort of attitude problem, her facial expression appeared so kind that Lloyd had to smile in greeting.

"Hi. Is Kahlila home?"

"You're looking at her," her smile widening and shifting slightly to one side.

Aw, man. Could she tell I was staring? No, "you're looking at her" is just an expression, idiot. "How ya doin'. I'm Lloyd, Dave Robinson's roommate. He had something come up at the last minute, so he asked me to come by and drop off these notes." He held up the folder in his right hand, as if displaying the notes made his visit legitimate.

"Oh! Well nice to meet you, Lloyd," she said as she extended her hand.

He took it, and was a little surprised by the firmness of the shake. *You'd expect someone who looked this fragile to have a weak grip.*

She pulled her hand away first. "Hold the door for one second. I need to get off the phone and print out the notes."

He propped the door open with his right hiking boot as he watched her disappear into a bedroom. He heard a door open, and expected to see her brown tank top materialize in front of him, but instead he saw a blue Franklin sweatshirt. This girl stopped in front of the door to inspect the visitor. He inspected her too, quickly surveying a skin color very close to his own, long hair, and a curvy figure that couldn't be hidden even in the sweats.

"Hi," she said as if it were simply an opening for Lloyd to explain himself and the nature of his visit.

"What's up. I'm just waiting for Kahlila to give me something."

"Oh," she replied, thoroughly bored, and continued down the hall without another word.

He was still trying to figure out what to make of her when someone's voice behind him made him jump.

"Excuse me," said a pair of the whitest, straightest teeth he'd ever seen. The sight of this third girl put Lloyd at ease. Kahlila was so striking that she made him nervous. The second girl's attitude made him uncomfortable. But this one trying to walk past him and into their apartment was so adorable that he wanted to give her a hug. Her smooth, chocolate colored baby face was framed by a short Halle Berry haircut. And she actually made Lloyd feel tall. She couldn't have been more than 5' 3" or so.

"I'm sorry. I'm all in your way," he said as he stepped aside to clear a path.

"That's okay. Can I help you with something?" Those pearly whites again.

"N'ah. I'm straight. Just waiting for Kahlila."

"Oh, okay. I'm her roommate, Robyn." She looked at her arms, which were filled with books, as if to apologize for not being able to shake his hand. "And you are . . ."

"My bad. Lloyd. Bryant." He was about to explain exactly why he was lingering in their doorway looking lost, but Kahlila suddenly joined them in their conversation and he was at a loss for words.

"Sorry, Lloyd. My Mac is so slow. I probably should have bought a PC. Hey, Robyn. Hope you were keeping Lloyd entertained."

"We actually just met, so I didn't have enough time to put together the full show."

Lloyd watched them just grinning at him and at each other, and he couldn't decide whose smile was cuter. Once he realized that he was probably grinning like an idiot as well, he decided that the whole thing needed to end.

"Well, thanks y'all. I'll be sure to get these notes to Dave, Kahlila. Nice meeting you, Robyn."

They waved simultaneously as he turned away and walked down the hall. *Lloyd. You're twenty-four years old. These girls are freshmen in college. What are you smiling for?* But he knew why. Because the only person he'd ever met who had a smile like theirs was in New York with some guy she met in her yoga class. He pushed open the front door of Booker T. Washington House with force. *I hate this fuckin' building.*

"Who the hell was that?" Dez shouted from her bedroom as soon as the door slammed.

"A friend of Dave's," Kahli shouted back from the hallway.

"Who the hell is Dave?" was the obvious next question from Desiree.

"Can y'all please stop shouting?" chimed in Shannon from the bathroom.

"Sorry," said Kahli, Dez, and Robyn all together.

Desiree came out of her room and met Kahli and Robyn in the hall. "Who's Dave?"

"The guy I'm working with this summer."

"Is he as geeky as his friend?" Dez made a face at the door as if Lloyd was still standing there.

"Desi, stop acting so stank," Robyn scolded. "He was kinda cute. His eyes were pretty."

"Pretty eyes? How could you see them behind the glasses?" Dez asked incredulously.

"And to answer your question," Kahli interjected, "No. Dave is not geeky. And he's taller than Lloyd. And browner. And more built. And . . ."

"O.K., player!" Dez said slyly, looking Kahli up and down. "How you gonna be looking at other men when you know you got Tarik?"

"Please! I can still look. Especially when the guy is like twenty-four years old and ain't thinking about nobody's Kahlila Bradford."

Kahli was suddenly ready to hit the books. The conversation was annoying her, and she was anxious to get her history reading done so that she could read Dave's notes.

She fake tossed her hair, and swiveled her hips around. "If you'll excuse me ladies, I have some business to conduct." She sashayed into her bedroom and shut the door behind her.

As soon as Kahli was seated at her desk, the door reopened. Robyn stared at her from the doorway.

"Bitch, do you forget we share a room? Don't be slammin' the door in my face!"

Kahli tossed a stuffed animal at her and they both sat down at their desks to prepare for the week ahead.

notes for summer program

kahlila-

i'm thinking that the program should have a theme of some sort. like base it around art or science or even hip hop. who knows.

writing skills are always low in urban schools. maybe focusing it around writing would be a good thing. if we can make it creative writing then maybe the kids will get into it. i'm thinking so many programs for minority students focus on science, business, etc. maybe something more liberal arts focused could be a nice change.

so hark says we have $10,000 which sounds like a lot but really it's not that much at all. once we pay ourselves, pay whatever staff we hire, buy supplies, arrange some field trips or whatever, there goes all the money. should we look into requesting additional funds, or finding a sponsor to match what coca-cola donated?

while we're on the subject of staff, how many people do we want to hire? do we want teachers by profession who are on summer vacation? or do we want college students working for us? combination of both?

where do we want to have the program? i'm sure we can find a place to house it at franklin. allowing the students to experience a college campus might be a good thing, especially if we're working with high school students. at the same time, are we privileging franklin with a sense of importance that it doesn't deserve? it might be better to have the program at whatever high school the kids attend.

how long should the program be? four weeks? six? eight? i'm thinking six. we want to give the students at least a few weeks to be couch potatoes in the summertime. and *i* might want a couple of those weeks as well.

i guess those are the major questions i've been thinking about. at least we have a few months to answer them all. how's wednesday at 4:30 for a meeting time? hark said we could use his office. let me know in class tuesday.

peace
dave

summer institute notes
dave,

i'm calling it a summer institute instead of a summer program because i think that the program should be academically focused and the title of the program should connote a rigorous curriculum. "institute" is flexible (since it kind of sounds like a mental hospital), but hopefully you understand what i mean in terms of terminology. kids think of very different things when they hear "summer camp" and when they hear "summer school." i don't want our program to be either of those things. camp seems like all play and no work, and school seems like the opposite, almost like a punishment.

i think that what we teach this summer is absolutely secondary to the atmosphere that is created within the program. more specifically:

- students in the program should feel as if they were chosen to be part of it, and that it is an honor to be part of the program. if that involves giving them a small stipend or whatever, i think it's worth it.
- staff needs to hold the highest expectations for these students. i mean that the work should not be geared to a lower level simply because these kids go to sucky schools. if our students are in grade 10, they should be getting 10th grade work. or maybe 11th or 12th.
- students should be exposed to things outside of their realm of experience. field trips outside of the city. language classes, perhaps. literature focused on subjects besides racism and violence.

• the program should function as a community—everyone must be fully committed and willing to work cooperatively with others. we should maybe target one school to recruit from, so that these kids can continue to work together and encourage each other once the program ends.

if this seems a little vague to you, this is how i think. logistics can come later, but i need to feel what we're creating before i can execute the details.

can't wait to talk more on wednesday,

kahlila

CHAPTER TEN

One day, I'm gonna have an office that looks like this. Dave had seen Dr. Harkonn's office many times, but it always served to amaze him nevertheless. The plush carpeting, the view of the skyline, the African art hung on the walls, the certificates and framed photographs on the shelves. And the books. Books on bookcases, on desks, piled in corners. It was the office of a true black intellectual.

It took five full seconds for Kahlila's mouth to close after her initial jaw-dropping survey of the room. She walked in behind Dave and slowly took a seat on one of the couches. She looked uncomfortable, sitting on the edge of her seat with her hands folded.

Dave smiled. "You can make yourself comfortable. The couch isn't gonna break if you put all your weight on it."

She looked embarrassed as she readjusted her position. He sat next to her on the couch and they both reached into their backpacks to take out the necessary materials to get down to business.

"So," said Kahlila as she sifted through her folder for Dave's notes, "Is everything resolved from Sunday night?"

Dave returned the question with a startled expression. *What the hell did Lloyd tell this girl about my issues with Joy?* "Uh, what do you mean?"

"Your friend said that something came up at the last minute . . ."

"Oh, right. Yeah, everything's straight." *I should have known Lloyd wasn't spreading my biz.* "So I really enjoyed your notes. Isn't it weird how . . ."

"How we both tackled such different aspects of the program?" Kahli finished. "I'm sorry. That was rude. Was that even what you were going to say?"

"That's exactly what I was going to say. You decided to focus on the feel of the program, or institute I should say. I concentrated on logistics."

"You don't see that as a problem, do you? Because I think it's sort of a strength, like we have all our bases covered."

"No, I completely agree. So what do you think our next steps should be?" Dave had to struggle to ask this question. He was so used to taking the lead when working on various projects, that it was hard to let go of the reins sometimes. *But this girl seems like she has her head on straight, and she deserves to be an equal partner.*

Kahli looked appreciative of the question. "Well, I was thinking that we could decide on what students we want to target, and design an application for them."

Dave tried to hide the relief on his face. "That was one of the things on the top of my list, too. I like what you said about targeting kids from the same school. How about Franklin City High?"

Kahli made a face as if to say that the suggestion didn't sit too well with her.

Before she could explain, Dave quickly added, "Unless you want to work with younger kids . . ."

"Actually, that's not it at all. I think high school sounds fine. Expose them to college life, treat them like adults, all that good stuff. But why Franklin City High?"

"I just figured Franklin City because it's the closest high school and the kids are definitely in need of some extra help.

"Dave, don't look so confused," Kahli said with a smile. "The idea was fine, but I was just thinking that maybe we could recruit from M.L. King High School. It's only a few blocks farther than Franklin City. And every time Franklin wants to do some kind of community outreach, they never do anything at King. So while the kids at Franklin City could benefit from the program, I bet the King kids could use our resources even more."

Damn, she actually looked scared to make that suggestion when it was a really good idea. "That makes a lot of sense, Kahli. I'm sorry—

can I call you Kahli? You almost tore Winston up for calling you that."

"Shutup. Of course you can. And I'd appreciate it if you refrained from bringing up Winston's name. Thank God he dropped Hark's class. I haven't seen him since that almost-fight outside the cafeteria. But anyhow, you wouldn't mind working with King?"

"Not at all. But since Franklin usually disses that school, the administration might not be too receptive to anything having to do with this university, you know what I'm saying?"

"I thought about that so I called them on Monday. The principal gave me the names of a few teachers who she thought could recommend some really good students. She said we could schedule an appointment to come to one of their staff meetings."

Yo, her shit is tight. I can't front. "Word? I'm impressed. I really am."

"Really? That means a lot. So if you trust me to handle getting students for the program, you could be working on something else."

"True, true. I'm thinking the kids are gonna want to know what they're getting into this summer. So how about I write up a program description and work on filling in some of the logistical blanks, like the actual site for the program, who's gonna work there, etc."

Something that he said must have sparked something in Kahli's brain because she hit Dave's leg pretty hard and exclaimed a fairly loud, "Oh yeah!"

"Was it something I said?" Dave looked like he was scared of another outburst.

"Yeah—the site for the program. I had an idea, and don't be afraid to tell me if it's crazy."

This girl is really funny. She's all composed and mature one minute, but she gets all hyped like a little kid the next. "What's your idea?"

"I was thinking that maybe the program could be a boarding school."

Yeah. She's crazy. "Like, they'd live here—at Franklin?"

"Yup! In Booker T. Washington House." She figured that she'd just keep talking until the idea sounded a little more feasible to Dave. "See, the house has all this extra money that they're not sure what to do with. Don't ask me how I know that, because it's supposed to be on the D.L. But anyhow, maybe they could match Coca-Cola's grant. That could solve our money problems. And no one lives in Booker T. during the summer anyhow. So if we hire a few R.A.'s and promise not to wreck the building, it'll be great publicity for the House. Think about it—the black dorm at Franklin takes in neighborhood kids for the summer? And think about how much the high school kids will love it."

Dave was definitely listening, but he wasn't completely sold. "I don't know, Kahli. It sounds like a huge responsibility. But at the same time, we could make sure they were getting their homework done if we had them 24/7."

"That's only one of the many advantages," Kahli said with a prodding head nod.

"Let me think about it?"

"Sure!" Kahli seemed surprised that Dave even agreed to consider it, and she couldn't stop smiling.

"So how have you enjoyed living in Booker T. House yourself this year?" *Why am I asking her this when the meeting could have been over?*

"I actually really like it. A lot of the freshmen don't because they say people are all up in your business. But I'm not doing anything that I need to hide so it doesn't matter."

"Yeah? You don't participate in any shady activities?"

"Nope. I'm pretty damn boring, actually."

"I doubt that. And I meant to ask you—who is this boyfriend you were talking about if you claim it's not el blanco?" *Dave, be quiet and stop being nosy. This isn't even your stylo to be up in somebody's mix.*

"You probably don't know him. He's an undergrad. A junior. Tarik Reynolds?"

"Reynolds. Reynolds," Dave muttered to himself a few times. "Yeah, that cat used to play basketball, right? Pretty boy?"

"Oh my goodness! I can't believe you said that. He is *not* a pretty boy."

"How do you figure?"

"Pretty boys are guys who spend more time getting ready in the morning than their girls. They have the perfect fades, the groomed facial hair, and the phat clothes. Tarik isn't like that."

"O.K. fine. But you just described Pretty Boy Type I," Dave explained wisely.

"There's a Type II?" Kahli asked, thoroughly amused.

"Of course. The natural pretty boy. He doesn't have to do anything to be pretty. He was simply born with pretty features."

"Oh, I see. And you think Tarik fits that description?"

"To a T. He's got the height, the build, the hair, the face. It's all there."

Kahlila crossed her legs and leaned in towards Dave, apparently interested. "So Dave, wouldn't you have to call yourself Type II too?" She sat back as if she'd made her case on that sentence alone.

"What?! Hell no. Yeah, I'm tall. But I ain't yellow, my hair's nappy, and I sure ain't got a six pack."

Kahli was tempted to argue the point further, but she just laughed instead. "Dave! You completely sidetracked me from my opinion of Booker T. House."

"My bad. I thought you were done." *Yeah, we need to wrap this up 'cuz Joy's about to be here any minute.*

"I was done, pretty much. But there's one thing I don't like about the House, and that's the name."

"You're fuckin' kidding me. Excuse my language, but I'm kinda trippin'."

"Why? You *like* the name?" Kahli looked worried that she might have offended him.

"N'ah. Just the opposite. I've been saying the exact same thing since I got to this school. I mean, why they gotta pick the safest negro to name the building after? I don't wanna call Booker T. a sellout . . ."

"Of course not," Kahli added. "'Cuz he lived in a different time and operated in the way he thought was best."

"Exactly. But at the same time, the building was only constructed in the 70's. Why not name it after someone more . . ."

"Contemporary? I agree. Like at Wesleyan they have . . ."

"Malcolm X House," they said together.

Kahli and Dave burst out laughing. "It was bound to happen, considering we kept interrupting each other," Kahli said.

"True. But I'm feeling you on that, though." *I think I'm gonna enjoy working with this . . .*

A knock on the door grinded Dave's thoughts to a halt.

Joy heard laughter as she walked down the hall in search of the office number that Dave had e-mailed her. It surprised her when she reached the correct door and the laughter got clearer. Joy knew Dave better than anyone, and he wasn't really a laugher. He cracked jokes, smiled a lot, but he was way too laid back to be cackling over anything. Her curiosity made her knock that much louder.

"Come in," shouted back Dave's familiar voice.

She opened the door with a slow deliberateness and took a moment to absorb the visuals. Dave sitting on a couch with a girl. She pretty much expected to see that. *I knew his coworker was a girl. And they have to sit together to go over stuff. On the same couch though?*

Her eyes zoomed in on the face of the girl sharing a couch with her boyfriend. The girl's face had an exotic look while still maintaining that "girl next door" appeal. She was wearing a green crocheted sweater with a tight brown shirt underneath, and a pair of wide leg brown jeans. Her hair was held back with a green scrunchie and green socks peeked out from her ankles. Joy took it all in and felt her heart rate accelerating. The worst part was the girl was staring back at her with such wide eyed innocence that she was forced to smile.

"Hey baby," said Dave from his position on the couch.

"What's up," Joy replied as she walked further into the room.

"Kahlila, this is my girl Joy."

Joy looked for a brief expression of disappointment on Kahlila's face, but she couldn't find one.

Kahli extended her hand immediately. "Nice to meet you, Joy."

"You too," she replied, eyeing Kahli as she rose from the couch. *At least her body isn't much to look at. Although Dave's not really a fan of thick girls.*

Kahli's hand gripped hers with a firmness that registered confidence and assurance. Dave had told Joy that his partner seemed to be on point and together. Joy hadn't figured that his wonder-student was smart *and* attractive. *Looks like I was dead wrong.*

Joy looked over at her boyfriend to see if he was taking in the full length view of his "work partner." But his eyes were still on Joy, and he seemed to be reading her mind.

"So are we all set for today, Kahli?" Dave's gaze was still focused on his girl.

"Yup," Kahli replied while packing up her things. "We can do some follow-up over e-mail."

"Sounds good. See you later."

"Bye, Dave. Nice meeting you, Joy."

"You too."

They watched her sling her backpack over one shoulder and walk out of the office. As soon as the door shut Joy say down next to Dave on the couch. "She seems nice . . ."

"She is."

"And pretty, too."

Dave smiled. "Really? I hadn't noticed."

Joy laughed and hit him with one of the sofa cushions. "Yeah, right. You guys are using nicknames already?"

"You don't know the half of it. When you're not around, I call her Pookie and she calls me Sugar Bear."

Joy leaned over and kissed him on the cheek.
He reached for her hand. "I love you."
"I love you more."

CHAPTER ELEVEN

Damn, this mirror needs cleaning. Specks of toothpaste and shaving cream splattered all over it. I can barely even see what I'm doing with these clippers. I think I'm pretty much done though. Not bad, actually. The barber would have gotten the edges a little better, but it's all good. The clothes on the bed look decent too. Khakis and a black button-up shirt. Not crazy dressy, but the most effort Kahli has ever seen me put out. Maybe I should wear a different shirt, like a polo or something. N'ah, fuck it. Valentine's Day only comes once a year. It can't hurt to wear some nice gear.

I'm a big fan of Valentine's Day. This hot water feels good as hell. The pressure is strong today. Trevor must have gotten out of the shower already. I know mad brothers can't stand this day because of all the required shit you gotta take care of. But all that ritual is really just part of the game. There goes the water. Guess Trev just got in. I hate this lukewarm sprinkling. It feels like somebody's spitting all over me.

Yeah, most niggas hate Valentine's Day. But it's really just an easy way to get bonus points with your girl. They don't want much–flowers, candy, a card with a sweet little message. Those corny gifts cash in lovely, too. I've had a few breakthroughs on February 14ths.

Lemme get out of this tub. I'm surprised the soap even washed off with this drippy ass shower. Yeah, my goal every other year was sex, or some variation of it. But I already got all that with Kahli and I'm still running around butt ass naked trying to make tonight phat. I hope letting Dez and Trev double date with us is a good idea.

Why am I wearing black boxers? It's like I'm trying to match my drawers to my outfit, like Kahli does all the time. Red instead? N'ah, that's hella corny, like I'm trying to do some kind of holiday theme. Hella. Where did I get that from? That's some old Cali shit.

But Dez and Trev should be cool. The two of them have been chillin' a lot lately, always nagging me and Kahli to do stuff with them. Thank God Kahli's not the cheesy type who always gotta be stuck to her girls. N'ah, she's more like me. She'd rather spend time with people one-on-one. But it makes sense to hook up with them today. Trevor has a car, and I didn't have the funds to be renting one. And plus, that dude is too hilarious so we'll probably be buggin' out all night.

That should do it. Hair cut, gear straight, and the room looks good for later. Lemme go knock on Trev's door. I should've swept this hallway earlier. It's hella dusty. There goes that hella again.

I'd better knock on Carl's door and remind him about that favor he has to do for me later on. Look at this nigga, sitting on the floor in his underwear playing Nintendo. Not even Playstation. The original Nintendo. No wonder he don't have nobody to chill with on Valentine's Day. I'd better not clown him though–he might pay me back by forgetting to do his part later tonight.

Why is Trevor taking so long to answer his door? Here he goes. Running late, as usual. Slapping on his cologne and putting on all his pretty-boy jewelry at the same time. He put on that blue shirt he bought at Structure the other day. Black pants, and damn–did he shine his shoes? They didn't look that bright last time he wore 'em.

Yo, I gotta ask–why is his bald ass pulling a hairbrush out of the back of his closet? He tells me it's for Dez, so she can do her hair in the morning. He ain't never gave her a brush any other night, I remind him. "But tonight's THE night," he stresses.

What do you know–Trevor the super-player been seeing this girl a month and still ain't hit it. I knew Desiree was gonna make him put in work. I tell him that it isn't a good idea to get there late, since he's all about trying to impress. That puts some fire under his ass. Finally—we're out.

I should have just taken Mom's camera at the beginning of the year. All these damn disposable cameras I'm buying, I could have bought a fuckin' camcorder by now. If I break a nail trying to open this package, I swear to God . . .

I'll just ask Robyn to open it. Hey, I didn't know she was doing Kahli's hair for tonight. If the camera weren't stuck in this plastic case, I'd take a picture of the two of them in the mirror, looking so serious about a hair-do. It looks good, though. I should have Robyn do mine sometime. Of course, Kahli still refuses to do anything but pull it back. But at least she twisted it up. I gotta give her props on the hairclip. She gives me her slanted smile and says thanks. She looks pretty. I'm not really a brown person but the long skirt looks nice. Is that suede? It goes well with the soft beige sweater.

Maybe I should have gone more conservative. A short red dress on Valentine's Day is kind of cheesy, I guess. "You look great," is coming out of Robyn's mouth with a big smile. She's a mind reader. I needed that. She takes the camera from me without my even having to ask. Does she look a little sad? It must suck having a long-distance relationship, having to rely on e-mail and occasional visits for romance. She looks cheery though, snapping pictures left and right. Kahli and I must look so stiff, standing here like mannequins. Why don't I just throw my arm around her or something? N'ah, too forced.

Shit! The door. That must be Trevor knocking all loud like his momma didn't teach him nothin'. This all of a sudden feels so weird, like when your prom date gets to your parent's house. Do you answer the door, or wait and make a pseudo-dramatic entrance? What if these idiots didn't dress up? I'll send them right home to go change. Kahli better have my back.

O.K. Robyn's making moves to get the door. Me and Kahli look like retards hiding out in this bedroom. I'd better say what's on my mind. Kahli agrees. As I'm walking out, a few dustballs are paving my way. Kind of like the rose bearers in Coming to America. Only filthy. I should make sure Tarik and Trevor don't come in. We should've cleaned before they got here.

The door is open, but I can't see them. Robyn's whistling, which is a good sign. What the hell are they sticking through the doorway? A red rose. I'm sure it's for Kahli. Tarik is sprung like that. My flower? For real? Lemme go grab this shit before Robyn tells me she was just kidding. My God. Trevor looks too fine. Oh yeah, Tarik looks cute too. But he doesn't have a flower. I feel kind of bad acting so gassed about it since Kahli doesn't have one. She looks happy for me though. Don't look too happy, girl. I know what Trevor thinks tonight is. Yeah, he's busting the "you look stunning" line. Keep that up Trev, and tonight might just be the night. Robyn, always thinking, snapping pictures as this whole scene goes down. Good, 'cuz I want to remember this feeling for a while. Cinderella moments don't happen at Franklin every day.

This waiter must be gay. He got way too much swish in his step for me. Whoever the bartender is hooked it up though. This Long Island is doin' its thing. I'm glad we went with mixed drinks instead of wine. Although women do love wine. Makes them all giggly and horny and shit. But it takes too much of it to have any effect. Look at Dez. She's already feeling her Brandy Alexander. And she's lookin' tasty as all hell in that dress.

Finally, the food's here. Why do nice restaurants think that it's classy to take a half hour to cook your food? You'd think that the expensive joints would have quicker equipment back in the kitchen. But yo, Tarik was right about Valentine's Day. I just decided at the last minute to buy that rose, and she was all giddy about it. Yeah, just keep up the romance and the jokes and her panties will be soaked by the time we get back to my place.

For real, though. Look at her. Hypothetically, could I see myself settling down with her if you were trying to do the commitment thing? She definitely has the looks–the face, the body. Tight. I wonder if she's smart. She never seems to be doing work. The only time I hear her talk about the library is when she's lying to Kahlila about where she's been. I don't know why she can't tell the girl she's at my crib. She's not even givin' me any. So what's the problem?

I can kind of see why she doesn't want to tell Kahlila, though. I could see her being all judgmental like, "Are you sure you can trust him?" and all that shit. Not to diss my nigga's girl or anything. She's cute. Not exactly my type, but cute. Not enough body for me. Although Tracy was kind of skinny. She had big titties though. Whatever. And I guess Tarik doesn't care that she's innocent. He's turning into a choir boy himself these days.

All right, I'm being too quiet. Let's get some juicy conversation in, here. I got it. I should suggest that we play "I Never." Someone says something like, "I've never had anal sex" and everyone who HAS had anal sex has to take a drink. Maybe I should have used a different example, because they're all staring at me like I'm crazy. What?! Dez is down for it. I'm feeling this girl. Kahlila looks kind of edgy. Probably 'cuz she ain't done shit interesting. And my boy looks a little nervous himself. I wonder how much he's told her about his sex life. The time we ran that train on that older girl back in high school? Definitely not. I don't even think he's told her that he used to fuck with that girl Shannon who lives with her. I'd better drop this idea before I ruin my boy's night.

I wonder what Desiree would do if I whispered to her that we should play by ourselves later tonight. What the hell. Go for it. Okay, player! Giving the sly little wink. You go, girl. Yeah, she's gonna need that brush tomorrow. 'cuz by the time we're through, her hair ain't gonna look nothin' nice. Where's that swishy waiter? I think we need another round of drinks.

I'm feeling those rum and cokes. This staircase is way too narrow for four people to be trying to rush up them at the same time. I'm getting a bit dizzy. Why did I get rum and coke? I should've ordered an amaretto sour. Why didn't that drink enter my head at the restaurant? I always think of good drinks when I get home from someplace. Just like I always think of good movies to rent when I'm sitting at home, but can never remember them when I'm at a video store.

Everybody's giggling and whispering, but I'm just trying to get to Tarik's room because my shoes are killing me and I need to take them off. I should have broken in these boots before I decided to wear them for a marathon evening.

It's weird to be in this house with Dez, watching her go off with Trevor while I head in another direction with Tarik. What do we say? "Have fun?" "See you in the morning?" Tarik has jokes about the two of them, talking about how Trev is gonna get lucky tonight. Whatever. Dez has only known that boy for a month. She ain't givin' him nothin'. I'll have to tell her tomorrow about Tarik's assumption. She'll think it's pretty funny.

Why is there music coming from Tarik's room? He's acting like he doesn't hear it. Just grinning like a damn fool. Why is he opening the door so slowly? Oh my God.

My eyes can't even take it all in at once. Candles lit everywhere. Red. White. They must be scented. I smell peppermint, and like a cherry-ish smell. It's yummy. Glad he didn't light incense. Did I ever tell him that I hate incense?

Rose petals. All over the floor. Some old Coming to America craziness. I'm loving it. Okay, Kahli. Don't get all teary. That would be hella corny. Hella. Robyn's South Central ass is rubbing off on me. What's playing on the stereo? ". . . 'cuz I never felt this way about lovin' . . ." I wonder if Tarik thought about the words or if he just figured he couldn't go wrong with Brian McKnight.

Shit. Is that a gift on the bed? Walk over to it and see, stupid. He wrapped it so nice, part of me doesn't even want to open it. Well, that's the stupid part of me. Let me open this thing. Wow. This stuffed animal matches my sweater exactly. He is so cute! And he's wearing a brown shirt–my favorite color. Yeah, Tarik's representing in a big way. Are these letters on the shirt? Oh my goodness–it says Kahlibear. I can't believe he did this. I can't believe it.

And he's actually apologizing for using mom's nickname for me. I didn't even think he knew it. I guess he listens more than I gave him credit for. I am so rude–I haven't even said anything since I walked in here. Thank you just ain't cuttin' it right now though. Wait a second–how did he get the candles lit and the music playing? I gotta ask. He's enjoying this–looking all smug and adorable. Okay, he's not gonna tell me. Trying to keep up the mystery. I'll humor him. He probably asked lard-ass Carl to do it. Charming is the only word I can use to describe him at this moment.

I'm in awe of the words he's speaking to me. Ready to make a commitment? I make him a better person? He feels honored that I let him into my life? I don't know if it's the alcohol or the words, but I am feeling him. I'm feeling all this. I want him. Right now. And as a boyfriend. Don't you think you've waited long enough to kiss him?

Nothing like the spoon position. The sex is over, you're a little sleepy, and your guy's arms are wrapped around your stomach and you can lean back into his body. It's great. Tonight was so wonderful. I'm gonna have to go home tomorrow and write down all the details before I forget. Tarik showed a side of himself I'd never seen before. He spoke poetry to me. His own poetry. He didn't even know he was doing it.

Am I murmuring out loud? I can barely hear myself, I'm so tired. I'm sure the drinks from earlier aren't helping. Oh, I guess I'm talking about how much I love his big bed. Whenever he tries to sleep over at Booker T., someone ends up on the floor.

Why is he asking me if I'm gonna live there next year? I guess he's tired of the uncomfortable nights. I do need to talk to Dez and Robyn about possible living options for next year. Hey, I wonder if he's ever thought about what me and Dave were talking about–the political implications of a house named after Booker T. Washington.

Okay, maybe bringing up this topic was a bad idea. My back is turned to him, but I can tell the expression on his face is blank. I'm weird, he tells me. All right Kal, try not to sound disappointed. You can't make him into someone he's not. He's already stretched himself for you. He's only so elastic.

Can I ever just be happy with what I have?

the dangling conversation

there's been something I've been meaning to say for a
while . . .
I love you.

air so thick the words get stuck
bare and suspended
waiting for you to grasp them, caress them, stroke them,
carry them with you always
in the back pocket of your mind.

air so thick the words get stuck
hanging naked in the atmosphere
- is it hot in here?
resonance of voice bolding offering itself
like an ancient sacrifice
breaking all rules of idolatry.

air so thick I barely breathe
feelings exposed, nowhere to hide.
why can't there be a return policy
on words spoken too soon
and regretted too late?

air thins out so suddenly I gasp.
my lungs expand as your hand
reaches for those scripted lines
that make everything fine . . .

I love you too.

CHAPTER TWELVE

To: drobinson@sociology.franklin.edu
From: kahlila@classof99.franklin.edu
Date: Feb 15, 1996 2:05 p.m.
Subject: where were you?

Message:
hey. missed you in class today. recovering from a crazy evening, perhaps? i know it was hard for me to get out of bed myself this morning.

-kahli

To: kahlila@classof99.franklin.edu
From: drobinson@sociology.franklin.edu
Date: Feb 15, 1996 2:43 p.m.
Subject: where were you?—Reply

Message:
are you spying on me now? how did you know i was working hard last night? i have my first midterm for my american civilizations class coming up and it's gonna be no joke. i threw on voice mail and didn't answer my phone. did you try to call me?

dave

To: drobinson@sociology.franklin.edu
From: kahlila@classof99.franklin.edu
Date: Feb 15, 1996 3:07 p.m.
Subject: where were you?–Reply—Reply

Message:
we are on two completely different pages. i thought you were "putting in work" for valentine's day, not some midterm. joy is an understanding woman! when you do want to meet next to plan some summer stuff?

-kahli

To: kahlila@classof99.franklin.edu
From: drobinson@sociology.franklin.edu
Date: Feb 15, 1996 3:43 p.m.
Subject: SHIT!!!

Message:
from the title, you should be able to guess that i did not clear my evening's plans with joy. i completely forgot about valentine's day. i'm gonna have to get back to you about a meeting time. i have some serious ass kissing to do. couldn't you have warned me earlier?

-dave

To: drobinson@sociology.franklin.edu
From: kahlila@classof99.franklin.edu
Date: Feb 15, 1996 4:16 p.m.
Subject: SHIT!!!—Reply

Message:

i hope your ass kissing skills are up to par. you need to write a poem or something. didn't you tell me lloyd writes poetry? you better get him to have some pity on you and whip you up a little something. devote today to saving your ass. i'll call you tomorrow.

-kahli

To: drobinson@sociology.franklin.edu
From: joy_rainer@yahoo.com
Date: Feb 15, 1996 4:18 p.m.
Subject: what do you want?

Message:
i got your page. i'm at work right now. since it's the middle of the day and you're calling me, it must be important. so i'm presuming you've remembered that yesterday was valentine's day. it's funny–i know you so well that i should have assumed that you never mentioned anything ahead of time because your mind was elsewhere. but the whole week leading up to the damn holiday i was thinking you were gonna surprise me. got last night off work, even. what's happening to us?

To: joy_rainer@yahoo.com
From: drobinson@sociology.franklin.edu
Date: Feb 15, 1996 5:01 p.m.
Subject: your forgiveness.

Message:
nothing is happening to us. we're fine. sweetheart, i've been busy beyond belief but that's no excuse. when i think of all the great valentine's days we've had in past years it hurts me

so much that i fucked this one up. e-mail is not cutting it for this occasion. what time do you get off work tonight? i'll be waiting at your apartment. please, baby. i love you.

To: drobinson@sociology.franklin.edu
From: joy_rainer@yahoo.com
Date: Feb 15, 1996 5:49 p.m.
Subject: your forgiveness.—Reply

Message:
7:00 tonight. bring food.

To: tarik@classof97.franklin.edu
From: kahlila@classof99.franklin.edu
Date: Feb 15, 1996 3:00 p.m.
Subject: you're a prince

Message:
hey you,
i've just been thinking about what crappy days some women had yesterday and i wanted to say thanks again. you made me feel like a princess..

kahli

To: kahlila@classof99.franklin.edu
From: tarik@classof97.franklin.edu
Date: Feb 15, 1996 3:31 p.m.
Subject: you're a prince–Reply

Message:
baby,

glad you enjoyed yourself last night. looked like trevor and dez had quite an evening as well. she didn't leave our place till noon. anyhow, i know you were a bit twisted when we got home but i wanted to make sure that you were cool with what i was saying, about wanting to be committed to you. i know you work early tomorrow morning. how about i stay at your place tonight?
tarik

To: kahlila@classof99.franklin.edu
cc: desiree@classof99.franklin.edu
From: robyn@classof99.franklin.edu
Date: Feb 15, 1996 3:36 p.m.
Subject: see y'all sunday night!

Message:
hey girls–y'all aren't the only women who get to have fun this time of year. jason called early this morning telling me he found a cheap flight on-line and that he'd pay for me to come down for the weekend. yeah, i know it's only thursday but i'm leaving in an hour. y'all got the number down at emory. peace, robyn

To: desiree@classof99.franklin.edu
From: kahlila@classof99.franklin.edu
Date: Feb 15, 1996 4:05 p.m.
Subject: have fun last night?

Message:
hey girlie–thought i'd run into you this morning but apparently you slept in. i had to leave the guys' house early to make my 10:30 class with hark. you wouldn't believe all the candles and flowers tarik had waiting for me in his room

when we got back from the restaurant. he told me he's ready for a committed relationship and i said okay. i'm actually really happy with him. i've been seeing him in a different light lately.

but why did that nigga say that trev was gonna get lucky last night. i had to inform him that it would take a lot more than a rose to get you to fall for trevor's game. why don't guys understand that you can sleep in someone's room without having sex?

aren't you so happy for robyn? she hasn't seen jason since christmas break.

later–kahli

To: kahlila@classof99.franklin.edu
From: desiree@classof99.franklin.edu
Date: Feb 15, 1996 4:28 p.m.
Subject: have fun last night?–Reply

Message:
yeah, last night was great, wasn't it? so tarik said trev got lucky, huh? niggas. see ya at home tonight. we'll talk then.
dez

p.s . . . yes, thank goodness for that plane ticket. i think robyn was going into jason withdrawal.

To: desiree@classof99.franklin.edu
From: kahlila@classof99.franklin.edu
Date: Feb 15, 1996 5:14 p.m.
Subject: have fun last night?–Reply–Reply
Message:

tarik's gonna be over tonight, so how about you come to the caf tomorrow after my shift is over and we can have lunch? you can let me know later.-k

To: kahlila@classof99.franklin.edu
From: joshuatravis@classof98.franklin.edu
Date: Feb 15, 1996 5:16 p.m.
Subject: valentine's day blows.

Message:
kal, how was your fuckin holiday. only i would manage to get dumped on february 14th. kristy calls me yesterday morning, telling me she thinks we need space. i'm not sensitive enough to her needs. and she's telling me this on v-day so that i won't go out of my way and do anything special for her that night. hello? i had to cancel the damn dinner reservations, and return that bracelet we picked out at the mall. what do you think–am i insensitive? man, fuck her. write back.

j.t.

To: joshuatravis@classof98.franklin.edu
From: kahlila@classof99.franklin.edu
Date: Feb 15, 1996 5:28 p.m.
Subject: valentine's day blows.–Reply

Message:
hon–considering how your holiday turned out, i don't think you want to know about mine. suffice it to say that it was probably the exact opposite of yours. i don't know what kristy's problem is. insensitive? i guess that depends on her meaning of the word. you're not mushy, sentimental, or in

touch with your feminine side. but you're kindhearted when it counts and you're sincere about your feelings. man, fuck her. let's have dinner tomorrow. call me tonight. just be prepared that tarik might answer.
kal

To: kahlila@classof99.franklin.edu
From: joshuatravis@classof98.franklin.edu
Date: Feb 15, 1996 6:12 p.m.
Subject: valentine's day blows.–Reply—Reply

Message:
so tarik's answering your phone now? i'd never let kristy do that in a million years. does that make me insensitive? i guess we can talk about it over dinner tomorrow. and tell tarik that y'all gotta come to my game saturday. cancel all other plans.

To: trevor2@classof97.franklin.edu
From: desiree@classof99.franklin.edu
Date: Feb 15, 1996 6:12 p.m.
Subject: hey

Message:
what's up, cutie. can we get together and talk about last night?
desiree

To: desiree@classof99.franklin.edu
From: trevor2@classof97.franklin.edu
Date: Feb 15, 1996 7:04 p.m.
Subject: hey–Reply
Message:

i'm kinda hemmed up tonight. and tomorrow i'm going to visit one of my boys at colgate. i'll check you when i get back.

To: angelabradford@aol.com
From: kahlila@classof99.franklin.edu
Date: Feb 15, 1996 7:23 p.m.
Subject: quick update

Message:
hi mommy. valentine's day was great. tarik and trevor took me and dez out to dinner and tarik got me this teddy wearing a shirt that says "kahlibear" on it. looks like we're an official couple now.

love,
me

To: kahlila@classof99.franklin.edu
From: angelabradford@aol.com
Date: Feb 15, 1996 8:16 p.m.
Subject: quick update–Reply

Message:
i didn't know that stuffed animals were replacing fraternity pins as symbols of "going steady." just kidding. he sounds like such a sweet boy. i'm glad you started giving him more of a chance. now i don't want to lecture, but make sure you're careful, kahlibear. men say they're faithful sometimes when they're not. even the best ones. so you do what you need to do and be safe. o.k. i'll stop now.
love,
mom

CHAPTER THIRTEEN

Dave opened the front door to his apartment building and encountered a bundled-up Kahlila, nose red, and smile wide.

"Why are you in such a good mood?" he asked, her smile contagious.

"I'm about to get out of the freezing cold, for one. And I just had a really fun dinner."

"Con quien?" he inquired as he motioned for her to follow him inside.

"I told you about that Spanish stuff. But I can deduce that your nosy ass is probably asking who my dinner companion was." Not yet in his apartment, Kahli already felt the heat from the hallway radiators and was peeling off her jacket, hat, and scarf.

"You're exactly right. So are you going to tell me?"

"I went out with J.T., if you must know."

Dave was ready to tease her about the outing, but he decided to let her into his apartment first. This was the first time they were meeting at Dave's house, and Kahli was looking around in the same way that she had the first time she saw Hark's office.

He allowed her to walk around the living room, following a few steps behind her to see what she took particular interest in. His place was always neat and clean, and though the furniture was donated by assorted members of his and Lloyd's friends and families, the pieces complimented each other in a way that was both eclectic and cozy.

She stopped in front of the massive bookcase in one corner of the room. "My goodness. Have you read all these books?"

"N'ah. Most of them are Lloyd's philosophy books. I keep most of mine in my bedroom. You can see the room, if you'd like."

She smiled. "That's okay, Dave. You're entitled to your privacy." She moved on to the keyboard standing upright, resting against the bookcase. It looked dusty and discarded.

"Don't tell me you play this thing. I would have never pegged you for a musician."

"Again, Lloyd. He's crazy talented. I haven't heard him play in a minute, but he definitely got skills."

After touring the kitchen and grabbing two cans of soda, they sat down on the living room couch.

"Now," Dave announced, leaning back and making himself comfortable, "Let's get back to business. What was the reason for this dinner date with le garcon blanc?"

Kahlila burst out laughing. She'd expected him to begin talking about the summer program, not about J.T. "I don't know whether to be impressed that you learned a French phrase for me, or offended that you're calling my best friend 'the white boy.'"

"Be impressed. Now spill it."

"There's nothing to spill. His girlfriend dumped him, and he was feeling down. I cheered him up, though."

"I'm sure you did," Dave replied, eyeing her from behind his soda can. "And where was your boyfriend while all of this cheering up was taking place?"

"He's out with his boys tonight. And Tarik is completely confident in our relationship, as he should be. He does everything he needs to do in order to feel secure. For instance, he actually remembers important holidays . . ."

Dave set his soda can down with force, pretending to be outraged. "I'll have you know that I saw Joy last night and ironed everything out. We're fine. Better than fine, actually."

Kahlila clapped her hands twice and sat up straight. "Terrific! Well, now that we're done playing 'Whose Relationship is Better?', can we get down to business?"

"Certainly. What's your update, chief?"

"Well, I went into King School on Wednesday and handed out your program description, and talked to this one teacher's class. The kids want more details. They want to know if the program is definitely gonna be residential, and what specific classes are going to be taught. Just calling it an enrichment program with a college prep focus isn't enough."

Dave sighed. "I hear you. We'd better figure some of this out tonight, then. Let's make some concrete decisions about the Summer Institute. It's definitely called the Summer Institute, right?"

"Right."

"And we agreed that we should do something more liberal arts focused than math and science."

"No doubt, especially if you're planning on asking *me* to teach something. I couldn't teach math if I tried."

"I'm sure you could, but we won't make you do it. I'd actually thought of a possible idea the other day; tell me what you think."

Kahli suddenly looked very serious, leaning forward and ready to listen intently to what he had to say.

"I thought that it would be phat if the kids could come out of the summer with something to show for it, like some type of end product. So what about publishing a newspaper or something?"

Kahlila's eyes brightened. "Or a literary magazine. Or a combination of both! That's fabulous."

"Why thank you, madam. I thought maybe you could teach the writing aspect, and I'm pretty good with computers. I could learn Pagemaker and Photoshop and design a publishing class."

"Perfect! And it really cuts down on our work because coming up with the theme of the publication could be the kids' job."

"Exactly. And I'm all for making our job easier. So how about I rewrite that program description over the next week or so?"

"Cool. And I'll make sure that the House Dean agrees to meet with me by the end of the week so I can tell these kids if they'll be living on campus or not."

Dave nodded. He'd told Kahli last week that if she got the dean of Booker T. Washington House to agree to house the students for the Summer Institute, that he'd go along with it. But he still had his doubts about the idea. "You realize that we'll have to hire Resident Advisors if the students live on campus."

"I know, don't worry." Kahli searched Dave's face for some signal of confidence in her plan. She didn't find one. She reached over and grabbed both of his hands. "Dave. Trust me. I won't let them burn down the building."

"Your hands are still cold from outside."

"Yeah. I tend to have cold extremities." She watched Dave as he watched her take her hands away and blow hot air into them.

Their eyes suddenly shifted to the apartment door, which was calling attention to itself due to the key that was jiggling the lock. The door swung open and Lloyd entered, looking cold and tired.

"What's up Lloyd. You remember Kahlila, my partner for that project Hark gave us?"

"Hi," Kahli said cheerfully. "How are you?"

Lloyd's eyes appeared as if they were adjusting to their environment, as his glasses defrosted and the picture of the two figures on the couch became clearer. "Cold as hell frozen over. It's ridiculous out there. But it's nice to see you again, Kahlila."

"You too. And you can call me Kahli, if you'd like."

He looked like he was seriously contemplating her offer. After a pause he said, "Actually, I prefer Kahlila. This may sound kind of random, but have you heard of Kahlil Gibran?"

"You know Gibran? That's who I was named after! He's my mom's favorite poet."

"Oh yeah?" Lloyd asked as he opened the door to his bedroom and tossed some of his belongings inside.

"Yeah. I wish she'd have just named me Kahlil instead of throwing the "a" on the end, but what can you do. Have you read any of his stuff?"

"All of it, actually," he responded as he joined them in the living room and sat on the chair near the couch.

Dave interjected. "Kahli, you know those people who know a little about everything?"

"Uh huh."

"Lloyd is not one of those people. He knows *a lot* about everything. Especially anything that can make him look smooth without appearing like he did it on purpose."

"Whatever, D. Don't listen to him, Kahlila."

"I'm not. But really—you know all his stuff? I've only read *The Prophet*. But I live by it. I'm still taking it all in and really grasping the meaning of what he's talking about. I'll move on to another one of his works once I get everything I can from this one."

"I don't think it's possible to exhaust *The Prophet*. So what's your favorite section?"

"Joy and Sorrow."

"No kidding. Mine too."

Dave watched a monologue for two unravel before his eyes between these two people who'd barely even met but appeared to have been practicing this recitation together all of their lives:

Kahlila: When you are joyous,

Lloyd: look deep into your heart

Kahlila: and you shall find it is only that which has given you sorrow

Lloyd: that is giving you joy.

Kahlila: When you are sorrowful,

Lloyd: look again in your heart

Kahlila: and you shall see that in truth you are weeping

Lloyd: for that which has been your delight.

They looked at each other, shaking their heads in awe at the depth of Gibran's words. Dave started clapping slowly, shaking *his* head at how strange both of them were.

They were paying him no mind.

"Yo, that joint is so true though," Lloyd commented.

"Everything he speaks on is true. It's mad simple, but you would have never thought to think about it that way. Like, nothing is going to make you miserable that doesn't also have the power to make you happy, and vice versa. The thing or person you once loved so much can very easily become the source of your anguish."

Dave listened without comment. *Yeah, I guess that is kinda true.* Trying not to think of Joy was becoming more and more difficult. He'd definitely been both the joy and the sorrow in his girlfriend's life lately. Their relationship had been so up and down these past few months, with every emotion felt ten times deeper because of all they'd experienced together over the years.

He tried to put those issues out of his mind and concentrate on Lloyd and Kahlila's conversation. She was asking him if he wrote poetry.

"Yeah. I used to write songs when I was more into my music. But I still jot down a few poems now and then. You?"

"A little. I mean, who doesn't?"

"I don't!" chimed in David, thoroughly amused by how artsy and literary the two of them were getting.

"Well you should start," advised Kahli. "Women are suckers for the lyrical."

Lloyd got up from his chair. "See Kahlila, Rico Suaves like Dave don't need to rely on the written word. They have the innate ability to win women over with their mere existences."

"You don't say . . ." said Kahli in fake amazement as she stared at Dave's skeptical expression.

"Whatever, Lloyd. Stop fuckin' around. Don't you have some work to do?"

"Yup," he answered, walking towards his bedroom. "But Kahlila . . ."

"Hmmm?"

"Be careful." Lloyd flashed a smile and closed the door behind him.

Dave wanted to come back with a smart comment, but he was also waiting to hear Kahli's reply.

"I think I'll be okay, Lloyd," she said dryly, though he was already out of earshot.

"Of course you'll be okay. You have enough to think about with a white boy and a pretty boy occupying all your time." Dave purposely avoided eye contact to keep himself from laughing.

"Don't make me strangle you with these cold hands of mine," Kahli threatened.

He was tempted to say something more, but he let it go.

They discussed the Institute for a while longer, and eventually moved on to other topics. Kahlila was asking him about his graduate degree.

"Ph.D's are no joke. When do you expect to be done?"

"With the dissertation and everything? I still have quite a few classes to take, so not for a few years yet."

Kahli shook her head in sympathy. "Hell no. I couldn't do it. Four years of *undergrad* seems like forever! I'm trying to see if I can take a semester or two off my time. If I take some summer classes I could probably . . ."

"Why are you in such a hurry to get things done?"

She thought about the question before she replied. "I only rush certain stages of my life, and I rush those so that I don't have to feel bad when I pause to relish in something unexpected."

He smirked before he retorted, "And what type of unexpected something might you pause to relish in these days?"

"Well, I sure could stay here all day," she whipped back, surprised at her own words.

He shifted his gaze downward for a moment before refocusing on her face, a face where a nonchalant expression was attempting to rest comfortably, but not quite succeeding. "No, miss. Since it's already evening, I'm afraid that as your elder I must advice you to go home and get a good night's sleep."

She commanded herself to smile cheerily. "Yes, sir," he retorted while giving a military salute. In a flash she was off of the couch, collecting her books, coat, and scarf in one quick motion. He felt like she was punishing him for cutting their banter short by leaving abruptly. As he fought to think of a comment to make in order to extend her visit, he knew her punishment was working.

"So when do you want to start working on the applications?" The question came out too quickly but he hoped she failed to notice.

His hurried inquiry did in fact escape her on account of her scarf being caught in her zipper. "What?" she murmured distractedly as she tugged at the snagged fibers.

"Never mind. I'll send you e-mail about it. Later, Kahli."

The scarf was finally free from the teeth and she flung it around her neck with a dramatic sweep. "Goodbye, Mr. Robinson," she said in a school-child sing-song voice as she let the door shut behind her.

CHAPTER FOURTEEN

"I'm home! Even more in love than when I left," Robyn shouted to no one in particular as she entered the suite on Sunday evening.

She walked down the tiny hallway and peeked in Desiree and Shannon's room. No one there. She continued to her bedroom and found Kahlila asleep at her desk.

"Wake up, girlie. I know you must have work to do!" Robyn said loudly as she shook Kahli's shoulder.

"Huh?" Kahli looked around disoriented as she removed her head from her desk and took in her surroundings. Once everything began to make sense, a huge grin took over her face. "Robyn! I missed you. How was Emory?"

"Emory? Like we left Jason's room more than twice. I've been on the campus a few times now and I still haven't seen much more than the Cafeteria and the video store." Robyn was running around their room at record pace, checking her voice mail, turning on her computer, unpacking her duffel bag.

Kahli watched her as she settled into being back at Franklin. "Wow Robyn, you'd think you wouldn't have any energy left after a three day sex marathon with Jason."

"Are you crazy?" Robyn said as she flopped down on her bed. "That *gives* me energy, girl. Do you notice anything different about me?"

Kahli squinted her eyes and studied her friend. Her haircut was the same—still short, shiny, and sassy. Her skin was always flawless, a glowing deep brown. Her dimple was in its normal place, her cheeky smile in tact. *She's such a clown, posing for me with her hand up to her face . . .*

"Oh, SHIT!!! What the hell is that on your finger?" Kahli

jumped up from her chair and ran over to inspect Robyn's hand. On her right ring finger was a gold band with an emerald stone.

"My Valentine's Day gift. Emerald is my birthstone," she informed, staring at the ring herself as she spoke.

"I can't believe he bought you jewelry."

"Why not? It's been three years, Kahli. I get jewelry every year. First was earrings. Then a bracelet. I wasn't sure if the ring was next, though. I thought he might go necklace or something. But it's all good."

"Sure is. Sounds like you had the perfect trip," said Kahli, making herself comfortable next to Robyn on the bed.

"Almost perfect," Robyn corrected. "Jason told me that he got offered some phat internship in Atlanta this summer. So he won't be in L.A. And if he's not gonna be there, I might as well stay at Franklin and get ahead with my science classes."

"That's what J.T.'s doing. Your family won't be upset?"

"N'ah. My sister's so happy to have the bedroom to herself, and my dad will support anything that involves doing well in school."

It always struck Kahli to hear Robyn say "my dad" in the exact same way that Kahli often said "my mom," or Dez would say "my parents." Robyn's mom had walked out on her family when Robyn was seven. Kahli had never heard of anything like that before. She'd had a lot of first hand experience with deadbeat fathers, but how could a mom do that to her kids?

"So, what did I miss this weekend?" Robyn asked cheerily, forcing Kahlila out of her daze.

"Not too much. Last night was the basketball game against Lehigh. We kicked ass. J.T. was having a bad night, though. Kristy dumped him on Valentine's Day."

Robyn gasped. "You're kidding! Why?"

Kahlila shrugged. "Beats me. She said something about his being insensitive. But it really came out of nowhere. I think she must have met someone else, although I would never tell him that."

"That's a shame. Poor kid."

"Yeah, I took him to dinner on Friday night. Tried to bring up his spirits."

Robyn raised her eyebrows. "And what did Mr. Reynolds say about that? After the way he showed up on Wednesday night all decked out, I thought he'd have you on permanent lock by the weekend."

Kahli looked down, embarrassed. "Well, to be honest, he kinda does. That night was pretty deep. He went all out, Robyn. And I'm completely happy with him. I adore him, actually . . . except . . ."

Robyn's eyes widened. "Don't tell me that you're catching feelings for J.T.!!"

Kahli stared back in shock. The mere thought of her and J.T. as a couple could only provoke one reaction: hysterical laughter. She laughed so hard that her eyes started watering, and soon she had Robyn laughing right along with her.

"Kahlila!" she reprimanded, punching her softly in the arm. "Seriously, you *did* have an except. And if it's not J.T., then who the fuck is it?"

She began intently picking lint off of Robyn's bedspread. "It's nobody, really. I just have a slight crush on someone. That's all."

Robyn slapped the back of the hand picking lint. "Tell me!"

Kahli started in on the serious task of picking at her fingernails. "That guy who I'm working with for Dr. Harkonn. Dave. I've developed this crazy crush on him! He's twenty-four with this girlfriend who he's had for like five years. And I've got this boyfriend who I've had for like five minutes, but he's a sweetheart. And I don't even want anything from Dave, but I love spending time with him."

"And this is a problem because . . ."

"What do you mean?"

"You're stressing out about this crush on a man, and he *is* a *man*, Kahlila, who you can't have and who you don't even want.

Do you honestly believe that once you commit to someone you stop noticing every other guy on earth?"

"It's more than noticing though, Robyn." Kahlila felt a sense of relief having confided in someone about Dave. Now that she'd started, she unraveled like a ball of yarn. "I look forward to meetings. I send unnecessary e-mail. I check out his clothes, I try to make him laugh . . ."

"Flirting is a necessary part of life." Robyn almost sounded like Hark to Kahli, schooling her on a key concept. "I love Jason. I can see myself spending the rest of my life with him. But it's not like I went dead when I came to that conclusion. Like, all of a sudden I became blind, deaf, and dumb to the existence of every other guy in the world. Flirting is even better when it's between two people who know that nothing can come of it."

Kahlila pondered Robyn's words. She'd never even thought of her interaction with David as "flirting" before. Was he flirting back when he teased her about Tarik, or clowned an outfit she was wearing?

Robyn waited for her roommate's reply, but she got none. "Well, from that little smirk on your face, it looks like you're starting to agree with me," Robyn said wisely.

"Yeah, I think I needed to hear a little bit of that good old Robyn Rationale."

"True. And what about the Desi Doctrine? What does *she* have to say about all this?"

Before Kahli answered the question, she got up from the bed, jogged down the hallway, and peeped into Desiree's room to make sure she wasn't home. She rejoined Robyn and spoke in a hushed tone despite Dez's not being in the suite. "I haven't talked to her about it. She's been acting really weird since Valentine's Day."

"Weird how?"

"Just really distant. I mean, that night was really fun and she seemed to really be feeling Trevor. The next day we exchanged some e-mail about it and I asked her to meet me for lunch that next day, Friday. When I got home she told me she didn't feel like meeting for lunch. And when I asked about things with Trevor, she said she didn't want to talk about that, either."

"That's doesn't sound like Dez at all. She usually loves to talk about men, especially when they're acting right. My hunch is that something shady must have gone down either that night or soon after."

Kahli looked skeptical. "You think? I'm not sure. Tarik hasn't mentioned anything about it."

"Kahli, you may be Tarik's girl. But loyalty to his boys is still a top priority. Anyhow, I'm sure Dez will perk up in the next few days. She's never been one to sweat a dude for too long."

After a sigh of satisfaction and a nod of agreement, the two girls sat at their desks and began to type away at their computers: Robyn checking her e-mail, and Kahlila working on a response paper for her history class.

"Hey Robyn," Kahli suddenly said, breaking the lulling sound of pressed keys and turned pages. "How come the only thing we ever talk about is the male species? We never talk about what we're studying, we rarely talk about our families, we sure as hell don't talk about current events. Occasionally music, sometimes a T.V. show . . ."

The tapping of the keyboard stopped. Robyn looked at her with a thoughtful expression. "That's a good point, chicky. So tell me something that has nothing to do with negros. And I'm saying negros in the male sense of the word, not the black sense."

Kahli's mind immediately shifted from the boring history assignment she was working on to one of her more interesting courses. "I'm really feeling Hark's class, and this summer project is becoming super important to me. Going into the King school and talking to those kids has been so fun. And now it looks like I'm gonna teach one of the classes at the Institute. I'm so excited about it."

"Wow," Robyn said, sounding impressed. "I can't believe you're going to teach those kids when they're only a few years younger than you. I'm sure you'll be great, though."

"Yeah. I thought about that. But I'm personally interviewing every applicant, and I'll ask them how they feel about having teachers only slightly older than they are. Oh! Guess what else?"

"What?"

"I'm gonna try to get the House Dean to agree to let the students live in this building for the summer."

"Really? The kids would love that. I remember how gassed I was when I got to stay at UCLA the summer after my junior year of high school. It was crazy, though. Our counselors were ready to kill us."

Kahli thought about how wary Dave was about having the kids on campus for that exact reason. "That's why I'm gonna have to hire an R.A. who can keep them in check."

Robyn completely turned her body away from her computer. "For the record, I would definitely be interested in that position. I went to a school like King, and I've done programs like your Institute. Since I'm staying on campus anyway, it sounds perfect."

"And for the record, you're hired. As long as I get permission for the kiddies to live here."

Robyn was beaming. "Don't you have to clear it with your partner Dave?"

Kahli smiled back. "I thought we agreed that this was a testosterone-free conversation." She suddenly felt very together. She'd randomly found the perfect R.A. for the Institute, and she'd completely rationalized her crush on Dave. Robyn Rationale was a great thing. Now as soon as she could get Dez talking again and find J.T. a new girl, everyone would be straight.

CHAPTER FIFTEEN

March 14th. Joy's twenty-fourth birthday. He made sure he didn't forget this time. It was raining, but it didn't damper their spirits. They cheerfully hopped in a cab and Dave uttered an address that Joy had never heard of. He'd found a little jazz club where they read poetry on Thursday nights–a little tribute to how they met. She loved it. "Remember how terrible those poets were at Lyrics? Whatever happened to that brown leather jacket you were wearing?" The evening was filled to overflowing with nostalgic rememberwhens.

David ordered coffee, as he had the first night they met. By the end of the night, when they threw open the door to her apartment, damp and chilly, he felt a buzz, a high that he hadn't felt in a long time. Joy looked so beautiful, her hair stuck to the edges of her oval face, her moist brown eyes looking at him with an appreciative gaze that melted his soul. He'd made her so happy tonight. And that made him tingle.

And he grabbed her as he had thousands of times before. He kissed her and remembered why he never tired of her kiss. Always new, but deliciously familiar. She effortlessly pinpointed the spot on his neck to breathe warm breath onto in order to make his spine shiver. She squeezed the exact section on his bicep that made his entire upper body tense up, and then she traced the line along his back that relaxed him again.

And their bodies knew and recognized each other, greeted each other, acknowledged the other's needs, and then provided those needs selflessly. He moved in the way that made her moan. She moaned in the way that made him cry out in joy. And they held each other in the still room as if their bodies joined together were a more natural state than their existing separately.

Dave laughed, breaking the silence of early, early morning.

"What?" Joy asked, feeling the rise and fall of his chest in her back as he chuckled.

"Kahli and I were just having a conversation about this the other day."

"About what?" she inquired, her voice even and smooth as butter.

"The spoon position–the way we're lying right now. Kahli was saying how it's the best, most comforting feeling on earth. And at this moment I can see where she's coming from."

Joy turned herself out of the spoon position, facing him and propping herself up on one elbow. "You don't think that's a little bit strange, David?"

"I mean, a little. But I don't think she literally meant that it was the *best* feeling in the entire world . . ."

"That's not what I meant," she interrupted, thoroughly exasperated. "I mean, why were you guys talking about that kind of stuff in the first place? What does that have to do with the project you're working on?"

"Well, it doesn't. But I didn't know that I wasn't allowed to ever digress from the topic of the Summer Institute," he answered, trying to hold in his defensiveness. But the statement came out edgy, and a bit too loud.

"Don't get like that. You just mention her a lot, that's all. And I can't pretend like I don't get little jealous feelings every once in a while." Joy turned her body back around, her eyes glued to her pale blue wallpaper.

Dave repositioned his arms around her waist and took in her body close to his. "Joy. She's a sweet girl. But she is just a girl. You're the woman in my life. Now go to sleep."

And she did. While Dave lay awake, staring at the white ceiling.

It often happened very late at night. When the thoughts started consuming his mind to the point where sleep was no longer an option. It started off as Dave thinking about the woman in his arms. Here was a woman lying next to him who did not possess an inch of flesh that he hadn't kissed. But he still felt like there was something much deeper about Joy that he didn't understand. Or, even more frightening, that there was nothing beneath the surface with which he needed to become familiar.

He thought about his last semester at Harvard, finding out that he'd been accepted to Franklin's Ph.D. program. He remembered his sadness, feeling his and Joy's relationship coming to a close. But there was also a sense of anticipation, of curiosity as to what else awaited him in the world. *Who* else awaited him. Visions of brilliant beautiful women in academic ivory towers intrigued him, increased his desire to leave Cambridge. To leave everything behind once he moved on. Still, he was sad. Joy was a soothing sort of drug that brought with it a drowsy pleasure. But Dave was ready for a stimulant.

It never happened. They never parted. Their separation was never meant to be. David felt his train of thought steering into regions where he preferred not to visit, and fought to redirect the path of his memory. *Maybe I should cook breakfast tomorrow morning. Do we have eggs in the house? I could always run and get some . . .* It was useless. The picture was becoming clearer. The rainy darkness almost two years earlier, a night not unlike this one. Joy's moistened eyes, adoring and pleading all at the same time. The look of terror that marred her usually serene face.

He sat up suddenly, hoping the physical movement would throw his thoughts off-track. Before he could tell if it proved effective, Joy's arms were wrapped around him. As if she knew not to ask, she instead placed her lips on his cheek, moving to his neck, chest, and back. Dave's relief increased with each caress. He was warm. He was with the woman he loved. He was safe again.

CHAPTER SIXTEEN

"Good morning," Desiree mumbled to the bus driver as she slowly climbed the steps onto the Number 32 downtown. She wasn't accustomed to being up this early, even on a Monday. She could think of a million places she would rather be on a Monday morning, with number one probably being her bed in a fetal position with Trevor curled up behind her. Nothing like the spoon position, Kahli always said.

But she wasn't snuggled up under her sheets. She was sitting alone in a single window seat on a chilly spring day. April Fools Day. *Maybe I'll wake up tomorrow and this will all be a dream.*

The physical sensation of eyes penetrating her skin caused her to turn from the window and assess the other passengers. An old light skinned lady with a long braid down her back like Desiree's grandma. A professional looking youngish white man with eyes the color of her favorite teacher back in high school. A teenage boy, reminding Dez of her little brother Desmond, decked out in Mecca gear from head to toe, trying to strike a cool pose in spite of his backpack full of textbooks. But none of the people brought her a sense of comfort. They were all staring at her, accusing her with their glares. She was a failure. She had let them down.

She closed her eyes to attempt to erase the vision of her persecutors. She reopened them and her glance fell on a mother and daughter sitting a few rows in front of her. The mother was facing the front of the bus, her hand protectively rubbing her young child's back while the little girl knelt on her seat backwards and looked directly at Desiree. The girl was probably two years old, with huge gray eyes and a curly frizzy reddish brown Afro. Her lips were pink and glossy like she'd just eaten candy or smeared on some Hellokitty cherry flavored chapstick. They parted to reveal a mouthful of baby teeth.

Everyone on this bus hates me except this little girl. Desiree felt an ice cool chill from all of the familiar strangers around her, but the warmth of the baby's smile penetrated her even deeper. She tasted the saltiness of her own tears before she realized she was crying. The child's animated face metamorphosed into one of great concern. She tapped her mother to get her to notice Desiree's anguish, but her mother just insisted that she turn around and face front.

Desiree casually brought her hand up to her face to wipe her tears. She did it slowly so as not to draw any attention to herself. *I wish Kahli were here.*

But just as quickly as she wanted her, she didn't. She thought about the way everyone at school called them "best friends, inseparable, mad tight." The only thing people *didn't* call them was "just alike." Even the dumbest person knew better than that.

But they were all dumb, really. Because Desiree and Kahlila certainly weren't best friends. True friendship meant more than eating every meal together, watching the same T.V. shows, dancing together at parties, sharing meaningless secrets about hook ups and break ups. What more does *real* friendship entail? *Whatever it is, me and Kahli ain't got it.*

What was unclear was who to blame for their superficial relationship. Herself, for acting too proud and important to ever need a shoulder to cry on? For playing her airhead role so well that she prevented any real intellectual discussion? *N'ah. Fuck that. It's Kahli's fault.* For acting like she's the only person around here capable of possessing any depth. For being too scared to admit that she doesn't always want to take the high road. That she'd love to skip class one day. Have a one night stand. Smoke some weed. *But then again, it's not like I'm telling Kahli how much I'm loving my Caribbean Lit class, or how some Friday nights I'd rather stay in and read instead of grinding in somebody's sweaty basement.*

As the bus started and stopped in commuter traffic, Desiree's mind paused on New Year's Eve night. Kahli had come down to visit her in D.C. and they'd planned on doing some hard core clubbing that evening. After being turned away from every spot in D.C. for being underage, they talked their way into an after hours jazz lounge.

They scanned the room, not even making an effort to hide the disappointment in their eyes as they registered faces of men old enough to be their dads. All eyes followed them to the booth they selected near the bar.

Desiree took out a pack of clove cigarettes and began to smoke one. She didn't smoke often, but it helped her buzz when she drank. And she was going to need all the help she could get with this crowd. Plus, she was in a jazz lounge. She knew she looked the part in her long black dress, her hair swept up, and a dark brown cigarette resting between her fingers.

Within five minutes, they had company. Michael was a junior at Georgetown—an English major from Michigan. Caramel colored with dark bedroom eyes and a smile that Billie D. would kill for. Desiree's intrigue only grew when he asked her where she bought her cloves. He sat smoking one of her cigarettes, explaining that he lost his boys at a crowded night club and he'd decided to roam on his own. Dez noticed Kahlila's eyes brightening upon hearing that. *She was a sucker for independent spirits.*

Suddenly Kahlila was asking him who his favorite author was and they immediately became entrenched in a heavy conversation about James Baldwin. Desiree knew she could have jumped in with her opinion of *Geovanni's Room*, but instead she took off her shoe and began running her toe along his leg under the table. *Am I really competing with Kahli for this guy's attention?* They'd never done that before. Part of Dez's being told her to stop, but another part conveyed to her the urgency of the situation. She had to win.

During a pause in Michael and Kahli's Black literature discussion, Desiree jumped in, throwing out several names of people she knew who went to Georgetown. Being that the black population at most universities was so small, they vibed on some folks they knew in common. She told a few funny stories about their mutual friends' high school antics and he laughed appreciatively. But she soon lost control again, sinking into the background of an animated debate about Hurston's use of vernacular.

Desiree decided to step her flirtation up a notch and found his hand under the table. She traced a few lines on his palm and played with his fingers. He managed to sneak a wink in her direction as a response.

Dez was feeling a little more on top of her game now and decided to run to the bathroom to check her makeup, maybe take her hair down. She excused herself and walked through the smoky room and down a small corridor. Someone called her name as she was about to push the bathroom door open. It was Michael.

Her heart stopped as he walked towards her, holding open the door to the restroom for her to walk through, and then following her inside. Luckily it was empty. With his back propped against the door so no one could enter, he gently pulled her towards him. His hands pressed on her bare back as he kissed her passionately. She was breathless when they separated. He flashed his beautiful smile and disappeared.

Michael and Kahli were chatting and laughing when she arrived back at the table. But she didn't care. She'd won.

As Dez took her seat, Michael stood up. Said he had to be going, that his boys were probably trippin' by now. He shook their hands and left. She was a little surprised that he didn't ask for her number, but whatever. He probably didn't want to offend Kahli. Desiree could just e-mail her peeps at Georgetown and get his info that way.

"So . . . he was interesting," Kahli said, breaking the silence.

"Definitely," Dez replied dreamily.

Kahli reached in her purse and pulled out a napkin. She threw the napkin on the table and motioned to it. Desiree noticed the black ink scrawled on one side. Slowly she came to the realization that Michael had given Kahlila his number.

"Think I should call him?" Kahli asked innocently.

But Desiree was tired of her innocent act. She knew she should be mad at Michael, but her fury was directed toward her friend. Had Kahli shown her the napkin just to show off that she'd won? Of course not—she didn't even know about the kiss in the bathroom. Dez managed to mumble a response about it being risky to call a guy she hardly knew. Kahli agreed and left the napkin on the table when they left the lounge.

Desiree, being the second one to rise from the table, snatched the napkin and stuffed it in her purse. She didn't know why she took it. Perhaps it could shed some light on the question she'd been asking herself more and more lately. *Why was Kahli always the chosen one?*

Later that night, as she smoothed out the crumpled napkin, she found her answer:

Intelligent. Beautiful. The epitome of class.
Wonderful meeting you,
Michael (202) 555-0989

Class. That word haunted her. Did she have no class for playing footsies under the table? For kissing a stranger in the ladies' room? If that's the case, she could only imagine what dear Michael would say if he saw her now.

"Next stop," she called out to the bus driver, her voice breaking.

There was no class in her lifeless shuffle down the street. And there was certainly no class in her destination.

CHAPTER SEVENTEEN

"Hi, Lloyd. Is Dave home? I'm supposed to meet him here at 3:30, but I'm early." Kahlila stood in the doorway of Lloyd and Dave's apartment building, wearing a cream sweater, a baby blue fleece vest over it, and a warm smile.

Lloyd, on the other hand, was wearing a dingy white T-shirt, an old pair of boxers, and a humiliated expression. "Um, no he's not here. But you can come in and wait, no problem." He opened the door wider as an invitation inside. The radiators in the hallways were no longer huffing and puffing. Winter was over, and mid-April brought with it lots of sunshine and a brisk but refreshing breeze.

As soon as they entered the apartment, Lloyd jogged down the hallway to put a pair of running pants over his shorts. Kahlila pretended not to notice his brief excursion to his bedroom, but she was secretly amused. *I wonder what he's so self conscious about. It's not like he answered the door naked. He should see what Tarik's boys look like when they come to the door sometimes. And lard-ass Carl definitely has more to be embarrassed about than Lloyd. I mean, Lloyd isn't Tyson Beckford, but there's at least a hint of a bicep.*

She walked into the kitchen, opened the refrigerator door, took out the pitcher of Kool Aid, and poured herself a glass. She tried to read Lloyd's facial expression, which fell somewhere between surprise at her boldness and relief at her comfort level. Kahlila was satisfied with his reaction. She'd wanted to make it clear that he didn't have to entertain her, that she was perfectly content amusing herself until Dave got home. *Not like I wouldn't welcome the company, but I'm sure he was busy doing something before I rang the bell.*

Despite her attempt to be the self-reliant guest, she was brightened when he joined her on the living room couch.

"So Ms. Bradford, how are those interesting roommates of yours? The one with the killer smile and the one with the killer stare."

Kahli sighed. "Well, Killer Smile is terrific. Teeth white as ever, grades high as ever, boyfriend representing as always."

"And Killer Stare?"

Another sigh. "Well, Desiree is a different story. She's been a different person these past few months. I think she's mad at me or something. Well, she's kind of weird around everybody, but she's especially distant with me." She noticed Lloyd's mouth poised to interrupt with a question, and she anticipated what it would be. "Yes, of course I've tried to talk to her. She says it's not me, that she's just been in a funk. I know things didn't work out with this guy Trevor she was liking, but I can't believe that's what has her down. You've seen her before. She's gorgeous!"

Lloyd nodded in agreement, although Kahli could tell that he was about to challenge something she said. But that's what she liked about Lloyd. He provided gentle support while offering food for thought. "Yeah, she's definitely attractive. But I can imagine that could get frustrating."

"What? Being beautiful?" Kahli asked, thoroughly confused.

"Well, being blessed with average at best appearance, I can only speculate," he smiled. "But it seems to me that if someone were always known as 'the pretty one,' that person's other qualities might go unnoticed."

"Other qualities like what?"

"I have no clue! *You're* her friend. You tell me."

Kahli stared at him blankly, a bit frustrated. *Damn. I thought Lloyd would come up with a better theory than this.* "I'm sure that Dez is not in a two-month long depression about being pretty. We were inseparable for five months. I can promise you Desiree Thomas has no problems with her external appearance."

"Maybe it's not the external," Lloyd pondered softly. He quickly perked up, hopped off of the couch. He walked over to his shelf of books, and instead of removing one, as Kahli had anticipated, he reached for his dusty keyboard.

"Don't tell me that you have a song written for this very occasion," Kahli teased. "My best friend's too sexy, it just breaks her heart . . ." she sang off-key.

Lloyd ignored her very unmelodic attempt at humor. He was busy wiping off the keys and finding an outlet to plug in the adapter. He finally got everything together and sat back down on the couch, the oversized keyboard resting on both of their laps.

"Now, I've seen you and Killer hanging out a few times before. Sometimes just the two of you and sometimes with other people. You two are very interesting, I must say."

"Where did you see us hanging out? I never saw you," she protested adamantly.

"Stop cutting me off. I have a point to make."

She obediently clamped her jaw shut and tilted her head to one side.

"As I was saying about you ladies–I don't know what Desiree's problem is. But here's my take on the two of you as friends." He pressed the power button on his keyboard, causing all sorts of red and green lights to appear. "Some people you just click with, you know? Like, you come together and the music's just right." He played two notes together that made a nice harmony. "That's a C and a G," he explained. "A perfect fifth."

"Other folks," he continued, "they might not blend as well. Maybe it's because y'all are too close. You need a little distance. A G sharp and an A, for example." He played those two keys, and Kahli made a face at the cluttered, unpleasant sound that came out of the speakers. "They're always all up on each other, so their music isn't beautiful. But they do manage to vibe pretty well when there are other folks around to relieve the tension." He kept his fingers on the same two notes as before, but added two more, and suddenly the chord sounded really funky, like something a jazz pianist would play. Kahli looked at Lloyd questioningly, very much interested but not quite clear on his point.

He picked up on her confusion and decided to speak in plainer terms. "I think that's what you and Desiree are. G sharp and A. You guys are too similar. You can get along in a social setting with other people around–parties, that kind of stuff. But when it's just the two of you, a feeling of competition sets in and you try to outdo each other. Show everyone whose sound is more beautiful."

Kahlila raised one eyebrow and looked at him sideways. "I hate to diss your music lesson, buddy, but you're way off with the Dez analysis. One, we're nothing alike. We're more like this!" and she played the highest and lowest notes on the keyboard together. "Two, we *never* compete. What are you talking about?"

"I learned long ago not to argue with people about their own tendencies," he said while pressing the power button again, making all the lights disappear.

Dave opened the door to the apartment just in time to see Lloyd returning the instrument to its place against the bookshelf. "Kahli, you actually got him to play that thing?" his tone was shocked and excited at the same time.

She looked in Lloyd's direction before she provided an answer. *What's that look on his face all about?* "Um, actually I didn't. Lloyd was just letting me fool around with it until you got here."

"Yup. And now you're here, D. So I'll check you later, Kahlila." They made eye contact for a split second, and she thought she caught a look of appreciation, but she couldn't be sure. Once he closed the bedroom door behind him, she didn't give it another moment's thought. Dave was home.

They quickly quizzed each other on the logistics of the next few weeks. Kahli had narrowed down the pool of students for the Institute based on the application Dave had written, and would be interviewing the finalists over the next few days. Dave had been working on getting some more money for the program, and succeeded in snagging a matching grant from Franklin's community service office. He'd done a few calculations and figured that they had enough money to pay himself and Kahli generously, and still have money to give the kids a small stipend. They'd have cash left over for field trips and costs of publication.

"I was thinking we should hit up Mr. Elliott and get Booker T. to pay Robyn's salary," Dave suggested.

In the past month, Kahli managed to erase all of Dave's doubts about making the Institute a residential program. Her persuasive skills began with Mr. Elliott, the House Dean, who was all hyped about having the King students live in the dorm by the end of his first meeting with Kahli. Once Mr. Elliott began talking about all the resources the kids would have by being in the House, specifically the seminar rooms, the computer room, and the library, Dave started getting excited about it right along with Kahli and Mr. Elliott. And after he met Robyn for a "formal hiring interview," he was sold that Booker T. was the perfect place to base the entire Institute, and that Robyn was an ideal R.A.

"He shouldn't have a problem with that," Kahli mused while making a note in her planner to send Mr. Elliott an e-mail. "So, where were you coming from when you walked in the door?"

"Joy's place. We went to church this morning."

Kahli looked him up and down suspiciously. "Wearing that?" He was dressed similarly to her, in a sweater and jeans.

"Damn, stop sweating me," he said slyly. "I had on a different pair of pants. Why do you look so surprised that I went to church?"

"I don't know. Just didn't see you as the church going type."

"Yeah, well Joy and I go whenever she's not working. There's a lot to be thankful for each week. I figure, why not go and celebrate with a bunch of happy black folks every Sunday . . . and I take it from that look you're giving me that *you're* definitely not the church going type."

"Definitely true. I mean, I'm pretty sure that I believe in God. But some things about religion just don't make sense! For example, what about people who live in parts of the world where the concept of God is never introduced? Do these people go to hell because they haven't accepted Christ as their personal savior? And what about kids? What's the rule with them? How old until you're accountable for your sins and stuff?"

Dave chuckled. "Interesting questions, Kahli. You're perfectly right, I think. Religion is man-made, and therefore flawed . . ."

". . . which is why I can't get into the whole church thing. I might as well just pray at home. Not like I do that too much, either. Except for when I'm in a crisis; then, I pray like mad. Am I just a total hypocrite?"

"Yeah. But at least you're honest enough to admit it. I mean, it's hard for most people to believe in something that seems irrational. Like when I first read *Beloved*, I had a hard time with it because I was trying to rationalize the existence of the spirit character. But once I accepted Beloved as a real entity, the rest of the book just made clicked for me. Am I making sense?"

"*You're* making sense, yes. But Morrison's book still never clicked for me. Maybe you have a point–I might be too much of a realist for my own good." Kahlila heard the words coming out of her mouth, but she knew she didn't really mean them. If she was such a realist, then why was a little voice telling her that it was possible for this mature, educated, handsome man to be staring at her at this very moment in a way that was in no way professional?

CHAPTER EIGHTEEN

To: angelabradford@aol.com
From: joshuatravis@classof98.franklin.edu
Date: April 8, 1996 10:15 a.m.
Subject: thanks, moms

Message:
ms. bradford-
just wanted to send a quick thanku e-mail for the cookies. kahli was pretty heated that you didn't send her any ;-). don't worry–i'll make sure i look out for her this summer (and i won't tell her that you told me to).
-joshua

To: steinway@prudential.org
From: kahlila@classof99.franklin.edu
Date: April 8, 1996 10:24 a.m.
Subject: j.t. update

Message:
hi mr. steinway–sorry i haven't e-mailed in a few weeks. it's been pretty hectic. i don't know if j.t. mentioned his chem midterm, but he did really well. got way above the mean. you know he always starts doing better once basketball season is over. he's been really upbeat lately, too. kristy is definitely a name of the past.

i'm doing well these days, too. i have a's in all of my classes so

far, except history. i'm thinking about a sociology or urban studies major. tarik's doing fine, too. i think he missed basketball this season more than he wants to admit. don't be surprised if you see him in uniform next year. i'm on my way to this high school off campus to interview some kids for my summer program. talk to you soon.
kal

To: kahlila@classof99.franklin.edu
From: drobinson@sociology.franklin.edu
Date: April 8, 1996 11:42 a.m.
Subject: hark! he summons . . .

Message:
excuse the pun in the subject line. i think i'm spending too much time around you lately :-). hark wants to meet with us after class tomorrow for an update of what we've been doing. about time, huh?

To: drobinson@sociology.franklin.edu
From: kahlila@classof99.franklin.edu
Date: April 8, 1996 12:02 p.m.
Subject: horrible pun.

Message:
a "hark! who goes there?" might have been more amusing. anyhow, i've been wondering when this man was gonna ask us where his ten thousand bucks was going.

so i decided to stay in booker t. house for sophomore year. after getting to know mr. elliott, i felt bad moving out. i'm definitely gonna be more involved in house activities next year. robyn's gonna live with me. desiree decided to move off-campus by herself. she told us it was to save money, but i'm not buying it.

see you tomorrow.

To: tarik@classof97.franklin.edu
From: kahlila@classof99.franklin.edu
Date: April 8, 1996 12:09 p.m.
Subject: lunch tomorrow

Message:
hey babe. i just found out that i have a meeting at noon so i'm gonna have to cancel on lunch. forgive me :-(.

To: tarik@classof97.franklin.edu
From: shannon@classof97.franklin.edu
Date: April 8, 1996 12:13 p.m.
Subject: (none)

Message:
hey, tarik. we were supposed to have a talk way back at the beginning of the semester. i haven't forgotten. you interested in getting together and hearing what i have to say?
shannon

To: shannon@classof97.franklin.edu
From: tarik@classof97.franklin.edu
Date: April 8, 1996 2:22 p.m.
Subject: very interested.

Message:
yeah. i'll get back to you on when i'm free. i shouldn't really have to say this, but don't mention this to kahli.

To: kahlila@classof99.franklin.edu
From: lloyd@philosophy.franklin.edu
Date: April 8, 1996 5:35 p.m.
Subject: hello

Message:
kahlil the second,

i rarely send e-mail, but i read this poem today in a harlem renaissance anthology and i thought you'd enjoy it:-
lloyd

La Vie C'est La Vie
by Jessie Redmon Fauset

On summer afternoons I sit
Quiescent by you in the park,
And idly watch the sunbeams gild
And tint the ash-trees' bark.

Or else I watch the squirrels frisk
And chaffer in the grassy lane;
And all the while I mark your voice
Breaking with love and pain.

I know a woman who would give
Her chance in hell to take my place;
To see the love-light in your eyes,
The love-glow on your face!

And there's a man whose lightest word
Can set my chilly blood afire;
Fulfillment of his least behest
Defines my life's desire.

But he will none of me, nor I

of you. Nor you of her. 'Tis said
The world is full of jests like these.-
I wish that I were dead.

To: lloyd@philosophy.franklin.edu
From: kahlila@classof99.franklin.edu
Date: April 8, 1996 7:53 p.m.
Subject: hello–Reply

Message:
what an ironic, depressing poem! truth be told, i do like it. but i'm curious as to why you were so sure i would.

it's an interesting piece, though unrealistically dramatic to me. i mean, that stuff rarely happens with such stabbing precision (i mean, everyone in this tight clique just narrowly missing their soulmate? come on, now).

thanks for sending it to me, though. my e-mail comes in prose 99 percent of the time. i enjoyed getting something different.
-kahlil the second (i like that!)

To: kahlila@classof99.franklin.edu
From: lloyd@philosophy.franklin.edu
Date: April 8, 1996 8:03 p.m.
Subject: you're welcome
Message:
glad you liked the poem. i'd have to disagree with your take on it, though. "the world is full of jests like these," kahlila. it's true. and if you haven't found yourself in a situation like this yet, count your blessings and pray your luck holds out for you. i'll be praying too. we need folks like you in the world who feel as if soulmates are found more often than not.
lloyd

CHAPTER NINETEEN

Dr. Howard Harkonn sat back in his chair, looking at the two individuals sitting before him with a critical expression. He hadn't spoken yet. Sometimes he liked to watch a little before he started meetings, to gage where people's heads were. David and Kahlila were sitting straight up in their seats, their mouths slightly turned up and ajar–ready to start joyfully gushing about their plans for how to spend Coca Cola's money. A quick inspection of their expressions told him it was going to be a good meeting, and only after he was satisfied with this fact did he utter his first words.

"Well, what have you got so far?"

He'd barely finished the question before answers came flying out of their mouths a mile a minute. He listened to the excitement in their voices more than the words that were being said, catching snippets of their fast chatter.

". . . looks like we'll have fourteen or fifteen students . . . individual attention . . . can't have too many if we have to watch them day and night . . ."

"some sort of publication . . . the kids can decide what type . . . design their own curriculum . . ."

"Summer Institute . . . didn't want the name to sound like a summer camp . . . they have to take the program seriously . . ."

Hark was surprised that Dave was actually sitting back, allowing Kahlila to speak about her contributions. Dave was usually the person who had to be in control. But it seemed as if they split responsibilities evenly, and Dave was calmly listening to his partner as she reported on her progress. Still, he looked relieved when she gave him the opportunity to take the reins.

" . . . we managed to get some more money . . . can get the kids backpacks, t-shirts . . . mad field trips . . . have to pay a printer to get the magazine made . . ."

He wanted to laugh at their admirable greed. Here he was, giving them 10,000 dollars, and they use their business savvy to get more money. *Funny that they didn't mention how much they think their salary should be. But good for them, using their resources to their advantage. They deserve a hefty chunk of change.*

". . . living in Booker T. Washington house . . . giving the kids opportunity to explore cultural issues . . . use the library in the building . . . discuss the implications of a 'black dorm' . . ."

He loved that they were simultaneously handling the nuts and bolts of the program, as well as thinking about important themes that they wanted to address with the students. Apparently, at least *two* people were listening to his lecture on combining theory and practice.

As they continued to talk, handing him spreadsheets and applications and interview questions, he began to focus on the two of them as a team. One picked up where the other left off. David laughed at her witty comments–had Hark ever seen him laugh like that before? They together infused each other with boundless energy.

He remembered his research partner during his graduate days at Yale. She had pushed him to think in ways that he hadn't before. Challenged him politically. Challenged him socially–forced him out of his serious shell and "brought the silly out of him," as she called it. That's still what she calls it, when the kids manage to get Daddy do his scary monster impression. *Bringing the silly out.*

And finally, they were done. Now they were leaning forward in their chairs, waiting for a sign of approval from their boss. He thought about making them sweat it out for a while, but he decided to be a nice guy.

"Excellent!" His voice boomed. "Do you need anything from me?" This was a trick question, and he hoped that they knew better than to ask him for anything other than a check. "Good," he said once they shook their heads no. "I have one more question for you, and then you're free to enjoy the rest of your day."

"What's up, Hark?" Dave asked.

"Do the two of you like the Fugees?" He enjoyed their looks of bewilderment at his abrupt subject change.

Kahli was the first to recover. "I personally think they're the bomb, I mean I think they're fantastic."

"Their new album came out recently and it's tight," Dave added.

"I'm aware of this," Hark said, almost offended that they thought he wouldn't know that *The Score* just dropped last month. "My wife won two tickets to their concert at some raffle they had at her job. We already have a benefit that we absolutely must attend, so I thought maybe the two of you would like them."

Their mouths simultaneously dropped as if they'd practiced synchronized surprise before the meeting. After the initial shock, Hark was bombarded with a thousand thank yous and we'd-love-tos. When he went into his wallet and pulled out the two tickets, David and Kahlila held them in their hands as if they were gold nuggets. They practically skipped out of his office. He chuckled as he watched them walk out, nudging each other excitedly. He sighed, suddenly feeling the urge to call his wife.

"Hello?" Tarik asked, breathless after running down the hall from Carl's room.

"Hey baby. Whatcha doin'?" Kahli asked, in a cute little girl voice.

"Playing video games. What's going on? How was your meeting today?"

"*So* good, actually. Dr. Harkonn gave me and Dave tickets to the Fugees concert downtown this Friday night!"

"Who the fuck is Dave?" Tarik's mind was now fully on the conversation, the Nintendo game he left behind long forgotten.

"Tarik, please. He's the grad student who I'm working on the summer program with. I told you that."

"Mm hmm. So I guess you're calling to cancel our plans for Friday night, like you canceled our lunch plans today."

"Baby," her voice pleading, "we don't have any plans for Friday."

"I guess you're right. We don't. I'll talk to you later, Kahlila." He hung up the phone.

"Hi, this is Shannon. You've reached my voice mail because I'm never home. But leave a message and I promise I'll get back to you soon." Beep.

"What's up, Shannon. This is Tarik. I thought maybe we could get together for that talk on Friday night. You might be able to answer a few questions for me. Give me a call. Peace."

"Hello?" Joy's voice was groggy and low.

"Sorry, baby. Did I wake you up?"

"Yeah. I have the late shift tonight so I was taking a nap."

"Oh. Well, I just wanted to tell you that me and Kahli met with Hark today . . ."

"Uh huh . . ." her tone anticipating something unpleasant.

"He gave us two tickets to see the Fugees Friday night."

"I see. And will you be going?"

"Not if you don't want me to," his response hesitant and unsure.

She laughed, her voice getting sharper and more alert by the second. "Sure, David. Make me the bad guy."

"That's not what I was . . ."

"Whatever. Look, just go. Hark will be offended if you don't use the ticket."

"That's what I was thinking," he agreed, the relief audible in his voice.

"Yeah. I'm sure that's what you were thinking. I'm going back to bed." She hung up the phone.

CHAPTER TWENTY

"Your soul is oftentimes a battlefield, upon which your reason and your judgement wage war against your passion and your appetite."
-Kahlil Gibran

"OOOOH, la la la la la la lalalalalalaaaaa, sweet ting!" Dave and Kahli burst into Dave's apartment, singing at the top of their lungs. They continued to bellow Fugees hits at maximum volume as they raided the refrigerator, looking for late night munchies. Soon a bedroom door opened and a sleepy Lloyd shuffled into the kitchen.

"Sorry!" Dave and Kahli said at the same time.

"How was it? And don't torture me with the details." Lloyd had been complaining of jealous pangs ever since they were blessed with the tickets. He'd seen Lauryn Hill sitting in the library at Columbia once and had yet to recover.

"Off the hook, for real," Dave said. "They put on a phat show. Lauryn sang her ass off, Wyclef was playing the guitar with his teeth, it was wild."

"I said no details," Lloyd whined, and headed back to bed.

They laughed at his drowsy bitterness as they settled into the living room couch.

"That was so nice of Hark to give us these tickets. I think he's really pleased with us," Kahli said with a contented smile.

"True, true," said Dave as he popped a Cheez-It into his mouth. "He's feeling the whole project. I can tell he's really pleased with himself for knowing that you were the best person for the job."

Kahli tried to hide her pleasure at the compliment. "Yeah

well, I just get really passionate about things that I think are worthwhile."

"Can I ask you a question?" Dave put the box of Cheez-Its on the coffee table in front of them.

"Shoot."

"How did you manage to get your shit so together in eighteen years?"

It was a useless endeavor to try and hide her pleasure at *this* compliment. Her grin was ear to ear as her cheeks glowed a deep red. "Trust me, I still have a ways to go," she replied as she grabbed the box off the coffee table and reopened it. "But I guess I *have* made some crazy strides."

"Hey, you can't just leave me hanging. You better share, girlie." He touched her arm like Mary would have done on an episode of 227.

Kahlila laughed at his unusual silliness. "O.K. I'll share. I think I was pretty conflicted a few years back. Being one of the only black people in a predominately white high school can take its toll. My freshman year, I felt like such an outcast socially. Everyone was starting to date and all that stuff, and I was just out of the loop. I needed some type of validation that I was normal, that I was pretty. So . . . I tried out for the cheerleading squad in tenth grade."

Dave's eyes widened a few millimeters. "You? A cheerleader?"

"Yup. Crazy, huh? J.T. and I had been cool before that, but we really got to know each other during basketball season, and that's the year we went out. That had a bunch of people talking, but I couldn't care less about what those white folks thought of me. I wasn't interested in their social life anymore. I wanted one of my own."

"So what did you do?" Dave asked, grabbing a cushion off of a nearby chair and propping it behind his head.

"Quit cheerleading. Joined the step squad. Yeah, I know it sounds minor, but it was like stepping into a different world–no pun intended. Step squad was all black–basically all of the black girls at the high school. I needed that base. It was like I finally found a safe space in this hostile environment. Not to mention that we were so good, that we took the cheerleaders' place at basketball games that year. The players voted–it was phat. I think J.T. swayed a lot of votes."

"I'm sure he did," Dave said, adjusting his pillow. "And twelfth grade?"

"Definitely the year of my intellectual growth. I'd always gotten good grades, but I never pushed myself to learn anything more than what my teachers presented. But once I realized what a Eurocentric curriculum they were pushing, I had to break out of that zone. I read all the time, anything I could get my hands on. And I looked around me. I started opening my eyes. I saw my neighborhood. And I saw how jacked up it was that I had to travel miles away from my own house to get a decent education."

"A true sociologist at heart," Dave said with a smile.

Kahli smiled back. "And I felt like I was missing something by leaving my community every day. So that's when I decided to spend a year where I would have been for four years if I hadn't gotten that scholarship: my neighborhood high school. I think that's the experience that has shaped me the most. It humbled me, and it placed the responsibility of changing things square on my shoulders."

"You're wise beyond your years, Kahli."

"Am I? If I were, I wouldn't be boring you with all this high school talk."

"It's cool. I went to high school once. Of course, I was there ten years ago, but it's all good." He gave her a reassuring pat on the shoulder.

But his comment only served to agitate her. She suddenly felt like an idiot, sitting in front of a mature adult, taking it back to cheerleading memories. She wanted to slap herself for even going there.

The high shrill of the phone halted Kahli's silent self-reprimand. Dave located the cordless between two couch cushions and answered the phone. "Hello? Hey, baby . . . It was really good, yeah . . . Let me call you back in a little while . . . I don't know, soon . . . Joy, let's talk about this when I call you back . . . Yeah . . . Yeah . . . N'ah. Bye."

Kahlila knew she shouldn't ask, but she had to. "Is everything okay? I could go . . ."

He heaved a long sigh as he rested the phone down. "For some reason, Joy is unreasonably concerned about our relationship . . . mine and yours."

"Really."

Dave looked surprised and mildly offended. "You don't sound at all shocked by what I just said."

"Dave, look at my jeans." She was wearing a pair of dark blue stretchy bellbottoms that fit very close until mid-calf, where they flared dramatically. They were one of the few tight pants that she owned, and they accentuated the little bit of figure that she possessed.

He scanned her from the waist down quickly. "What about them?"

"Is this the first time you're seeing them?"

"N'ah."

"When did I wear them before?"

Dave looked absolutely perplexed, but answered obediently. "That time me and Joy ran into you on your way to that Q party. Now what does this have to do with anything?"

For the first time since she made his acquaintance, Kahli felt older and wiser than Dave. "It has everything to do with Joy's suspicion. The only wardrobe you should have memorized is hers. Just one of the many reasons why her head is probably spinning about us." She unfolded herself from her position on the couch and walked to the bathroom. From where Dave was sitting, it looked like she was swinging her hips more than usual.

As he sat alone in the living room, he felt very betrayed. By both of them. *How is Joy gonna be illin' on the phone like that just because Kahli's here. She really doesn't trust me after all these years? And how is Kahli gonna set me up to make me feel like I'm noticing shit I shouldn't be?*

Kahli stood in the bathroom staring at herself in the mirror. She was smirking. She'd been bluffing about the jeans. She didn't really think that he noticed what she looked like, never mind what she wore.

But he had. It meant something. It had to.

She returned to the living room and noticed the troubled look on Dave's face. His refusal to make eye contact told her loud and clear that she'd pushed too far. She mumbled something about being tired and wanting to call the Franklin shuttle to take her home. He didn't argue, and stared at the ceiling as she dialed the numbers on the cordless phone.

"Does Kahlila know about us?" Shannon had just arrived at Tarik's house. He'd walked her up the stairs to his room. She looked around quickly, and then sat down on the edge of his bed. They hadn't exchanged two words up to this point, and he wasn't prepared for the question that she posed when she did decide to open her mouth.

"What's to know?" he asked nonchalantly, choosing to take the seat near his desk instead of joining her on the bed.

"Um, that we fucked? Many times, as a matter of fact."

"Our freshman year!" Tarik reminded her.

"So it doesn't count?" Shannon asked angrily.

"It sure doesn't count as anything serious. We were just having fun, enjoying ourselves. Why should I tell Kahli about it?"

Shannon looked poised to answer that question, but then changed her mind. "Tarik, do you remember why we stopped chilling freshman year?"

"Honestly, no Shannon I don't."

She proceeded as if he hadn't answered at all. "You told me that I was the type of person you could see yourself settling down with. But you weren't ready for a relationship. And it wasn't fair for us to be sleeping together, knowing that you couldn't commit."

It did start to sound familiar to Tarik once Shannon started talking. He'd used that line a few times, usually when he started getting bored or when someone was beginning to take up too much of his time. "Look, I'm sorry for that . . ."

Again she continued like he hadn't spoken. "So now you've grown up. You're ready for a real relationship. And who do you decide to get with? Some freshman who doesn't even deserve your loyalty."

Here's what he had been waiting for. The inside information. "What do you mean? Has she been seeing somebody else?"

"How the hell am I supposed to know? I'm never in that room!"

Tarik was ready to explode. She'd set him up. She didn't know shit about what his girlfriend had been doing. She was just trying to start trouble so that she and Tarik could pick up where they left off two years ago. He looked at her as if he were seeing her for the first time. Her braids were pulled away from her face, accentuating her high cheekbones and cat-like eyes. Her lips always looked like they were slightly puckered, and they looked even more so than usual as he stared.

Now what? This girl was sitting in his room wearing a seductive expression with absolutely nothing to report, but seemingly with no place else to be. She didn't look like she was planning on leaving anytime soon either. As a matter of fact, she was removing her button-up sweater, revealing a red tank top that exposed a very flat stomach and a very sexy belly button ring.

She noticed him looking at her navel. "Yeah, it wasn't there the last time you saw my tummy. Did you want to get a closer look?"

Tarik stood up turned in 10 different directions, but Shannon's eyes met his everywhere he looked. At any other time in his life, if he was getting that look from a girl, he'd take it as a green light to start peeling off her clothes.

But this time was different. Yes, Shannon looked good. Yes,

she was clearly down. Yes, she was even in the running for the best sex he'd ever had. But no–she wasn't Kahli.

"Shannon, I think you need to leave."

Instead of walking out of his room, she walked closer to him, so close that if she leaned forward a few centimeters, her lips would be grazing his neck.

"Why? Am I tempting you?"

Shit. Why doesn't her breath stink so I can just be turned off. "Whatever. Stop playin'. I'll just check you later." He took a step back as he spoke.

Her smile disappeared. "Actually Tarik, I'll check you now. You wanna try and act like you ain't feelin' me but I know you better than that. You can't tell me you don't remember how good it was. Don't think I bought that shit you told me about not being ready for a relationship. And don't think I buy this Mr. Nice Guy act you're putting on with Kahlila. You're just not the commitment type. But you do like to have fun. And so do I. So stop fuckin' acting like you want me to leave, okay?"

Tarik felt his anger bubbling. *What is this bitch tryin' to say–that I'm just all about getting mine, that I can't love nobody?* He was about to give her a piece of his mind when she reached for his zipper. Tarik was speechless as Shannon unfastened his belt and pants and reached inside.

His mind was working overtime, concocting foul comments to spit her way that would make her feel like trash. But his body wasn't cooperating. He could utter nothing except a moan as she got down on her knees and began exploring the content of his boxers with her tongue.

This is unbelievable. Shit like this never happened to me when I was single. He forced a mental picture of Kahli into his mind. Kahli, who never went down on him unless he asked. Kahli, who lately seemed more passionate about her summer job than she was about him. Kahli, whom he knew he loved but refused to tell because something told him she wouldn't say it back.

He practically ripped his T-shirt, pulling it off fast and furiously. Shannon looked up at him and smiled.

Fuck it. Might as well give her what she came here for.

CHAPTER TWENTY-ONE

As Kahlila turned the hallway on the fourth floor of Booker T. Washington House, she noticed a figure turning the key in her door. For split second she thought it might be Robyn, but she quickly remembered that she was in Atlanta for the weekend. It was one of those nights when she needed a girlfriend to come home and talk to, and for months Robyn was the only person who was filling that role. Desiree was practically a stranger to her, and inexplicably so.

Once she realized that the person in the hallway was Shannon, her disappointment increased. But she forced a pleasant expression as she reached the door just as Shannon was opening it.

Shannon greeted her with a grin. "Hey, Kahli! Where are you coming from at . . ." she looked at her watch–"two thirty in the morning?"

Is she on crack? Kahlila was blown away by Shannon's friendliness, and decided to pounce on it before it disappeared again. She returned the smile and said, "I went to a Fugees concert. It was really phat. Where are you coming from?"

"Trust me, hon. You don't want to know." And with that mysterious comment, she walked into her bedroom and shut the door.

That girl couldn't shake her shadiness if she tried. Kahli just shook her head in amusement as she headed into her own bedroom and picked up the phone to call Tarik. The fantasy part of the evening was over. *Time for me to get back to reality. And a pretty damn good reality it is, anyhow.*

Desiree was in bed under her covers when Shannon entered their bedroom. Dez's eyes were closed, but she hadn't slept through the night in months. She was wide awake as Shannon changed into a T-shirt and shorts, and then walked around the room searching for her cordless phone.

Desiree listened to the numbers being dialed, a little excited that she was about to hear a conversation between her roommate and another person. She'd never even seen Shannon using that phone before, except to check her messages.

"Hi, it's me," Shannon's voice came out in practically a whisper. "What are you doing? Oh, really? I just saw your girl on the way into our room, actually . . . Anyhow, get off the phone, I wanna talk to you . . . What? I know you're not gonna try to act like nothing happened . . . You really haven't changed at all. You're just gonna fuck me and go on living your perfect little life with your perfect little girl . . . Tarik? Tarik! Hello??"

Shannon was still staring at the phone in disbelief, only half hearing the dial tone, when she heard rustling from the other side of the room. She didn't even acknowledge Desiree as she got out of bed, figuring that she probably had to go use the bathroom. But Desiree stopped right in front of her, forcing her to hang up the phone and pay attention. "You nasty ass fucking whore. I'm going to Kahli's room right now, and please be somewhere else when I get back."

Shannon's jaw dropped, partly due to Desiree's insult, but more because of the fact that the girl spoke at all. She hadn't heard Desiree open her mouth in at least a month, and now that she did, it scared her. Her voice was lower and sadder than it had been. And something about it made her put on a pair of jeans, call her girlfriend, and ask to stay over for the night. Maybe the week.

Desiree walked into Kahli's room without knocking. She was curled up on her bed, the phone cradled under her chin. Her eyes got very large as she made out the shadow in her doorway.

"Hang up the phone. I gotta talk to you." She walked in and sat down at Kahli's desk.

"Tarik? Lemme call you back. Okay, honey." She turned off the phone and sat up on her bed.

Desiree recounted the words she just heard Shannon speak on the phone with no emotion at all. It was as if she were reading back the transcript of the call, adding no additional comments or tokens of sympathy. If she saw Kahlila's tears, she didn't acknowledge them. When she was finished, she rose up from the chair and began walking towards the door.

Kahlila stopped her with a broken cry. "Dez. Please stay." Trying to pull herself together, she added, "I could really use a friend right now."

Desiree's eyes looked lifeless, as she looked at Kahlila but didn't even see her. "I know, Kahli. But I'm really not in the position to be that person. Call J.T.–you know he'll be there for you."

"But what if I don't want J.T.? I need you, Dez!" Kahlila's voice was desperate.

"I'm sorry," Desiree said in almost a whisper.

"So when are you gonna let me help *you?*" Kahli shouted to her as she walked out of the door.

There was no answer as Desiree's footsteps echoed down the hallway.

Kahlila picked up the phone and pressed Memory 3.

"Hey sweetheart," Tarik answered, guessing it was Kahlila.

"Fuck you. On second thought, fuck Shannon. Oh no wait, I guess you already did that, didn't you?"

"Kahli . . ."

"Don't say my name. Don't call me. Don't even look at me if I'm unfortunate enough to run into your sorry ass on the street. You and that shady bitch deserve each other." She slammed down the phone, and hysterically sobbed well into the night.

april showers

lies stacked high as a tower
that's collapsed upon itself,
no longer have the power
to pretend I can not see.
I have to take control
and walk away while I still can
before you steal my soul
and take control of me.

everything to lose,
nothing more to gain,
no more blinding sunshine—
just the rain . . .

watch the heavy rainfall
from the warm dry room.
want to make the phone call
but I know I should move on.

getting hot up in this place,
open air will cool me down.
feel the water hit my face,
wash my tears till they're all gone.

teardrops from heaven
begin to soothe my pain.
no one understands me—
but the rain.

CHAPTER TWENTY-TWO

"Yesterday is but today's memory and tomorrow is today's dream."
-Kahlil Gibran

"Men are just natural born assholes," Kahli announced as she downed a shot of Bacardi Limon.

J.T. simply chuckled as he stared at the mess in front of him. On his bedroom rug were assorted bottles of alcohol, an array of shot glasses, scattered playing cards, and in the middle of the mayhem, a very drunk Kal. It had been quite a long day. Kal had called him early that morning, reporting last night's events. J.T. couldn't believe it. He'd trusted Tarik to act right, and T had to go fuck up a good thing.

He had quickly gotten dressed and met Kahlila at the closest subway station. They took the train downtown and went to IHOP for breakfast. Kal attacked her omelet with her fork as she relayed how Tarik talked to her last night as if he had done nothing wrong. And how Desiree wouldn't even stick around after she dropped the news that he'd slept with Shannon. J.T. just shook his head as he stuffed huge quantities of pancakes and syrup into his mouth.

After breakfast, Kahlila figured she could use some therapeutic shopping time, so they headed to the mall. After two tank tops, a pair of sandals, a photo album, and a Tracy Chapman CD, Kal decided that she needed to refuel. The twosome hit the Food Court and she continued on her verbal rampage as she vehemently dipped her fries in sweet and sour sauce.

They shopped a bit more after their Burger King break, this

time for J.T. Kal ran through department stores like a woman possessed, throwing shirts and pants at him and ordering him to try them on. J.T. absolutely hated dressing rooms, but he knew better than to argue. He surrendered his credit card to the saleswoman as Kal told him what items to purchase, knowing that he'd be back at Macy's the next day to return everything.

Finally they ended up at J.T.'s house off-campus. Kahlila rarely visited his house because it was always so loud and filthy. Living with seven guys did not make for a tranquil environment, that was for sure. But today, she said that she would rather face the shouting and dirt than go back to her room. Robyn was still in Atlanta and Desiree was locked in her room as usual. And she didn't know what she would do if she ran into Shannon.

And so they began an afternoon and evening of drinking games. Egyptian Ratscrew, Kings, and lots of other card games that J.T.'s teammates had taught him. Soon they got bored with that and borrowed board games from the other guys in the house, finding inventive ways to incorporate drinking into the standard rules. Scrabble: with consequences. Monopoly: the next level. After a few hours, they were tapped out of ideas. The only other games one could play that involved alcohol were sexual, and there was no way they were going there.

Which caused them to put their cards and gamepieces down, and simply engage in conversation. And this was more difficult than it sounded, due to the levels of liquor in their systems. But they babbled happily, Kahli cheerfully condemning the male species and J.T. contentedly letting the insults slide.

"Except you, of course," Kahli corrected her previous blanket statement. "You're not an asshole. And neither is Dave."

"Enough about this Dave dude! Is he the idiot who told you to buy a Tracy Chapman CD?" J.T. gathered up the cards on the rug and began to shuffle them.

"Actually, no. That was Lloyd. And *he* isn't an asshole either. Thanks for reminding me." She grabbed the cards from his hand and began lining them up on the rug for a game of solitaire.

"Damn Kal, all these men you keep talking about—I can't figure out why you're even sweating this Tarik thing. Just get with one of those other cats."

"Cats? Hello, you're a white boy from Boston. What the hell is 'cats' all about?"

He turned a bit pink, embarrassed at getting called out on his slang. "Yeah, I got that from your boy Trevor. Or Desiree's boy, I should say."

"I think I can pretty much state for a fact that Dez and Trev are over. I don't know much about that girl these days, but they definitely seem to be history." She slapped down cards on top of each other, quickly grew bored, and ran over to her shopping bags in the corner of the room to give her purchases a second look.

J.T. groaned. "Please don't tell me that you're gonna try on those clothes again."

"No, even better–I want to play my CD," she said as she walked over to his stereo and started pushing buttons.

"Great. Well, what number is Fast Car? I like that song," said J.T., trying to make the most out of an unpleasant musical situation.

"J.T.! That was like three CD's ago, back in the eighties." Her forehead wrinkled as she struggled to figure out the workings of his stereo. "Will you give me a hand over here? The only thing I know how to do is play the radio."

He laughed. "I guess you'd better choose a station, then."

Kahlila was about to begin a major argument about it, but she liked the song on the radio and decided to wait until she was home alone to listen to Tracy.

She danced around the room to Ol' Dirty Bastard and Mariah as J.T. leafed through a sports magazine. He had to be pretty drunk to dance, and obviously he hadn't downed enough shots to feel comfortable doing his Steinway rendition of the cabbage patch.

Kal lost quite a bit of steam after three songs, and collapsed on the bed next to him. She stared at the Janet Jackson poster on his ceiling until everything went black.

"Kal. Kal!" J.T. was shaking her shoulder. We fell asleep–wake up."

"Shit! What time is it? I have an early meeting with Dave tomorrow." She jumped out of bed too quickly and had to grab his dresser for support. She suddenly didn't feel too well.

"It's almost midnight. Want me to walk you home?"

"Why? I can just take the shuttle."

"My boy Earl on the J.V. team lives in your building, and he just got a new game for Playstation. I'm trying to get on it tonight."

"My God. Is this what your life gets reduced to when you break up with someone?" She tried to hide a smile.

J.T. ran at her full speed and suddenly she was thrown over his shoulder. He started spinning her around. "Are you trying to say that I've become pathetic since me and Kristy broke up? Think carefully before you answer." He lifted her off of his shoulder and held her in the air by her waist, poised to slam her down on the bed if she responded incorrectly.

"Yes, I'm saying that you are quite pitiful. Now if you wanna throw me down and cause me to throw up on your bed, that's your business."

He hesitated. "You're bluffing," he decided. "You're not gonna puke," he said as he tossed her gently onto the mattress. He was hoping that she would strike back, and give him an excuse to toss her around some more. But she put on her shoes and jacket instead. As much as he hated to think about Kristy, he did miss their play fighting sessions. Kal just wasn't the wrestling type. He put Kristy's silly giggle out of his head, grabbed his windbreaker and his wallet, and followed Kal out of his bedroom.

J.T. was right–Kal wasn't going to vomit. But his spinning her around like that didn't do anything positive for her headache. By the time they started walking home, the streets were revolving before her eyes and she was tripping over her own feet.

At last they reached Booker T. House, and they stood outside as Kahlila tried to pull herself together. Even in her drunken state, she knew better than to walk into the dorm acting the fool. By lunch the next day, everyone would hear about how J.T. Steinway had to practically carry Kahlila Bradford to her room because she was so depressed about Tarik Reynolds, and who knows what the two of them did once they went upstairs.

"Joshua," Kahlila whined as she searched her pockets for her I.D. card, "how the hell am I gonna make it up the steps to the third floor?"

He reached into her jacket pocket and produced the card she was looking for. "Want me to carry you?"

He grabbed for her waist and she swatted his hand away before she turned around and opened the front door of the building. Once her back was turned to him, he was about to grab for her again when he felt a pair of eyes on him. He turned around and noticed a guy standing too far away for him to recognize. The stranger quickly looked away once he caught J.T.'s eyes, and hurried on a path parallel to Booker T. House. J.T. managed to get a closer look as the person continued nearer to them, but the face still didn't look familiar.

By the time he walked into the building and asked Kahlila to peek out of the door to identify the suspect, he was just a distant shadow.

Thank God she didn't see me. Dave sat on his bed, still fully dressed, staring at the digital clock. 12:58. He'd seen them a half hour ago. Joy was working the late-late shift at the hospital, and he left her apartment a little after she did. He'd stuck around to check out a few videos on B.E.T.'s Midnight Love before he began the walk back to his apartment.

He wasn't sure exactly when he ran into them. At some point on his walk he just looked up, and there they were. They were too far for him to hear their voices, but he recognized her, even from the back. She was wearing her tan spring pea coat, and a pair of matching tan shoes that Dave always teased her about. Her walk wasn't her usual walk, which clued him in on what she'd been doing all night.

Her companion wasn't too hard to deduce. Tall, white hands, brown hair—cut short on the sides and gelled sort of spiky on the top: that was definitely her boy J.T. Where were they coming from so late? And where were they heading?

They had almost made it inside the dorm when J.T. spotted him in the distance. Dave knew that he should turn away, walk in the opposite direction. But he had to walk closer, to see if J.T. went inside with her. And sure enough, they walked into the building together.

Why should he care, anyhow? Maybe because he'd never pegged Kahli for the cheating type. Tarik was supposed to be her man, and there she was being much more than friends with J.T. He'd seen J.T. trying to put his arms around her, and Kahli wouldn't let him. She probably didn't want any folks in the dorm to see them all up on each other.

Still, he could be jumping to conclusions. Kahli did volunteer the whole history of her and J.T. to Dave, and it really sounded like they were more like brother and sister than anything else. Not to mention that either way, it wasn't any of his business.

While he silently repeated to himself to stay out of it, he felt his own feet taking him out of his apartment and down the deserted street, in the direction of Booker T. House.

Kahlila didn't know how she made it up the stairs. J.T. had gotten off on the second floor to play video games, and she must have scaled that last flight on sheer willpower. She threw open the apartment door and found her way to her bedroom. Her bed had never looked so inviting. Falling on it and finding sleep was the only way to make her head stop spinning and her stomach stop churning. She threw herself down onto her salvation and passed out within seconds.

The next thing she remembered were her eyes jerking open to see a tall figure leaving her room. "J.T.?" she called out, her eyes still glazed over from her brief nap. She glanced at the clock. She hadn't even been sleeping for an hour.

"N'ah. It's me–Dave." He turned around slowly, his eyes lowered.

"What . . . how did you get in here?" She sat up, looking down at herself to see if she was decent. Sometimes when she was really tossed she'd walk into her room, strip off all her clothes, and pass out. But thank goodness, she still had on the clothes she'd worn all day.

"The apartment door was open, and so was the door to your bedroom. Sorry to have scared you, Kahli. I was just checking to make sure you were okay." He stayed poised in his spot at the doorway, unsure whether to leave or to come back into the room.

"Oh. I take it that you somehow heard about me and Tarik . . ."

He forgot himself and walked over to Robyn's empty bed, sitting at the foot. "What about you and Tarik?"

"Long story short: he fucked my roommate. Not Desiree, and not Robyn. The other one. So we're through."

"Word? That's some real shit right there. Yo Kahli, I'm really sorry." He wanted to ask a follow-up question: so was J.T. her new man already? But he couldn't form the question in a smooth enough way for it to sound casual.

"Yeah, well . . . wait a minute! If you didn't know about me and Tarik, then why did you come by? You've never even been to my room before. Must have been something important to show up in the middle of the night."

Her interrogation was long enough for Dave to catch a whiff of all the alcohol she'd been drinking earlier, which triggered a good excuse in his brain. "See, I saw you stumbling home earlier, and it looked like you'd been puttin' down way too many drinks tonight. I wanted to check that you made it home safely."

Kahli's face softened, apparently touched that he was concerned. "So why didn't you just call?"

"I did," he lied. "No one answered, which was why I came over. I mean, I didn't know if you were on your way home or not when I saw you, but in case you were heading this way and never made it . . ."

"So you only saw *me* walking? You didn't see J.T. with me?"

Dave put on a confused expression. "He was with you? I didn't see him. But I passed by really quickly. I was in a car."

Now it was Kahli's turn to look perplexed. "A car? Whose car?"

"Look, it's late and I shouldn't even have woken you up in the first place. You need some sleep. But for real, Kahli, you don't need to be drinking like that, no matter how depressed you are. Nothing good comes from it, do you hear me? Nothing." His voice got louder and sterner with each passing word, as Kahli's pupils got wider and wider.

"Yes, sir! Damn, you sound like my father. Well, you don't sound like *my* father, but somebody's father." She slid back under the covers, pouting and curling herself up into a little ball.

Dave rose from her bed and headed towards the door. "I just give a shit, that's all," he muttered. Kahlila was snoring before the door shut behind him.

Kahli overslept the next morning. She was supposed to be at Dave's by 11 o'clock, but it was 11:15 when her eyes opened for the first time. She fumbled for her phone and dialed Dave's number.

"Hello," Dave's voice materialized after two rings.

"Hi, it's Kahli. I'm so sorry, but I just woke up. I can be there in an hour." She got out of bed as she spoke, relieved that her head was allowing her to walk without pounding like it had last night.

"That's cool. I'm having a slow start this morning, too."

"Really? What did you do last night? I drank way too much

for my own good, hanging out with J.T. Mad drama with Tarik–I'll have to tell you about it when I come over."

Dave's mouth dropped. Was she really asking him where he was last night? Had she truly forgotten that they'd seen each other, that he was in her room? Relief flooded his body. He'd been struggling all morning to think about how he was going to handle any more questions that arose about the whole incident last night. "Uh oh, sounds like you have a story and a half for me. Just come by when you're ready. I'm not going anywhere."

"O.K. Bye." She hung up and opened the door to her bedroom, walking down the hallway of their tiny suite to the bathroom. No Shannon, no Dez. Thank goodness. Suddenly, Kahli turned back and looked at her bedroom door. It had been closed all night? She swore she'd left it open when she collapsed on her bed.

That's it, she vowed. *No more heavy drinking. Nothing good comes from it. Nothing.*

PART TWO

CHAPTER ONE

The campus was drenched in sunlight as Kahlila stepped out of the Earth Science building. Her geology final exam was exactly what the professor had promised, and she knew she aced it. But that was just frosting on the cake. The real treat was that she was done. With classes. With papers. With tests. With freshman year.

A speeding bullet would definitely lose a race to my first year of college, it went flying by so fast. Kahli could barely believe how much had happened in nine months. She made a best friend and lost her; she found a boyfriend and lost him. But she'd also gained so much that couldn't be lost, and she decided to think about those positives as she strolled the main campus on her way to the Caf.

Classes had been better than she'd ever expected. Everyone had warned her that going to a large university such as Franklin would mean huge lecture halls and teachers who didn't know her name. Sure, she had a few of those types of classes, but she also had people like Hark who saw her unique talents and got to know her, not her social security number.

The students at Franklin were great, too. All the black people said hello to each other when they were walking around campus. It was a little thing, but it was something that she immediately noticed when she visited. She was used to avoiding eye contact with people when she walked down the street in her neighborhood; she never wanted to give a guy an invitation to start kicking game or have some gangster girl thinking that she had beef. But after Kahli started working at her neighborhood high school, she began to love walking around near her house because she knew everyone and she felt good greeting them. It was just a continuation of that at Franklin.

Having nice acquaintances was important, but having trustworthy friends meant ten times more. She and Robyn had grown so close, and she could always trust Robyn to tell it to her straight. And even though Desiree withdrew from everyone and everything second semester, she still told Kahli what happened with Tarik and Shannon. It was then that Kahli knew that whatever Dez was going through had nothing to do with her, even though it prohibited her from reaching out to other people. She wanted to try to talk to her one more time before the summer, but Desiree's last final had been a few days prior to Kahlila's, and by the time Kahli looked up from studying, there were Desiree's parents, carrying out all her stuff to the car. Dez put on a good act in front of them, being cheery and hugging her roommates goodbye. Kahli and Robyn played the roles too, not wanting to sell out their friend. Because she was still their friend–no matter what.

Kahli knew that she was blessed when it came to friends, including the guys. J.T. was the best anybody could ask for, and now she had Lloyd and Dave, too. It was just as she began thinking about Dave that she spotted him in the distance, sitting on a campus bench with Joy. She quickly touched her hair to make sure it was smooth, and rubbed her lips together to check if she had on lip gloss. Her strides got more confident: longer, with more swagger. Doof! She stumbled on one of the raised bricks on her path. It never failed. *It could have been worse. At least he didn't . . .*

"We saw that!" Dave shouted from twenty five feet away, stomping his feet in hearty laughter. Kahlila pretended to turn and walk in the opposite direction before continuing on her path towards the smiling couple.

"I should hope you two saw that," Kahli said once she reached the bench where they were seated. "I did it on purpose to give you guys a laugh."

"It worked," said Joy, smiling but not particularly friendly. Her tone was more sarcastic than anything, causing Dave to shoot her a reprimanding look. Kahli could feel Joy's eyes looking her up and down, which she really didn't mind. After all, she was doing the exact same thing. She assessed Joy's full package for about three seconds, as she had every other time they encountered one another. She always came up with the same results: a face that looked quite young, due to her bangs and Bambi eyes; perfect skin; perfect smile. *Damn her.*

Okay, she's still grilling me and Dave's looking uncomfortable. I'd better bounce. "Well, I gotta run. See you later." Kahlila didn't wait for a response before she continued on her way, careful not to trip as she briskly headed down campus.

Joy continued to watch Kahlila as the streams of students in the distance absorbed her. "She sure left in a hurry," she deadpanned, staring at her short painted nails.

Dave waited in silence until Joy returned her eyes to his face. His expression was sad and frustrated at the same time. "This has really got to stop, baby."

"So make it stop, David," her eyes returning to her fingers.

Dave took a deep breath, careful of his next words. "Joy, I can't make something stop that exists only in your head. Damn it, what do you want me to do? I'm gonna be with the girl every day this summer. So are you and I gonna have this argument twice as often?"

She wearily rested her forehead on one palm. "I don't know, Dave. I can't help how I feel. It's like I need you to prove to me that we're okay as a couple."

"And how can I do that?" he asked desperately, taking her free hand in his.

"Let's see other people." It was out of Joy's mouth before she'd even thought about its full meaning, and she couldn't stop herself once she'd started. "In my most irrational moments I sometimes think that you would date this girl if you could somehow manage to do it without being the bad guy. So if we agree to see other people, and you still don't show any interest in her, I feel like my worries will disappear."

He returned Joy's hand to her lap and released it. "You're crazy, Joy. You want to make sure we're okay by breaking up?"

"I didn't say anything about breaking up. I just said we could try an open relationship," she replied, not even really knowing why she was still trying to convince him to do it when she didn't want it herself.

"It's the same thing. It would mean that we're not committed to each other anymore." Suddenly Dave's facial expression cheered, as if a new pleasant thought ran through his mind. "You're just bullshitting," he said knowingly, as if he'd just solved a murder mystery. "You just want me to say that I don't want to do it. Well I'm saying it, so you can just cancel this whole stupid suggestion."

Warm relief spread throughout Joy's body. She wanted to slap herself for playing that kind of game. What was she thinking? She was suddenly anxious to change the subject. "Fine, Dave. Whatever. So are you hungry? We could go to my place and fix some . . ."

The residual crease of frustration in Dave's forehead was replaced with laugh lines as he chuckled at her attempt to erase their conversation. "You're hilarious. I knew you were bluffing the whole time. I mean, really. See other people? And who in the world would *you* go out with?"

Joy's flood of relief instantaneously turned to rushing rage. "Excuse me, but there was life before you, Dave. It's not like I'm nothing if you're not here."

Dave's eyes filled with outrage and confusion. "What the hell are you talking about? I'm not suggesting that you can't live without me. As a matter of fact, I'm starting to think that you might want to. What I'm asking you is who you're so pressed to go out with, since you seem to want to get rid of me?"

Her eyes narrowed, her mouth in a straight line. "Don't try to flip this on me. You're the one who has feelings for someone else. Not me."

"Here we go again. Joy, who's the one talking about an open relationship?"

"Who's the one lying about their feelings for someone else?" Her voice increased in pitch with every word. "Honesty is a good thing. So just be true about your feelings, sleep with her and get it over with!"

Dave suddenly rose from the bench. "What the fuck. You're crazy. I can't argue with nonsense. It's like I don't even recognize you when you act like this. If you want us to have an open relationship, then fine. It starts now. Watch–Kahlila will still remain a friend, and a friend only. Then maybe we can put an end to these damn fights."

Joy looked down at the ground, embarrassed that she'd let herself get that emotional. Passers-by were beginning to stare. "Okay. And I'm sorry for blowing up like that. And honey, I do want to make it clear that there is no one out there for me. You're it. So I'm not gonna see anybody else."

Dave looked past her as he swung his backpack on his shoulder. "Do whatever you need to do, Joy. I'll talk to you later." He followed Kahli's path as Joy watched him until he disappeared.

CHAPTER TWO

To: angelabradford@aol.com
From: kahlila@classof99.franklin.edu
Date: June 2, 1996 8:39 p.m.
Subject: back at school

Message:
hi mom-

i'm back safe and sound. my room in booker t. was all ready and waiting. me and robyn have our own bedrooms, which is nice. she'll be back from l.a. in a few days.

i had a really good time while i was home. i'm glad we got to spend some time together. it's been a while since spring break when i was last in boston.

love
kahlibear

To: drobinson@sociology.franklin.edu
From: kahlila@classof99.franklin.edu
Date: June 2, 1996 8:45 p.m.
Subject: hey you

Message:
whatzup-
i'm back from boston. what have you been doing over the past few weeks?

To: kahlila@classof99.franklin.edu
From: drobinson@sociology.franklin.edu
Date: June 2, 1996 10:14 p.m.
Subject: hey you—Reply

Message:
welcome back. haven't been doing too much. recovering from the semester. making some business plans for this month. you know the kids don't get out of regular school until the end of june, so in the meantime i have workshops scheduled for us with members of various franklin departments to get their feedback on our plans for the institute. i'll come by and drop off a tentative schedule, and check out your new room. let me know when is good for you.

To: angelabradford@aol.com
From: kahlila@classof99.franklin.edu
Date: June 3, 1996 1:32 p.m.
Subject: confession

Message:
hi mom-

it's funny–when i told you about dave, i think i kinda downplayed how i was feeling about him. but as soon as i stepped off the plane yesterday, it really hit me. i just couldn't wait to get to the dorm and e-mail him so we could schedule time to see each other. and i also realized that my excitement about this summer is only partly related to the work with the institute. i think i'm just super-excited to see him every day. we're supposed to get together later today to catch up on business stuff. i'll let you know how it goes.
To: kahlila@classof99.franilin.edu
From: angelabradford@aol.com

Date: June 3, 1996 3:54 p.m.
Subject: confession—Reply

Message:
kahlibear,

first, i'm so thrilled that you're sharing these feelings with me. i can't remember when you've ever done this before. you certainly never bubbled over like this with tarik. this dave character must be pretty special. and i hate to kill your high, but there is a problem with this whole relationship. it's not his age, either. it's the fact that he does have a girlfriend. and if you never listen to anything i say, listen now. if you attempt to steal this man from his girlfriend, you'll never be taken seriously by him. after all, how can you expect to have a loyal relationship with him if you were the person who destroyed his last loyal relationship?

so please honey, have patience. don't rush life. you have a bad habit of doing that. he's not going anywhere, and neither are you. be a friend to him, and nothing more.

love,
your worried mother

To: angelabradford@aol.com
From: kahlila@classof99.franklin.edu
Date: June 4, 1996 11:10 a.m.
Subject: turn of events

Message:
mom,

i read your e-mail last night right before dave came over and i vowed to listen to your advice, but the most amazing thing happened. first, when he arrived at my door, he gave me a big hug. and i didn't realize it till that point, but we've never even hugged before!

anyhow, that isn't even the best part. we were catching up on what's been going on since i've been in boston, and guess what he told me? HE AND JOY DECIDED TO SEE OTHER PEOPLE!!! isn't that great? so it means that i don't have to just be his friend anymore, right? please say yes!

love
kahlibear

To: kahlila@classof99.franklin.edu
From: angelabradford@aol.com
Date: June 4, 1996 12:02 p.m.
Subject: turn of events—Reply

Message:
sweetheart,

as much as i want to tell you that you're now allowed to pursue your heart's desire, i must once again urge you to wait. do you want to be the girl he runs to as soon as his very serious relationship alters its state? think in the long term, and being the girl of the moment suddenly doesn't sound very appealing, now does it?

i'm guessing that he didn't tell you what the reason was for their making the decision to date other people. regardless of the reason, keep in mind that they didn't decide to stop seeing each other, which means that they still feel deeply for one another. there's only room for one person per heart at a time, and this may not be your time. just slow down, darling.

love
mom

To: kahlila@classof99.franklin.edu
From: drobinson@sociology.franklin.edu
Date: June 4, 1996 2:19 p.m.
Subject: check this

Message:
kahli-

we have a lunch conference tomorrow at noon with a groups of undergrads who work in the community service office. they want to know what we're doing and if they can help. honestly, i don't know if i want a bunch of white franklin students all up in our institute, but they mean well and i figure we can do lunch.
peace
dave

To: angelabradford@aol.com
From: kahlila@classof99.franklin.edu
Date: June 5, 1996 3:28 p.m.
Subject: feeling crazy

Message:
mom-

what a day. dave and i had a catered lunch in the community service office with fifteen franklin students who wanted to be down with our institute. we were basically explaining the goals of the program and they were all awed and speechless, pretty much sweating us. they wanted to know if they could do anything to help, and we decided to possibly host a career day or something at some point during the summer.

the conversation then got sidetracked when one girl (white of course) said something about the king school students lacking functional families! lemme try to remember the quote exactly . . . "well, how could you expect anything but failure from children who come from homes with no fathers? I mean, dysfunction breeds dysfunction."

mom, i can't even remember exactly what i said; i can just remember what i felt. my heart started pounding, my head got hot, and my food started doing weird things in my stomach. i forgot myself and went off. i told her that she shouldn't even be permitted to work with kids and that she was perpetuating the racism that franklin was famous for. In the midst of my spiel, dave grabbed me and pulled me out of the conference room. i was almost in tears, i was so angry. he told me that he understood, but he also made it clear that since i was in a leadership position and was supposed to serve as a discussion facilitator, going off on the girl was not permissible. as he was talking, he held my hand really tight and my head stopped pounding.

it was a weird experience. i don't really know how i feel about it. if it happened again, i don't know if i could act differently. and though the memory of dave holding my hand will stay with me for a while, i'm kinda embarrassed that i showed my immaturity. i'm trying to make him forget the fact that i'm eighteen, not rub it in.

talk to you later
love
kahlibear

p.s . . . robyn's back from l.a.! i'm excited–it was getting kind of lonely living by myself. she and jason got to spend some q.t. before he headed back to emory for the summer.

To: kahlila@classof99.franklin.edu
From: lloyd@philosophy.franklin.edu
Date: June 7, 1996 9:30 a.m.
Subject: how've you been?

Message:
kahlila,

how are you? you haven't been by the crib since you came back from beantown. what are your plans for tonight? it's friday evening so i know you must have something going on. but in case you don't, dave's going to the movies with joy if you want to stop by and catch up. hit me back.

later
lloyd

To: lloyd@philosophy.franklin.edu
From: kahlila@classof99.franklin.edu
Date: June 7, 1996 11:11 a.m.
Subject: good to hear from you!

Message:
hi lloyd,

i've been meaning to come by but lately dave's been coming to my place for planning since robyn lives with me and she's part of the institute as well. soon we'll be decorating the place for when the kids start living here, and it will really be crazy.

tonight i'm supposed to be chilling with j.t., since he's been complaining that i have no time for him anymore. but i'll call you tomorrow–you should swing by and check the place out the next time dave comes over.

peace
kahlila

To: kahlila@classof99.franklin.edu
From: lloyd@philosophy.franklin.edu
Date: June 7, 1996 1:02 p.m
Subject: good to hear from you!–Reply

Message:
>but i'll call you tomorrow–you should swing by and check the place out the next time dave comes over.

thanks for the invite, but it's all good. booker t. house really isn't my favorite place to be. i'll catch you later.-lloyd

To: jedwards@emory.edu
From: robyn@classof99.franklin.edu
Date: June 11, 1996 2:00 p.m.
Subject: sittin up in my room . . .

Message:
hey baby,

i'm sitting here daydreaming about you and the last time we were together. this activity has become an almost hourly

routine. orgo is kicking my ass, but i knew it would. luckily, the job is laid back so far. the kids don't start the program until the end of the month, so we've basically just been planning. kahli and that dude dave i was telling about seem to be getting pretty tight. i predict serious sexual activity by the end of the summer. anyhow, you haven't been up to franklin in a minute. how about you check on-line for any cheap tickets for this weekend or the next one? i miss you!-
me

To: robyn@classof99.franklin.edu
From: jedwards@emory.edu
Date: June 11, 1996 6:30 p.m.
Subject: sittin up in my room—Reply

Message:
robster-

this internship is kicking my ass, sweetheart. a visit just ain't gonna happen till at least july. do you need me to send you some naked pictures of myself to hold you over until then? :-) glad to hear that kahli's in contention for some good lovin. that tarik situation was real jacked. she deserves better. miss you too.–jay

To: angelabradford@aol.com
From: kahlila@classof99.franklin.edu
Date: June 13, 1996 10:01 a.m.
Subject: great mood

Message:
mom,
i know you must be tired of my saying this, but i had the

most amazing talk with dave last night. we were talking about desiree, and how weird she was acting last semester. he just broke it down how i have to reach out to her, no matter how much she shuts me out. i just have to keep trying because she needs me. talking about dez with so much compassion in his voice just reminded me what a sensitive, wonderful person he is.

so i'm gonna e-mail desiree today. it's not like i didn't want to do it before, but now i feel like i have to. it's like he put this urgency on it. i swear, i'm at my best around him. not in the way that i'm trying to be something i'm not, but meaning that it's this natural feeling–everything about myself that is real and good just flows out in his presence.

love ya
k.b.

To: kahlila@classof99.franklin.edu
From: angelabradford@aol.com
Date: June 13, 1996 10:43 a.m.
Subject: great mood—Reply

Message:
kahlibear,

did it ever occur to you that you might just bring out the best in him as well? don't shortchange yourself, honey.

and please, finish school before you run off and marry this man, okay?

smile
mom

To: desiree@classof99.franklin.edu
From: kahlila@classof99.franklin.edu
Date: June 13, 1996 5: 39 p.m.
Subject: hey, it's me

Message:
dez,

hopefully you're checking your e-mail over the summer. i guess i just have two questions: 1) are you okay? and 2) are we okay?

robyn and i are living together in bookert. this summer, and it just ain't the same without you, girl. i can't believe you'll be off campus next year.

you have to understand that i'm here WHENEVER you want to talk. i'm not going anywhere, and i'm not letting you disappear either.
love,
kahli

To: kahlila@classof99.franklin.edu
From: desiree@classof99.franklin.edu
Date: June 14, 1996 3:20 p.m.
Subject: hey, it's me–Reply

Message:
kahli,

i am checking my e-mail, as you can see. i don't have it at home, but i'm taking a class at hopkins, so i get on-line when i'm on campus.

i'm okay. not great, but okay. not the same person i was, but okay. i need this summer to process and sort of hide. but hopefully next semester we can get reacquainted.

till then
desiree

To: drobinson@sociology.franklin.edu
From: kahlila@classof99.franklin.edu
Date: June 14, 1996 7:40 p.m.
Subject: dez update

Message:
dave,
so dez e-mailed me back and she sounds allright, but distant. at least she wrote back, i guess. she says she's taking a summer class, so i'm thinking maybe she failed a class last semester. but the class is at johns hopkins. isn't it hard to take classes there? i'm clueless. anyhow, i do feel better for writing her, so thanks.

see you tomorrow
kahli

To: drobinson@sociology.franklin.edu
From: joy_rainer@yahoo.com
Date: June 17, 1996 12:19 p.m.
Subject: is e-mail the only way to reach you?

Message:
dave,

you really need a pager. you're never home. anyway, just wanted to run this by you–how about having a cookout for the 4th of July? we can have it in the park, and invite whoever's around for the holiday. we never do things like that anymore. call me.

joy

To: joy_rainer@yahoo.com
From: drobinson@sociology.franklin.edu
Date: June 17, 1996 3:14 p.m.
Subject: is e-mail the only way to reach you?—Reply

Message:
hey love, i'm feeling your idea of a cookout. i'm e-mailing instead of calling because i'm on the run between meetings. we're actually going downtown today to pick up backpacks for the kids. hark got us the van from the community service center.

on a different note, your lightening up about the whole kahli issue hasn't gone unnoticed. thanks. it's been nice just chilling with you, stress free. maybe this seeing other people thing, without actually seeing other people, was the answer.
later, dave

To: drobinson@sociology.franklin.edu
From: joy_rainer@yahoo.com
Date: June 17, 1996 10:10 p.m.
Subject: a couple issues . . .

Message:
baby,

two things: invite kahli to the cookout. tell her to bring whoever. i'm a big girl, i can handle it.

also, i can't believe you still feel like we're doing this "see other people" thing! it was just an argument, honey, and we haven't talked about it since that day. i just want it to be us. i guess we can talk about this later.

love
joy

To: angelabradford@aol.com
From: kahlila@classof99.franklin.edu
Date: June 19, 1996 9:30 p.m.
Subject: kahli the idiot
Message:
hey mom,

i got an embarrassing story for you. so we were in the basement of booker t. house, storing the supplies we bought for the kids, when out of the blue, dave asks me, "what are you doing for the fourth of july?"

now i'm envisioning these images of the two of us on some beach, sipping on lemonade or something. and i'm all upset because i already have plans. but before i can play myself, he continues, "because joy and i are having a cookout and i thought you might want to come and bring robyn or whoever."

how wack is that? not only did he suggest that i spend a holiday with him and his girlfriend, but it didn't even cross his mind that i had a man to bring! so of course i had to play up my plans. i replied, "oh thanks, but j.t. and i are taking a trip to the jersey shore for a couple of days. i figured i'd need a release before the institute starts the next week."

of course, i failed to mention that we were meeting j.t.'s dad there, and that the trip is a mini-high school reunion. oh well .You were really right, mom. joy is still clearly an issue, so i'd better respect that.

love,
k.b.

To: robyn@classof99.franklin.edu
From: joshuatravis@classof98.franklin.edu
Date: June 21, 1996 4:58 p.m.
Subject: question

Message:
robyn,

kal's birthday is july 6th. what do you think we should do? we'll be back from jersey by then–any ideas?

j.t.

To: joshuatravis@classof98.franklin.edu
From: robyn@classof99.franklin.edu
Date: June 22, 1996 11:01 a.m.
Subject: question—Reply

Message:
j.t.-

how about we do something sorta chill, like take her out to eat or something? i know something that will make her birthday mad special. i'll call you to discuss details.

later
robyn

To: kahlila@classof99.franklin.edu
From: angelabradford@aol.com
Date: June 24, 1996 6:15 p.m.
Subject: pack your bags . . .

Message:
kahlila,
i just got a letter from your dad in the mail. enclosed is a ticket to spain. start learning some spanish, because the trip is at the end of the summer, between the time the institute ends and fall semester begins. it will be just the two of you. should be wonderful.

mom

To: angelabradford@aol.com
From: kahlila@classof99.franklin.edu
Date: June 24, 1996 8:20 p.m.
Subject: pack your bags . . . —Reply

Message:
mommy,

WHAT?! i can't go away with that man by myself! what will we talk about? this is crazy! did he say why he wanted me to

go, or what exactly we would be doing? forget e-mail–i'm about to call you at home.
To: drobinson@sociology.franklin.edu
From: kahlila@classof99.franklin.edu
Date: July 2, 1996 9:30 a.m.
Subject: peace out
Message:
dave,

just e-mailing to say goodbye before i leave for jersey. i'll be back Friday. page j.t. with any program emergencies–800-555-3903. have a good fourth of july. check in on robyn for me.

kahli

p.s . . . we never really got a chance to discuss this spain trip further. my mom sent the letter that she got from my dad. it doesn't really shed any light on the situation. but it doesn't look i have much choice as to whether or not i'm going.

To: robyn@classof99.franklin.edu
From: drobinson@sociology.franklin.edu
Date: July 3, 1996 11:33 a.m.
Subject: you're invited (even w/o your girl)

Message:
robyn,

i know kahli's on her lovely beach getaway, but i just wanted to let you know that you're still welcome at our cookout tomorrow. call me if you need details on how to get there.

peace

dave
To: jedwards@emory.edu
From: robyn@classof99.franklin.edu
Date: July 4, 1996 8:42 p.m.
Subject: happy holiday, honey

Message:
jason,

so the holiday didn't turn out to be depressing. i thought i'd be sitting in the house, bitter that you couldn't come up and see me. i was still bitter, but at least i wasn't in the house :-). i went to a cookout at the park that kahli's love interest dave was having. it was actually mad cool. good food, nice people. i hate to admit, but dave's girl joy is really sweet. she's pretty too, although i think kahli's prettier. their friends were real chill. it was nice hanging with people who are a little more mature than the undergrads i'm around all the time. dave's roommate lloyd is hella cool, and we were kickin it for a while. i'm trying to convince him to do some work at the institute with music (he plays the piano). anyhow, the best part of the day was that dave agreed to come out with us on saturday night for kahli's birthday. she's gonna be hella surprised. actually, i should probably tell her ahead of time cuz if she looks like a scrub, she'll be heated.

anyhow, call me later.
i love you,
robyn

To: robyn@classof99.franklin.edu
From: jedwards@emory.edu
Date: July 4, 1996 9:10 p.m.
Subject: whatever, man

Message:
well damn robyn,
between lloyd and the rest of those cool folks you met, you probably don't need me to come up there at all, do you? whatever. i can't call you tonight cuz i have an intern meeting.

To: jedwards@emory.edu
From: robyn@classof99.franklin.edu
Date: July 4, 1996 10:02 p.m.
Subject: whatever is right!

Message:
jason,

are you kidding me? this is not some shit that needs to be addressed over e-mail. i can't believe it needs to be addressed at all. call me when you get in from your meeting. i don't care how late it is.

robyn

To: angelabradford@aol.com
From: kahlila@classof99.franklin.edu
Date: July 5th, 1996 11:50 p.m.
Subject: all smiles

Message:
mom,

life is ridiculously great right now. jersey shore was really fun. saw a bunch of people from high school, had great weather, relaxed on the beach . . . it was awesome (sorry for the lingo–j.t. over-exposure). when i got back, i had this e-mail from an alias called "the wish-granters:"

>kahlila bradford,

>you've been selected to receive the phattest birthday ever. j.t., robyn, and dave request your presence at o'dowds tavern on the evening of july 6th, 1996. expect more details over the course of the day.

i was blown away. i can't believe that the four of us are going out. i'm excited, but kinda worried that we won't have anything to talk about. what if it's super awkward? well, i'll let you know on sunday how it turned out. and don't worry, i won't drink too much.

love,
k.b.

CHAPTER THREE

Kahlila felt the butterflies in her stomach as she approached O'Dowd's Tavern with Robyn, J.T., and Dave. *Please don't card us. Dave will really think we're a bunch of kids if that happens.*

She tried to appear confident as they approached the door. J.T. opened it and led the way. No one even looked up at them. Kahlila heaved a light sigh of relief.

She took a moment to take in her environment. *Not much to look at, that's for sure.* Her eyes slowly adjusted to the dim lighting. It wasn't romantically dim, but just dim enough that you couldn't play any card games without bringing a flashlight. The bar was fairly crowded with older white men drinking various brews on tap. Even though almost all of the stools were occupied, no one was really speaking to each other. They were either all strangers, or had hung around O'Dowds so much that there was nothing left to talk about. The bartender didn't exactly blend with the rest of the scene. She was young and Latina, and seemed to have too much life in her for the crowd that she served. Only one couple occupied a booth, and they got up to leave as soon as Kahlila turned their way. Billy Joel was playing on the juke box, which was acceptable music for Kahlila. From the look on Dave's face however, he seemed to think otherwise.

"All right, guys. Dave, you and Kahli grab a table, and me and Robyn will hook up the drinks. K-Love, be prepared to get wasted, sweetheart." He winked, grabbed Robyn by the wrist, and dragged her towards the bar.

"I can't believe I'm in here," Dave muttered almost to himself as he and Kahlila slid into a booth at the back of the shadowy room.

"*You* can't? I'm the one who just turned nineteen and I'm chillin' up in here like it ain't no thing! Why are *you* so surprised to find yourself in here?"

"It's just been a while, that's all." He glanced around, taking in the atmosphere, or lack thereof. "Your friend clearly knows all the high-class joints though, Kahlila."

She giggled. "Yeah, J.T. has been frequenting seedy Irish Taverns since high school in Beantown."

He hesitated, opened his mouth to speak, and then shut it again. Finally, he began a sentence, the words rushing out as if to avoid his changing his mind about uttering them. "I don't know, it seems like you two . . ."

"All right, party animals. I got some of those fruity-assed mixed drinks for the ladies, and Dave—we're just gonna chug down some beer if that's okay with you." J.T. seemed to arrive at the table out of thin air bearing a pitcher of beer and two mugs. Robyn wasn't too far behind with color-filled glasses for herself and Kahlila.

The two of them sat down on the other side of the booth and J.T. began to pour the beer. David stared at his own mug as the beer was being poured, but remained silent.

Kahlila noticed his strange expression.

Maybe I should tell him that he doesn't have to drink. I don't want him to feel pressured. "Dave, I thought you weren't a drinker."

"I'm not," he replied slowly, still not shifting his gaze. "But I can handle a beer on your birthday." He smiled and patted her hand. She forced her body not to respond to the unexpected touch.

"Kal, I like him already!" J.T. and Dave clinked their mugs together and the festivities began.

Time flowed faster than foamy beer from pitchers and they talked and laughed the night away. J.T. had eventually convinced Robyn and Kahlila to step up to shots ("Hey, the juice is just filler anyway,") but he and Dave stuck to the beer. Dave definitely had more than one, but J.T. was putting them away noticeably faster.

The alcohol hit Kahlila so quickly that she didn't even think to wonder at the fact that her friends had anything to say to each other at all. If she had been in her right mind, she would have maintained her anxiety that the night would be an awkward disaster. But she was liquored up and completely carefree.

Conversation was plentiful but light. J.T. and Dave talked basketball while Robyn and Kahlila discussed how drunk they were. They all as a group discussed Franklin: their expectations as to what their experiences would be and how the reality stacked up in comparison. Robyn expected to be so steeped in work for her premed classes that she wouldn't have time to miss Jason in Atlanta. J.T. thought that basketball would be so important to him that the long bus rides and grueling practices wouldn't phase him. Dave presumed that Franklin would attract people who were passionate about gaining knowledge, but it seemed like everyone was about getting out and making money.

Kahlila interrupted, "Well, didn't you find people who were passionate about learning at Harvard?"

"Nah. I found people who were pressed to show other people how much they'd learned. There's a difference." He picked up his mug and took a big swig. "So Ms. Bradford, you've yet to share with us what *you* expected out of this place."

Before she even realized what she was saying, she declared, "I expected to fall head over heels in love."

"Ah! The classic find-a-husband mission. I thought you were above that, Kal," J.T. said, shaking his finger in Kahlila's direction.

"I didn't say I wanted a husband, Joshua Travis. Like, Dave said he wanted to find people passionate about learning. I wanted to find folks who were passionate about passion. I wanted to feel so much for someone that I couldn't see straight. Get swept off my feet, y'know?"

J.T. waved off her comments. "Well, I guess Tarik fucking your roommate kind of messed up that warm fuzzy fantasy. This is getting way too cheesy for me. New topic, guys."

Again, Dave touched Kahlila's hand. "Don't worry. You have lots of time to find that passion."

Kahlila turned toward him and searched his eyes. "Do I?"

She was startled by a soft kick under the table. "Come to the bathroom with me," said Robyn as she scooted out of the booth and headed away from the table. Kahlila jumped up and followed her without a word to J.T. or Dave.

When they reached the bathroom, they realized that it was a potty-for-one. They looked at each other, shrugged, and ran in together. When Kahlila shut the door behind her, she immediately hugged her friend. "I am having so much fun!!!"

"I can tell. That's why I called you in here. Listen, I really like Dave for you, Kahli. I definitely sense the vibes between you two. But play it cool. Don't push him away. You were crossing that line when I kicked you. There's something holding him back, and if you're too direct, he'll be forced to walk away from you."

"Robyn, I don't know if this is 'cuz I'm really drunk, but right now you sound like the wisest soul on earth. So I'm gonna listen. But guess what?"

"What?"

"I need to pee."

Robyn burst into laughter. "Okay, hon. I'll wait for you outside."

Robyn and Kahlila rejoined their two male companions, who were wearing huge grins on their faces. Robyn eyed them suspiciously. "What's so funny?"

"No Robyn," J.T. replied, "The question is not 'what's so funny,' but 'what would be so FUN right now?' Me and my partner here have figured out an answer."

"More like J.T. has figured it out by himself and I'm just laughing at him," Dave corrected.

"Well don't leave us hanging!" Kahlila almost shouted, and then covered her mouth when she realized how loud she was being.

"Damn girl, settle down. I'm about to reveal my marvelous idea: Let's play Truth or Dare!!"

"Aw, hell no!!" protested Robyn and Kahlila at the exact same time.

"Well, J.T., I think we know what they were practicing in the bathroom all that time," commented Dave with a smile.

"Oh stop the theatrics, ladies. It'll be fun!" J.T. was clearing all of the pitchers, mugs, and glasses to the side of the table, as if they needed all the room they could get to play the game effectively.

"And Dave, you agreed to this juvenile activity?" Kahlila asked with an elbow to his arm.

J.T. spoke before Dave had a chance to answer. "Of course he did, Special K. He may be like 40 years old, but he can still have a little fun." Sudden smile. "Man, you know I'm playing with you."

"It's cool," Dave said, and they gave each other pounds across the table. Kahlila and Robyn looked at each other in amusement. Kahlila's buzz was wearing off and she was finally able to realize the bizarre nature of it all. *I can't believe these two are bonding.*

Robyn was the one to give in. "Fuck it. Let's play. But it's getting late. So I vote for one round of Truth or Dare, and then let's go home."

Dave nodded in agreement. "Yeah, it's way past my bedtime."

J.T. looked like he was going to explode from excitement. "I know how it is for you old heads, Dave. We'll keep it brief just for you. So everyone gets to pose one Truth or Dare. Who goes first?"

"How about we allow the birthday girl the honors?" Dave asked the question in a way that made Kahlila's cheeks turn warm. She decided not to go for the obvious and instead opted to direct the question at someone implication-free.

"Robyn. Truth or Dare?"

"Uh oh! She turns against her best friend!!" J.T. struggled for dramatic effect.

Robyn and Kahlila avoided eye contact for a short moment. *Best friends?* Neither one of them ever thought of themselves as filling that role for the other. But at the same time that it sounded strange to hear it, the notion wasn't as strange as it would have been just a few months earlier.

"Girl, you already know everything about me. I'll take a dare, please."

A drum roll on the table from J.T. provided the musical accompaniment while Kahlila thought of a dare.

"I got it! See that forty-something Irish-looking dude sitting at the bar by himself with the Guinness in his hand? Go over there and talk to him. And don't come back to this table without his phone number." Kahlila looked very serious as she gave the instructions, but she burst into a grin when she saw the look of horror on Robyn's face.

"So much for looking out for a friend, Kahli," Robyn fake frowned.

"Come on! I let you off easy. I could have made you do a strip tease on this table."

"That's what I'm talking about!!!" J.T. started rubbing his hands together like someone just placed a seven-course meal in front of him.

Kahlila rolled her eyes. "Joshua, can you please spare the dramatics for just a moment?"

Dave patted her leg. "Give him a break, Kahlila. It wouldn't be college without drama. Hell, it wouldn't be life without it."

She attempted to look down at his hand on her leg in order to mentally imprint the memory. But he moved it before she could casually glance downwards.

"Yeah! So let's get this show on the road. Robyn get your butt on over to Mr. O'Flaherty over there." J.T. began scooting her out of the seat with his butt.

Kahlila and Dave laughed as Robyn slowly walked towards the bar. She was sitting on the stool next to O'Flaherty before he even noticed she was there. The three of them watched as he did a double take to see this random black girl sitting next to him, apparently wanting to strike up a conversation.

J.T. decided to play Dick Vitale from their booth in the corner. "O.K. folks. The game has begun. We have a smile from Robyn, and a quick return grin—or is it a grimace—from

O'Flaherty. She's talking at a comfortable pace, and now she's motioning to her teammates on the bench. He's waving to us. Should be wave back? That's an affirmative on the waving. O'Flaherty's getting the bartender's attention. Is Robyn getting a free drink out of this dare? Sure looks like it. And she scores!! One fruity-assed beverage on the house!!!"

"But still no phone number," Kahlila reminded him.

"But that's where you're wrong, Kal. Not only did the bartender serve Robyn a drink, but she also provided a pen and a napkin. Lucky for her you picked a literate subject, because he is writing down his info as we speak."

"Wow, Kal. Your girl got skills." Dave watched intently as Robyn closed the deal.

"And who gave you permission to use that nickname, David?"

"And who told you to say my name like my mother does, Ms. Bradford?"

Robyn arrived back at the table in time to hear the latter part of their conversation. "Kahli, is he giving you trouble?"

"A little. But let me see this napkin." She snatched it from Robyn's fingers. "Sean, huh? Is this a real phone number?"

"Does it matter? I sure ain't using it!" Robyn was happy as a clam, sipping on her newly acquired drink. "So Dave, since you're giving my girl a hard time . . . Truth or Dare?"

"Well, let me think about this. There is no way in hell that I'm getting naked or kicking game to some random white girl, no offense J.T. So since you can't back out of a dare, I'll have to take truth for $200 please, Alex."

"Excellent. So here's my question: you know how Kahlila was talking about that love stuff earlier, all that blinding passion mumbo jumbo?"

Kahlila stared at Robyn nervously. *Oh my God, what is this girl going to ask him??*

"Yeah," Dave replied skeptically.

"My question is, have you found that all-out, no-holds-barred passion with your girlfriend?" Robyn's hand found Kahlila's under the table. Kahlila squeezed it appreciatively.

"Joy?"

"No Dave, your *other* girlfriend. Now stop stalling and answer the question."

The table was the quietest it had been all night. Even J.T. donned a serious expression as he waited for Dave to respond.

Kahlila was still holding onto Robyn's hand. *Do I even want to know the answer to this question?*

Dave exhaled deeply. "No. I haven't. J.T. Truth or dare?"

The two girls released hands abruptly. It was the answer Kahlila wanted to hear, but she wasn't excited, as she thought she would be. The sadness in his voice, the resignation—it prevented her from being happy that he hadn't found "it" with Joy. She was still grappling with her feelings when J.T.'s loud bellow jolted her back to the task at hand.

"GIMME A DARE, MAN!!"

Dave paused before he responded. "Honestly J.T., the whole point of a dare is to embarrass the person and for you, I don't know if that's possible. Let's ask someone who knows you a little better . . . Ms. Bradford, do you have any suggestions?"

Kahlila forced herself to move past Dave's recent confession. *Just because he and Joy aren't swinging from the chandeliers doesn't mean they don't love each other.* "Well, since Joshua was so excited about the notion of someone dancing on the table for us, how about you make him perform a little strip tease right on this little space he cleared?"

J.T. tried to hide his mortification with a smart comeback. "Darling, if you wanted to see me naked all you had to do was ask."

Dave took the burden off of Kahlila to answer. "I like that one. And J.T., even if Kahlila wants to see you naked, I don't. So the dance will do. No actual stripping necessary. And let's not contaminate the drinks. You can skip the getting on the table part."

Robyn faked disappointment. "Damn, and I was getting all riled up, too."

"Well don't be disappointed yet, Robyn," Dave warned. "*You* get to select the music for J.T.'s performance."

"Word? Come with me, you little striptease," Robyn pulled J.T. up from the booth by his arm. "We're gonna pick a song for you to shake your booty to. I hope you got rhythm."

"Are you kidding? I turned down Alvin Ailey to play ball at Franklin!" J.T. beamed at his three companions, hoping that someone would give him props for even knowing who Alvin Ailey was. No one did. Instead, Robyn toted him off to the jukebox.

Kahlila was suddenly alone at the table with Dave and felt like she had to take advantage of it. *Quick, say something!!* "Dave, I really want to thank you for hanging out with us tonight. I hope you're not regretting you came."

"Hell no! I'm having a good time. The sleepiness is starting to set in right about now, but other than that I'm straight chillin'. Your friends are very cool. Robyn is real nice and your boy is straight hilarious."

My boy? "Yeah, well they must have found a song 'cuz here they come."

Before Kahlila could even ask what song they agreed on, Tina Turner's voice wafted out of the speakers.

"All the men come in these places/ And the men are all they same/ You don't look at their faces/ You don't even ask their name . . ."

J.T. was swinging his hips and sticking out his non-existent butt pseudo-seductively in front of their booth. Robyn stood behind him in hysterics, and Kahlila and Dave faced him with their mouths hanging open. He slowly unbuttoned his short-sleeved checkered shirt, exposing his white wife-beater tank underneath.

"I'm your private dancer/ A dancer for money/ Do what you want me to do/ I'm your private dancer/ Dancer for money/ Any old music will do . . ."

At the outset of Tina's chorus, J.T. ripped off his shirt, swinging it over his head and tossing it in Kahlila's face. When Kahlila removed the checkers from her eyes, she saw Robyn raising her eyebrows appreciatively at J.T.'s biceps. Even Kahli couldn't help but stare at his chiseled arms, and his chest bulging through his tank. She glanced at Dave, who was shaking his head in amazement at J.T.'s routine.

J.T. quickly grew tired of his own one-man show, and halted in the middle of Tina's second verse. "O.K. ladies, that's all you get. Being that sexy gets tiring."

The foursome was soon seated once more, waiting for the last truth or dare so they could go home. J.T. leaned in closer as he posed the question. "K-Love, what'll it be?"

Do I really want J.T. making me answer some embarrassing question in front of Dave? "Dare."

"Kahlila Renee Bradford, I dare you to . . ."

She stopped breathing.

"kiss . . ."

Her heart stopped.

"me."

"YOU?" Kahlila and Robyn repeated together.

"Y'all got that talking at the same time thing down to a science," Dave said, looking down at the table in front of him.

"Don't they?" J.T. agreed. "Sweetheart, no Truth or Dare is complete without someone having to kiss someone else. I thought it would be impolite to throw you on someone who's spoken for. Therefore, you're stuck with me. So let's go. Switch seats with Robyn."

Kahlila and Robyn slowly exchanged places, still in disbelief at what was about to occur. Kahlila slid into the booth and turned to face J.T. "So kiss me, damn it!" She smiled, trying to lighten the mood.

"It's your dare. *You* gotta lean in," J.T. commanded.

I could kill this boy. He's gonna make this as difficult as possible. What the hell is Dave thinking right now? O.K. let me not make this a bigger deal than it actually is. I'll just do it and stop hesitating.

She leaned in, her lips landing softly on his mouth. He placed his hand behind her head and deepened the intensity of the kiss. Kahlila was shocked at the feeling of familiarity that swept over her. She hadn't touched J.T. since the tenth grade, but she remembered that hand gently massaging her the back of her neck whenever they kissed. And then it was over. When she opened her eyes and looked around her, two stunned pairs of eyes were waiting to meet hers.

Dave was the first to speak. "So, on that note . . ."

"Yeah. Time to go," Robyn finished.

They collected their things and for the first time that evening, an uncomfortable silence settled around the table.

The tension subsided a bit by the time they reached the cool air outside. Robyn turned to J.T. suddenly. "I have something important to ask you. Joshua Travis, will you be *my* private dancer?"

J.T. immediately began chasing her at full speed down the street. Kahlila and Dave looked at each other and smiled. They were alone again. She knew she only had half a block before they took separate paths back home. This time, her question was prepared.

"So Dave, what was it that you were going to say earlier this evening, back when J.T. and Robyn were getting drinks?"

"Never mind. I think I've figured it out on my own. But this is my stop. I'll see you Monday. Happy birthday, Kahli. Thanks for inviting me." He extended his hand.

"Thanks for coming," and she took his hand in hers. She held it as she began to continue backwards down the street. Their arms stretched until their hands broke free.

"Good night!" she shouted with her back turned as she ran to catch up to Robyn and J.T.

She couldn't hear if he answered.

CHAPTER FOUR

The next morning, Kahli awoke with a dreamy smile plastered to her face. She'd had a great nineteenth birthday, and she wasn't ready for it to be over. She looked over at her clock. 11:20. It was Sunday, her last day of freedom before the summer program began. She decided that she was entitled to take her time getting out of bed.

Kahli let last night's events replay on her mental video screen, pausing and rewinding points that she liked best. Dave touching her hand and her leg were definitely pause-worthy moments. The kiss with J.T.–she didn't know what to do with that, so she just fast forwarded past it.

She was jolted back to regularly scheduled programming by the phone's loud ring. She picked it up quickly so as not to wake up Robyn, whom she presumed was sleeping in the other room. "Hello?" she answered in a groggy voice.

"It's me, Special K. How'd you enjoy your birthday festivities?" J.T.'s voice perked her up immediately.

"Honestly, hon—it was my best birthday ever."

"I could tell. That old dude has you sprung like a well."

"J.T.! Dave is not the reason that my birthday was such a success."

"Well, his being there sure helped a little bit. There's no need to be all defensive though, Kahli. He was mad cool for a senior citizen," he said teasingly.

Kahlila pretended to take offense, but she appreciated the vote of approval from her friend. "He is not old!" she protested, hoping J.T. couldn't detect her smile through the phone lines.

"You're right—he's not old . . . compared to our parents. I'm just kidding, sweetheart. But you've definitely been holding back on me—what the hell is going on between you two?"

"By your definition, absolutely nothing," she said in an almost motherly tone.

"What's my definition?" he asked defensively.

"We're not having sex. We're not even messing around. So therefore, in your horny little brain, nothing is going on."

"Oh, why didn't you tell me you were gonna take it to that emotional bond bullshit? Just give me a minute to wake up my sensitive side. O.K.—he's up and alert. Proceed."

Kahlila thought about arguing with him a little more, but she was really dying to talk about it so she dropped the sarcasm. "I don't know, J.T. I've never been in anything like this before."

"You haven't been in much of anything before," he quickly interjected.

"True. But I'm now an official sexual being, complete with trifling relationships and the whole nine. Still, I've never felt a connection like this with anyone."

"Should I be offended here? You always get pissed at me when I talk about some girl who's threatening your position in my life."

"Is that why you made me kiss you in front of him and Robyn? To mark your turf?"

"Kal, you have so much to learn. Did you not see the look on your boy's face when you kissed me? His eyes turned green, he was so jealous. It was a test, and he failed. Or passed, depending on how you want to look at it."

"He really looked jealous?" Kahlila's voice raised an octave.

"Yeah. But let's go back to how I don't feel special anymore . . ."

"J.T.—no one is taking your place. Ever. I need you to give me advice, at least until I have my first orgasm. That was a joke. Laugh, damn it."

He gave in and chuckled. "Well, at the rate things are going for you, it looks like we'll be buddies for life."

"O.K., shut up and let me finish. Now you and I definitely connect, and we have that complete honesty vibe going. And you're gonna be a part of my life forever. My mom has practically adopted you, for God's sake! But with Dave and me, it's like I feel like I've known him forever too, when it's only been like six months. We have the same passions, you know? And the way I feel when he smiles at me, or when he laughs at my jokes, or when he nods like he really understands what I'm talking about—I just want to melt. It's crazy."

"It does sound crazy. And mushy. Look, this is getting way too sentimental for me. You really need to attack this guy. He's just waiting for you to make the move."

"But Robyn told me to take it slow!!"

"I see her point—that's why I didn't dare you to kiss *him* last night. You don't want to scare him off. At the same time, he needs an excuse to give in. He admitted it himself—Joy isn't the one. But that's still his girl. So you have to find a happy medium that allows you to break them up without being the bad guy." J.T. was quickly falling into his rare "relationship-expert" mode.

"Actually J.T., I don't have to break them up. Joy already told him that he could see other people."

"WHAT??" Kahlila had to take the phone away from her ear because J.T. was talking so loudly. "Then you need to go over there right now and rip his clothes off."

"Joshua Travis, you know that ain't even my style."

"That's your problem. You don't have a style. You're just a straight-up wimp. A chicken, even."

Kahlila could usually accept any criticism that J.T. dished out, but the name calling was too much for her. "A chicken? I've been the one pushing the envelope for months!"

"Ooooh, by doing what? Making some suggestive comments that he could easily pretend not to notice? Please. Let's see him pretend not to notice a half-naked you in his apartment."

At the same time that Kahlila was recovering from J.T.'s blows to her ego, she was intrigued by the point he was making. "All right, all right. Tell me more," she requested begrudgingly.

"Kal, when you take off those ridiculous hippie clothes you insist on wearing all the time, you're actually working with some decent raw material. You're a little on the thin side, but you've got the essentials."

"I can't believe I'm listening to this."

"Yes you can. You're loving it. Anyhow, guys are extremely weak when it comes to blatant physical advances. Touch him a little, show some skin—you're in there."

"In *where*, exactly? J.T., I'm not trying to just get in his pants and be done with it. I actually want to be with him in a serious kind of way. Not that I'd expect *you* to understand."

J.T. was hardly scathed by the comment. "You're such an amateur. The guy already likes you—I saw it with my own eyes. But he's having a hard time seeing your little freshman ass as a possible companion in the sheets. So as soon as you can flip it and show him you're a complete woman," and he stifled a giggle, "you'll be all set."

"See, you can't even call me a woman without laughing. How am I supposed to convince someone five years older than I am?" Her voice was gaining a nasal quality, a high pitched tone that she assumed whenever she was feeling helpless.

"First of all, make sure you don't start that whining bullshit. It's annoying as fuck. Next, just be confident in yourself, Kal. He wants you. He just doesn't know if he wants to act on his feelings. You have to make it so that he has no choice in the matter. And I can give you no more instruction than that. The rest is up to you."

Dead air traveled through the phone line as Kahlila absorbed everything he'd said. J.T. wondered if he'd been too tough with her.

"Hey you." He decided to test the waters to see if she was upset with him.

"Yeah?'

"You know you're my little K.B. Toy, don't you?"

She grinned. "I know."

Kahlila thought about J.T.'s advice all day. She and Robyn went to IHOP for a late breakfast, but Kahli purposely focused on other subjects. She was sick of talking about Dave to other people. It was time for her to decide exactly what route she wanted to take, and to make that decision all by herself.

Instead of talking about men, they talked about the first day of the Institute. All morning would be move-in, which Robyn would assume all responsibility for. Then came their first house meeting, and classes would meet that afternoon. While Robyn was anxious about handling any possible roommate drama, Kahli was petrified about her first day of teaching. They finally decided to stop talking about it because the chatter was just making them more nervous.

That night, Kahli sat at her desk, looking over her lesson plan for tomorrow. Without even thinking it through, she picked up her phone and dialed Dave's number.

"Hello?" Dave asked after two rings.

"Hey. It's me."

"What's up. You all recovered from the celebration?"

"Yeah, I'm straight. Not even a hangover this morning."

"Glad to hear it. You sound kind of weird though."

"Really?" Kahli asked, a bit pleased that he noticed her anxiety over the phone. "Well, I *am* kinda nervous."

"About tomorrow?"

"Yeah. Crazy, huh?"

"Are you kidding? I can't even sleep 'cuz I'm playing out all these scenarios in my head."

"Um, you probably can't sleep because it's only 9:30."

"Well, I thought I'd need all the sleep I could get considering we're gonna be with the kids tomorrow."

"Dave, you're 24, not 84. I think you can handle 15 teenagers."

"Hey, weren't you the one who called *me* all nervous? Why you trying to make me feel stupid when I tell you I feel the same way?"

"Because picking on you makes me feel better!"

"Oh. Well then pick away."

Kahli smiled. "Allrighty then, I'll continue picking on you while simultaneously taking your mind off the kids. Why come you couldn't ask me a simple question last night? You scared of me or something?"

Dave quickly countered with, "Why come you can't speak English? N'ah-seriously though, what are you talking about?"

Kahli sighed, suddenly questioning her decision to even bring up last night at all. "Forget it, Dave. I was just talking about how it seemed like you kept wanting to ask me something and you never did. And then at the end of the night you said that you'd figured it out, whatever that means."

"Oh, that," he said, pretending that she jogged his memory. "I was just wondering what the real deal is with you and J.T., but the kiss pretty much sealed my opinion."

Kahli was horrified. She couldn't let Dave think that there was something going on with J.T. Before she could even think out her response fully, she asked, "If I tell you something, do you promise not to laugh?"

"I promise," he answered, somewhat dreading what she was about to say.

"J.T. has this crazy idea that we like each other. Me and you."

"Really." This was not the confession that Dave was expecting.

"Yeah," Kahli continued, "And he thought it would be funny to see if you got jealous or something last night. I know it's stupid, but that's really what was going on."

Dave was suddenly tongue tied. He didn't like where this conversation was going, but he wasn't ready to change the subject either. "Um, I guess I've heard of crazier things. But listen Kahli, I gotta run. Don't stress about tomorrow, okay? If I know you at all, you'll be the bomb teacher."

"Same to you."

"Later."

"Bye, Dave." Kahli pressed the off button on her phone. *What the hell was that conversation? How am I supposed to interpret that?*

She quickly shook those questions out of her mind. *Stop analyzing everything. You have two months of spending every day with this man. If something is meant to happen, it will.*

Kahli felt the butterflies in her stomach as she returned her attention to her lesson plan. She didn't even try to analyze the source of her nervousness. She just knew that she couldn't wait until tomorrow.

CHAPTER FIVE

Robyn's official job on the first morning of the Summer Institute was to stand in the lobby in case any students had questions or problems. No one counted on the students being so on top of things. They all arrived by 9:15 with enough clothes, appliances, and toiletries to last them an entire year, never mind six weeks. Each student had at least one parent, grandparent, aunt, or uncle in tow, and for quite a few of them, move-in was an entire family excursion.

Robyn felt absolutely useless as she watched the chaos around her. She introduced herself as new families appeared, informing the students of the house meeting at noon. The responses were polite, yet somewhat disinterested, as the kids were more concerned with seeing their rooms than anything else.

Suddenly, after what seemed like an endless parade of suitcases, floor fans, televisions, and stereos, it was 10:30. All of the extraneous family members were gone. It was suddenly quiet. The hallways were empty.

Robyn walked through the long halls, listening for any muffled conversations floating out from the suites. There were none. She remembered the first awkward minutes of meeting Dez and Kahlila when they moved into Booker T. House. There was so much to ask, and so much to talk about, but nowhere to really begin.

With that wave of nostalgia, Robyn made her first administrative decision of the summer. Dave and Kahli had allocated her a budget for "house activities." She was to organize programs for the residents in order to enhance their academic and social experience. *It looks to me like these kids need some social assistance right now.*

Immediately, Robyn was knocking on doors, inviting students

to a free breakfast at McDonalds across the street. Within fifteen minutes, Robyn and the fifteen students at the Institute were getting acquainted over Egg McMuffins and Sausage Biscuits.

They stayed at McDonalds until it was time for the house meeting, at which time they all walked into the multi-purpose room in a fit of hysterical laughter. Kahlila and Dave were waiting for them, somewhat shocked at the familiarity between the students already. Robyn tossed the pair a quick wink as she joined them at the front of the room. The kids seemed to sense that playtime was over, and they quickly quieted down and waited for the meeting to begin.

Dave was the first to speak. "Hey y'all, I'm not feelin' the setup of this room. How about we move these chairs into a circle?" The students obediently began shifting their chairs into a new formation. Once everyone was resituated, Dave continued. "Anytime we meet as a group at the Institute, we'll sit in a circle. That way everybody can be seen by everybody else, heard by everyone else, and no one is in a position of importance over anybody else. Cool?" Heads nodded around the circle.

"Word. My name's Dave Robinson–yeah, like the hoops player–and I'm probably the one person who most of you haven't met yet. Kahlila handled the interviews so you've all talked to her, and you met Robyn this morning, so I'll just tell you a little bit about myself quickly. I'm a graduate student at Franklin, so I already went to college for my bachelor's degree and now I'm going for my Ph. D. I study sociology, which means I study why things in society are the way that they are. I'm from Jersey–anybody here from Jersey?" One girl raised her hand, a cute bashful smile on her face. "That's straight. Anyhow, I'm really amped to meet all of you. I'm gonna be teaching your publishing class this summer. We'll be putting together some type of magazine, which means you'll have to work with different computer programs. Anybody good with computers?" Seven students raised their hands eagerly. "True? Well I'm counting on y'all to back me up, because we'll all be kind of learning as we go. Anyhow, I'm gonna hand this over to Kahli," he said, motioning to his left.

Kahlila was wearing a relaxed smile, although the butterflies in her stomach were flittering all over the place. *These kids are listening to us like we know what we're doing. This is crazy. We're in over our heads.* "Hi, everyone. It's good to see everyone again. Everybody moved in?" Head nods. "Any move-in problems?" Head shakes. "Good. I don't have too much to say. I'm gonna have Robyn go over schedule stuff and general rules in a minute. All I wanted to say was that we are really excited about this summer. We've been planning for this since January, and it's finally here. I don't think we could have found a better group of students, either. We read a lot of applications, then narrowed it down to thirty people for interviews, and the fifteen of you stood out. You should feel really good, because we feel really good to have you here. Robyn?"

"O.K. guys," Robyn said with a genuine grin, apparently much more at ease than she was earlier that morning. "You all know me at this point. Let me just outline what a general weekday will be like for you. Wake-up is at 8:00. Breakfast is in the campus dining hall at 9:00. Kahlila's class is at 10, Dave's class is at 11. You have a break from 12 till 2, during which time you'll eat lunch, run errands, whatever. From 2 till 4 is time to work on independent projects relating to the magazine. Writing, computer work, meetings with your teachers, that kind of thing. 4 to 6 is free time, where you have access to anything on campus. You can use the gym, the music rooms, all kinds of stuff. Dinner is at 6, study hall is from 7 to 9. Free time till 11, at which time you have to check in with me, and then you're bound to the building for the rest of the night. Any questions?" She didn't really expect them to ask any. She was sure that most of them had a million questions, but it was still early. No one wanted to be the first one to question the rules.

She continued after a brief pause. "Basic rule: nothing is optional. You can't skip meals, class, study hall, or check-in. I won't even get into any other disciplinary rules, 'cuz I know there won't be any problems. Kahlila, Dave, you have anything to add?"

They looked at each other and shrugged. "N'ah," Dave answered, "Except that we're not following the usual schedule today. After this, you'll go to Kahli's class for a half hour, then to my class for a half hour. We'll have a late lunch where we'll play some games, get to know each other, and I'll fill you in on the rest of the day's schedule at that time. You can follow Kahlila into Seminar Room A." The students cohesively rose from their chairs and headed toward the door. "Hey y'all!" Dave called, in a voice louder than usual. All the students turned around in surprise. "You *are* allowed to talk, you know," he said with a smile. Nervous laughter floated back to him as they walked out.

Five minutes later, Kahli was all alone. Well, she wasn't truly alone. There were fifteen other bodies in the room with her. But she felt completely by herself. The kids already knew to move the chairs in the seminar room into circle formation, and Kahlila used that time to flip through her notes and collect her thoughts. It wasn't working. And she was running out of stalling time. The last chair was moving into place. They were all looking at her to begin. She inhaled and exhaled. *Here we go.*

"It's so great to have all of you in class finally, after the interviews, meetings, and everything else leading up to this Institute. Welcome. I'd tell you the name of this class, but it doesn't have one." Kahli enjoyed the looks of confusion on the fifteen faces in front of her. She paused for a moment before she continued.

"This class is what you make it. I have an agenda, and I can tell you what it is. My major goal is for all of you to grow as writers. But this class won't focus on grammar. You will read and write though, probably more than you ever have. We have six weeks, and I have fifteen works of literature that I want to get to."

"Fifteen books?" shouted Marcus, a boy sitting directly across from Kahli. "Now I know you our English teacher and everything, but let me give you a math lesson. There ain't no way we readin' fifteen books in six weeks."

Kahli laughed, as did the students. "Well, maybe not fifteen entire novels. But snippets from all of them? It's possible."

"Are these books good at least?" one girl asked skeptically.

"That's something you'll have to judge for yourself. Hopefully, even if you don't like them all, you'll be able to take something from it. And I also chose things that are pretty popular in academic circles, so that you can become familiar with these books before college." Kahli scanned the room for non-verbal responses to her answer. They seemed to perk up upon hearing the word "college," as if it suddenly hit them that this class was legitimate. It encouraged her to continue. "Shakespeare, Hemingway, Hurston, Fitzgerald . . . those are just some of the authors I would like to get to. But let's say that we get stuck on something. We start talking about Booker T. Washington and just can't stop. That's fine with me. As long as our minds are working, we don't have to stick to the plan."

The same girl spoke up again. "So what's required out of this class, like in terms of papers and stuff?"

"Well, you'll have to keep a journal, and you'll have short response papers to do after you complete the night's assigned reading. You'll also be working on a piece for the magazine that you'll be putting together this summer. That's your independent project. You'll be meeting with me on a one-on-one basis regarding that writing assignment." Kahli pretended not to see two of the boys nudging each other upon hearing that they'd have to meet with her "one-on-one."

"Enough of me talking. Let's have our first of many intellectual discussions. I'm passing around a sheet with a excerpt from *The Prophet* by Kahlil Gibran. Anybody heard of him before?" She received blank stares and raised eyebrows as responses. "Okay, then. Anyhow, in this piece he's talking about teachers. Take a moment to read it to yourself."

She watched them as they pored over the strip of paper intently. Some of the students wanted to show off their literacy skills, and seemed to treat the assignment as a race to see who could read the sentence the fastest. They looked up quickly, waiting for everyone else to finish. Others reviewed the sentence a few times, attempting to decipher what may have been cryptic for them the first time.

"If he is indeed wise, he does not bid you enter the house of his wisdom, but rather leads you to the threshold of your own mind."

Once Kahli was satisfied that everyone had examined the sentence, she asked her question. "Thoughts?"

Dead silence. Heads started pointing downwards, avoiding eye contact. Kahli knew that tactic. She'd been a student herself for too many years not to recognize the tricks students had so they didn't have to answer a question. She'd never stood in Hark's shoes before, but she was quickly learning that it wasn't always a fun place to be. Seconds elapsed, and it seemed like hours as Kahli waited for a voice, any voice. *What if no one answers? Was this over their heads? Maybe I should have started with something more straightforward.*

Just as Kahlila was about to break the silence herself, she was rescued. A soft spoken girl was speaking in a hushed tone. "I kinda get the first part, but I'm not sure what the second part means."

Kahli thought she might explode from happiness. "Well why don't you tell us what the first part means to you."

The girl began her answer in the same quiet voice she started with, but as she continued to speak, her voice grew, as did her confidence, as did–Kahli sensed–a degree of anger. "I feel like it's sayin' that some teachers, they be acting like it's all about them, you know what I'm sayin'? Like we should be sweating them 'cuz they got a degree from whatever school and they have all this knowledge. Like we should be hanging on their words or something. So like "the house of wisdom," right, that means that some teachers want you to be little versions of them."

Okay, so clearly this wasn't over their heads after all. "Anyone want to respond to Rayna? And when you respond, try to connect what she's saying with the second part of Gibran's quote, the part she was a little fuzzy on." Kahli gave her a look of thanks before she took the next comment.

"I definitely know what Rayna's talkin' about with those teachers who be actin' like they all that. They got mad ones like that at King, and they don't even know anything! Got their degree from North Bumblefuck community college and still think they the shit." The other students wanted to laugh, Kahli could tell, but they weren't sure whether they were allowed to.

O.K., *Anthony's testing me. He wants to see what he can get away with in here.* "All right Anthony, where are you going with this? And when you continue, see if you can manage to articulate your point just as clearly minus the language," she said pointedly.

"My B, Kahli. Anyway, the good teachers don't be actin' like that. They let you talk about stuff in class without them always having to butt in to make their own points. They listen to what you have to say if you know more about something than they do. So that's what the second part of the quote means." He picked up the strip of paper and quickly re-read it. "Yeah, they 'lead you to the threshold of your own mind.'"

"Well said. Is anybody still unclear?" No hands. "It's really okay if you're a bit confused. This isn't easy stuff." Five hands. Kahli smiled. "Does someone else want to give it a try?"

For the next twenty minutes, Kahli got to sit back and watch. Watch them talk about the words on the page, about their own teachers, about what it means to come to the threshold of one's own mind. Doesn't threshold mean limit? How do you reach your limit? Does that mean you can't learn anything more? That you can't grow anymore? She resisted the urge to butt in, remembering what Anthony said about good teachers.

Monica, the outspoken girl who was asking the questions earlier, decided to throw a curve ball into the discussion. "I got a question for y'all. Why the teacher gotta be a 'he?' Most of teachers I know are women anyhow. That seems a little bit sexist to me."

Jermaine, who hadn't said anything up to this point, sucked his teeth and rolled his eyes. "You're trippin'. The dude is tryin' to write so that it sounds good. He's supposed to write "he or she" all the time? That's wack. And plus, just 'cuz most *school*teachers are women doesn't mean that most teachers in general are women."

Monica was ready to attack, apparently alarmed that someone actually had the nerve to disagree with her. "And what's the difference between schoolteachers and teachers in general? That makes no sense."

"Ain't your parents teachers? And coaches? And friends? Everybody's a teacher sometimes. Am I right, Kahli?"

Kahlila was a little thrown, being unexpectedly addressed, but she pulled it together. "In this class, as long as you can argue your point well, you're right. So yes, you are right. But so is Monica. I like what you said though Jermaine about teachers not just being found in the classroom. You can be a teacher anywhere. And you can be a student anywhere too. Which leads us to the homework assignment for tonight." There was a collective groan from the group. Kahlila was suddenly feeling quite comfortable in her pseudo-teacher role.

"For homework, I'd like you to write about two experiences: one where you were in the position of teacher, one when you were the learner. And both experiences have to have occurred outside of school. Questions?"

"Do we have to type it?" Justin asked.

"Yup. There are fifteen computers in this building. Everything has to be typed all summer, except for your journal." Another collective groan. "Other questions?"

"How long does it have to be?" Three students asked at the same time.

Kahlila hadn't thought about that. "Um, as long as you need it to be to convey the experience as clearly as possible."

"Word? That's the bomb!" Raheem shouted out.

"See Raheem, don't be a lazy delinquent up in here, writing three lines just 'cuz she didn't say how long it had to be," Latisha warned, calling him out. Everyone laughed.

Kahli brought them back to order. "If no one has any more questions, you can head to Dave's class, which meets in the computer room."

"I have one more question," Marcus interjected. "That dude who wrote that sentence, his name is Kahlil?"

"Yes. Kahlil Gibran," Kahli answered, unsure of his line of questioning.

"That sounds a lot like your name. Is that why you picked him, 'cuz he's like your favorite writer or something?" She was about to respond, but he didn't let her. "'Cuz if you picked him because you like him so much, aren't you making us enter your own house of wisdom, instead of leading us to the thresholds of our own minds?"

Kahli's jaw dropped. She was speechless, but Nicole spoke for her. "You're dumb, Marcus. She may have chosen that writer 'cuz she likes him, but she didn't tell us what to think about it. She let us come to our own conclusions, which is what Gibran was talking about."

Marcus grinned a devilish grin. "I know. I was just trying to mess with our teacher's head a little bit. I'm just playin' Kahli."

"It's all good, Marcus. We're gonna have a good time this summer. I can tell already. See you all later."

She sat in the room, truly alone this time, for a few minutes. She couldn't believe it. She was a real teacher. Gibran had told her so. And more importantly, so had her students.

"How was Kahli's class?" Dave asked, once everyone was seated at a computer station.

He was bombarded with "Cools" and "Goods," and he tried to hide his pleasure. *I knew she would do a good job. I don't know what she was trippin' about.*

Just as Dave was about to give them an overview on what they were doing in class that day, Anthony spoke up. "She talks like a white girl, though!"

And with that one comment, the class divided. Some of the students were agreeing with Anthony, shouting "True!" and "Yeah!" Others were clearly embarrassed by his comment, muttering, "Anthony, shutup!" or "No sir!"

Hark had once told Dave about seizing teachable moments. They may not be lessons that you plan, but they're priceless. Dave thought he may have just stumbled into one.

"All right everybody," he said, waving his hands in the air. "Settle down. Let's talk about this. So Anthony, Kahli talks like a white girl, huh?"

Anthony suddenly looked very conscious of fifteen pairs of eyes on him. "Well, yeah. It's not a bad thing, though. It was just an observation."

Dave resisted inserting his own opinion, and opened it up to the group. "What do the rest of you think about Anthony's comment?" He watched in near-awe as the students managed to ask all of the important questions without his prompting. What exactly does "acting white" mean? Why does "speaking proper" suggest that you're somehow betraying your race? On the other hand, isn't it important to be able to use and understand slang? But shouldn't you be able to use both?

Once they reached this point in the conversation, Dave interrupted them to tell them some theories a few Franklin professors had on the ability to "code switch," or adapt your speech according to your environment. Then he tried to segway into the magazine. "Guys, this has been a really good discussion, and I'm glad we had it. But we were supposed to brainstorm themes for the magazine today. Anyone have any ideas?"

Nicole raised her hand. "What about stuff like this?"

"Stuff like what?" Dave asked, a bit confused.

"Like what we were just talking about. Acting white and stuff. Judgements that people make. Stereotypes, I guess." She looked around for non-verbal support, which she received in the form of nods and smiles.

"That's real cool. So how about we go with—is it Nicole?—yeah, Nicole's idea for a moment. What are other possible topics related to the theme of stereotyping?"

"Oh I got one, definitely," said Marcus. "What about the fact that just 'cuz I'm tall and black people think I gotta play basketball?"

Toya sucked her teeth. "Marc, you *do* play basketball."

"I hear that, Marcus," Dave interjected, "So how about we all think about that theme for tomorrow and brainstorm some other ones as well. Homework tonight: go on-line and find different articles. Print out three very different types and bring them in. Questions?"

"Do they have to be boring, like the New York Times or some crap?" Anthony asked, dreading the answer.

Dave laughed. "N'ah. You can go to the Vibe website if you want, or ESPN." Anthony's face lit up like a Christmas tree; it was like he'd never heard a teacher say before that he could actually do something fun for credit.

Anthony's enthusiasm suddenly made Dave's pulse race with excitement as he thought about the possibilities for this summer. As the students started talking amongst themselves and packing up their things, he glanced towards the door. Kahli was standing in the doorway wearing his same excited expression.

Dave didn't even attempt to analyze why his heart was racing. It could have been how well the first day of class just went. It could have been how hot it was in that computer room. But as he and Kahli shared big smiles and bright eyes, he just knew that he couldn't wait until tomorrow. And the next day. And the day after that.

CHAPTER SIX

Robyn was absolutely exhausted. Between Organic Chemistry during the day and watching fifteen adolescents at night, she felt like she didn't have a minute to sleep. So at the precise moment that a movement in the doorway of the Booker T. library caught her eye, she had been trying to catch a quick doze.

Since she was supposed to be monitoring study hall, she quickly snapped to attention, ready to bawl out one of the kids for trying to sneak out early. But she caught herself in time, realizing that the movement at the door was not a student, but Lloyd. She smiled, eased out of her chair, and walked into the hallway, shutting the door behind her.

They exchanged a hug and a few compliments. Lloyd looked different from the last time Robyn had seen him. He had gotten a little color due to the recent scorching weather, his browner skin making his eyes look even lighter. And his hair was the shortest she had ever seen it, even though she would have preferred it even shorter. But it did have a semblance of a fade, which was better than the mini-fro he'd been rocking since she met him. Robyn's hair was actually different too; she was letting it grow out a little, allowing the sides to angle toward her chin and leaving it a bit shorter in the back.

"What brings you around these parts, Lloyd? I can count the times I've seen you in this building. One . . . yup, I'm done counting," Robyn laughed.

"Yeah, I'm not a big fan of the House. But I was passing by after catching dinner and I figured I'd stop in and say hi," Lloyd explained as he seated himself on a couch in the lounge.

"Well Dave and Kahli are at some meeting, so you're stuck with me," Robyn said, joining him.

"I should be so unlucky more often," Lloyd responded, almost to himself.

She was surprised by the almost suave comment. The response drove her eyes to examine him once more, picking up more and more attractive qualities with each scan up and down his frame. She heard his voice, but it sounded almost distant, even though he was sitting two feet away from her. "Hmmm? I'm sorry, what did you say?"

"I was asking you how you liked your job so far."

"Oh, it's going really well. The kids are a trip, for real. It's just a lot more work than I thought it would be, and I'm kinda stressing with this class I'm taking, too."

"I hear that. Is your stress starting to affect other areas of your life?" He squinted his eyes a little, as if you suggest that this question deserved serious consideration.

"What do you mean?" she asked, although she knew.

"Like with Jason. Is it hard not having much time to talk or visit?"

"It *has* been pretty rough lately. He's stressed out too, so we both have very little patience with each other. But that's my baby, though. These issues are just temporary. We've been through worse." She brightened as she listened to her own words. She'd

actually been agonizing about Jason for a little while now, and was surprised at her ability to sound so positive. She made a mental note to call him during her next free moment.

"So y'all got that serious love thang goin' on, huh? Bumps in the road just come and go, but the road keeps on and on." Lloyd simulated the road with his hand as he described it.

Robyn smiled. "Something like that, I guess. Yeah. Exactly that, I would say."

"Love is that natural drug, isn't it?" She was about to answer, but he didn't wait. "What do you think the best thing is about being in love?"

She had been buying into his romanticized spiel, but that question snapped her back into her usual practical Robyn Rationale.

"First of all, there ain't shit that's good about being in love if the person doesn't love you back. Now, if you're lucky enough to have that mutual thing, which I am, then it's ALL good."

"Like what–be specific."

She seemed taken aback at the request. "Oh. I don't know . . . being able to sit in silence without feeling the need to break it."

"That IS a good one. I used to be on the phone with Sonia and we'd both be doing our school work, not saying a damn thing." He shocked himself with his casual reference to Sonia, a name that he seldom spoke anymore. What was even stranger was that Robyn already knew who she was. They had talked about her during their first real conversation at the Fourth of July cookout.

"Are you serious? I thought Jason and I were bad, watching T.V. on the phone and then falling asleep, running up the bill for no reason."

"Yeah, we used to do that too. I got another one for you though–not having to plan real dates all the time."

"See? That's some old typical male reasoning. How come you can't do nothing for your girl anymore once the relationship is official?" She folded her arms, waiting for him to defend himself.

"Whoa there, tiger, settle down. I'm just saying that you don't have to go out *all the time*. You can be content doing almost anything without there being this pressure to entertain the other person."

"Mmm hmmm," Robyn replied, still looking skeptical. "What about not having to care about what you look like anymore? That's a good one."

Now it was Lloyd's time to look disbelieving. "Well, that one's pretty much a mute point when you look how you do."

Her cheeks turned a deep mahogany as she retorted, "Please, Lloyd. You haven't seen me anywhere near my worst. Wait till I put on my head scarf at night."

"That's not unattractive," he corrected. "Merely Afrocentric."

"Ha! More like Aunt Jemima-centric. How about this–that

you can listen to your friends complain about their love woes and feel secretly smug. Is that terrible?"

"Not at all! Everyone feels it. You can be there for them as they deal with their drama, but you're still thinking, 'Thank God it isn't me!'"

"Yeah, I know I think exactly that about Kahli all the time. She's going on and on about Dave, wondering if it's ever gonna happen, and I'm just thinking . . . oh my goodness." Robyn put her hand up to her mouth, her eyes growing wide. "From the look on your face, I'm guessing that you didn't know."

Lloyd quickly shut his mouth, recovering from the jaw drop he experienced after hearing Robyn's words. "Know what, exactly?" he asked, hoping that he'd misunderstood.

"How she feels about Dave," Robyn answered in almost question-like form.

"Well, she never actually told me, but it's pretty obvious."

"Yeah, I guess it is, huh?" Robyn said laughing, apparently relieved that she finally had someone with whom she could discuss the whole issue. "So do you think it's ever gonna happen between those two?"

"I couldn't tell you," he answered in a forced casual tone. "Things with Dave and Joy are pretty serious, and very complicated. But Kahlila's the kind of girl that could change what seems to be unchangeable." He was looking at something imaginary in the distance as he spoke, and it took him a moment to realize that Robyn hadn't responded. When he refocused, he saw her regarding him very strangely, as if she'd noticed something she'd never seen before.

"Uh huh," she finally said slowly. "Well let me get back to these kids before they decide to sneak out of study hall."

"All right. Nice talking to you, Robyn."

"You too," she called as she jogged back inside the library.

Lloyd's mind was racing overtime. Kahlila likes Dave. Kahlila likes Dave. It's not like he'd never thought about it. Why wouldn't she have feelings for Dave? He was a good looking brother with a good head on his shoulders. But still, he had Joy. And Kahlila never struck Lloyd as someone who would accept playing second to anybody. *And with me, she would never have to.*

CHAPTER SEVEN

Dear dad,

I'm falling in love with these kids more and more with each passing day. I know it sounds crazy that I'm calling them kids. They're 15 through 17, and I'm 19. Maybe I'm still a kid, too. Who knows.

None of them were friends when the program started. It struck me as weird at first because all the black people at my high school knew each other. But I guess it's a different situation when your high school is entirely black. All of the kids we selected rolled in different circles, which was a complete coincidence. I'd thought about "socially engineering" the acceptance process so as not to create cliques, but it worked out by itself.

They're quickly bonding. The program seems to be too small for them to self segregate. There are only two: girls and guys. They spend their free time differently. The boys work out, play video games. The girls shop and sit around chatting. Of course there are little romances brewing already, but I like the fact that the girls haven't started any of that petty drama over males that our gender is so famous for.

Gotta go prep for tomorrow's class.
Love,
Kahlila

Dear dad,

I'm shocked by how easily my class flows. Everyone said that the kids would be impossible to control and that I'd have a lot of trouble with classroom management. But i don't have to manage or control anybody. They all want to be here, which I think is the key to this whole thing.

And they're amazing writers, dad. Yeah, some of their basic technical skills need work. But they draw pictures with words. I wish I could express myself as well as some of them.

Dave is doing a terrific job. He has them so hyped about this magazine. They feel like they can really say something with this publication. He's totally empowered them. I guess I'm doing a good job, too. But they make it fun for me.

All the boys have crushes on Robyn–it's really cute. They get in her business about Jason all the time. I think it's pretty funny that they feel as if they can talk to Robyn about her personal life, but they don't do that with me, because I'm their teacher. It's crazy how Dave and I have managed to assume these teacher positions so convincingly when we're just learning as we go.

Love,
Kahlila

Dear dad,

I'm sick of calling them "these kids." You have to learn their names. They are wonderful and unique, and it's only right that I share them with you.

Raheem and Marcus are King's star basketball players. Well, they will be next year. There were a bunch of seniors who were getting all the playing time, but now that they've graduated, the team will be counting on Heem and Marc to step up. And it's all they talk about.

Since all of the students live in Booker T. House and eat in one of the dining halls on campus, we had to get them Franklin I.D.'s. The I.D.'s get them into the dorm, the cafeteria, and also the gym. Heem and Marc love going to the gym and wrecking shop on all those "Franklin fools who swear they got game." Everyone, especially the white kids, worships them there. I think this college exposure is doing them a world of good.

Till next time
Kahlila

Dear dad,

Jermaine is one who deserves an entire novel written about him, never mind one letter. He got under my skin so much (in a good way) when I met him that I broke my own rules to let him into the program. I'll explain–see, I first met Jermaine when his sister latisha was interviewing for the institute. He doesn't go to King, but he happened to be around that day after school and I let him sit in on our interview. By the end of the hour, I knew that I had to work with both of them this summer.

Jermaine isn't tall, but he's the most muscular fifteen year old I've ever met. He'd gotten in a lot of trouble a few years back when he punched one of his middle school teachers in the face. He swears the teacher kicked him first, and honestly I believe him. The stories I've heard about some of these schools lead me to think that nothing is impossible.

But because of the incident he was expelled from the city's public schools and his mom struggles to keep him in a private school right outside the city. I can tell he's battling between the roughneck image and the prep school prototype. I remember how hard it was for me to establish an identity in high school, and I can imagine that the environment would be even more traumatic for a black male.

Anyhow, having him in the program has turned out fine. The other day, he came to my class in a really bad mood. He'd just gotten off the phone with a friend and the conversation clearly had him upset. He took it out on me and refused to work in the discussion groups I'd set up for class that day. I asked him to leave the room until he was ready to participate, and he never came back. The next day, he was actually scared to come back to class because he was afraid I'd be mad. So he sent his sister to test the waters. After I assured Latisha that I wasn't angry, she convinced him to come to class. Afterwards, he explained to me that his boy had been shot the day before. Luckily, his friend is going to be okay, but he was mad at himself for not being there to help his boy. "Help your boy?" I asked. "Even your big ol' melon head isn't weapon enough against a gun!" He laughed as he left the room.

Latisha is something else herself. She is one of the smartest people I've ever met. If I were a junior in high school, I would do anything to make her my best friend. She keeps everyone in the entire program in line without ever having to do more than raise an eyebrow. The funniest thing about her ability to keep folks in check is the fact that she's only 4'10"! She's a natural born leader, though. She thinks it's all her experience as a supervisor at Burger King, but I think it's instinctual. Oh yeah, and about her Burger King job–guess how much she made last year before taxes? Seven thousand bucks! Do you know how many hours you have to put in at burger king to earn that kind of money? And homegirl still manages to make the phat grades. Their mother must be doing something right.

Love,
Kahlila

Dear dad,

It seems like I'm always trying to hold back the laughter when I'm around the kids, because they're all hilarious in their own way. Two of the students stand out in particular though. Justin is always providing comic relief. He's the only student in the program who isn't black. There are only a few non-black students at King in general, most of them being Latino or Vietnamese. Justin is the only white boy in the entire school. And he's straight chillin'.

I guess by now, Justin's used to being an anomaly. His mom and siblings comprise the only white family in his entire neighborhood. He's developed a few coping mechanisms. One is that he's put a lot of work into his athletic craft. He will also be helping Heem and Marc keep king's winning basketball record next season. He also plays football (wide receiver).

His second coping mechanism is humor. He embraces every nickname the kids give him: Beastie Boy, Vanilla Ice,

Casper, Snowflake, the list goes on. It's impossible for him not to stand out (he's not even one of those dark haired, Italian looking white guys. He's blond and blue eyed), so being the class clown allows him to receive the attention on his own terms.

Being that everyone else in the program is black, many times in class we'll end up talking about racial issues, and many kids begin to speak negatively about white people. Justin either 1)pretends to act offended, 2)joins in with his own "white folk ain't shit" comments, or 3)simply inserts a haughty and pointed "Ahem!"

I don't want it to sound like Justin is an outsider by any means, because he's not. Like his peers, he is a consumer of black pop culture and immerses himself in rap lyrics and Nike clothing. He's also a girl magnet, or so I hear, which doesn't surprise me. Girls like novelty. I'm no exception. But I'm digressing . . .

It marvels me how accepting and welcoming we can be as a black community. I think of the experience that one would have as the only black student in a white school. Justin has told me that he, during school hours, can sometimes forget that he's white. I don't believe it's ever possible for the reverse to happen. At least it wasn't for me.

The second student who cracks me up is Monica. She's really just straight rude. But she's so funny that she gets away with it. Unfortunately, I'm her favorite target. She loves making fun of me. But I must admit that I love it too. Her biggest topic of criticism is my clothing. "Mm, mm, mm. Kahlila. Was it still dark when you got dressed this morning? Or was you just rushing?" Other times she asks a question that's a little more subtle. "Kahli, you sure like them sandals, huh?" I answer, "Yeah, Mon. I do." She starts nodding and gives a cool, "That's nice." For the rest of the day I'm asking people if my shoes look okay.

Maybe I let her throw the insults my way because Dave will sometimes stick up for me if he's around, which makes it all worthwhile. He'll say, "Yo Monica, chill out. Her bellbottoms aren't bad. They were actually in style–thirty years ago," at which point they'll both start dying of laughter, giving each other pounds. But then when we're alone he'll make sure to say, "You know I was playing about the pants, right?" Wow, I'm really digressing now. These letters are supposed to be about the kids.

Love,
Kahlila

Dear dad,

The most amazing thing happened today. I've been having one-on-one meetings with the kids as they've been deciding what they want to write about for the summer publication. The theme is going to be stereotypes, and the students are going in all different directions with it. Today I had a meeting with Rayna, a senior with a good chance of being class valedictorian this year.

So we're talking about possible ideas for her composition and she busts out with, "Well, I guess I could write about how people view me differently once they find out about Devon." So of course I ask her who Devon is. "My son," she answers. Dad, I'm surprised I was able to even form any words in the face of such shock, but the questions just began pouring out of my mouth a mile a minute.

She told me that her son is going to be a year in August, and that her grandmother watches him while she does this program. She said that she didn't want to tell me about Devon during the interview because she was afraid it would hurt her chances of getting in.

As she explained what a typical day in her life was like during the school year (dropping off Devon at her grandmother's, going to school, picking up her son, doing her homework, looking after him, working on weekends), I realized how little I've lived. How I've yet to be responsible for anyone, barely even myself. Knowing that someone would always be there to catch me. Could I even deal with having to catch someone else?

Apparently no one in the program knows about Devon. She transferred to King after she had the baby so she could start over. She's a beautiful girl, and a lot of the guys want to talk to her. But they presume that she has a man since she goes home whenever she has a few free hours. Little do they know how right they are.

Love,
Kahlila

CHAPTER EIGHT

As Kahlila munched on her chicken nuggets and french fries, she could barely believe that she was in New York City with fifteen kids, Lloyd, and Dave. It had all happened so fast that her head was still spinning. A few weeks before, Kahli was leading a discussion on various types of prejudice and she came to the startling realization that almost every one of the King students was completely homophobic. While they sat bemoaning the fact that their skin color was keeping them oppressed, they would quickly become the oppressors with nonchalant mentions of "faggots, dykes, homos, and butt munchers." As soon as class was over, Kahli headed over to the library to find a book that would serve to enlighten them in some way. She didn't have any luck. When she tried to talk to Dave, he was barely any better than the kids. While he didn't use the same offensive terms, he didn't understand Kahli's urgency in remedying the situation. "That's just the way kids talk," he rationalized. So Kahli decided to take the issue to someone a bit more sensitive.

Lloyd turned out to be an even better resource than she had hoped. Apparently, a gay friend who played saxophone with him in a band back at Columbia had just sent him an e-mail raving about RENT, a new musical on Broadway. Not only did it address issues of homosexuality and AIDS awareness, but the music was supposed to be stellar. Kahlila was on the phone with the theater the same day, pleading her case and trying to get a hefty group discount. It only took her twenty minutes. Two weekends later, they were on a rented bus, headed to the Big Apple.

The kids knew they were going to see a show, but Kahlila was secretive about all of the details. She also decided to be a softie and allow the kids to get to The City early enough to give them a bit of free time. When they arrived downtown, the persuasive teenagers convinced her to let them go off on their own, as long as they agreed to meet back by 1:00. Lloyd and Dave assured her that they would be fine, but Kahli wished that Robyn were with them to give her expert opinion. But she had an Orgo exam Monday and couldn't afford to lose precious hours of study time.

Still, things seemed to be going smoothly despite her absence, and at 1:05 p.m., as Kahli popped her last french fry into her mouth, the last group of stragglers entered McDonalds. She tried not to make her sigh of relief too audible, but Lloyd and Dave threw knowing looks her way regardless. Each chaperone was seated at a different table, surrounded by kids. At Kahli's table, Nikki, Rayna and Shahid were in a heated argument, something about O.D.B. vs. Busta Rhymes. Kahli was quickly bored with that conversation, and looked toward Lloyd's table, anxious to see how he was getting along with the kids. He seemed pretty comfortable chatting it up with Marcus, Anthony, and Justin. She was about to turn away when she noticed him remove himself from the conversation with one abrupt head jerk.

Kahli followed Lloyd's open mouthed gaze to the condiment stand. Her eyes landed on a girl who was no less than stunning. Even in her ripped jeans and Columbia tank top, she was striking. Kahli rarely took notice of beautiful girls, partly because she thought that one could build an inferiority complex that way, and also because Kahli set a high standard for beauty. Most of the women who reached that standard were black women, but this woman wasn't black, though she was definitely a person of color. Her olive-beige skin glowed and her dark hair shone. Her eyes were wide set, and Kahli could see her eyelashes from where she was sitting, which was about fifteen feet away. Her cheekbones were chiseled, her lips red and full. Her arms showed definition, and a strip of exposed stomach revealed abs of steel. Kahli guessed that she must exercise a great deal, considering the Super Size milkshake in one hand and the apple pie in the other.

She was suddenly flooded with embarrassment because this girl was staring back, clearly having detected that Kahlila was watching her. But after a prolonged awkward moment, Kahli realized that it wasn't *her* stare that the girl felt. It was Lloyd's. The girl's jaw dropped as she walked over to him. Kahli gaped as well as she put the pieces together. Columbia logo. Beautiful girl. South Asian looking. This has gotta be . . .

"Sonia," Lloyd said almost sadly as he got up to give her a hug and a kiss on the cheek.

Sonia, on the other hand, was all smiles and laughs. "I can't believe this! What are you doing in the city? I thought you'd be upstate, or at school."

"Well I am. At school, I mean. I'm just in New York for the day. Some friends of mine are running a summer program and they needed an extra chaperone. We're going to see RENT." He was looking not in her eyes, but at her hands, which were decorated with gold rings.

"Really? You'll love it. Rishi and I saw it last month." Kahli didn't know who Rishi was, but from the expression on Lloyd's face she could guess that it was Sonia's new man. He looked thrown. She could almost see the wheels in his head turning as he fought for the appropriate response. It wasn't coming. The period of silence grew. Finally Sonia spoke again. "So where are your friends? I'd love to meet them."

"Right here," Kahli surprised herself by answering loudly. Sonia and Lloyd both turned in her direction, equally startled. She got up from her table and was manning Lloyd's side in seconds flat. If Lloyd was speechless before, he was completely tongue tied at this point.

Kahli took control of the situation immediately. "You must be Sonia. I've heard a lot about you," she said, extending her hand.

Sonia accepted the hand warily. "And you are . . ." she said in a voice that fought to sound friendly.

"Oh, I'm sorry. Kahlila Bradford. Lloyd's . . . friend. Very good friend." She slipped her arm under Lloyd's, a simultaneous gesture of both ownership and property. It had taken a while for Lloyd to see what Kahli was up to, but it finally clicked. They exchanged a wordless look and he tightly gripped Kahli's arm with his.

Thus began a five minute exchange of polite nothingness, where Kahli made up a dab of realistic fiction explaining how she and Lloyd met. According to Kahli, she met Lloyd when he was T.A'ing her seminar fall semester (she also threw in the fib that she was a senior philosophy major at Franklin). As Sonia cordially asked questions, attempting to mask the fire in her eyes, Kahli convincingly played the role of significant other with her words and body language.

She suddenly began to wonder what the kids were thinking about this whole charade. She sneaked a subtle look around her to find fifteen amused faces that had clearly deduced exactly what was going on. They'd apparently decided that Lloyd was a cool guy, unworthy of their blowing up his spot for the fun of it. So they stayed quiet.

It was then that she finally noticed Dave. He'd been sitting only two tables away from her with Latisha, Monica, and Jermaine, yet she hadn't noticed him since she'd first spotted Sonia. It was strange. She had never been in such close proximity with Dave before without being conscious of his presence. When he even entered a room where Kahli was, her breath would quicken. Awareness of her movements would increase. But for those few minutes, he hadn't even been there. It was bizarre.

But now he was back and Kahlila was intent on trying to read his facial expression. He'd definitely taken in the whole spectacle: the Sonia/Lloyd renunion, Kahli trying to save the day, Sonia's reaction. *What is that look on his face? Amusement? No, that's not it. Confusion? Nope, he clearly understands what's going on. Anger? That's it. He actually looks mad. But why? Is he pissed off that we tricked Sonia? But why would he have Sonia's back over his boy's? Or maybe he's heated because Lloyd didn't introduce him? No, Dave's not the type to care. Well if I keep looking his way, Sonia's gonna get suspicious. Focus, Kahli. Focus.*

Dave knew that Kahli had just caught him glaring, but he didn't care. His mind was too busy racing for him to hide his feelings with false facial expressions. *Yo, I can't believe Kahli's doing this shit. All up on him, grabbing his arm, rubbing it even. Sonia's definitely buying it too, trying to look all polite while her eyes are burning. I guess it's cool, "cuz Lloyd's looking like the man right now when a few minutes ago it was clear he was struggling. Sonia is mad fly, though. I'd seen pictures, but damn. Lloyd's a bit of a Type II pretty boy, but still—mad props to him on that one.*

Kahli is playing this girlfriend role to a T. Staring at Lloyd adoringly while he's talking to Sonia, pulling lint out of his hair. I've never seen her in this mode before. I wonder what type of girlfriend she's really like. She doesn't strike me as the super attentive type, although she did buy me that herbal tea stuff the time I had the flu. Would she be needy? N'ah, not needy like Joy is. She wouldn't be one to be questioning her place. If she was with a dude, she'd have to know that she was the one and only. I could tell that about her from when she was with Tarik. But she's still young. She'd have to be needy to some extent. She's still trying to figure out who she is. But then again, so am I. So maybe we could figure it out together.

Together. Together. What the hell am I thinking about? Me and Kahli as anything more than what we are now is a bad idea. Forget bad idea, it just ain't gonna happen. I'm with Joy, and I love Joy. And who's to say that Kahli's thinking about me either? Right now, she seems ten times more into Lloyd than she is into me. But still, the possibility of us being together crossed my mind. I'm still thinking about it! So what does that mean?

I need to talk to somebody about this. But who? I can't risk anything getting back to Joy, or to Kahli for that matter. And Lloyd and Kahli have gotten cool lately. If I talk to him, he might let it slip. Maybe I need to talk to one of these King kids. They're always cracking jokes about me and Kahli anyhow. O.K. I'm bugging out for real now. Confessing feelings to a bunch of adolescents? Chill.

They got to the theater with little time to spare. By the time they were all seated in their balcony seats, they barely had time to leaf through the program before the first deafening chords of electric guitar sounded and the performance began. As if the eighteen of them were being controlled by one mind, they simultaneously leaned forward in their seats, visibly captured by the sights and sounds.

All except Lloyd. He wasn't watching the stage. He was watching Kahlila. Lloyd watched *her* watch the stage, her expression of wonderment perhaps more beautiful than the performance itself. A shiver of excitement went through him as he remembered her stroking his arm earlier. Of course, he knew it was all a show, much like the one they were now watching. But it was still real enough to be thrilling as he burned the image into his mind.

"How do you document real life, when real life's getting more like fiction each day?"

He forced himself to turn away from her profile before she caught him staring. He tried to concentrate on the acting, singing, and movement on stage, but his mind was spinning as he replayed the day's events. How many people live in New York? A few million, right? Then how in the world did he and Sonia end up at the same McDonalds? *The girl doesn't even eat red meat! Fate is a cruel woman when she wants to be.*

"How do you leave the past behind, when it keeps finding ways to get to your heart? It reaches way down deep and tears you inside out till you're torn apart. Rent!"

He briefly attempted to calculate the odds of running into Sonia the way that he did, but quickly remembered the reason he dropped Calculus as an undergrad. A mathematical mind he did not have. A musical mind–that was another story. By the middle of RENT's first number, he'd forgotten: about Sonia, Kahlila, everything. The performers had managed to get his attention. The chords, the lyrics, the voices–he couldn't think about his mundane problems anymore. All he could think about was the music. *I used to write music this good. What happened?* But he knew what happened. His heart got broken. And the music stopped.

"How do you write a song when the chords sound wrong, though they once sounded right and rare?"

He jumped in his seat, both confused and excited by the words being sung. It was as if these performers were speaking only to him. "Lloyd!" they were screaming. "Create! Find a way." *But how?* How could he just begin playing and writing music again after so long?

He felt a hand on his thigh. A warm hand with light pressure. Kahlila. "You okay?" He merely nodded; he couldn't speak even if he wanted to. He'd, in that moment, found his solution: he could write for her.

"One song, he had the world at his feet. Glory, in the eyes of a young girl, a young girl."

He was truly excited, his energy building with each passing note he heard. Although he didn't want the musical to end, he still couldn't wait to be back in his bedroom with his keyboard.

When was the last time he played a whole song? When was the last time he even sung a note? He imagined the release that would come over him once he allowed himself that outlet of expression again.

"Find glory–in a song that rings true, truth like a blazing fire, an eternal flame."

The magic disappeared within seconds of the house lights coming on, signaling intermission. The stillness of the audience and vibrancy of the stage was replaced by hundreds of voices buzzing and what seemed like thousands of people heading towards the restrooms. But among the party of eighteen in the balcony, nobody moved.

Kahlila decided to listen to the kids' conversation with her eyes closed, something she occasionally did when they all ate lunch together, or watched T.V. in the evenings. In this manner she could be an observer without being a participant. Snippets of voices became clearer as soon as her eyelids shut.

"So what does everyone think so far?" *Dave's voice. Definitely.*

"I didn't know that Broadway shows had this many black people in them!" *Jermaine.*

"Well, they don't *all* have this many, silly." *Latisha.*

"I think Mimi's a bomb singer." *Nikki.*

"Forget her singing! She's fly as hell." *Justin or Anthony. Can't tell.*

"Yo, is Angel a guy or a girl?" *O.K. That's Anthony. It was Justin before.*

Laughter. "You couldn't tell, dawg? He's a flamer, man. Drag queen. All that." *Marc.*

"Word? That's deep."

"Why is that deep?" *Lloyd.*

"I don't know, just the way him and that other dude seemed to really be in love and all that. It was strange, like they were a real couple . . ."

"What do you mean by real?"

"Like a guy and a girl."

"Anthony's an ass. You can be a real couple if you're two guys, or two girls." *Monica.*

"But that's not cool though, for real." *Shahid.*

"Yo, be quiet. That's why Kahlila took us to see this show in the first place. 'Cuz she thinks we're gay bashers. She's mad sensitive, y'all. Maybe she's a lesbian herself!" *Monica's buggin. She knows I'm listening, too.*

Roars of laughter. "After the way she was all up on Lloyd today at McDonalds? I don't think so!" *Rayna.* "It don't matter though, Kahli. Even if you are, we still love you."

I guess it's my turn to say something. "That's all I wanted from you in the first place, Rayna."

David was sitting in the seat directly behind Kahli, and leaned forward in his seat so that his lips were centimeters from her ear. "Mission accomplished, captain."

She didn't turn around, afraid that her beaming grin would give her away—both to the kids, and to Dave.

CHAPTER NINE

To: desiree@classof99.franklin.edu
From: tarik@classof97.franklin.edu
Date: July 30, 1996 4:16 p.m.
Subject: long time

Message:
dez-

whatsup. how is everything. i hope this summer has given you a chance to sort of get back into the swing of things. i know how real last semester was for you.

i must admit though that i'm mailing you for selfish reasons. i feel like we were pretty cool last year through kahli and that you could possibly help me out. as you know, i fucked up big time with the whole shannon thing. last semester kahli said she never even wanted to see my face again, so i kept my distance, trying to give her some time to cool off. but it's been months and i'm not thinking about her any less. i really want to try to make things right and be with her again.

so, as her confidante, do you have any suggestions? i know things got a bit tense between you two, but you still understand her. what should i do? write? call?

thanks in advance
tarik

To: tarik@classof97.franklin.edu
From: desiree@classof99.franklin.edu
Date: July 31, 1996 10:18 a.m.
Subject: long time—Reply

Message:
tarik,

i'm okay. hanging in there. anyhow, i wouldn't advise you to call or write kahlila right now. she's at school running some program and with her being so busy, it will be easy for her to brush you off as someone she doesn't have time for. wait until the fall. talk to her face to face and let her see the pain in your eyes (if you're hurting as much as you say you are). in the meantime, think of the perfect thing to say and enjoy the rest of your summer.

desiree

To: joy_rainer@yahoo.com
From: drobinson@sociology.franklin.edu
Date: July 31, 1996 12:02 p.m.
Subject: quick favor

Message:
hey babe,

what's going on? i can't believe how crazy our schedules have been lately. i can't wait to see you tomorrow night.

yo, can you do something for me in the meantime? the kids have decided they want to have a dance and they've been so great, we're gonna let them do it. doesn't your girl amber have a man who's a d.j? can you get his number for me? the dance is this friday so we're kinda in a tight spot.

thanks
dave

To: drobinson@sociology.franklin.edu
From: joy_rainer@yahoo.com
Date: July 31, 1996 2:41 p.m.
Subject: no problem

Message:
hi honey,

i called amber for you. pedro's number is 555-9780. it's so cute that the kids want to have a dance. i remember those days. anyway, i've been hearing so much about these students of yours, maybe i can call in sick friday and go to the dance with you so i can meet them.

see you tomorrow
joy

To: joy_rainer@yahoo.com
From: drobinson@sociology.franklin.edu
Date: July 31, 1996 5:40 p.m.
Subject: no problem—Reply

Message:
babe,

thanks for doing that so quickly. i actually don't need to call him after all, though. one of the kids just told me that he wants to d.j. and his boy has the tables and everything. as for coming to the dance, we told the kids that they can only have this party if they didn't invite any outside people (to avoid any potential drama), so therefore they made us promise to do the same. but i didn't know you wanted to meet them. if that's the case you can come sit in on a class of mine anytime.

love
dave

To: lloyd@philosophy.franklin.edu
From: robyn@classof99.franklin.edu
Date: July 31, 1996 5:58 p.m.
Subject: i want details!

Message:
so . . . kahlila told me about your little role playing exercise in new york. sounds like sonia was sufficiently shocked. i won't be surprised if you get a phone call within the next week or so. how did it feel seeing her again? was it a major setback?

by the way, i reminded dave to tell you about the dance the kids are having on friday night. but in case he forgot, they all made sure to tell us that they wanted you to come. so consider yourself invited. and wear a suit–it's semi formal.

To: robyn@classof99.franklin.edu
From: lloyd@philosophy.franklin.edu
Date: July 31, 1996 7:09 p.m.
Subject: i want details!—Reply
Message:
it's funny that you said sonia would be calling, because i did

indeed have a message from her last night. i haven't called back yet, nor do i plan to. i know she's gonna ask for further details about my "relationship" with kahlila, and i'm not really trying to extend the lie any further than it's already gone.

as for your question about how it felt to see her, it felt . . . okay. at first, i was a bit numb. so many images came rushing back to me, and i was a little overwhelmed. but as soon as she mentioned her new man, and kahlila came over and did her thing, it all just became so absurd that i couldn't take any of it too seriously. in that moment i think i also realized that there is life after sonia. there are women as wonderful as she is. more so, most likely.

so you'll never guess what i did that night. i played my keyboard. for the first time in over a year. i've barely stopped since. i'm finally feeling like myself again, robyn. i guess that's occasion to celebrate, so you can tell the kids i'll be at their shindig friday.

To: lloyd@philosophy.franklin.edu
From: kahlila@classof99.franklin.edu
Date: August 1, 1996 8:13 a.m.
Subject: 8:00 2nite okay?

Message:
whatzup lloyd,

i know i said i could be to your place at 7, but we have some last minute planning to do for this dance tomorrow. so unless i hear from you, i'll assume 8:00 is okay.
peace
kahlila

To: drobinson@sociology.franklin.edu
From: kahlila@classof99.franklin.edu
Date: August 1, 1996 8:24 a.m.
Subject: we're mad silly

Message:
dave,

i can't believe i'm sending e-mail when i'm gonna see you in like an hour. and the hilarious thing is you'll probably respond. :-)

so have you heard lloyd playing that keyboard in his room lately? he seems really excited about getting into his music again. will you be at the crib when i come over there tonight to hear his new song?

To: kahlila@classof99.franklin.edu
From: drobinson@sociology.franklin.edu
Date: August 1, 1996 10:28 a.m.
Subject: we're mad silly–Reply

Message:
sup–didn't get a chance to talk to you at breakfast. i was rapping to maine about his article for the magazine, and time flew. you're teaching your class right now. by the way, the kids are feeling your unit on poetry. they were talking about it in my class yesterday.

lloyd hasn't mentioned anything about a new song yet. i've actually only heard him playing a little bit, and he turns down the volume real low and shuts his door. guess he's not ready to make a public appearance yet. i actually won't be home tonight, so you'll have to let me know how he sounds.

that's interesting that he asked you to hear the song, though. should i be jealous? :-)

To: drobinson@sociology.franklin.edu
From: kahlila@classof99.franklin.edu
Date: August 1, 1996 11:33 a.m.
Subject: we're mad silly–Reply-Reply

Message:
> that's interesting that he asked you to hear the song, though. should i be jealous? :-)

i doubt it. i'm sure you're still lloyd's best buddy.

To: kahlila@classof99.franklin.edu
From: drobinson@sociology.franklin.edu
Date: August 1, 1996 11:40 a.m.
Subject: (none)

Message:
>> that's interesting that he asked you to hear the song, though. should i be jealous? :-)
>i doubt it. i'm sure you're still lloyd's best buddy.

that wasn't what i meant.
later

CHAPTER TEN

Lloyd had played out the scenario in his head about thirty times before she'd arrived. There had been thirty different endings, all of them positive. In one of them she heard the song and wept. In another one, he hadn't even finished the song and she was already ripping her clothes off.

But here she was, and this was the only scenario that counted. They sat in the living room, Kahlila on the oversized chair and Lloyd on the couch. Already his vision was messed up. In all thirty scenarios, they were sharing the couch. *Damn.*

He'd agonized over whether he should engage in small talk when she arrived, waiting before he played the song. But he eventually decided on the direct approach, the keyboard ready and waiting as soon as she walked in the door. So when she entered and sat down, (he'd envisioned that she'd have to take off her jacket, but he forgot that it was hot as hell outside, even at night), he leaned forward to meet the keyboard sitting on the coffee table, and he began. They'd barely even said hello.

Successive eighth notes flowed from his fingers, the pedal attachment blending them together to sustain haunting chords. His voice was merely another instrument, coming in to accompany the piano and not overpower it. His voice was rich and deep yet hurting and broken all at the same time.

> see me/ see me for who I am/ see me for what I can be to you/
> if you want me to

hear me/ hear me and what I say/ let me have my way/ with you/ just let me do/ what I feel/ what I feel is more real/ than anything before

if fate deals/ a way to seal/ our fates as one/ I will kneel/ in thanks for the one I adore

see my face/ hear my words/ feel my love/ come to your senses baby/ open your eyes

you might be surprised/ to see me/ i've been here all along/ singing this song . . .

Lloyd stopped suddenly, looking sheepish. The fingers that a few moments ago were massaging the keys of his synthesizer were now fidgeting in his lap. "That's all I have so far. I'm not really sure where it's going."

Kahlila opened her eyes slowly. She looked as if she hadn't been ready for the song to end. "Lloyd. That was unreal. Listening to that was more than just listening to some random song. It was an actual physical, emotional experience. I never even knew you sang!"

Wow. That was almost the exact response from Scenario #17. Lloyd smiled in appreciation.

Kahli's expression grew compassionate. "You must really love her, huh?"

Huh? "Love who?"

"Sonia. I mean, I saw her and how you reacted to her. She really is unbelievably beautiful. If her personality at all matches her exterior, I can definitely see why you're still hurting."

Well God damned. I knew things were going too well. I gotta nip this perception of me still love-sick over Sonia in the bud. "Actually Kahlila, I am completely over her."

She looked relieved. "I am so glad to hear it. She was a fool for letting you go in the first place. And what's the point of holding on to someone who doesn't even appreciate you? Like with your song—if whoever you're singing to doesn't see you, hear you, or feel you when you're all up in her face, then it's time to move on."

Why is she grinning like she's cracking jokes? She's really just bringing me to my senses. I am standing right in front of this girl and she doesn't even see me. "True, true. You're absolutely right, Kahlila. Why sweat those who aren't sweatin' you back? I mean, you might as well just hope they're happy with someone else, you know? 'Cuz really, who are you to try to get in the way? They're not feeling you anyhow, so what's the point of trying to mess up what they really want? True. That's a really good point."

"Um, Lloyd? Why so bitter?"

"What do you mean?" The question rushed out in his nervousness.

"This rambling of yours sounds personal. If it ain't about Sonia, who is it?" Lloyd's delayed response and contorted facial expression forced Kahlila to take back the question. "Actually, don't even worry about it. A man's got a right to privacy." But she'd already come to her own conclusion. *Robyn. It's got to be. And he's scared to tell her 'cuz of Jason.*

Kahli decided to change the subject since Lloyd was looking extremely uncomfortable. "But I do know that your song is off the hook and I want to hear updates as you work on it. Deal?"

"Deal." Lloyd looked as sincere as he possibly could while promising to keep Kahlila included in his musical process. But he knew that he would never play a song for her again after tonight. She said it herself. *I gotta stop wasting my time being invisible.*

CHAPTER ELEVEN

Dave noticed that his suit jacket was fitting a little tighter than it had when he last wore it. As he took in his reflection in the full length mirror, it did appear as if his shoulders had gotten a bit broader, and his muscles were thickening. He'd always worked out his fair share, but lately he'd stepped up his regiment. J.T. had him on a new routine at the gym. They'd been lifting together since a few days after Kahli's birthday.

The two ran into each other that next Tuesday on their way into Johnson Gymnasium and ended up on the same team in a pickup basketball game. They kicked ass. On their walk out, as they recounted a few of the game's key highlights, discussion moved towards the weight room. Dave expressed an interest in switching up his routine, so J.T. offered to show him the program that Coach Myers put him on. Since that day, they'd met three times a week without fail.

What Dave didn't know was that when J.T. told Kahlila about his newfound gym buddy, she was absolutely ecstatic. "J.T., you'll have to get some info for me–find out how things are going with Joy, and if you can, try to gage his feelings for me while you're at it." J.T. informed her that she was crazy, that his and Dave's conversations were limited to sports and music. Maybe an occasional mention of a cute girl on the Stairmaster, but that's as far as discussions on women traveled.

What J.T. didn't know was that Dave was often tempted to mention Kahli as they did their squats or as he spotted J.T. at the bench press. But he hadn't quite perfected an entry that was subtle enough. "So, you think Kahli's over the whole Tarik thing? How do you know for sure–is she seeing someone new?" Dave knew that question was stupid, because if Kahli had a new man she would have told him herself. The question he really wanted to pose was this one: *Is Kahli down if I am*?

Dave had a strange feeling as he looked at his own reflection. He didn't know why, but he strongly felt as if that unasked question would indeed get answered. Tonight.

Robyn was giving Kahli an odd look as Kahlila emerged from their bathroom wrapped in a towel, her hair dripping onto the floor. "Sorry about the puddle. I'll clean it up," said Kahlila, attempting to anticipate the source of the gaze.

"Whatever. Yo, why don't you leave your hair like that tonight?" Robyn's eyes were locked on Kahlila's jet black curls. Her hair cascaded past her shoulders in corkscrew-like ringlets.

"Like this? Just out, and out of control?" Kahli asked incredulously.

"It's not out of control, Kahli. It looks really good. If you're worried about it getting frizzy, that's nothing a little gel can't prevent. I'll hook it up for you."

Kahli still looked skeptical, but she reluctantly agreed. "All right. Just let me put my robe on and you can do your thing." She walked into their bedroom and turned on the stereo. "So what are you wearing?" she shouted over the noise to Robyn, who was still in the hallway.

"Does it matter? There ain't nobody there for me. Those kids stare at my butt too much as it is. I'm not wearing a thing to encourage any more of it. Conservative is my look for the evening. Now you, on the other hand, need to impress the hell out of your boy. Has Dave ever seen you dressed up before?"

Kahli reemerged from the bedroom in a robe and slippers. "Nope. Sure hasn't. So you think he'll like this whole curly hair look, huh?"

"Definitely," said Robyn, examining Kahli's locks more closely.

"Damn, chick, where the hell did you get this hair from? This ain't no normal black girl stuff."

"My dad, I guess," she answered, her eyes shifting downward. Quickly, her expression brightened again. "So are you gonna make me a diva or what?"

"Girl, if he ain't droolin' tonight, he's never gonna. And that's the truth."

Dave smiled as he looked around the multi-purpose room. It was hardly recognizable. He'd finally figured out a way to put those eager Franklin students from the community service office to good use. They'd decorated, bought snacks, and done all the things that he, Kahli, and Robyn hadn't wanted to do.

And the kids were loving it. They'd been acting crazy all day, especially the girls, running to CVS to buy last minute items, coming to class with curlers in their hair. But it had all paid off. The kids looked on point. As Raheem walked over, Dave had to give him a pound on his pin-striped vest. Dave didn't think the kid owned anything that lacked a swoosh.

He was talking to Raheem about Marcus's surprising D.J. skills when Heem's attention was suddenly diverted. "Yo Dave, check it out. By the door. Can you handle it?"

Dave followed the motion of Raheem's head nod and his mouth dropped where his eyes stopped. It was a figure he knew, but had for so long commanded himself not to acknowledge. The dress: a deep maroon silky second skin, hugging a modestly curved figure and then flowing out from the knee to the floor. The thin straps revealing a long elegant neck and tantalizing bare shoulders. All of the exposed skin absolutely glowing. The refined glamour of the gown juxtaposing a gorgeous frenzy of wild black curls. It was breathtaking. No. He couldn't handle it.

By the time he'd taken it all in, Heem had left his side to get his homies. When Dave finally regained the composure to walk over and greet Kahlila, it was too late. She was surrounded by a circle of kids: the boys whistling and shouting good natured comments, the girls playing in her hair and slathering on compliments like Jergens lotion. He had never felt so lost. He was floating out of his body when a voice pulled him back to the tiled floor. "I take it you approve of Kahlila's new look."

Lloyd. Dave had never been so happy to see him in his life. "What's going on man," Dave said, feeling himself getting grounded once more. "Yo, she looks . . . damn. I never knew, well I guess I did know, but . . . what's that look for?"

"Yo man, I'm kind of struggling right now. I kind of want to put you on to something, but I'm not completely sure if it's a good idea." Lloyd wasn't being completely truthful. He knew that Dave liked Kahlila. The way Dave was gazing at her made everything crystal. And if Dave did indeed like her, then Lloyd should no doubt tell him that she felt the same way. Lloyd's real struggle was whether he was ready to wholeheartedly abandon the prospect of Kahlila being *his* girl, as opposed to "the girl my roommate's kicking it with."

"Well, you gotta put me down now that you brought it up. I'm sayin', that's just not cool otherwise." As Dave spoke, he stole occasional glances in Kahli's direction to see if the crowd had died down. It was dissipating.

Be the bigger person, Lloyd. Do it. "True. Here it is—she likes you. Kahli, I mean."

Lloyd now had David's full attention. "She told you this?"

"N'ah. Robyn did. Kahli doesn't talk to me about it at all. But it's definitely true." He waited for a response until he couldn't wait anymore. "So what are you trying to do?"

"What do you mean, what am I gonna do? I have a girl, dawg." A crease in Dave's forehead had developed and was deepening.

"But aren't y'all supposed to be seeing other people?"

"Sort of. But we haven't been actually doing it. Yo, check it, I'm gonna go outside and get some air. I'll be back in a while." He absentmindedly set his drink on the closest table and headed out the door.

Lloyd exhaled a deep sigh of relief. *He isn't gonna go for it. He's gonna stay with Joy.* Now Lloyd's conscience was clean without his having to sacrifice anything, which is what he wanted all along. He decided to find Robyn; suddenly, he felt like dancing.

At first, Kahli was disappointed that Dave hadn't come over to her as soon as she got to the dance. But she quickly developed a coping mechanism. As she flitted around, chatting and dancing, she invented a sort of game. An alternate existence of sorts. In this world that Kahli created, she and Dave are a couple–one of those comfortable couples who don't have to be up under each other all night. They mingle in their own individual social circles, knowing that later on in the evening it would just be the two of them, snuggled up under the sheets.

Of course, this dream was hard to maintain considering that there were only twenty people at the whole dance. Only about three or four social circles existed at a time. And after an hour of absolutely no contact with Dave, Kahli was getting the distinct impression that he was avoiding her. Actually, he seemed to be avoiding everyone. Half the time he wasn't even in the room, and when he did come in, he blended into a corner or stood by the turntables helping Marc pull records.

Finally she decided that she was being an idiot. *I think being at this high school dance has thrown me back a few years. He's not some random boy. He's Dave. If I want to say hello, I should just go over there.* She took long strides over to him, reaching him just as he bent over a crate of records. When he stood back up, he jumped slightly at the sight of her.

"Hey," she said cheerily.

"What's up." Awkward silence. "I like your hair."

"Thanks. Do you like it enough to dance with me?" *Where the hell did that question come from? That one just slipped out.*

Awkward silence again. He was thinking. "Sure. Let's dance."

They walked onto the dance floor in the middle of "Ice Cream," but as soon as they got into dancing position, the music came to a screeching halt and Marc's voice was booming through the speakers. "Change of pace, y'all! This one's for the teachers on the dance floor."

Kahli's cheeks turned the color of her dress as Marc began to play Faith Evans' "Kissing You." She was about to tell Dave that they didn't have to go through with the dance when she felt his arms encircle her waist. Electricity ran through her fingers as she placed tentative hands on the back of his neck. They began to move to the bassline, laughing and shaking their heads at all of their students cheering them on. Dave and Kahli yelled for the kids to be quiet but they were honestly glad for the diversion. If it weren't for the students, they'd have to look at each other, and neither one of them was quite prepared to cross that invisible line.

Dave didn't look in her eyes even as he began to speak. "You know what's hilarious about this whole situation?"

"Um, what *isn't* hilarious about this situation?"

"True, good point. But I was gonna say that I don't even dance."

"You're not dancing," said Kahlila wisely. "You're swaying."

Dave smiled and finally looked her square in the face. "Oh. Well am I swaying okay?"

"You're swaying more than okay," she answered, returning the smile.

Lloyd was forcing himself to look at everything *but* the dancing couple in the center of the room. He noticed that the sign above the refreshment table was misspelled. He noticed that Nikki had a run in her stockings. He noticed that Rayna and Anthony were suddenly missing in action. But nothing helped. Every ounce of his being was fully aware that Kahli and Dave were wrapped up in each other, on display for all of their friends and students to see.

To make matters worse, he saw Robyn approaching him excitedly. He would have been glad to talk to her at any moment except this one. He had a sinking feeling that she was going to be spewing some cheerful garbage about the scene he was watching. It took less than ten seconds to prove his theory correct.

"Lloyd," she whispered anxiously, "They are really groovin' out there! I mean, serious sexual tension. We should help them out."

"What would you suggest, Robyn–wheeling in a bed for them?" His voice was monotonous.

She laughed. "You're silly. Here's what I'm thinking. Kahli and I are supposed to stay and clean since Dave got here early to set up. How about I tell Kahli she can leave now so that she's free to chill with Dave?"

"And where are they gonna do this chilling?"

"At your place. So you need to stay with me for a while and help me clean this room. That cool?" Her eyes were beaming with enthusiasm.

"Yup. Cool."

"Phat. I'll tell her as soon as they stop dancing."

Dave watched Kahlila from afar as she talked to some of the students in an attempt to find Rayna and Anthony. *I should have told her that her dress looked nice, not just her hair. Hair is so specific. I wonder if she got the message that everything about her is on point tonight.* He stared as Robyn approached Kahlila and pulled her aside. In less than a minute, Kahila was back at Dave's side.

"What's going on?"

"Robyn found Rayna and Anthony. They were outside on some romantic stroll, which seems harmless enough. And Robyn's going to Atlanta tomorrow which means I have to watch these kids all weekend. So she gave me the rest of tonight off."

Word. "Word? So you want to come back to the crib and hang out for a minute?"

"Sure," she answered as nonchalantly as possible. She sauntered out of the building with him, her toes throbbing from the pressure of her high heeled sandal. But she felt no pain. She was floating.

CHAPTER TWELVE

"There is no future, there is no past. I live this moment as my last."

-RENT

The whole time they were talking in the living room at Dave's house, Kahlila's mind was elsewhere. She was holding up her end of the conversation, even inserting a witty comment on occasion. But the wheels in her brain were turning fast as she tried to get up the courage to actually speak her mind. She knew the moment would come when the conversation would thin out and her exit would be imminent. She felt the urgency of the situation. *If I don't make a move tonight, it's never gonna happen. All of the pieces are in place, and if I let this opportunity go, there may never be another one.* Her mind flashed the lyrics to a song from Rent, which wasn't surprising considering how often she played the soundtrack.

"There's only us, only tonight. We must let go to know what's right. No other course, no other way, no day but today."

As predicted, the moment came for her to go home. Her mind registered his voice saying something about calling the shuttle service. They both rose from the couch. They looked at each other. *Deep breath. This is it. No day but today.*

"Look. I don't want to leave, okay? There. I said it." Her heart was pounding inside of her chest so hard that it actually hurt. She felt like he could hear her breathing, so she took in shallow swallows of air and let them out a little bit at a time. Why hadn't he responded yet? How much time had passed? He was still just looking at her. She tried to read his eyes. She wouldn't call it staring exactly, but his eyes were definitely fixed on hers. *Why won't he speak? This is ridiculous.* She'd said it, and he didn't say anything back. It was time to go. She broke the gaze and reached for the door.

The pressure on her free arm almost made her jump. She looked at her arm and Dave's hand was gripping it tightly. He was also looking at her arm, as if he couldn't believe that he just grabbed for it.

Their eyes connected again. Dave knew that it was his turn to speak. "I don't want you to leave either, Kahli." His grip loosened a bit, but he didn't let go.

Kahlila was tempted to leave anyway. It was so perfect, this moment that she had been waiting for all summer, all last semester, all her life. It could never be repeated or recreated. She was overwhelmed by the intensity of her own thoughts, running a mile a minute through her head.

"Wow. We've never gotten this far before. What happens now?" she finally asked, attempting to lighten the mood.

"Whatever you want to happen." His hand moved up and down her arm, stroking her as she stepped closer to him. He pulled her in until she was nestled against his chest.

Kahlila's heart had still been racing when Dave said he wanted her to stay. Her stomach was fluttering as he rubbed her arm. But as soon as she wrapped her own arms around his waist and found the crevice in his chest where her head fit like a puzzle, a calm spread throughout her body. She pulled away enough to see his face. He was even more handsome this close. She smiled a little, and traced his lips with her finger. She rose up on her toes, tilted her head, and kissed him.

It was Dave who was nervous now. Who was this *woman* standing in front of him all of a sudden, taking control, and kissing him like a pro? Her lips were soft and seductive as they moved from his mouth to his cheek to his ear. "Be careful, little one. You're about to go somewhere you might not be ready for," he warned, trying to reduce his anxiety with humor.

Kahlila pulled away and looked him dead in the eyes. The serious expression that met his smile slapped the grin off his face. She stepped out of the embrace, took his hand, and walked through the living room, down the hallway, and stopped outside of his bedroom. "I'm ready. I've been ready. But I don't want to push you. So if you want to do this, you have to be the one to open the door."

Without hesitation, he turned the knob.

David throwing the door open. His pulling her into the room. Their arms wrapped around each other. Their lips meeting and exploring faces, necks, shoulders. Kahlila's pulling David's shirt over his head. Laughing softly as it gets stuck. Falling on the bed. Slipping off slacks and a crimson dress. Kissing bare skin. Leaving no stone unturned. Pause. "You know there's only one line left to cross, right?" Nodding.

It was all a blur two hours later as they lay in bed naked watching Soul Train. David stole glances when she wasn't paying attention. The light from the TV reflected on her glistening body that was only half wrapped in sheets. She really was beautiful. He'd forced himself not to recognize it for so long, but now that he had, he couldn't stop looking at her.

Kahlila kept replaying the evening in her head. One line left to cross. And they crossed it. She almost didn't recognize herself in her flashbacks of what occurred. Was that her being bold, going after what she wanted and getting it? Was that her throwing her head back in ecstasy and crying out for more? She sure couldn't say that she acted that way with Tarik. She actually couldn't remember anything she'd ever said to Tarik during sex–well, maybe little things like, "You got condoms?" or "Move over, I'm about to fall off the bed." But never the good pillow talk like, "Oh God, yes! Please don't stop." Her red-toned skin turned a little redder just thinking about it.

But it's not like Dave was exactly being himself either. "Can I kiss you here? And here? What about right here?" Making her giggle as he blew lightly on her stomach. And then he had said the strangest thing, Kahlila remembered. She still couldn't figure it out. After it was all over and Kahlila lay on his chest with her eyes closed, Dave said in almost a whisper, "Damn, I'd missed you." Though she heard him quite clearly, she wanted him to elaborate so she purred, "Hmm?" in his ear. Suddenly he seemed to get very alert. "Huh? Nothing. Nothing."

Kahlila replayed that dialogue specifically in her head a few times as she pretended to concentrate on the hoochies shaking their bodies to the music, trying their best to get on camera. Her expression grew more and more pensive as she analyzed the comment. Dave took notice and decided to do something about that thoughtful gaze she was sporting.

He quickly rolled over and pinned Kahlila on the bed by her arms. "So. If I've learned anything tonight, it's that you're ticklish. Now how can I use that information to my advantage?" He held up one finger to her face menacingly. "Now it looks like a harmless finger, doesn't it? But when I place it right here," and he quickly jabbed her in the side, "Or right here," and he reached down to trace the soles of her feet, "It becomes a negotiating tool."

Kahlila was in hysterics. "Stop!! Dave, stop!! Please, Dave. What do you want??" He was loving it but he stopped because she was really getting loud and he thought he just heard Lloyd walk in the front door. When she finally calmed down, she was lying in the fetal position on the bed, still suspicious that he might run a sneak attack.

Dave looked at her with fake sympathy. "You really are pitiful, you know that? I'll let you off easy. Are you thirsty?" Kahlila nodded. "Good. Since I won the tickle battle, you're in charge of getting drinks from the kitchen."

Kahlila was once again composed, and ready to participate in the verbal exchange. “I wouldn’t call that all-out assault a battle. I’d call it abuse. And you didn’t have to do all that to get me to bring you something to drink. You just had to ask, idiot.”

“Who you calling an idiot, wimp? You’re the one who’s scared of this,” he said holding up the guilty index finger. At the sight of the finger, she gave a little yelp, jumped up, threw on his t-shirt, and quickly ran out of the room.

She giggled all the way to the hallway, where she walked directly into Lloyd on his way to his bedroom. She looked up at him with mild surprise, opened her arms, slipped them underneath his and squeezed his waist as tightly as she possibly could. “I love you so much, Lloyd. I am so happy right now!” She kissed his cheek and skipped off to the kitchen.

David stared at the ceiling while Kahlila was out of the room. He had always believed that the answers to the future lay somewhere in the past. But there had never before been anyone in his life like Kahlila. And she sure as hell seemed like an answer to something, the piece in the puzzle that had been missing before she walked into his world. Damn, he’d missed her. And he hadn’t even known her.

Lloyd didn’t speak a word until he reached his room. He put all of his Sade CD’s into his stereo, hit the random select button, and flopped down on his bed. “Nice going, Lloyd,” he said to no one in particular. Soft talking and laughter drifted into his room until he fell asleep to a woman singing about a bulletproof soul.

Dave awoke the next morning with the sun. It was as if one word burst into his thought pattern along with daybreak: Joy. She wasn’t anywhere to be found a few hours before. But with the new day came . . . was it clarity? Or confusion? He thought for hours. Joy. Kahli. Joy. Kahli. Before he knew it, the clock said 8:30 and when he looked over at the figure beside him, her eyes were staring right back at him.

"Soooo . . . Dave."

"So Kahli."

She sat up abruptly, exposing her bare chest momentarily before pulling the sheet up to her neck. "So before you get super uncomfortable, let me say something. It's Saturday morning. We don't have to see each other again, or even speak for that matter, until Monday. How about we take that time to get our thoughts together. Sound good?"

He exhaled deeply. "Sounds real good, Kal."

"I thought you might say that," Kahli responded with a wink. She slipped out of bed and began a scavenger hunt for her underwear. "Just one favor," she called out from her position under the bed.

"Anything."

"Can I borrow some clothes for the trip home? Nothing is more embarrassing than an early morning walk of shame in formalwear."

Dave chuckled. "For being so understanding about things, you can have the shirt off my back if you want it."

"Um, hon, you don't have a shirt on at all. So how about you get your lazy ass out of bed and find me something stunning to put on."

He heaved a sigh and slowly threw one leg, then the other, over the side of the bed. "Question: are you gonna actually put on at-shirt, running pants, and those high ass sandals you had on last night?"

"Shit! I didn't think of that. I guess I gotta put back on the dress then, huh?"

"Guess so," he answered somewhat distractedly, forcing himself not to stare as Kahlila fastened her strapless bra. "You can take a shower here before you go, if you want."

She pondered the offer for a moment, and then grabbed her dress from a corner of the room. “You know what? That’s okay. The longer I stay, the harder it’ll be to leave. I’ll just jump in the shower at my place.”

He wasn’t ready for the disappointment that filled him when she declined his offer. It scared him. And then she was dressed, heading out of his bedroom. He followed in a pair of shorts and socks. They reached the door too quickly. He wasn’t ready to say goodbye. How should he say goodbye, anyway? A hug? A kiss?

But Kahli didn’t even give him enough time to make a decision. “See you Monday.” Her smile was cheery but her eyes pleading as she backed into the hallway. She closed the door and Dave was left staring at the doorknob.

Do I hurt someone today? Or do I hurt someone Monday? There was no way around it. Dave knew that someone wasn’t going to be happy by the end of all this. And as selfish as it seemed, he prayed to God that it wouldn’t be him.

)4-SKER

CHAPTER THIRTEEN

To: robyn@classof99.franklin.edu
From: kahlila@classof99.franklin.edu
Date: August 3, 1996 10:02 a.m.
Subject: HELP!!!

Message:
hey, you'll get this when you get to jason's. okay, i spent the night there. well, i guess you know that. and it happened–we did it. it was great.

but now i'm stressed. i think i handled myself really well this morning. i told him that he could take a few days to process everything and i'd stay out of his way. he seemed pretty relieved. do you think that was okay?

i think i need to get out of this room because if i'm here, i'll be tempted to call. write back please!

love
kahli

To: joshuatravis@classof98.franklin.edu
From: kahlila@classof99.franklin.edu
Date: August 3, 1996 10:16 a.m.
Subject: BIG NEWS

Message:

i know you're studying all weekend. let's meet for lunch near the library. we gotta talk about me and dave–yeah, major progress. major.-kal

To: kahlila@classof99.franklin.edu
From: joshuatravis@classof98.franklin.edu
Date: August 3, 1996 10:40 a.m.
Subject: BIG NEWS–Reply

Message:
you fucked him? please tell me you did. lord knows you need some ass. yeah kal! never thought you'd get the guts to jump him. congrats. meet me in front of the library at 1:00. and in the meantime, please don't go messing everything up, calling him and asking him about his "feelings." please.-j.t.

To: kahlila@classof99.franklin.edu
From: robyn@classof99.franklin.edu
Date: August 3, 1996 2:04 p.m.
Subject: HELP!!–Reply

Message:
girl, i can't believe it. i wish i were there to talk to you about it in person. first, mad props on how you handled things this morning. very mature. you were right not to stress him.

i don't want to be the spoiler here, but i feel like i have tell you not to get your hopes up. lloyd was just telling me last night that dave still seemed to care about joy a whole lot. have you thought about how you're gonna handle being around him if he decides that he doesn't want to pursue anything more with you?

keep me posted on everything
robyn

To: lloyd@philosophy.franklin.edu
From: kahlila@classof99.franklin.edu
Date: August 3, 1996 3:19 p.m.
Subject: thoughts?

Message:
hey lloyd,

sorry if i weirded you out last night. i guess everything is finally out in the open. i would've told you how i felt about your friend a long time ago, except i didn't want to put you in the middle. i still don't, so i guess i'll shut up now.

kahlila

To: robyn@classof99.franklin.edu
From: kahlila@classof99.franklin.edu
Date: August 3, 1996 5:38 p.m.
Subject: new developments

Message:
no word from dave. but an update on public opinion. i had lunch with j.t. and he's in complete agreement with you. i've been in the library with him all day since then, reading some of the magazine submissions for the institute. they're really good, actually.

but check this e-mail i got from lloyd. i know i shouldn't have done this, but i e-mailed him subtly (or not so subtly) feeling him out on the dave issue. here's his response:

>don't take this the wrong way, kahlila, but i just can't think about any of this right now.
>-lloyd

now i'm thinking one of two things. 1) he knows that i'm about to get dissed and doesn't have the heart to tell me. 2) he's upset about something else.

believe it or not, i'm leaning towards #2. and i know you're gonna say i'm insane, but i think he's upset that you're in atlanta. we can discuss this when you get back, but i have this weird feeling that lloyd likes you. he played this song for me the other day and it was clearly for someone he has really strong feelings towards, and as i'm putting more and more pieces together . . . you're definitely that person.

anyhow, i'm gonna run home and check on the students. j.t. is gonna spend the night in your room tonight, to insure that i don't fold and contact mr. robinson. i'll e-mail you tomorrow.

luv
kahli

To: robyn@classof99.franklin.edu
From: kahlila@classof99.franklin.edu
Date: August 4, 1996 4:02 p.m.
Subject: it's me (fwd)

Message:
okay, robyn–you're probably on your way back here as i'm sending this. and i'm probably a big traitor for forwarding you his message to me but i'm bursting and i have to share,

even if only electronically. you're the only person i'm sending this to (j.t. read it over my shoulder already; he's still at our place). i just got this from dave about three minutes ago:

>kahli,

>

>i appreciate your giving me some time to sort some things out before further proceeding. thank you for not pressing for instantaneous answers. like i've always said, you are mature beyond your years.

>

>but i have kept you in the dark long enough, and don't think for a moment that this hasn't been all that i've been thinking about for the past two days.

>

>let me get to the point. friday night was this eruption of feelings i'd kept inside for a long time. now that they're out, i can't suppress them. i want a chance to explore things with you further, beyond friendship. things between joy and me are over. please don't ask for details. they're painful and unnecessary to rehash.

>

>i'm sorry that i'm being a punk, conveying all this over e-mail. but suddenly i feel really nervous about talking to you, like i'm back in grade school or something. don't write back. i'll just see you tomorrow. i hope you'll allow me to greet you with a kiss.

>

>dave

CHAPTER FOURTEEN

With that one e-mail from Dave, it became official. Dave and Kahlila. It spread like wildfire. During lunchtime on Monday, one of the students at the Institute had spotted them holding hands. By study hall, it was all anyone was talking about.

"I knew it! I saw it building up all summer," said Latisha wisely.

"Whatever, Tish. We all saw it at the dance. They were so adorable when they were dancing!" Nikki said in a daydreamy tone.

"Well I, for one, am not happy about it," said Raheem. "Dave's steppin' on my toes! As soon as this Institute was over, Kahli was gonna be my woman. She just didn't know it yet." He reached over to give his boys a few pounds as everyone doubled over in laughter.

Robyn watched them all talking from the doorway of the library. She'd been smiling when the conversation first began, but the kids suddenly became a little blurry. That's when she realized she had tears in her eyes. *Damn it, I can't let the kids see me like this.* She quickly turned to run to the bathroom and she walked straight into Lloyd's chest.

"Whoa!" Lloyd exclaimed, grabbing her by the arms. "Where are you going in such a . . . Robyn? What's wrong?"

It was all Robyn needed–a face wearing a truly concerned expression. She'd held it in long enough, and she knew that the moment had come to break down. She buried her face in Lloyd's chest and cried.

Lloyd was thoroughly thrown, but he tried to think rationally. He knew that Robyn wouldn't want the kids to see her crying, so he tried to lead her away from the room as he hugged her.

Then he attempted to figure out her motivation for crying. Friends? Family? Boyfriend? *Wait, didn't she go to Atlanta this weekend?*

"Is this about Jason?" he asked gently.

Robyn was sobbing too hard to answer verbally, but he felt her head nodding up and down on his chest. He led her into a seminar room and they sat down. He gave her a few moments to wipe her eyes, sniffle, and breathe. He knew a story was coming, and sure enough, it was.

"So I went down to Atlanta this weekend to surprise Jason. He'd been so busy with his internship, I thought he'd appreciate the visit. I called him when I got on campus, and I could tell right away that it wasn't gonna be a good visit. He sounded . . . weird. When I got to his dorm room, it wasn't how it usually is between us. He was being so distant. I tried to chalk it up to his being stressed with his job, but that wasn't it. We were pretty much just existing in the same space.

"Saturday afternoon, I got an e-mail from Kahli updating me on these new Dave developments. I told Jason, thinking he'd be all excited for Kahli. But he was barely listening to my story. Just then, there was a knock on the door. Jason didn't answer it. 'Aren't you gonna answer it?' I asked him. He told me to just ignore it, that it was probably another intern bothering him about work.

"But the person kept knocking. And it sounded like that angry kind of knock. Then I hear her voice: 'Open the door, Jason!'"

Lloyd sighed. He suddenly saw where this story was headed.

"So he has no choice at this point but to open the door. As soon as he turns the knob, this girl's pushing her way inside, walking all up in my face! Talking about, 'So this is your girl, huh? The one that you supposedly deaded it with last month? You're full of shit, Jason.'

"Lloyd, I didn't know who to direct my anger at. Her, for acting all ghetto and trifling up in my face, or him for making ME feel like the other woman. I guess I decided on him, because before I even knew what I was doing, I was pounding on Jason with my fists. He was trying to grab my arms, and the girl–I later found out her name is Monica–just laughed as she left the room. She kind of reminded me of Shannon, our old roommate, the way she was so damn evil.

"He finally let me beat on him a little bit, but it didn't help. I just collapsed on the bed crying. At first, all my yelling had to do with how stupid he made me look. But then I realized that my looking like the dumb girlfriend was only the tip of the iceberg. I mean, I'd planned to marry this guy. We'd named our kids already. Now, none of that's gonna happen. My future is completely unplanned without Jason. He changed my entire life by messing with this girl."

Lloyd listened carefully, processing her words thoroughly before responding. "So why is that bad, Robyn? I understand that you're hurting more than you ever have right now, and forgiving him clearly isn't an option for you."

"You got that right. Four years, and he still wants to cheat? What type of life am I gonna have with a guy like that?"

"That makes a lot of sense. But what you said about your future . . . Robyn, you're how old?"

"Eighteen," she answered softly, a bit embarrassed by the low number.

"Eighteen. Your future should not be written already. It should be a book full of pages with no writing. Remember that. I know it's hard, 'cuz I have a hard time thinking that way myself. But it's true."

"I hear that. But you know what else I was thinking? I deserve this shit. Here I was, all gung ho about Dave and Kahlila getting together, not even thinking about Joy's feelings. Does anyone know how she's doing right now? She probably feels a lot like I do . . ."

"Robyn," Lloyd began, but didn't quite know how to finish. She had a good point. Dave hadn't mentioned Joy at all to him since the night of the dance, and Lloyd wasn't about to ask him. All he could muster was, "Things will look up. I promise. And if you need to talk, I'm here."

She looked at him intently. "You know that works both ways,

Lloyd. If you need to talk . . . I mean, I know it hasn't been easy for you, watching the two new lovebirds flitting around campus, and soon your apartment."

"What do you mean?" he asked without blinking.

"You can stop playing the role, Lloyd. It did take me a second, but I know how you feel about Kahli. It finally clicked when we were cleaning up after the party. Excuse my language, but you were looking hurt the fuck up. And then Kahli was saying to me how you didn't seem too amped about her and Dave . . ."

"You haven't said anything to her, have you?"

"No, of course not. In fact, she's invented her own explanation for the whole thing. Are you ready for this one?" She managed her first smile of the day.

"Tell me."

"She thinks you're in love with me, and you were salty this weekend because I was in Atlanta visiting Jason." She paused, waiting for his reaction.

"Shut up," he said in disbelief.

She laughed. "And when I tell her about Jason, it's only gonna get worse. She'll be all gassed to hook us up. That way she can start planning the double wedding."

At the sound of the word "wedding," Lloyd's heart sank even further. Robyn put her arm around him, and they walked back to study hall. It would have been difficult for the kids to tell which person was providing support for the other.

full emptiness

you reach your fingers
so deep inside my soul
massage my insides
tickle my essence

then
once the feel of you
consuming me becomes comfortable
you yank your hand out
leaving me barren.

CHAPTER FIFTEEN

Kahli and Dave decided to take a night off from seeing each other. Dave wanted to work on tightening up the notes he'd been writing about the Institute, and Kahli needed to do a final edit of the students' submissions for their magazine. Plus, she wanted to spend some alone time with Robyn.

When Kahli learned about Jason and Robyn's break up, she felt absolutely terrible. Here she'd been, chasing Robyn down with stories of newfound romance, and meanwhile Robyn's world had been falling apart. It had been a week since then, and most of Kahli's social time in that week was spent at Dave's apartment. Sometimes it was just the two of them hanging out, but more often Lloyd and Robyn joined the party, making a fun foursome. It was the perfect balance: Kahli knew Robyn needed her friends more than ever, and she also knew that spending time with Dave was a must.

Their most hilarious evening was when they tried their hand at gourmet cooking. Between the four of them, their most ambitious domestic efforts to date included pasta, pancakes, and chicken breasts. But they daringly boiled lobsters, baked casseroles, and whipped souflees. Most of their concoctions had fallen flat, but the jokes were plentiful and the smiles abundant.

Kahli had hatched a plan to get Lloyd and Robyn together, but she didn't want to push it too much right away. Robyn needed a little time being single before she rushed into a new relationship. She knew that Robyn was still hurting and she decided to take her out for drinks tonight, without the guys.

She was ready to leave for the bar, but Robyn wanted to get in another half hour of studying. Her Orgo final was rapidly approaching. Kahli looked around the room for things to occupy her until it was time to leave. She noticed her journal poking out from under her bed. It had been abandoned that past week. She'd been having too much fun to pause and record it all.

She picked it up and flipped through it. For the past few months, many of her entries had been addressed to Dave. She didn't know why; she had no plans of ever showing him her words, but an invisible audience made expressing herself easier.

-How do I resolve this problem–I have these feelings for you and they're not going away. I know you're with someone else and I understand that you're trying make it work. But I don't believe that you're happy. If I did, I might be able to write you off as a lost cause. But as much as you try to remain a closed book, I think I know you fairly well, and you don't seem happy to me. You seem like someone who feels as if he has no other choice but comfort and stability, so you're just going to go with it.

-What are you feeling when I touch your hand or get up to leave your apartment? Sometimes I think I know. Sometimes I wonder if you know how deep it is. Why am I not looking for a new guy to take Tarik's place? Why am I so excited about this upcoming summer job? Why do I lie awake so many nights? What would you do if you knew that the answer to all these questions is you?

-The smallest things give me satisfaction. Watching you from a distance helping someone after Hark's class. Hanging up after a good phone conversation. Getting an unexpected e-mail. It doesn't take much from you to make me happy. When we're talking and you look directly into my eyes, nothing else matters. Sometimes

Joy doesn't even matter. Sometimes I convince myself that we have something that you and her don't. But only sometimes.

-Now that the Institute has started, I'm seeing even more of your giving side. You feel the need to take care of everything and everybody. Who is taking care of you? I feel like you need just as much support as the people who you reach out to. There is nothing I want to do more than to give it to you. Supporting you and being proud of you makes me feel good.

-I just read the proposal for your dissertation. I love that you can write an essay where you put John Dewey and Malcom X together and it makes sense. I love that you even know who John Dewey is. I love your loyalty, even if it's the reason why you're not with me. I love that you're hesitant to let people in, because it makes it more special when you do decide to open up. I love that things matter to you—in a serious way. I love that you're socially conscious, and you're not afraid to act in order to make change.

-I feel like you're too good for me. I feel like I'm perfect for you. I feel like this will never happen. But I feel like it has to. Because where else will I find everything I ever wanted wrapped up into one person? If you came to me tomorrow and told me that I was the one you wanted, I would be so happy, but at the same time, I wouldn't be shocked. I think I'll be more surprised if I wake up one day and I'm fifty years old, and I don't know where you are or what you've been doing for the past quarter century. I don't know what to do if we never try.

Kahli shuddered as she finished her last entry, shocked by the fact that she was now living her greatest fantasy. But it didn't feel nearly as good as she thought it would. First, Joy was a forbidden topic between them. It couldn't be healthy to have taboo subject matter a week into their relationship.

Second, Kahli was frightened by the intensity of her own feelings. Although the past week with Dave had been better than a dream, she feared that her feelings about him were not completely reciprocated. Part of her knew that was crazy, considering the fact that he ended a five year relationship for her. But still, Robyn and J.T. kept reminding her not to push him about commitment. "He may just be all about having fun right now," Robyn warned. "You might still be young in his eyes," J.T. cautioned. "He may not see you as girlfriend potential just yet."

Their words echoed in her ears as she closed the journal. "Kahli," Robyn called from her bedroom. "You ready to go?"

"Yup," she shouted back. She wanted to call Dave and check in before they left, but she forced herself not to. She would listen to her friends. *I'm not gonna smother him. I'd rather give him a little space than lose him completely.*

As I Watch

by Rayna Boswell

I watch women watch me
when I am alone.
My confident walk
and eloquent talk
bring looks of approval
from passers by.
"A bright star," they say.
"She'll go far," they say.

I watch women watch me
when I have him
with me,
as I push his stroller
or fix his bottle.
Some look to shame me
with their gaze of condemnation.
Others remember when they
were the girl being watched
when they weren't alone.
And a tear may form
before they turn away,
trying to forget.

Women,
you who reproach me with your eyes,
you who pity me with your tears,
DON'T.
"I'll still go far," I say.
Amen.

CHAPTER SIXTEEN

J.T. and Dave went through their lifting routine in unusual quiet. They hadn't met up to work out since Dave and Kahli became Dave-n-Kahli. J.T. had been locked up in the library studying for his summer session finals, and Dave's schedule was off as the Institute was winding down and his free time was often occupied with Kahlila. Now that the men had finally gotten back into their ritual, there was a new tension. And it wasn't going away, even after tons were lifted and pounds of sweat were shed.

"So, I guess I'll be the one to break the code of silence," J.T. said with an uneasy smile. Dave knew what he was referring to before he continued. "So . . . Kal. You and Kal. I'm happy for you guys, man. I mean, it's about time, you know?

Dave grinned, relieved that the ice had finally been cracked. "Yeah, I know. It's been a long time coming . . ."

"But D," J.T. interrupted, "I just gotta say this. Kal told me that you know about how long she's had feelings for you and all that. I just want you to know that I was never working out with you just to get information for her. You know, acting as some kind of spy."

Dave burst out laughing. "Yo, that never even crossed my mind. But now that you mention it . . . sike. I'm just playin'."

"For real though," J.T. said, a furrow still in his brow, "Whatever happens between you two, I'm staying out of it. Unless you intentionally hurt her. Then I'll have to kick your ass." He forced a look of mock seriousness, and then suddenly switched back to his usual jovial self.

"Word. That sounds fair." They exchanged a pound and went back to the program. After a set of squats, Dave broke the silence.

"So is it out of order to ask you about the relationship between you and Kahli? Back in high school, I mean."

J.T.'s face was emotionless as he gave the question time to marinate. After a few moments, he placed the free weight he'd picked up back on the ground, and sat forward. Dave did the same. "What do you want to know?"

Dave gave the matter some consideration. "Why it ended. I'll be blunt. For a while, a long while, I thought you and Kahli still liked each other." J.T. motioned to interrupt, but Dave dismissed the effort with his hand. "I know it's not true now, but it's still strange to me. How two people who so clearly vibe and care for each other so much would decide not to be together . . ."

"We didn't decide," said J.T. plainly. "The decision was made for us."

Dave pondered the meaning of his statement. Did their parents force them to end it? No, that couldn't be. Kahli was always telling him about how much her mom loves J.T., and how Mr. Steinway just adores her to death.

J.T. continued before Dave could contemplate further. "We were fifteen. Trying to act as if people's opinions of us didn't matter. But they did, more than we knew." He hesitated. "Yo D, if I'm gonna tell you this you have to promise that nothing will get reported back to Kal. Most of this stuff she doesn't even know. I understand if you're not comfortable keeping secrets from her . . ."

"You got my word."

Satisfied, J.T. heaved a sigh before he resumed. "I was an athlete, cool with everybody. White, black–as long as you had game, you were my boy for real. So when shit started up with Kal, I didn't really think that much of it. I mean, I'm not gonna say that I didn't notice she was black. That would be stupid. But it just wasn't a big deal.

"So my teammates noticed us hanging out together after games–she was a cheerleader–and I started getting comments. From the white guys, it was shit like, 'Didn't know you had the fever, J.T.'

Now that shocked me 'cuz they used to talk about cute black girls all the time. They'd just never dated any.

"The black guys were saying stuff too. Little things: 'Yo J.T.–we only got like five fly honeys in the whole damn school. Why you gotta take 20% of our stock?" J.T. laughed despite himself as he thought back on the silliness of the statement, and Dave chuckled as well. "Anyhow, it was just comment after comment, every practice, every lunch period. It wasn't unbearable, but it got to me."

"Do you think Kahli was experiencing similar treatment?" asked Dave.

J.T. shook his head vigorously. "Definitely not. I can't really explain why, but people didn't stress her about it. But that's not to say she wasn't dealing with her own shit."

"With herself, you mean," Dave interjected.

"Exactly. I can't even pretend to know what being black at a mostly white school feels like, but it doesn't always feel good, I know that. And sometimes I could feel Kahli's discomfort around me, whether it was her eyes, her body language . . . I could just tell. And she was going through this whole image shift, too. The books she read, movies she saw, music–they started to change. And her friends got–well, browner. And here I was, the white boyfriend. You see what I'm saying?"

"No doubt," answered Dave, the situation becoming clear.

"But we stuck it out for a while because we really liked each other, and because neither of us wanted to be the first to mention the dreaded topic of race.

"Finally though, it all came to a head. I was in the locker room late one night, just me and my boy Dan. He was talkin' shit, as he's done since kindergarten. Somehow Kal got mixed into the conversation. He was like, 'I don't get how you're still with that black chick. I thought you were tryin' to get laid at first, but this has been goin' on too long. I mean, I know she's not your typical black girl. Like real dark skin and bushy hair and all that, but still. It's just not something you need to be doing when there are so many white girls who'll gladly give up the goods."

Dave closed his eyes, almost wishing he hadn't asked to hear the story. "So what'd you do?"

"Punched him. Fucked his jaw all up. Said see-ya-later to a dude I thought was a good friend."

"That took strength."

"Not really," J.T. admitted. "It was a reflex reaction. But I knew after that: I wouldn't always be able to be strong every time. And I wanted out. Luckily, I think Kal had reached her breaking point at that time also. We never discussed the issue; I never even told her about Dan. But we just began backing away from each other.

"Within a month, our relationship had completely changed form. She was suddenly my sister, my lil' homie. And everybody at school loved it! Thought it was cute as hell. It doesn't make sense."

"But when you think about it, it does," Dave said slowly. "Folks want to act like they're forward thinkers, good people at heart. But they can't erase what history taught their parents to hate. But anyhow–and you don't have to answer this if you don't want to–if Kahli were white . . ." He knew he didn't have to finish the question.

J.T. understood and exhaled. "I'd have probably put a ring on her finger by now."

It was fierce honestly, so fierce that it stung a little. But Dave was grateful for it. "So I guess it all worked out in my favor, huh?"

J.T. laughed. "Guess so, man." They picked up their free weights and resumed their routine.

I Know

by Latisha Davis

He is young, big, and black. You might see him in the early hours of morning on the upper level of the subway station any Monday, Tuesday, Wednesday, Thursday, or Friday. He is probably alone, his dark, dark eyes darting this way and that, and perhaps he catches your eye. You are staring. He is not very tall, but he is built, and those black baggy pants make him look even bigger. His pants match his jacket, which matches his skin, and he is scowling. Though it is warm, you shiver. His hair stands a foot high, proud, erect, rising above the crowds of people milling around the station. Yet he stands still, not a move, not even a twitch. You gape. Your gaze moves slowly to his eyes, which are huge and hypnotizing. You can tell that his eyes have never crinkled with laughter or shed a tear. The sun glints on his earring and you notice the huge gold ornamentation in his left ear, and the smaller one in his right. You shake your head in disgust and return your persecuting glare to those unfeeling eyes. He finally acknowledges your staring with a puzzled expression, and you turn away in fear.

Several others will notice him while he waits—sometimes for five minutes, sometimes for a half hour. You may think you know a lot about him from that quick glance. But you do not. I do. I should. He's my brother.

I know that he is waiting at the subway station for the carpool to take him to the upscale private school that he attends to have a headstart on college. I know that he is scowling because the carpool is late, as usual, and because he hates wearing dark colored pants to follow the school dress code. I know that he is too busy trying to get good grades in order to keep his scholarship to bother getting a haircut. And I've known his eyes both to crinkle and to well with water. I've seen him laugh at a story I tell for hours on end. And I've watched him try to hold in the giggles while his girlfriend's mom is calling him a "nice young man." I know that just a few days before you saw him, he was crying. Crying for a friend who had been shot four times by a group of guys dressed in white with short hair and naked ears. I know.

Sometimes when I'm walking the two blocks home from my bus stop, I approach a man wearing dark clothes and a solemn expression. I am tempted to cross the street in fear. But then I think of my brother and I relax. I keep walking. We pass each other. I know I'm safe.

CHAPTER SEVENTEEN

Kahlila looked around the house of Dr. Howard Harkonn as she absentmindedly stuffed Cajun chicken into her mouth. Hark's house was merely an extension of his office (or vice versa), his living room packed with books and loaded with unusual souvenirs from the most exotic places. She loved everything in his home, and loved being there. When Dave and Kahli were invited for dinner to look at the rough draft of the student magazine, they didn't know whether to tell Hark about their newfound relationship. They instead decided to let it speak for itself.

When they arrived on his steps, Dave was standing behind Kahlila with his hands on her waist. Hark merely lifted an eyebrow when he opened the door. He then introduced his wife in a tone that was clearly reserved for non-campus functions. It was softer, warmer.

His wife was a social worker at a residential program for boys. She used to be a history professor, but she explained her change of venue. "While Howard has managed to find satisfaction in university life, I hated it. My calling was elsewhere. Your Institute sounds absolutely amazing. How are you two enjoying the actual teaching experience?"

"It's really rewarding," said Dave, "although since I teach the kids desktop publishing, we don't get to have as much intellectual exploration as I would like. Kahlila does though, and the kids respond to her like she's been teaching for twenty years."

Kahlila flashed him a look of appreciation before modestly correcting him. "I think the kids were just waiting for a space where they could exchange and process ideas, and my classroom just happened to be it."

Hark had been frowning the entire conversation. "I'm sorry to interject here people, but what the hell is going on with you two?"

Kahli flushed red and Dave smiled. "What do you mean, Hark?"

"Are y'all dating or something?" The frown still present.

"Something like that," Kahli answered, looking smugly at Dave.

Hark burst into a rare grin. "Fabulous! I'll take all the credit at the wedding. Now let's eat."

During dinner, Kahli was quieter than she usually was around Hark and Dave. Normally, when the three of them were in a room, ideas were bouncing off walls faster than she had time to digest them. But this evening she wasn't interested in Hark's thoughts on improving urban education, or Dave's opinion of Franklin's role in the community.

She was staring at Hark and at his wife. His wife was beautiful, but understated. She sat back and watched her husband as he pontificated, inserting an occasional subtle yet brilliant comment when she felt it necessary. She was balancing her roles as host, mother, and wife with a grace that Kahli had never really seen, and Hark thanked her for her burden with an adoring gaze to which his wife seemed quite accustomed.

Kahlila wanted their life. She wanted the handsome, sensitive, intelligent husband who still managed to stay down to earth. She wanted the two beautiful children, and the adoring gaze.

And then she looked at Dave, who was looking back at her. The connection was brief, three seconds perhaps, but it racked Kahli's equilibrium. Her blood turned hot and her heart stuttered, and she suddenly felt catapulted into adulthood by the mere idea of there being potential for such happiness in her world. With Dave, even. And not happiness of the fleeting kind. Grown up happiness.

Dave and Kahlila decided to walk home. It was a beautiful night. They walked in contented quiet for several minutes before Kahli broke the silence. "Hark's a great father, isn't he?"

"Yeah. He is." A pause. "Why don't you tell me about your dad, Kahli?" Dave didn't know what motivated him to ask. Maybe it was that he felt as if he was getting to know her so well, but the deal with her dad was a subject that always went untouched. He knew that she didn't grow up with him, and he knew about the upcoming trip to Spain, but that was about it.

Kahli didn't look at him as she recounted the story. Instead, she told it as if she were reading a book report, or reciting a biography for Black History Month.

Sarju Rivers was born in England to an Indian woman and a black man from Trinidad. His mother's family disowned her when she had a black child. Sarju's father had gone back to the islands, and his mom was alone. Her family agreed to accept her back if she gave up Sarju for adoption. He lived in a foster home until age three, at which time he was adopted by a British family. They were very kind to him, and renamed him Sam, a name he went by until he reunited with his mother at age sixteen.

He never met his father, which Kahli thought should have inspired him to be a better father than he was. But then again, history does have a way of repeating itself. He came to the United States for college, where he met Kahlila's mom. By the time Kahli was born, he was back in London and they never heard a word from him until she was thirteen.

In those years he'd become a well known writer of travel books, and on Kahli's thirteenth birthday, he sent two tickets to Florence for a week in August. He'd arranged everything; Kahli and her mom stayed in a beautiful hotel, and he met them just one time for breakfast during the whole vacation. Since that time, every summer he sent them tickets to various countries, always meeting them for a few hours on each journey. It was bizarre, to say the least.

He never had any other children, and Kahlila would have felt better if he had. If he had another family, she could excuse his disinterest in her life. But he didn't. And that made the whole thing worse.

Sarju could never be pinned down to one location. Kahli didn't even know where he lived when he wasn't traveling. But he promised that he was going to make it to her high school graduation no matter what. He didn't. Kahlila hadn't spoken to him since. He sent a card of "explanation," but she never responded. Their trip to Spain would be their first communication in two years.

David was silent for a few minutes. It was strange, stranger than fiction. And he had questions, but was wary to ask them. She told the history of her father with such detachment; he didn't want to force her to feel the pain that she'd clearly pushed down deep inside. But he couldn't fight it anymore. He had to know.

"Kahli, don't get mad, but in your room, I've seen letters on your desk to your dad. I knew you weren't close, but I thought you at least talked to him."

Her eyes flashed with something for a moment, though he couldn't tell what it was. Anger? Embarrassment? Sadness? "I don't send those. It's just a journal, really. But I write my feelings best when I feel like I'm writing to someone."

"Oh," was all Dave could say, feeling an overwhelming desire to hold her hand, which he did. "So have you ever wondered what your life would be like if your dad had been around?"

"Sometimes I think about it. Like, I'll watch the Cosby Show reruns and just sweat Cliff Huxtable. He is the quintessential dad, with his crazy sweaters, love of peknuckle and penchant for hoagies. And the man was always home! He'd occasionally run out to deliver a baby, but he'd be back in time to teach Theo a lesson or to give Vanessa's boyfriend the third degree.

"Now that I'm older, I can watch Bill Cosby playing that role, and appreciate just that–the character he's playing. But before, it was much more than that. I wanted to be Rudy as he gave all her friends pony rides or as he held her by her feet trying to take off her snowsuit.

"I still feel a pang of jealousy though, when friends of mine take their Huxtable existences for granted. But then I have to remember–who lives a charmed life? J.T. has his dad, but barely remembers his mom. Same for Robyn. Dez has both her parents, but clearly she's not hunky dory. As a matter of fact, the only person I know personifying the American Dream . . . is you, Dave Robinson."

Dave nodded slowly. "I think about that a lot–how blessed I've been to have two parents who love me and love each other. Raised me and big sis in a boring peaceful Jersey suburb. I've gotten the best schooling, been extremely fortunate with the women I've dated," he paused to kiss her hand, "am in good health, have yet to deal with the death of a loved one . . . and that's when I start to feel guilty."

"For being blessed when others aren't?"

"No . . . for still feeling unsatisfied with my life."

Kahlila looked at him for a long time with an earnestness that almost made him feel uncomfortable. "Dave, you should not feel guilty. You want to do great things and you won't be fulfilled until you do. I'd be worried if the mere fact of being born into some degree of privilege was solely satisfying to you."

"True, but I don't know how much of my restlessness was a desire to make social change. If that were the case, how come I've been so at peace with myself since you've entered my life?"

"Because we're changing the world, Dave. We're training 15 kids to be the future leaders of America."

He laughed. "I don't know if we're changing the world Kahli, but you are definitely changing mine."

A Love Story
by an anonymous King Student

It all started innocently enough. We'd exchange brief gazes during Spanish class. Then we were partnered to practice conversation. *Hola*, he said. *Me llamo John*, he said. We started to hang out after school, sneaking of course. My parents would go crazy if they knew. Stolen kisses behind gigantic trees. On the cheek at first. But then . . .

I love him. But with him comes trouble. He's not my type. People wouldn't understand us being together. At the same time, it's hard living a lie. Claiming that we're just good friends, that I would never cross that line.

I inhale him, and he refreshes and contaminates my lungs at the same time. When I exhale, he fails to exit. He's seeped into the crevices in my brain. He's crept through my veins, reaching my heart and then gripping it, inducing a tortured beat. He is undetectable, invisible. But he is everywhere. The gas I breathe is strains of his eyes, his voice, his lips. I want him gone because he chokes me, but I can't survive without his presence. Sometimes I hold my breath but then I gasp hard, desperate for him. More of him enters me then, overtaking my previous perception of who I was and what comprised me. It's a toxic paradox–John as sustenance, John as poison. A dilemma greater than words, greater than air.

What are you thinking as you read this? Am I over dramatizing? Maybe you're thinking that my affair with John is sweet? A classic high school silly forbidden romance?

One more thing I forgot to mention. I'm a guy. Has the sweet turned sour?

Just recognize: your closed mind causes my heart ache.

CHAPTER EIGHTEEN

Friday night, Dave and Kahli decided to stay in. That afternoon had been the final day of the Summer Institute. That morning they had a little ceremony where each student got their plaque and stipend. It was touching; the kids made very thoughtful speeches and their families went crazy with photographs. Move-out was tomorrow. They knew they were in for a hectic morning, so they wanted to take it easy. Kahlila sat between Dave's legs on the bed as they listened to Groove Theory and as Dave tried to work out a kink in Kahli's neck.

"I knew I shouldn't have agreed to jump double dutch with the kids today," Kahlila said as she cocked her head to one side. They had an outdoor lunch after the "mini-graduation," and it had turned into a straight down-home cookout.

"Baby, only you could play a game strictly concerned with leg movement and still manage to hurt your neck," he replied, dodging a playful hit from Kahli.

He continued the massage as she cheerfully chatted about the kids and their drama. She then shifted to grown-up gossip, telling Dave her theory about Lloyd's crush on Robyn. Dave, wearing a smirk, listened silently, thoroughly amused at Kahli's soliloquy. She talked as if she'd been putting pieces together like she was Nancy Drew or something. Dave hadn't really noticed Lloyd showing Robyn any more attention than he even showed Kahli, but he thought it best not to argue. He instead concentrated on his fingers, kneading her collarbone and shoulders.

"Hmmm, that feels good," she purred.

"Really? How does this feel?" He scooted his body closer to

hers so that he could encircle her waist with his arms. He nestled his cheek into hers and breathed softly onto her neck.

In a flash, Kahlila was completely turned around, kneeling on either side of his legs, caressing his face with her palms. Something in her stomach welled up as she stared into his eyes and he stared back and neither blinked.

Seconds later, her legs were wrapped tightly around his body and they were caught up in a passionate kiss. But Kahlila couldn't stop smiling, her smile actually forcing her to pull back from the kiss.

"What's wrong?" Dave looked concerned as he held her face in his hands.

She paused before answering his question, as if she were considering whether to confess exactly what was on her mind. "It's funny—I've walked along the sandy white beaches of St. Thomas, ridden a mule to the top of Santorini, sampled wines in Napa Valley . . ."

"Kahli, are you rubbing in my face the fact that I've never been on a plane before?"

"Let me finish. What I'm saying is that of everywhere I've been, everything I've seen, you know what my favorite place is?"

"I don't even have a guess, sweetheart."

"This room. This bed. With you."

"What a coincidence. We share a favorite travel destination."

"I'd like to confirm my reservation, please."

"Baby, you're booked for as long as you want to stay."

They stayed in that position for a while, their bodies facing one another as their heads rested on each others' shoulders.

"I can't believe that summer is almost over," Dave murmured.

"Yeah. I talked to my mom today and she's gonna come down a few days before school starts to help me move into the new place. We'll come back together when I get back from Spain."

"Word? Moms is coming?" Dave jerked his head back.

"Yeah . . ." Kahlila eyed him warily, not sure of what was coming next.

"So . . . I get to meet her, right?"

Kahlila was rarely speechless. But hearing this man say that he wanted to meet the most important person in her life just ripped out any words in her throat that were even thinking about forming sound. *He doesn't just see me as a little girl. And he doesn't just see me as a fun, fleeting fling. He doesn't see me as anything less than what I view him to be . . .*

Her thoughts were carrying her away as Dave wiped a tear from her cheek with his finger. "Oh, Kahli . . ." he whispered softly.

David rocked her back and forth as she buried her head deep in his shoulder.

CHAPTER NINETEEN

Kahlila was checking her e-mail when she heard a knock at the door. She thought of who it might be as she ran to get it. Robyn possibly, if she forgot her keys. Maybe J.T. dropping by to tell her how his Biochem final went. If he was stopping by, it must mean that it either went really well or really . . .

My God. She wouldn't have guessed correctly in a million years. Standing in her doorway was Joy, and from the look on her face, she hadn't come to the wrong apartment.

"Sorry to come by unannounced. Can I talk to you?" Joy didn't sound angry, only tired.

Kahlila was still speechless, so she motioned for her to come in. She led Joy to the living room, a space that was never used. Kahli and Robyn always entertained company in their bedrooms, since the T.V.'s, stereos, and computers were there. Their living room, especially since it was only a summer residence, wasn't even decorated; the only objects adorning the room were a couch, a wooden chair, and a lamp–all of which came with the suite. Kahli was embarrassed at her blatantly collegiate lifestyle, but Joy seemed quite oblivious to her surroundings. She was focused on something more important. She sat on the wooden chair, Kahlila sitting opposite her on the couch.

"I'm gonna get right to it," Joy said, looking Kahlila right in the eyes. "I'm not here to cause drama . . . well, maybe I am. I want to know how you feel about David."

Kahli was relieved at the easy question. "I feel very strongly for him."

"Do you feel as much as I do for him?"

Kahli sighed. She should have known the questions would get

more difficult. "I guess I can't say. I don't know you, or what you feel."

"He's everything. He's my rock. I'm floating in space without him. All I'm saying is that if this is some exciting affair with an older guy for you, and that's all it is, let him go."

Let him go? "Joy, if he wants to leave, he can."

"Maybe he thinks I won't take him back after what he did, after the way he left it."

Kahli was tempted to ask exactly *how* Dave chose to end things, but she fought back the urge. "Well that's something for you to discuss with him, not with me."

"I'm talking to you because I thought that maybe you'd understand. Maybe you've been in love once and can know how I feel right now." She waited for Kahlila to respond, and when she didn't, she pressed on. "In a room full of people, I'm lonely for David. I don't think you understand."

"Joy, I do understand because I feel the same way about him."

Exasperation filled Joy's face and body as she dug her fingers into her hairline and pushed her bangs off her face. She stayed frozen in this position while Kahli tried her hardest not to stare.

Joy had a scar across her forehead about two inches long. It had clearly been deep, requiring many stiches. Now it was a fairly wide strip significantly lighter than her normal complexion. It wasn't ugly; it wasn't horrible. But something told Kahli that the circumstances behind it were both those things.

Suddenly Joy became aware of where Kahli's gaze was pinned. She combed down her bangs with her fingers and rose to leave.

"Look, forget I came, okay? I thought I could talk to you woman to woman. My mistake was forgetting you're just a little girl."

The insult barely registered with Kahlila. Her mind was still on Joy's face. *How long had she had the scar? Was she planning on hiding it forever? Why did she look so horrified that I saw it?*

Kahli found her voice and calmly replied. "No. You figured you'd try and catch me before I fell in love with him. Problem is, you're too late."

Joy walked out of Kahli's apartment without even closing the door behind her. Kahli wanted to close it but she couldn't move. *Joy can barely function without him.* Kahli felt for her, but there was nothing she could do. *Would I be any better if Dave broke up with me right now?* She forced herself to get that thought out of her head.

She instead focused on whether or not she would tell Dave about Joy's visit. That's what Joy wanted—for Dave to know that she was still pining away for him. She didn't want to give Joy the satisfaction. *But is that the real reason I'm considering keeping this from Dave?*

Deep down, Kahlila knew what she was afraid of. Maybe the fact that Joy still wanted him back was all Dave needed to hear. He might run back to her.

Kahli, you're truly an ass. That man is going nowhere. If you want a grown up relationship, act like an adult. Hide nothing. Share everything.

With long strides she walked to the front door and shut it. She went into her bedroom and dialed Dave's number. She mentally constructed her message while she waited for the tone.

"Hey baby. I know you're going out with Lloyd tonight, but come over afterwards. Please. I'll be up. We gotta talk. Bye, sweetie."

Dave listened to her story without interrupting. Joy's plea, her dramatic exit, the whole deal. He was moved, Kahli could tell. It hurt him to hear that people were fighting and hurting because of him. And he said that. "She's hurt too much because of me already."

"Joy?" Kahli asked, trying not to sound confrontational.

He knew he had to explain. It was time. "Kahli, there's something I haven't told you. Haven't told too many people, actually. And I need you to listen without interrupting."

She was already waiting in attentive silence with those pleading eyes that he adored so much. He took a deep breath.

"It was June of 94. We'd just graduated, me from Harvard and

Joy from B.C. I was so excited about coming to Franklin, you just don't know. I'd enjoyed my time in Boston, especially once I met Joy. But I was ready to move on. Joy and I hadn't really spoken about what she was gonna do that next year–Boston has a lot of good hospitals, and they were kinda sweatin' her, but she didn't seem like she really wanted to stay up there. I had this feeling that she was waiting for me to ask her to come with me to Franklin. But I wasn't ready for all that. I wanted my freedom.

"I knew that me and Joy had to have a serious conversation very soon, but my parents were up from Jersey, and my sister had flown up from North Carolina. They kept me busy around graduation time, which made it easy to put off telling her that I wanted to break up. I barely even introduced Joy to them. I tried to act like I just didn't have time, but I could tell that Joy knew. It was just that she'd never met my family before, so why have them meet when I was planning to end it anyhow? But Joy could always read me, and she was real quiet when I picked her up on graduation night to go out and celebrate with some friends of mine.

"We all went to a bar, a place I never went being that I didn't drink. But it was my last night seeing those cats, so I decided to stop by for a little while. Joy got a glass of wine, which she sometimes did. I noticed how quickly she relaxed once she started sipping. She seemed to be forgetting about the day's events, how hurt she'd felt when I kept my family away from her.

"I was jealous of her smile. She was just laughing, making small talk with my friends, having a good time. I couldn't enjoy myself. I knew I had to tell her that it was over. She needed to accept one of those jobs in Boston, or maybe go back to Seattle and find something there. I couldn't lead her on to think that she could come with me. I made up my mind to tell her that night.

"All my friends at the bar were having a ball, and they decided to do a couple of tequilla shots for old times' sake. I don't know why I took one. Maybe because I'd always wondered what the whole drinking hype was all about. Maybe because I wanted to have that same relaxed feeling that Joy had once she drank her wine. Maybe I needed a glass of courage to tell Joy how I really felt. Whatever the reason, I downed the shot with a lick of salt and a suck of lime. And that was it. We left soon after that.

"Joy was so quiet in the car. Her smile had disappeared as soon as we left my friends. It had begun to rain when we were at the bar. The roads were slippery. We weren't speaking to each other. The radio was off, and the car was silent. I looked over at her and she was looking back at me. Her eyes were so sad, they were begging me not to do what I was about to do. I wanted to look away but I couldn't. I never saw the curve in the road. Soon we were skidding and the tree stopped the car dead in its tracks.

"I had a driver's side air bag and walked away from the accident. Joy didn't. Her head smashed the windshield and she broke both her legs. That was the worst summer of my life. She was in the hospital for a month. I visited every day. She never blamed me. An angry word never came out of her mouth. And we never talked about what would have happened if the car hadn't skidded. I took care of her until her legs were out of the casts, and then she drove me down to Franklin. We got an apartment here together, and she got a job at the hospital in no time.

"This year, we decided that we needed a bit more space so we decided to live apart. But that's how we got where we were when you came into my life."

Kahli's thoughts were spinning away from her. She couldn't believe it. The story was something from a T.V. movie, not from real life. The life of her boyfriend, even. *And is he even my boyfriend?* She had so many questions, she didn't know where to begin.

"Damn. Did you have to go to court?"

"I had my license revoked for six months. They didn't really go buckwild about pressing serious charges because my blood alcohol level was still under the legal limit. Go figure. Not to mention that Joy was hardly cooperating with the investigators."

"It's so crazy, Dave. It's like, everything is a big mess but at the same time it's all so much clearer . . ."

"Like what?"

Kahli's words poured from her lips like gravy. "Like why you guys were together so long when you clearly weren't happy, and . . ."

"Hold up," Dave interrupted, sitting up straighter. "Who said we weren't happy?"

"I don't mean that you were miserable," she corrected herself hurriedly. "It's just that guilt can cause . . ."

"I wasn't with Joy out of guilt, Kahlila. I didn't tell you this whole story to explain why we stayed together. I wanted you to understand how deep our relationship is."

"Is?" Kahli's chest was pounding.

"Was. I mean was." He was silent for a moment. "Look, Kahli, you're young. You don't know a thing about serious relationships. I'm not saying that to hurt your feelings, but so you'll understand."

"Understand what?" she asked desperately.

"That feelings don't just vanish overnight. That love lingers. Isn't that what Joy was trying to say to you today?"

Kahlila's eyes were starting to burn. She knew that the stinging would stop if she just let herself cry, but she didn't want to give him any more ammunition to fuel his new "Kahli's a kid" theory. "David, do you want to be with Joy?" She tried not to show her fear, but her voice betrayed her with a crack.

Dave's voice rose in frustration. "Did I say I wanted to be with her? Don't put words in my mouth!" Finally, as he heard the volume of his words increase and as Robyn's bedroom door clicked shut, he recognized that things had gotten out of hand. He stood up from her bed. So did Kahlila.

"I'm sorry for getting loud," he said in an almost whisper.

"That's okay," Kahli's voice virtually inaudible.

"I'ma call you later." Dave walked out of her room and the apartment. Kahli's lips ached from the missing kiss goodbye.

CHAPTER TWENTY

Be logical. Approach this as you would any other problem. Figure pros and cons. Make a list, even. And that's what Dave decided to do. Not a list, really, but some preliminary notes on the issue. He sat at his desk, planner in hand, agonizing over his predicament in absurdly rational form. Hark had taught him about strength based models, solving problems by examining positives. He chose to approach this dilemma in that manner, jotting down only strengths that the two women possessed.

KAHLI—beautiful inside and out, common interests, intellectual, sense of humor, outgoing, confident. i feel alive when i'm with her. she makes me want to do more. become more. achieve more. people look at us when we walk down the street. we make strangers smile. not afraid to argue or disagree with me. i've found a level of passion with her that i've never known before.

JOY—the strangest, most fragile combination of strength and dependence. radiates with goodness. i complete joy; together we make sense. she gives a quiet support that elevates me as a person. she doesn't feel the need to be showy or to impress. loves unconditionally. nurturing. will make a great mother someday.

He stared at his notes. And stared. And stared. And then he wrote.

Kahlila lay on her back staring at the white low ceiling of her dorm room. She no longer had the urge to cry. Nor did she have the urge to move. She could lie there for hours. Which she did.

At midnight, Robyn passed Kahli's open door on the way to the bathroom, noticed her friend, and joined her on the bed. "I heard most of it," she admitted. "Wanna talk?"

"I don't wanna lose him, Robyn. What do I do?"

"Well, why do you think you might lose him?"

"Didn't you hear him today? 'Feelings don't disappear. Love lingers, Kahlila.'"

"True, but so what? I still love Jason. Would I get back with him? Hell no. The only reason you got over Tarik so fast is because you didn't love him. The rest of us are fucked up for months. Years, even."

"But I love Dave. I do. And I can't lose him."

"Have you told him? That you love him, I mean."

"Hello?!" Kahli exclaimed, sitting up. "Who's been the person telling me not to overwhelm him?"

"I know, I know. But things are different now. What if he's thinking about getting back with Joy just because he thinks she loves him more than anyone else could? I mean the girl rolled on you at your crib, asking you to leave him. That's some crazy stuff. You need to make it clear that you're just as crazy about him."

"So I just tell him. 'Dave, I love you?'"

"You say whatever you gotta say to keep him. You guys are right together." And with that, she got up and walked down the hall to the bathroom. When she passed the bedroom again, Kahlila was writing furiously.

8/19/96
Dave,

So . . . our first fight. It's late and I want to call but we can talk tomorrow. Just figured I'd get my thoughts down on paper so I wouldn't forget anything I wanted to say when I do see you.

First, I wanna apologize for thinking that I understood a situation that I couldn't possibly comprehend. You trusted me enough to tell me about the accident and instead of giving a listening ear I gave an earful of bullshit. I'm sorry. Though this is no excuse, I think I was feeling threatened by Joy's visit and wanted to diminish what you guys had.

As I think about that now, the notion of needing to belittle your and Joy's relationship to elevate ours, I of course feel like a complete idiot. I would be a fool not to recognize what the two of us have. We don't even have to say anything to each other to know. But even though we don't, I still plan to say exactly how I feel the next time I see you.

For now, I'll have to settle for lying here with all of my little memories of you and of us. Even though I miss you to death when you're not with me at night, I like to lie here in my bed sometimes and remember the kiss from earlier in the day, or the joke you told me last week, or the time you first looked at me and I saw exactly what you were thinking. I close my eyes and see you teaching your class. I feel you brushing my hair. I hear you whispering my name.

I used to lie in bed late at night and create these fabulous fairy tale fantasies about some perfect man and all of these adventures he would take me on. I don't need those anymore. And I know that when my memories lose their clarity and blur with the passing of time, I'll always have new ones to wrap around me in the dark.

Kahlila

CHAPTER TWENTY-ONE

Dave left a message on Kahli's voice mail telling her to come over at six o'clock the next day. She couldn't decipher his tone, but she'd already made up her mind that his tone didn't matter. She was going to declare her love at six p.m. and that was that. She was *not* going to lose him.

She missed the King students a lot that day. She longed for their chatter, their smiles, their frowns. They could have kept her occupied until that night. But they were back at their homes, enjoying the last two weeks of summer. She wouldn't see them again until the magazines were all printed and she went to King High School to distribute them. Would Dave go with her? Would they still be together in three weeks? She was leaving for Spain in a few days. What would that do to their suddenly fragile relationship?

Six o'clock at long last arrived. She stood at his doorstep like an abandoned puppy. He opened the door and took her in. He offered her food and drink, which she refused. They stood in the center of the living room. Her mouth was poised.

"I wrote you a letter," he said suddenly. "Just to get my thoughts on paper so I could say things exactly how I wanted to. But now I'm thinking that I can't say them verbally."

A letter? We were thinking alike. It must be a sign. Should I give him mine? It might be easier that just blurting everything out. She fished in her jacket pocket in hopes of finding the note. She felt the paper's folds with her fingers. She hadn't even remembered putting the letter there. *It's fate.*

"I wrote you one too," she responded anxiously, pulling out the white lined square. He looked at it inquisitively, slowly taking it from her extended hand. He then walked over to a corner of the living room to read it. He didn't give her his letter to read. But when she sat down on the couch, there was a piece of paper on the coffee table with her name on the top. She quickly took the sheet and began reading, while he read his from across the room.

Kahlila,

I'm writing because I don't wanna call this late at night and have this conversation but there are some things I need to say.

First, I'm truly sorry for the way I blew up today. You probably thought you were being helpful by offering your opinion about Joy. I just wasn't ready to hear anything about my relationship with Joy from you. I was ready to talk, but I wasn't ready to hear anything back.

While I wanted to apologize, the main reason I'm writing this is because I've been thinking about a lot of shit since you left my apartment.

After hours of sitting immobile at my desk, I realized this—I caused Joy more pain than she ever deserved. We weren't perfect, but I owed her a better explanation than the one I gave, which was practically nothing.

And it's not just about owing her something. I realized just how much I miss her. Just talking about her to you brought back how much we've been through. I don't know if I'm ready for it all to end. And if she's coming to your door asking you leave me alone, then apparently she isn't either. I'm sorry, Kahli. You are more special than you will ever know. But you deserve someone with a lot less baggage. I need to try and work things out with Joy. Understand that I'm not trying to hurt you. But it would just end up hurting more later when more time has passed and Joy still comes to me in my dreams.

Dave

They looked up from their pieces of paper and their eyes met, both pairs shocked and wounded.

Kahlila stood up from her seat and walked closer to Dave. She crumpled the letter very slowly and deliberately into a tight ball. She brought the fist that held the piece of paper way back, and then hurled it with all her might at his chest. So hard that her shoulder felt like it momentarily popped out of the socket. But her effort was in vain. The lightweight paper & ink ball softly patted Dave's shirt and fell to the floor. She'd wanted it to reach inside his ribcage, rip out his heart, and slash his vocal chords. Maybe then he could understand how she felt at this exact moment. She had no words to speak. Her only weapon had been that letter, and it failed her. Now her hands were empty, swinging useless by her side. There was nothing left to do except to turn around and walk out. She had no energy left to slam the door behind her.

She ran home. Maybe if she ran fast enough she would jolt out of this nightmare and everything would be the way it was two days ago. Her mind raced faster than her legs as raindrops began to spatter on the ground.

Coward. Was he gonna tell me face to face that he wanted Joy back, or was he gonna send me home to read that letter? And I was gonna gather the courage to tell this man I love him? No, wait. Don't feel bad. At least I was going to be honest. This fucking coward wrote me a full page of bullshit. He doesn't want Joy. He wants the safety and the comfort that she represents—someone who's going to stand by him in spite of anything. Doesn't he fucking know that I would do the same? This coward is afraid to wait and find out.

Or maybe not, Kal. Maybe you're the damn coward who's too scared to face the truth. You were just the break he needed before he committed to Joy forever. And that's all you were. My God, that hurts more than I thought it would. The truth hurts. I can't breathe. Maybe if I'd told him how I felt earlier, he would have changed his mind. Fuck it. Doesn't matter anyhow. What did Frost write? "Nothing gold can stay." Sounds about right. Joy comes to him in his dreams. More like his nightmares. He screams her name when he sits up suddenly in the middle of the night in a cold sweat. But when I lie awake after the sunrise watching him sleep peacefully, it's my name that he murmurs over and over.

seasons

summer's warmth
that glows your skin
and glistens your pores,
and summer's brightness
that blues the skies
and squints your eyes

can be as cold and dark
as late november nights.

for loneliness transcends all seasons.

tossing and turning
in bed mid-august,
even the sweat
can make you shiver.

CHAPTER TWENTY-TWO

Dave walked purposefully across damp grass and slicked pavement, concentrating on his destination. Joy. The one who stood timidly outside that horrible poetry lounge. The one who spent so many more hours a week than she had to on her hospital rotations in college because of all the lonely patients who loved her company. The one who still buys treats for the children at the hospital and wears a smile even after a day of changing bedpans. The one who wiped his eyes as he sat on *her* hospital bed crying, begging for her forgiveness and wishing that it was him who had gotten hurt instead of her. The one who changed her life plans for him. The one who knows the exact spot on his back to massage after he plays ball. The one who has nicknames for most of his body parts. The one who knows every one of his favorite foods. The one. . . .

He reached her door and knocked on it hard. The walk had done him good. Thinking about all of those memories reminded him why he was at Joy's door and not anywhere else. Joy opened the door and stared. Dave was soaked, his windbreaker providing little protection from the downpour outside. She motioned for him to come inside. As they stood just inside the door to her apartment, she unzipped the jacket and took it off for him. She hung it on the coat rack and walked into her bedroom to get one of his old t-shirts for him to put on. When she came back with one, he was standing in the exact same spot. She tossed him the shirt and sat on the couch, looking in the opposite direction as he took off his wet shirt and put on the dry one. When she couldn't take it anymore and had to look at him again, there was a tear in the corner of his left eye.

He hadn't spoken a word yet. Neither had she. But she knew why he was at her door, and he knew that she knew. Joy had planned everything she wanted to say to him if she was ever presented with the chance to take him back. Her mind raced as she tried to figure out where to start. Should she address the fact that he was willing to throw away five years with her for five months of knowing Kahlila? Or that he never even had the decency to express his doubts until he was ready to leave? Should she talk about her pain—that she hasn't slept through the night for two weeks, that she cries at work, that she considered moving back out west to her family? Or maybe she should make *him* talk—ask him what his feelings were for that little girl exactly. Ask him what she had that made him leave.

Her mouth was poised, ready to attack him with a slew of insults and inquisitions. He reached up to his eye to catch the water. Joy found her voice.

"I missed you. Oh God, I missed you David."

He joined her on the couch and took her in his arms. She'd been crying into that t-shirt she gave him for weeks, only half believing that he might one day wear it again.

PART THREE

CHAPTER ONE

Angela Bradford had just pulled away from Booker T. Washington House, the long trip home on 95 North awaiting her. Kahli waved from the sidewalk fighting back the tears. Her mind had been occupied during the two days that her mom had been there. They'd unpacked her things, decorated her room, explored new restaurants–kept as busy as humanly possible. But now she was gone and Kahli was alone until Robyn returned from L.A. the next day.

She turned to go back into the dorm, but changed her mind and started walking toward the campus green. She looked down at her bronzed bare legs as they strode the pavement. She imagined what passers by were seeing when they looked at her. Skin glowing from the Spanish sun, hair wild and curly, curves enhanced from two weeks of fattening foods. Eyes sad.

She tried to fancy herself as a tragic fictional character. Some lovely woman tortured by heartache. Perhaps Janie from *Their Eyes Were Watching God.* Yes, she was Janie as she returned to her hometown after Tea Cake, the love of her life, was killed. But Dave wasn't dead. He'd just decided that he didn't want her anymore. She quickly abandoned the literary comparison.

Think happy thoughts, Kal. Spain. That was definitely a pleasant memory. As one man exited her life, another entered. She met her dad at the airport in Madrid, and things had been awkward until dinnertime. Something during the meal had caused her to think of Dave. Maybe it was the food, since Dave loved spicy dishes. More likely it was probably nothing more significant than her loving him and not being able to exorcise him from her mind. She couldn't remember. Something triggered it, and she just snapped.

She started bawling over her plate of paella, much to her father's alarm.

They talked all night–about Dave, about love, and most importantly, about the two of them. Father and daughter. Strangers. There were pounds of tears shed and profuse apologies uttered and they woke up the next day refreshed and ready to begin a new chapter.

Kahli smiled. The walk had done her good and she was ready to face the empty apartment. She turned dead in her tracks and walked right into a gray t-shirt with a chiseled chest beneath it. She didn't even have to look up; she knew the feel anywhere. "Tarik," she stated in a monotone.

The sight of Kahlila caused a ripple in Tarik's stomach. He hadn't seen her since early May, although he stared at her picture all summer. It was a picture of the two of them on Valentine's Day. Robyn had made them pose despite protest, and they stood in front of the bathroom door, which was slightly ajar. It looked like a typical high school prom pose, except that a toilet and shower curtain substituted for the usual piano and balloons.

Tarik's name was all she managed to say, because as soon as he moved past the initial shock of running into her, he started talking. And talking. It was evident that he saw this as his golden opportunity to argue his case. And quite a case it was. Kahli only caught snippets as her mind drifted.

"You look gorgeous. I mean, you always did, but I've never seen your hair . . ."

"No excuse for what happened with Shannon . . ."

"Threw away the best thing that had ever . . ."

"Willing to start from scratch . . . take our time . . . won't rush you . . ."

Booker T. House was in plain view and Kahli wanted to finish this conversation before he asked to take it inside. It was clear that she would have to interrupt if she wanted to get a word in. "Tarik, listen to me," she said commandingly, grabbing his arm and halting mid-step.

She took advantage of his startled silence. "I completely forgive you for last semester." It hurt her to see the look of sheer joy on his face, knowing that his expression would soon change. "I forgive you because I feel as if it was partly my fault." His look turned questioning as she continued. "I'm not saying that I drove you to sleep with Shannon, but I am saying that my heart wasn't in the relationship. Yours was. And that wasn't fair."

Tarik's eyes were wounded as he spoke. "So where was your heart, Kahli, if it wasn't with me?"

Kahli looked down and began to ramble. She told him everything. The crush on turning to love, the brief relationship, the confusing end, the remaining pain. When she finished, she looked up to meet a look of anger, hurt, and perplexity.

"I know that look, Tarik," she said sympathetically. "I've been feeling it every day for weeks."

He nodded, understanding although he didn't want to.

"But hey," she said more brightly, "La Vie C'est La Vie."

"Huh?" Tarik was lost.

"N'ah. Never mind. It's a poem I thought of that just made sense to me at this moment." She thought for a second, and then asked impulsively, "Do you want to come in? There's no reason why we can't be friends."

"Yeah there is," he quickly responded. "Because I don't want that. Friendship is not what I need from you. I guess I should have known I wasn't gonna win in all this. Dez warned me . . ."

Desiree. Kahli hadn't even thought about her since her return to campus. She was suddenly overwhelmed with a desire to see her. "You spoke to Desiree? When?"

"I saw her yesterday. She seems much better. We talked for a minute about you and about Trevor . . ."

"Trevor? What about him?"

"I just told her how I cut him off once he told me about everything. I mean, me and Trev go way back, but I can't be boys with no nigga who ain't gonna support his girl when things get rough. From the way he told it to me, it was almost like that asshole took pride in the fact that he just wrote her a check and then wrote her off . . ."

A check? Why would Trevor be giving Desiree money? "Shit. Oh my God. I'm sorry, Tarik. I gotta go. Do you know where Desiree's apartment is?"

He quickly realized what just happened. She hadn't known. Desiree hadn't told her. "Yeah. Highland Court. Her name's listed on the outside door."

She was running before he even finished. She yelled a thank you over her back and tore down campus.

CHAPTER TWO

Kahli pressed the bell over and over again. She was breathless from running and teary from the thought of it. How could she have been so dense? It all made sense. Desiree was pregnant. Desiree was pregnant.

And suddenly, Desiree stood before her. Everything flooded Kahlila at once. Her selfishness, focusing on Tarik and Shannon last semester. Putting Dez out of her mind during the summertime because she was having such a great time with Dave. She deserved no kindness whatsoever, but there was Desiree with a smile. She couldn't remember the last time she'd seen her smile. When she outstretched her arms, Kahli collapsed into them and cried. And they stood there in the doorway sobbing, the months and months of tension and silence washing away as cars drove by and people walked past them.

"I know," was all Kahlila could say when they finally went inside Desiree's apartment and sat down on the bed.

Desiree looked relieved. "Good. I wouldn't have known how to say it anyhow."

Kahli was unsure of what to say next. "Do you wanna talk about it?"

"I thought Trevor might have been the one. I really did. When this happened, I wasn't even all that scared or traumatized. If I was, I probably would have broken down and told you. But I was all composed, taking the issue to him so we could discuss the next steps." Her voice starting breaking.

"It was worse than I could have ever imagined. He became so cold, so unfeeling. He was a different person. He questioned if it was his, Kahlila. Damn it if I didn't feel like the star of an after-school special." She forced a smile. "I didn't sleep that first night after I told him. I got out my journal and wrote and wrote."

"I didn't even know you kept a journal," Kahlila murmured.

"There's a lot you don't know about me." There was no anger in her voice, and no bitterness. She was merely stating a truth, and all Kahlila could do was nod.

"So what did you write about?" She suddenly longed to fill in all the missing pieces of Desiree's persona.

"I made a list. Not a pro or con list. Not a list of options. Nothing like that. I made a list of things that Trevor never said to me. If he'd said even one of these things, I might have felt like I could have gone through with it."

"Having the baby?" *Oh God, I shouldn't have said "baby."*

"Yeah," Desiree replied in an almost whisper. She got off her bed, hoisted up her mattress, and took out a large tattered sketchbook with a solid black cover. As she repositioned herself on the bed, she flipped through the pages, clearly looking for something.

Kahlila stared. Photograph collages, lines arranged into poems, light sketches in pencil, all flashed quickly before her eyes as the pages turned. She was still staring when Desiree placed the book in her hands. Kahlila shifted her gaze downward and began reading the words on the page.

-You are so smart.
-Whatever you decide, I'm right here to support you.
-I knew you were special the first time I saw you.
-It wasn't just sex to me.

"It *was* just sex to him, though. He'd wined and dined me until I finally caved in on Valentine's Day, and then he was done," she said, taking back her book and leafing through the pages some more.

"I feel horrible that I never even gave you the room to tell me the truth about what happened that night." Kahli closed her eyes, remembering the naïve e-mail she'd sent Dez all those months ago.

"I just felt like you'd think I was being a skank if you knew I slept with him after a month. And I definitely felt like you'd judge me if you knew about the pregnancy. Especially once I decided to . . . well, not to, I should say. I struggled though, sitting in this room and writing everything I felt." She turned to the back of her sketchbook and pulled out a piece of folded paper stuck between two pages, and handed it to Kahli.

heart heavy with emptiness
belly full with life

the guilt of altering nature
or the burden of a lifetime reminder . . .

which will swallow me whole?

"Kahli, I walked around with the poem in my pocket for a week. Clearly you know what I decided. I decided to be selfish. To make it easier on myself. Trevor hurt me, and now I was supposed to muster up all the love I had left to give to a little person? I decided that would be too much effort for someone as selfish as me . . ." She couldn't continue. She covered her face with her hands.

"Desi, no. I won't let you do that to yourself. There is no easy way out in a situation like this. And being selfish? Well, I guess you could look at it that way. But we're young. We're allowed to be selfish. And who's to say that the other decision wouldn't have been selfish. I mean, are you really ready for that kind of responsibility?"

"Damn Kahli, you sound like my mom."

"So you told her?"

"Yeah. After it was all over. She couldn't believe I went through it by myself."

"I can't either."

"I didn't want to. Sometimes I was so close to running into your bedroom and telling you everything. But then I'd think about it some more, and I wouldn't let myself."

"But why, Dez?"

"Because it would just confirm it."

"Confirm what?"

"That you were better than me. You were smarter, more responsible, the good one. The golden child, or the copper child I should say." She bitterly smiled again, looking at Kahlila's skin that was even more bronzed than usual.

Kahlila's jaw dropped. "I can't believe this. You honestly felt like that? Desiree, do you know how many times we stood next to each other in front of the mirror, getting ready to go somewhere, and I just wished I could look like you? Have your confidence? Have that magnetism that would make guys fall to their knees?"

"See, that's just it!" Desiree protested. "It's always about that. Yeah, guys like light skin and long hair. So what? Do they ever ask me about James Baldwin or call me the epitome of class?"

Kahlila was baffled for a moment by the reference, until memories of Michael on New Year's Eve came flooding back. *Wow. Lloyd had been right after all.* "Dez, you're more than a pretty face. You know that."

"Maybe *I* know it, yes. But do you? Did you know that I wrote a poem late that New Year's night once you went to sleep? Did you know I got funded to take a writing class at Hopkins this summer? Did you know that Trevor is only the third guy I've been with?" Her eyes were beginning to moisten.

"That's not fair, Dez! You never shared any of that with me. You drew a picture of yourself and let me color it in any way I wanted. Dez is the one who hates school, who loves men. Kahli is the one . . ."

"Kahli is America's sweetheart," Desiree finished. "Loves school, turns bad boys into gentlemen, works with kids . . ."

"Whatever, Dez. Kahli is also boring. Dull. Predictable. Dispensable."

"Hey," Desiree said, wiping her eyes, "I'll trade you. No problem!"

Kahlila smiled. "Deal."

Desiree's eyes suddenly clouded with confusion. "Wait a minute, though. What do you mean, you're dispensable? You have to understand that I never meant to throw away our friendship."

"I know that, hon. I was more talking about the fact that I got dumped by my first real love."

"What?!" Desiree was incredulous. "You can't honestly think that you loved Tarik. You barely even wanted him when you had him. And to refresh your memory, he may have cheated, but *you* dumped him, remember?"

"True," Kahli smirked, "but I wasn't talking about Tarik."

Desiree's eyes glistened with intrigue and residue sadness. "Girl. What the hell did I miss this summer?"

And so Kahlila recounted tales of Fugees concerts, school dances, late night conversations, confrontations with ex-girlfriends, and sheer heartbreak. They giggled and sniffled as Kahli shared the details of what she thought was to be forever and as Desiree read poems from her sketchbook.

It was five o'clock in the morning when Dez made up the couch for Kahli to go to sleep. "You know what, Kahli?"

"What, hon?"

"Maybe we did switch places tonight. I'm the intellectual, reading my poems. And you're the hoochie, talking about your hot affair with your T.A! I could get used to this."

Kahli smiled a tired smile. "So could I. Good night."

"Good night."

CHAPTER THREE

Lloyd knew he was a glutton for punishment for doing it. He hadn't even told Robyn when he made the decision. But it was something he knew he had to do. He was going to tell Kahlila the truth about his feelings for her.

Maybe the timing wasn't right. She was still reeling from the drama with Dave, and she was stressed about declaring her major. *But is the timing ever right with us?* He was tired of waiting. The time was now.

One thing giving him pause was how Dave might react to Lloyd's getting involved with Kahli. But he consoled himself with the fact that Dave pretty much abandoned all claims on her when he discarded her with no warning.

Then he told himself that it didn't matter if Dave would get upset about Lloyd's feelings for Kahli, because Dave would never know. It wasn't like Kahli was going to reciprocate them. He was going to get played. But he had to do it, just to know that he tried. He couldn't live knowing that he never put it out there. *For God's sake, the girl has spent the past two months thinking I'm in love with her roommate.*

Since Kahli returned from Spain, Lloyd had to overcome his bitterness towards Booker T. Washington house. That was where she and Robyn lived, and it wasn't like they could come to Lloyd and Dave's apartment anymore. That happy foursome had abruptly crumbled. So two weeks into the school year, he sat on the chair in Kahli's room, on the verge of confessing his love. Robyn was at a pre-med society meeting, and Lloyd knew he had at least a few hours of alone time.

He decided to test the waters before diving head first. "I don't know if this is gonna upset you, but Dave wanted me to tell you that he sent the magazine to the printer yesterday."

"Oh my goodness, Lloyd. I am getting a bit tired of people tip-toeing around me when it comes to Dave Robinson. I mean, we worked together. Our paths will inevitably cross. I can't pretend he doesn't exist, nor can I mourn his loss forever. So from now on, if possible, please refrain from the using the piteous tone whenever you mention your boy. Understand?"

Lloyd understood. He got it in the way that one catches a cool breeze on a stiflingly still day. Her words washed over him and he felt rejuvenated. He was hearing her say that Dave was no longer her focus, her raison d'etre. And he had to take advantage of this line of thinking. She hadn't thought this way about Dave since he'd known her. *It could make all the difference.*

"Understood. So let's change the subject altogether. Tell me about the Flamenco dancing you saw in Spain."

She shrugged. "Not much to tell, really. Beautiful women in beautiful costumes, clapping out complicated rhythms with castanets."

This was the moment–for him to tell her that he could write a song about her in Seville: Kahlila the Flamenco Dancer. Her hair pulled back so tight that her eyes slant up, slicked so shiny that he can see his own awed reflection. Her cheeks painted crimson, her lips smeared with red and lined with black. Her body encased in satiny rainbow colors as it gracefully swirls from side to side, altering the patterns in her dress. Her castanets sounding a playful beat while her high heels stomp out a hypnotizing bass, causing her audience to stare with dazed smiles. He wanted to tell her about the fire in his toes and the smoke rising up his legs, making him want to jump on stage right with her, fall into her step, grab her waist and spin her until she feels dizzy with happiness and can no longer remember past painful days pre-pretty polka dots.

The words were making their way to Lloyd's tongue, some rushing ahead and others straggling behind. When they were lined up in order at last, he opened his mouth to utter his vision . . .

"But you know what I remember about Spain the most?" Kahlila asked suddenly. "It wasn't the flamenco. It was the cork oak."

"The what?" Lloyd managed to respond.

"The cork oak. It's just like what it sounds: a tree used to make cork, like for wine bottles and bulletin boards. It's planted and left to grow for 20 years, completely unattended. Then, out of nowhere, man comes and peels the outer layer from the tree for his own purposes. The oak is left exposed, a bright white color. Soon it turns honey colored, to deep red, to a brownish black. Then when it starts looking like it once did, about six years later, someone else comes along and strips it again!"

Lloyd was half listening, staring at the stripes on her bedspread. They started to blur together as his mind turned, trying to make sense of what was happening. Did she really start this random rambling right when he was about to confess his feelings for her? Was she doing it on purpose?

"He stripped me, Lloyd," Kahlila cried, yanking him from his thoughts. Her face had been clear only seconds before, but now streams of tears were creating a road map on her face as they crisscrossed and intersected. "Bare. Opened me up, exposed my insides, and left. Left me in the forest naked–white and innocent." Her sobbing had reached the point where she couldn't continue speaking. But she quickly took a deep breath, exhaled, and continued.

"I guess eventually I'll get darker, hardened. And then six years from now, someone else will come along and strip me again." She began clearing the road map away and she wiped her face with the back of her hand.

He knew that he should hold her, stroke her hair and tell her that she was going to be okay, that she would grow strong again in time. But he didn't. He couldn't. He squeezed his own hands together tightly as Kahlila composed herself.

"I am so sorry, Lloyd," she sniffed, "for unloading on you like this. You must think I'm such a fool."

He finally got the strength to join her on the bed and place his hand on her shoulder. “Believe me, Kahlila. I understand more than you know.”

CHAPTER FOUR

"So let's find a bar so dark we forget who we are, and all the scars of the nevers and maybes die."

-RENT

Lloyd recounted his failed attempt at love on the phone with Robyn the next day.

"So she just started bawling right in front of you? Geez Louise, I'm sorry," said Robyn, trying to offer support and eat her Ramen noodles at the same time.

"It's all good. It was my last ditch effort. I'm done."

"You do realize that it's hilarious how you're done before you've even started. You never even told the girl how you felt."

"Why make things awkward for her? It would change things."

"You're probably right to call it quits. Not because you don't deserve her, but just because her heart's kinda occupied right now. You know how it is."

"True. Hey, how have you been holding up?"

"Barely. I could use a pick-me-upper."

"Idea–let's go get bent somewhere. Let the alcohol seep in, and the problems float out. What do you say?"

"I'm down."

Two drunk friends stumble into the guy's apartment. The guy's roommate isn't home. He sits on the couch while she turns on the stereo. She joins him on the couch. He places one leg in her lap. She takes off his shoes. His feet are funky. They laugh. She moves to get away from them, crawling up his body, resting on his chest. He comments on the smell of black women's hair–always the faint smell of hair grease. She says that hers must smell like smoke from the bar. He says it doesn't. She smells his, massaging her fingers through the wooly mass. Her face moves past his to return to his chest, but she doesn't make it. Their lips meet. Once they meet, they can't separate. Well, briefly, to explore other body parts: necks, shoulders, chests, arms. Always returning to the mouth. She wraps her legs around his waist. He hoists her off the couch and they take the adventure down the hallway. Her knee scrapes the wall on the trip. It hurts. They laugh. They reach the bedroom, where the remainder of their clothes come off, with the exception of his white socks. Frustration mounts as the urge to push the envelope increases. She volunteers a condom from her purse. He runs to the living room to get it, and returns in seconds flat. It's on now. Excitement builds. Sweat builds. Pain builds. Pleasure builds.

Then they lie exhausted, hot, reflective. Not about the act, but what drove them to it. And who they were trying to forget. He breaks the oppressive quiet. "What do you miss most about your life?" he asks. She feels the hot tears coming as she lets her mind rest on him. Not the him with his arms around her. The him with the hold on her soul. "It's okay to cry," he says. So she does. Silently. "We've hurt a lot these past few months, haven't we," says he softly. She answers that a middle aged angel is probably looking down at them, chuckling at their petty problems. Once silence sets in, she turns around and faces him. He kisses her forehead. It's the kiss of the evening she'll never forget.

CHAPTER FIVE

Classes had Dave and Lloyd stressed already, so they decided to head to a nearby bar and grille for a relaxing drink. For Dave, that meant a ginger ale, but he was still happy to get out of the house. Lately, his only visits out of the apartment were Joy's place and the library. He hadn't even dare hit the gym out of fear of seeing J.T. He'd never meant to break his promise.

"So what was up with Robyn leaving the apartment this morning? We didn't get a chance to talk about it." Dave had made a mental note to bring up this topic as soon as he had Lloyd alone. He couldn't believe it earlier that day when he saw Robyn walk into their bathroom wearing only a t-shirt. He flashed back to the several conversations he'd had with Kahli prophesizing Robyn's and Lloyd's eventual hook-up.

Lloyd knew the question was coming, and he had a prepared statement. "We're friends. That's it. You can't make something more than it is."

"I hear that, dawg. Sometimes playing with the line is ten times better than crossing it." He was tempted to say more, to ask more, but he stopped there. Lloyd appreciated Dave's brevity. He really didn't mind telling him what went down exactly, but he wanted to protect Robyn's privacy. It was one of those inexplicable, isolated incidents that never needed to be repeated, or even discussed.

They sat without speaking for a while, sipping on their drinks. Dave asked suddenly, "So you guys still talk, right? You and Kahli?"

"Yeah," Lloyd answered a bit defensively. *Don't tell me he's gonna ask me not to speak to her anymore.*

"Do me a favor? Just let me know how she's doing every once

in a while. I need to know that she's okay." He mumbled the last sentence, as if reluctant to admit his concern.

"Yeah, I'll do that. But why can't you inquire about her well being yourself?"

"You know I can't do that, man. I owe it to Joy to keep my word about not communicating with Kahli."

"Don't you think you owe *Kahli* anything?" His question was without accusation, a mere inquiry.

But something beneath the shine in Lloyd's eyes shamed David. *Isn't this supposed to be my boy? Where exactly is his loyalty these days?* "God damn, Lloyd!!" Dave whispered with as much fury as a whisper could contain. "You don't think I feel like shit? But what the hell am I supposed to do?"

It was the angriest Lloyd had ever heard him sound, but it didn't change Lloyd's demeanor whatsoever. He reached in his pocket for his wallet, pulled out a ten dollar bill, laid it on the table, and rose to leave. "Do what you gotta do, man." He began to walk towards the door, when he suddenly turned back around. Dave wasn't looking at him, but at his half empty glass of ginger ale.

He was still staring at his glass when he saw Lloyd's hand drop something on the table. A small white square sat on the brown wood surface, and again Lloyd turned and deserted the area.

David reached for the white square, his stomach anxious without his knowing why. Kahli's face greeted him as he flipped it over. The blue sky, the white beach, the green water–they were all gray and lifeless behind her stunning image. Her eyes were squinted as they fielded the burning yellow sun. They were the eyes that stared at him so many times in nothing short of adoration. Her mouth was closed; there was not even a hint of a smile. Her lips were even slightly pouting, calling to his memory the hundreds of kisses she'd managed to administer within those few short weeks. Her nose was wet, not from the perspiration of Spanish summer heat, but from the water that had just fallen from Dave's eye.

He reached in his wallet, found a companion for Lloyd's

bill, stuffed Kahli's visage into an empty compartment, and walked home.

He turned the key in the lock, wondering if he was going to run into his roommate before he went to sleep. Had they just had their first fight tonight? Part of him wanted to resolve it right away, but another part also wanted nothing more than to be alone in his room.

Lloyd was sitting on the living room couch with the keyboard balanced in his lap. It wasn't turned on, and he pressed notes into soundless chords. He began talking as soon as Dave walked in, almost as if he had been in conversation with himself before Dave entered.

"Don't fill a vase with flowers unless you plan to replace them when they die, D. Kahli was that vase, and you filled her up with all types of hopes, swelled her up with happiness she'd only dreamt about. Then you removed all of it. Simple as that. Once a vase gets perfect red roses, it can't go back to daisies and dandelions. It would rather stand empty, secretly praying that one day it will be deemed worthy enough to hold such beauty again. She's waiting, D. And you can't just leave her hanging."

David breathed in and out one long time before he walked any closer to his friend on the couch. As he took his steps, he went in his wallet and extracted the picture of Kahli. He put it down on the coffee table. "I hear everything you're saying, man. I hear you. I don't need this picture though. She's all up in my head regardless, you know what I'm sayin'? But you're a good friend, homes. To both of us."

They exchanged a pound, and with it sealed for Lloyd an understanding that Dave did know Lloyd's feelings for Kahlila after all. But Dave only knew them because he felt them himself.

CHAPTER SIX

"And let today embrace the past with remembrance and the future with longing."

-Kahil Gibran

Urban education. She'd done it. Invented her own major. Hark had helped her perfect the written proposal for the sociology department. As she met the undergraduate chair of the department to discuss the logistics, she hoped that she might run into Dave on her way out of the building. But she hadn't. She hadn't seen him at all since she walked out of his apartment one month before. Now she walked into her dorm trying to focus on her day's victory and erase her overwhelming feeling of disappointment.

Her heart stopped when she saw his handwriting. His child-like print was scrawled on a post-it, stuck to a magazine which had been slid under her door. The artwork on the front of the magazine was expertly drawn by Justin, a simple word in brilliant colors: TRUTH. For a moment she forgot Dave's note as she beamed with pride at her kids' finished product. But only for a moment. Her eyes refocused on the post-it:

Kahlila,

Sorry the printing took so long. I changed my submission at the last minute and held things up. I'll handle getting the copies to the kids.

Dave

"Well damn, Dave," she said out loud. "Can you sound any more distant?" She tossed the magazine, along with her body, onto her bed. Her gaze fell on the walls. The pictures on the walls stared back. *Me and Mom in Martha's Vineyard. Me and J.T. at his last high school basketball game. Me, Robyn, and Desiree on move-in day freshman year.*

Kahlila, alone with her two-dimensional memories, was surrounded by love.

She'd never realized it before, but she didn't even own a picture of Dave. But if she closed her eyes, her vision of him was clearer than any 35 millimeter could capture. Dave studiously taking notes in class. Dave in his suit, laughing with their kids in the middle of the multi-purpose room. Dave lying next to her sleeping.

Looking at the pictures in her bedroom, Kahlila could detect the bonds that connected her to the people in the photographs.

-Her mom's hand resting gently yet protectively on her shoulder, her gaze on Kahlila instead of on the person who was taking the picture.

-J.T., still sweaty from playing the best game of his career, pushing through the crowded bleachers to hug his Special K. His dad whipped out his camera and snapped the shot while J.T. swung Kal in the air as she laughed hysterically.

-Kahli, Robyn and Desiree, not yet comfortable with one another, still strangers assigned to the same room, but desperate to become friends. Their arms around each other in an attempt to break the ice as all three of them hoped the same thing: that they wouldn't have to go through freshman year alone.

When she retreated to the memory bank in the back of her mind and sifted through the still images of her and David, she looked for evidence of that same love that she felt from all of the other people who meant so much to her. His smiles, his winks, his arms around her, his worried expressions, his hands holding her face in his palms. *A picture is worth a thousand words.*

It was then that she knew. He was not okay with saying goodbye. He wasn't fine with the way he left things. He missed her. He thought about her. He wondered how she was holding up. He hoped she didn't hate him. He hoped she didn't still love him. But then he prayed that she did.

She smiled for the first time in weeks, and reached for the magazine, its glossy cover calling her to open it. Though she momentarily tried to fight the urge, Dave's piece was the first thing that she turned to. Her eyes moistened as she scanned his words, shaking her head in disbelief at what she was reading. After she finished, she closed the magazine with a satisfied sigh. Then she rose from the bed, grabbed her keys, and headed out the door. Her friends were waiting for her at the Caf.

Love Lesson 101
by Dave Robinson

People have stereotypes about so many things. Race, class, gender–every group is given a set of characteristics to which they are supposed to adhere.

But there are all kinds of stereotypes. For instance, people make a lot of assumptions about love.

Love is magical; love is easy; love is for the person who mans your side from day to day; love is something that can be expressed through words, through touch.

But the truth is that love isn't always magical. Sometimes you'll realize you love somebody and it's not even someone who you're allowed to have feelings for. Other times you'll love someone, even if you don't like them. Love isn't a perfect science, and it doesn't even always feel good.

And so love isn't easy. Sometimes it involves making sacrifices for the person that you love. Sacrificing some of your habits so the person will love you more. Sacrificing friends so the person will trust you more. Sacrificing honesty to spare feelings. Sacrificing freedom to provide support.

People think of your true love as the person you spend the most time with. This isn't always the case. Sometimes you carry a love stronger than life itself for a person who's passed on. Other times you love someone who you can't be next to for whatever reason. Yes, usually you do feel love for the person whose eyes meet yours every morning. But you can also love the person whose eyes meet yours when you close them each night.

People try to convey love through verbal expressions and physical advances. What do those things really mean? Love is something you feel deep inside you–a fluttering in your stomach when that person surprises you at your door. A warm feeling that spreads through your chest when that person smiles at you. How do you convey those feelings to a loved one? You don't. You just have to hope that they know. And often, they don't.

No one may be telling you. No one may be holding you. You might not catch an adoring glance. You may not feel a warm hand enclosing your own. But you are loved. You have to believe that. It ain't storybook, but it's real.